The Mountains of Arabia: A voyage to Pluto.

The Mountains of Arabia

A Journey to Pluto

Patrick Worthington

Amazon Kindle

Dedication:

To the First Legion.eu family. A crew of gamers gave me expert advice and support for this book. And deadly players that gave me many painful deaths on the battlefield of Karkand!

Further dedication to Rohtez, Sunnyghost, and Default-Swedish who were the first to buy my book. And to Jane Scott, with the fondest memories, who also bought this book.

And to my brothers Ronald and Robert and my nieces and nephew, Romena, Natesa, and Renzo.

Table of Contents.

Rendezvous

Chapter One

Nancy Darkstrider, captain of the deep-space scout ship, Copernicus, spoke into her computer. "Captain's log: We entered the Pluto system at 1115 hours, October 12, 2117, C.E. So far, there has been no repetition of the signal other probes have triggered." Nancy glanced around the bridge of the Copernicus. In front of her were the ship's young navigator and communication officers, Chris Tripper and Jane Franke. To her right was her old Academy classmate, Spiro Leonidas, known to the crew as 'Spock' for his rigid manner. She could see the engine deck on her monitor. Busily working were the two inseparable engineers, Jason Riley and Francis Book. Nancy rubbed her tired eyes and looked at the main bridge screen. The minor planet Pluto filled her view and gradually grew as she watched.

The famous 'heart' glowed in the lower part of the globe.

"Broadcast on all frequencies, Yeoman Franke," ordered Darkstrider, "see if you can elicit a response." Jane glanced over her shoulder. "I've been doing that since we entered the Pluto system, captain. So far, nothing." Leonidas looked up from his science station. "It would have been too lucky to get a signal, captain. The last two probes were unsuccessful." Tripper chuckled, "Always thought Vulcans didn't believe in luck?" Leonidas replied deadpan, "I wouldn't know, Mr. Tripper since I was born in the Martian colonies." Nancy said, "If we are all finished with the jokes, perhaps we can get some work done."

Captain Darkstrider returned her attention to the main bridge screen. The older officer marveled at Pluto's multi-variegated surface of deep blacks competing with verdigris greens and liquid oranges. The left lobe of the 'heart' glowed white while the broken right lobe shimmered icy blue. Thoughtfully, Nancy let her eyes wander over the planet. *"What secrets does that silent world hold?"* she wondered.

"All right, Mr. Tripper, steady as she goes."

Silently, on its hydrogen ram-jets, the 1500 meter, one million metric ton Copernicus glided through the velvet curtains of space. The distant sun glowed off the glossy segments of the oval head, tapered midsection, and bulky propulsion units. Like a bolt of lacy cloth, the Milky Way unfurled across the heavens. In the vast array of Orion, the excellent ruby star Betelgeuse glowed majestically. Other constellations coiled like luminous dragons.

Leonidas reported 65,000 kilometers from Pluto, "We're approaching the outermost moon's orbit, Hydra, Captain. It will cross our path in five minutes." Nancy replied, "All right, Mr. Tripper, full stop." Tripper's hands moved on his controls. "Full stop,

Captain." In engineering, Jason Riley remarked to Francis Book, "We've come to a complete stop. I wonder what's going on?" Book studied a bank of instruments. "Who knows?" Five minutes later, from the left of the main screen, a hurling object burst into view. It tumbled over itself in greens and oranges.

"Pluto's largest minor moon, Hydra, irregularly shaped fifty-five kilometers by forty km," said navigational officer Tripper. The bridge crew watched as Hydra crossed their view with a tumultuous roll. Captain Darkstrider noticed a dark patch on the moon's surface and frowned. "What is that circular, dark region, Mr. Leonidas?" asked Nancy. "It's approximately ten kilometers in diameter, Captain Darkstrider, origin unknown," replied the First Officer. "H'm-mm," mused Nancy, "could be worth a look later." As Hydra left the main bridge screen, Captain Darkstrider ordered, "All right, Mr. Tripper, steady as she goes." Tripper confirmed, "Steady as she goes, Captain."

Fifteen minutes later, Leonidas announced, "58,000 kilometers. We're crossing the orbit of the moon Kerberos." Nancy spoke. "Put it on the long-range scan." Then, on the screen, Kerberos came into view. The small moon appeared to be an irregular dumbbell. "Kerberos, Plutonian moon," intoned Leonidas, "12 kilometers by 4.5 km." Tripper spoke over his shoulder, "Interesting fact, Captain. After Kerberos's discovery in 2011, the actor William Shatner, who played Captain James T. Kirk in the old T.V. series 'Star Trek,' proposed the name 'Vulcan' for the moon." Yeoman Franke darted a mischievous look at the science station. "What do you think of that, Mr. Leonidas?" Spiro smiled slightly. "Fascinating," replied the First Officer. "Thanks for the history lesson, Mr. Tripper," remarked Captain Darkstrider dryly.

A short time later, Leonidas announced, "49,000 kilometers, captain. The orbit of the moon Nix, 54 kilometers by 41 km." The bridge crew looked up. "Full stop, Mr. Tripper," said Captain Darkstrider. "Full stop it is, Captain," replied Tripper. However, the crew only had a short time to get started. From the left of the main screen erupted a sizeable grey object which rolled chaotically. "Look at that large purple splotch on its surface," pointed out Yeoman Franke. "Centred on a crater," observed Leonidas, "most interesting." For several minutes, Copernicus's team watched the strange object until it left their sight. Then, firing up its engines, the massive ship continued.

Now the routine announcement came. "46,000 kilometers, captain. Within the orbit of the moon Styx. The dimensions of the moon are 5 kilometers by 7 km. It is the smallest of Pluto's moons," said the First Officer. "Nix, Styx?" whispered Tripper to Franke, "Imaginative names." Franke smiled back, making a kissing motion. "Long-range scan, Mr. Leonidas," ordered Darkstrider. The tiny moon sprang into sight. It was a vivid white object with streaks of blue and green on its surface. "Water ice with components of nitrogen and methane," reported Leonidas. "Shatner tweeted the name of Romulus for this one, captain," said Tripper. "Creative mind, give him that," answered Nancy. "What's a tweet?" asked Franke. "I'll tell you later, Jane," promised Tripper.

"We're now inside the orbits of the smaller moons, Captain Darkstrider," reported Leonidas. "That leaves just the large satellite." The captain habitually tapped her cheek. "Charon," replied Nancy. "Precisely," said the First Officer. "Charon, referencing a Greek mythological figure: The ferryman of the dead." Darkstrider leaned forward intently, studying the bridge screen. "Cheerful prospect," joked Tripper. "Well, where is it?" complained Franke. "I can't see it." At that moment, from behind Pluto, an ominous grey orb appeared. "Oh, I see it now," said Franke.

"Charon," said Leonidas, "1212 kilometers in diameter. It orbits Pluto at a distance of 19,500 km." Nancy strained her eyes. "Long-range scan, Mr. Leonidas," ordered Captain Darkstrider. The grey surface of Charon filled the screen. A vast, dark area dominated the North Pole. "The north pole of Charon has a cap made of tholins and organic macro-molecules," intoned Leonidas in a monotone voice. "Formed from methane, nitrogen gases released from the atmosphere of Pluto." The area swam into view, looking like a bloody mouth. "Mordor," breathed Yeoman Franke in an awed voice. "Yes, Mordor, crewman Franke," replied Leonidas, "from 'Lord of the Rings.'" From the crew's viewpoint, a large canyon circled its equator. "What was the name of that canyon, Mr. Leonidas?" asked Nancy. "Serenity Chasma," came the reply from the First Officer, "over a thousand kilometers long and sixty km wide. Much larger than the Grand Canyon back on Earth." At the mention of Earth, a small sigh came from the younger crew members. "Very well," said the captain briskly, "Mr. Tripper put us in Geo-synchronous orbit around Pluto, one diameter distance. Orientated on the center of the heart and North and South poles." Tripper acknowledged, "Pluto orbit, Captain."

The Copernicus sailed serenely towards its long-awaited rendezvous with the minor planet Pluto. Behind the trim ship, the small Plutonian moons continued their intricate dance. The crew watched as Pluto filled the main viewer on the bridge and then crowded everything else out. Slowly, the glowing 'Heart' grew larger and larger. Finally, the First Officer's voice intoned, "The heart of Pluto. Named Tombaugh Regio after Clyde Tombaugh, the astronomer who discovered Pluto in 1930. Left of the 'Heart' that extended, dark area is called 'The Whale', or more properly 'Cthulhu Regio.' To the right of the 'Heart,' the smaller dark region is called 'Krun Macula.' The region named after Krun, the most illustrious of the five Mandaean lords of the underworld."

Smoothly, navigator Tripper put the Copernicus in orbit around Pluto. "Pluto orbit achieved, Captain Darkstrider," said Tripper. Everybody on the bridge glanced at the captain at this momentous announcement. Riley and Book paused in their work in the engine room and looked at their viewers to see their captain's reaction. "Well," said Nancy Darkstrider, "we're here."

The crew gathered in the main conference room several hours after the captain's orders. Communication officer Jane Franke unpinned her blonde hair, letting it cascade down her back. A pout crossed her lovely face. "Why would she call a meeting and not show up?" she complained. Navigator Chris Tripper glanced over as he rubbed his brown, crewcut hair. "Captain's privilege Jane. And shouldn't you be wearing your hair up on duty?" Jane shrugged. "It's a meeting. We're off duty, Chris." Jason Riley, the black assistant engineer, remarked, "It must be important to get Francis and me out of engineering. The ship is on automatic." The First Nations chief engineer, Book, echoed, "Yeah, the first time since we left Titan station." First Officer Spiro Leonidas said, "Believe me, Engineer Riley, if Captain Darkstrider called a meeting, it's important." Chris Tripper asked, "You've known the Captain for a long time, haven't you, Mr. Leonidas?" Leonidas looked up from his computer console. "The Captain and I met at The Academy thirty-five years ago." Franke laughed, saying, "I can't even imagine thirty-five years!"

The door whisked open. A moment later and Captain Darkstrider marched in. "Sorry I'm late, Captain's privilege." Chris Tripper glanced at Jane Franke, who made a tiny moue at him. Nancy paused at the coffee machine. Pouring herself a cup, the captain sat at the head of the conference table. "You're probably wondering why I called the entire crew to this meeting." Captain Darkstrider moved her green eyes around the table, pausing fractionally at Franke's unbound hair. "This is a momentous occasion. For the first time in history, humans are orbiting Pluto. The next thing is to decide what we're going to do next." Leonidas asked, "Pardon me for saying this, captain, but don't you have orders from Star Command?"

Darkstrider replied, "Yes, orders, but not how to accomplish them. They have left those details to me." Captain Darkstrider paused for a moment and then continued. "First, Copernicus is to map all bodies in the Plutonian system. Second, find and identify the source of the beacon recorded previously." Into the hush that followed, Chris Tripper interjected, "Piece of cake!" Nancy settled her gaze on the younger officer. "Precisely, Mr. Tripper," replied the captain. "Mr. Leonidas, can you show us what we know so far?" Leonidas replied, "Affirmative, Captain." The First Officer worked at his computer console for a moment, and a hologram of Pluto appeared hanging above the table. The ice planet revolved slowly in locked orbit with its grey companion Charon. Pluto's outer moons whirled around its parent as twinkling fireflies. "2015 C.E., the probe New Horizons passed through the Pluto system." On the holographic image, a yellow line sketched a path through the moons and close to Pluto. "In 2042 C.E., the next satellite reached Pluto." An orange line appeared close to the yellow one. "Over the next fifty years, three more probes passed through the Pluto system." Green, red, and blue lines appeared on the holographic map. "Then, in 2098 C.E., a satellite triggered a signal from somewhere on Pluto's surface." A purple line appeared with the other colored ones. "In 2101 C.E., another probe triggered the same response." A pink line passed close to the purple one. "Finally, in 2105 and 2107 C.E., NASA launched two satellites to orbit Pluto." A gold bar and a silver line appeared and circled Pluto. "Both failed to trigger a response and crashed into the surface for unknown reasons." In the holo map, the two lines touched the face of Pluto and disappeared.

"Well," said the captain, "there you have it. Nine probes and satellites have entered the Pluto system in the last one hundred and two years. Mr. Leonidas, could linguists tell us anything of that signal?" The First Officer replied, "Negative, captain. Despite exhaustive analysis, the signal remained undeciphered. A complete blank." The crew mused that information over. "Do we know why those last two probes crashed, captain?" asked assistant engineer Riley. "They were supposed to orbit Pluto for years but crashed almost immediately." Darkstrider replied, "No, Mr. Riley, that's one mystery we hope to solve while we are here."

Captain Darkstrider paused and examined each of her crew members. With some trepidation, several stared back. Finally, the captain said, "I've assigned teams to explore Pluto's moons. Tripper and Franke will take Shuttle One, map, and explore Charon, Pluto's large satellite." Chris and Jane exchanged glances of delight. Nancy turned to her two engineers. "Book and Riley will take Shuttle Two and map the four outer moons. You two get out of the engine room and have some fun." The two engineers looked startled and then grinned widely. "Thanks for the vote of confidence, captain," said Book. "Same here!" exclaimed Riley. Captain Darkstrider shrugged. "I know you have had extensive training in exploration and shuttle piloting. I have every confidence in all of you." The captain looked to her right at Leonidas, the First Officer. "While the teams are away, Mr. Leonidas and I will map the surface of Pluto. Hopefully, by the time we finish, we will have turned something up. OK, this meeting is over." The four younger crew members filed out. Leonidas paused and remarked, "I'm surprised you said nothing about Franke's hair, Captain." A small smile crossed the captain's face.

"We're five billion kilometers from home. I think we can relax regs a bit." With a slight nod, the First Officer turned and left the room. Captain Darkstrider propped her elbows on the table and rested her chin on her hands. She contemplated the holographic display of Pluto and its five moons as they swirled above the table. An intense gleam glowed in her beautiful green eyes.

Two hours later, Nancy lay on her back in her cabin bunk. Hands behind her head, she contemplated what the future held. Restlessly, the captain swung her legs over the side of her bunk, went to her computer station, and sat down. She turned on the screen and punched in a program. A holographic image of a twenty-year-old youth who strongly resembled Nancy appeared. "Hi, mom! Your son Greg is speaking from the academy. So far, classes are going fine. My astrophysics and math are weak, but they always were. Guess it runs in the family. I graduate in two more years, and then it's out into space! I must tell you, mom, how proud I am that they have selected you to command the first trip to Pluto! My classmates are always asking me questions about you and your mission. I tell them it's top secret, and I can't divulge any information. They don't know if I'm kidding or not! Well, I have to keep this short, so one more thing. Don't take any risks, and come home safe! Love you, mom! Greg out." Nancy shut off her screen, and her emerald eyes saw nothing for a while. Far below, the heart of Pluto gleamed silently in the reflected sunlight.

The following day, the crew assembled on the shuttle deck of the Copernicus. The two engineers, Riley and Book, and the navigator and communication officers, Tripper and Franke, stood in front of the ship's two shuttles. They all wore flight suits and held helmets under their arms. They all hid excitement under an air of nonchalance. Captain Darkstrider and her first officer, Leonidas, stood in front of the two couples.

Nancy Darkstrider spoke, "Well, here we are. I have briefed you on your missions and know what to do. Map the satellites thoroughly. We don't know what we're looking for, but I'm sure the scientists back on Titan and Earth will appreciate accurate information. Questions?"

Chris spoke up, "Can we land, captain?" By his side, Franke looked at Tripper with apprehension in her eyes. Captain Darkstrider said, "I leave that up to you. Charon is big enough that a landing should not be a problem. The other moons are moving much more swiftly and are much smaller. Riley, Book, I would use your discretion on attempting a landing. Remember, if you crash the shuttle, it will be challenging to attempt a rescue. Any more questions?" There were none.

Captain Darkstrider, "Very well, then off you go, and good luck!" Silently, the two couples entered the shuttles, and after several seconds, the hatches closed. After the last look, Nancy and Spiro left the hangar deck and exited its door.

Ten minutes later, the Captain and the First Officer watched the shuttle deck viewscreen. Captain Darkstrider, "Evacuate the atmosphere on the shuttle deck, First Officer." Leonidas pushed a button on his board, "Atmosphere purged, captain. Five minutes." On the viewscreen, an ample red light began to strobe on the shuttle deck. After five minutes, the light turned green. Nancy keyed her mike. "Cleared for liftoff. Proceed when ready." The captain's view changed to the outside of the ship. Slowly, a massive exit port appeared on the side of the vessel. The first one, and then the other shuttle, appeared in the opening and moved silently into space. Involuntarily, both Leonidas and Darkstrider exhaled their breaths. "Both shuttles are now clear of the ship, captain," reported Leonidas. "I have sowed the wind to reap the whirlwind," replied Nancy. Leonidas looked at the captain curiously but said nothing.

Aboard Shuttle Two, Riley and Book enthusiastically plotted a course to their first aim, Pluto's most minor planet, Styx. "16 kilometers by 9 kilometers by 8 km," said Francis Book. "Not much to it is there, Jason." Riley replied, "Well, big things come in small packages, Francis. Maybe we'll find something." The tiny moon grew in their view screen until it filled it blinding white. "Orbit in ten seconds, on my mark," intoned Francis. Then, with consummate skill, Book matched the movement of Styx. Silently, the shuttle glided over the moon's smooth surface. Blue and green streaks streaked down its side. "Frozen nitrogen and methane, just like Leonidas reported," said Riley. "Yeah, oddly beautiful, isn't it," replied Book.

Hours went by as the two engineers mapped every meter of the moon's surface. Riley stretched at the controls. "Do you think we'll find something, Francis?" asked Riley. "This moon is just one frozen snowball." Jason replied, "It doesn't matter if we find anything. It's important to map everything while we have the chance."

Riley got up and put his hand on Book's shoulder. "Think of it, Francis. We're the first people ever to get out this far. Mapping unfamiliar terrain, seeing things no one has ever seen before. 5 billion kilometers out, and it took six months from Titan station to get here. Look at the sun out there. It looks like a bright star. I don't know Francis; I feel lonely. We cut the rest of humanity off. And this is a one-shot deal too. We only got here so fast by using Uranus and Neptune to sling-shot us to a higher velocity. The planets won't align like this for another 150 years. We've got two months to map Pluto and its moons, find the source of the signals, and then go back to Earth. Piece of cake." Francis laughed, "Piece of cake! Even if we don't find the source of the signals, we'll go down in the history books. First surveyors of Pluto's moons. Not bad for a pair of second-rate engineers passed up for promotion."

For a time, the two men were silent, busy making the last few circuits of Styx, mapping as they went. Then, finally, Francis Book frowned. "Jason, do you notice something odd about those stripes?" Riley replied, "Now that you mention it, I do. Some pattern that I can't put my finger on." Book said, "It doesn't matter if we can't figure it out. Leonidas can run it through the computer on Copernicus. If there is a pattern, the Nav computer can sort it." Riley asked, "I wonder how Franke and Tripper are making out on Charon?" Francis replied, "Making out is the operative word." The two men laughed as Styx continued its slow dance around Pluto, as it had for the last 4 billion years.

"Orbit around Charon in ten seconds, Chris," said Jane Franke. "Good piloting, Jane," replied Chris Tripper. "Glad they taught you how to pilot a shuttle and communications at the academy." Jane said, "It was an elective subject. I thought it might come in handy one day." Tripper replied, "You thought right, sweetie." The shuttle settled into orbit around the greyish-brown orb that was Pluto's largest moon. Franke and Tripper gazed at the surface of Charon as it unfolded below them. Long ridges dominated plains that and pocketed with meteorite craters. Elongated grabens or canyons snaked all over its terrain, bespeaking a possible volcanic past. On the North Pole, the brownish-red patch of Mordor crouched like a malignant spider.

"That's a large canyon," exclaimed Jane as it passed below them. "Serenity Chasma," replied Tripper. "It's a pull-apart fault." Franke complained, "What the hell does that mean?" Chris answered patiently, "It means that Serenity Chasma formed because of a subsurface ocean on Charon, which expanded as it froze," Franke asked crossly, "Where do you learn this stuff, Chris?" Tripper replied, "I learned it by studying, asking questions, and reading books."

Franke laughed, "You read Chris? I thought the only books you read were Captain Galaxy Space Adventures." Tripper asked, "Have I told you how much I admire your sledgehammer wit, Jane?" Franke said seductively, "That's not all you admire, Tripper."

Fifteen minutes later, the shuttle passed over another chasma. "Another large canyon," said Chris. "But I forget what it's called." Jane replied, "Argo Chasma.

Reaches a depth of 9 km, with cliffs that may rival Verona Rupes on Miranda, Uranus's smallest moon, for the title of the tallest cliff in the solar system." Tripper exclaimed, "How on earth did you know that?" Jane replied," Oh, I googled it just now." Tripper remarked, "These grabens, or canyons, extend around the equator for at least 1,000 km. Macross, Tardis, and Nostromo Chasma are the other large canyons." Jane said, "Charon's color reminds me of Earth's moon." Chris asked, "Remember that night at Tranquillity City last year, Jane?" Franke replied, "I'll say I do. We're lucky we didn't get arrested at The Lunatic Bar." Chris pointed out, "We got arrested, Jane." Franke answered, frowning, "Oh, that's right, I remember now."

An hour later, the shuttle was gliding over the Southern Hemisphere. "I'm picking up many craters, Chris," reported Franke. "Yes," replied Tripper. "Kirk, Nemo, Spock, Sulu, and Uhura. To name a few." Jane turned her head in astonishment, her blond mane flying. "What an incredible list of names. Someone sure is into science fiction." Chris reached over and stroked Jane's cheek. "I think astronomers are a bunch of Trekkie and Doctor Who fans at heart."

A dark area near Charon's South pole drew Jane's attention. "What's that, Chris?" she asked. "Morder is at the North Pole, isn't it?" The red splotch looked like a pool of blood. "Yes," replied Chris. "That's Gallifrey Macula. Like Mordor, made of tholins and organic macromolecules blown from Pluto. The large chasma crossing it is Tardis, the Timeship from Doctor Who." An hour later, an area of several chasma appeared. "Cataclysmic conditions tore it apart as if in some distant war. Conquest, War, Famine, and Death Chasmas," said Tripper. "Named for the Four Horsemen of the Apocalypse. That enormous crater is Armstrong. Named for Neil Armstrong, the first human to have walked on the moon." Then, finally, a large plain crept into view. "Vulcan Planum," said Tripper. "The only large plain on Charon. It's home to the tallest mountains in Charon. Clarke, Kubrick and Butler Mons." For a while, the two were silent, looking at the vast silent plain dotted with craters. "It's eerie, Chris," said Franke." I keep reminding myself that we are the first humans to see these features. And that we're billions of kilometers away from home." Tripper replied, "Yeah, we're as far out as humanity has ever gotten. And likely to reach for the next one hundred years. We're making history, as no doubt Book and Riley are saying right now."

Back on the ship, Captain Darkstrider and First Officer Spiro Leonidas were on the bridge. Nancy viewed through the viewscreen at Pluto, passing slowly below. "Any word on our shuttle teams?" she asked. "Book and Riley are finishing their mapping of Styx," replied Leonidas. "Their data is being fed into the Nav computer." The captain glanced at her first officer. "Did they find anything interesting?" asked Nancy. "Yes," replied Spiro. "Riley says they think there is a pattern in the nitrogen and methane stripes on the moon's surface."

Finally, the captain ordered, "Well, analyze the pattern; they might be right. Anything from Franke and Tripper?" The First Officer replied, "Nothing yet, captain. But they have a lot more area to cover. So it might be hours before the check-in." Nancy muttered, "If they can only concentrate on their work and not themselves."

Darkstrider swiveled her chair to face Spiro. "When do you estimate the mapping on Pluto will be complete?" she asked. "The ship is surveying in a ten-kilometer-wide grid pattern," replied Leonidas. "It will take a month to map all 16.7 million square kilometers." Nancy swiveled her chair back to the viewscreen just as a large, dark area passed below Pluto's surface. "It looks like a black whale," said Darkstrider. "Cthulhu Macula," remarked Spiro. "At 2,990 kilometers long, it is the largest of the ten maculae on Pluto." The captain asked, "What causes it to be so dark?" Leonidas replied, "The color results from a tar made of complex hydrocarbons called tholins. Forming from methane and nitrogen interacting with ultraviolet light and cosmic rays." Darkstrider replied, "Yes, I remember you mentioned tholins before. You said Pluto's atmosphere released the particles that caused Morder on Charon's surface. So where did the name of Cthulhu come from, anyway?" The first officer replied, "It comes from the fiction writer H. P. Lovecraft's short story The Call of Cthulhu. An evil entity is hibernating in an underwater city." The captain rubbed her chin reflectively. "An underwater city? That rings a bell somehow."

As Copernicus moved further into its orbit, two long lines appeared on the dark mass. "What are those two lines, Mr. Leonidas? Ditches?" The answer came, "That is correct, captain. Beatrice Fossa and Virgil Fossa. Beatrice visits Hell and asks Virgil to guide Dante in Dante's Inferno. In The Devine Comedy, Virgil, Dante's guide through Hell and Purgatory." Darkstrider remarked dryly, "Dante sure got around, didn't he?" The first officer's only reaction was to arch an eyebrow. "You may also note several large and small craters in the whale," pointed Leonidas. "Oort, K. Edgeworth, Elliot, Brinton, Harrington, and H. Smith."

A roughly circular dark area now hovered into view. "We are now seeing the first of the Brass Knuckles," informed Spiro. "Six black splotches spaced roughly equidistant from each other. The first is Meng-p'o, after a Buddhist goddess who caused the dead to forget their past lives." Two more dark areas now appeared. "Vucub-Came and Hun-Came," intoned Leonidas. "After a pair of death gods in the Popol Vuh text of the K'che' Maya." A large black patch appeared below. "Balrog Macula," said Spiro solemnly. "I know this one," replied Nancy. "From J. R. R. Tolkien's Lord of the Rings. A demon that almost killed Gandalf." The first officer replied, "Correct, Captain. The largest of the brass knuckles and the second-largest maculae after Cthulhu." A small dark spot came into the field of sight. "Ala," said Leonidas, "smallest of the Brass Knuckles, named after the most important deity of the Ibo people of Nigeria. It means Earth in their language." The panorama unfolded to reveal a large rectangular patch. "Krun Macula," reported Spiro, "named after a lord of the underworld in the Mandaean religion of southern Iraq. The easternmost and last of the brass knuckles."

Above the Krun Macula, Nancy could see a shimmering blue field. "Turn the viewscreen to wide aspect, Mr. Leonidas." The view jumped back to reveal a large blue icy vista. "The left lobe of Tombaugh Regio," reported the First Officer. Named after Clyde Tombaugh, who discovered Pluto in 1930. To the left, that large brown area is Tartarus Dorsa, the pit of Hell in Greek mythology." Then, slowly, a blinding white lobe swam into their vision—Icy-white in its frigidness. "Sputnik Planitia," intoned the First Officer. "The left lobe of Pluto's heart. So huge that it was the only feature that the Hubble telescope could see. Albeit as a featureless blob." Darkstrider said, "Remarkable, isn't it? That a moon could have a heart on its surface. I've read that there was general disbelief when the New Horizon's photos first showed the heart." Leonidas continued, "Sputnik Planitia is a high-reflective ice-covered basin about 1,050 by 800 km in area. It's surface of irregular polygons separated by troughs, convection cells in the nitrogen ice."

Captain Darkstrider stared at the scintillating ice field beneath her eyes for a time. "What do you think caused the formation of Pluto's heart?" she asked. "Sputnik Planitia likely originated because of an impact from a large body that subsequently collected volatile ices," Spiro answered. "The size of the affecting object might be between 150 to 300 kilometers." Nancy remarked, "Luckily, it didn't smash the planet to bits." The First Officer noted, "They estimated the ice surface to be about 180,000 years old. The dense, volatile nitrogen ice accumulation would make Sputnik Planitia a positive gravity anomaly." Nancy ran her hand across her forehead thoughtfully. "I seem to remember another explanation for the anomaly during the briefing at Titan Station." Spiro Leonidas turned in his chair and faced the captain. "Yes," he said. "Such an affecting body created if the explanation for the positive gravity anomaly would need a subsurface liquid water ocean below Pluto's water-ice crust." Darkstrider answered, "I remember now. A liquid ocean out here! Is such a thing possible?" The First Officer's reply was immediate. "Not only possible but highly probable." Far beneath them, Pluto's heart's blue and white lobes sparkled in a phantasm glow.

"Nyx, the Greek goddess of the night," said Francis Book. "Seems appropriate, looking at it, doesn't it, Jason?" Riley glanced over at his companion and then at the greyish, jelly-bean-shaped moon as their shuttle approached. "Orbit in ten seconds," reported Riley. "Three, two, one. Lock. Nyx orbit achieved." The two men relaxed and stretched as their ship began moving across the smooth surface of the small celestial object. "Nyx," intoned Francis. "The Greek goddess of darkness and mother of Charon, the ferryman of Hades." The engineers watched the grey surface unfold below them. "49.8 km × 33.2 km × 31.1 km I'm reading on my screen," remarked Francis Book. "That matches what is in Copernicus's data banks." Jason replied, "At least it's bigger than Styx." Finally, a sizeable reddish area centered on a crater came into view. "Hello," said Francis, "what do we have here?" Jason replied, "According to the data banks, I think it to be an enormous impact crater, where the reddish material ejected from underneath Nix's water ice layer and deposited on its surface. It's approximately 18 kilometers across." Silently, the ship soared across the red maelstrom that filled their viewscreen. "It look's like Dante's Inferno down there," commented Riley. "Yeah," replied Francis. "The gateway to Hell."

Francis Book's hands danced over the controls, rapidly adjusting the shuttle's orbit over the tumbling moon. The ship moved in precise parallel segments, mapping every square meter of the satellite's monotone surface. "I still can't believe we're here, Jason," said Book. "Four thousand engineers in the fleet, and they all applied for this mission. And we got it. Why were we chosen? There were other guys more qualified, more experienced, and had seniority. Why us?"

"Just before we left, one of my friends said this was a suicide mission," Riley replied. "I thought it was a case of sour grapes, but now I'm unsure. Copernicus is such an old ship for such an important mission. And why was the door into the propulsion units sealed off from engineering? I don't buy that story that they were afraid of radiation leaks. Something doesn't add up." Jason was silent as he peered at his viewscreen and monitored his instrument panel. Long columns of figures paraded across his sight. "You're not saying why you don't like that sealed door, Francis," said Book. "Spit it out."

Riley turned his head defiantly, and an angry expression crossed his face. "All right, I will," he replied. "I keep hearing noises on the other side of the doors. Something is back there, I tell you, Book." Francis shook his head, "You hear the engines' sounds sometimes. And why is it I never heard these sounds? Why is it only when you're alone that you listen to them?" Book moved the ship into a new search pattern. The shuttle seamlessly adjusted its path in response to Francis' instructions. "I don't know, Francis," admitted Jason. "Oh, maybe you're right. Maybe I hear things. Things get spooky on these deep-space missions." Francis said, "If you're that concerned, why don't you talk to Spock?" Jason replied, "I did; he said to talk to the captain if I thought it was that important." An amused smile crossed Francis's brown face. "And did you?" Riley replied grimly, "Not in your life."

"I can't believe how huge that canyon is, Chris," said Jane Franke as their shuttle passed over Argo Chasma. "700 kilometers long, Jane," replied Tripper. "Almost three times as long as the Grand Canyon back on Earth. It's big, all right, but nothing as large as Valles Marineris on Mars. That's 3,000 kilometers long and as much as 600 km wide and 8 kilometers deep." Jane sat silent for a while as the massive rent on the moon's surface unfurled below them. "8 kilometers deep, you say," said Franke. "So our chasma has it beat by one click then." Chris laughed and playfully punched Jane on her shoulder. "Oh, it's our canyon now, Jane?" Franke hit Tripper in his shoulder with rather more force. "Why not? We're the first people to map it. Why can't it be ours, Chris?" Chris massaged his shoulder thoughtfully and glanced at the rent far below. "You might have a point, Jane," he admitted.

The two were silent for a while as they maneuvered their craft above the moon's desolate surface, carefully mapping and studying the data stream. Their hands gracefully moved over the controls in an intricate, practiced pattern. "You know Chris," said Jane. "When you spoke about Valles Marineris, it got me thinking. Remember the last time we were on Mars two years ago and that trip we took with the Martian Colony Tours?" Tripper glanced at his beautiful companion and then returned his gaze to his work. "Of course, I remember," he replied. "We shuttled right into the canyon and flew the entire length below the planet's surface. Incredible scenery." Franke tapped her cheek thoughtfully, "Why don't we do the same thing, Chris." Tripper arched his back in surprise, "What? Take our shuttle right into the canyon, below its rim?" Jane replied, "Why not? Argo is 30 kilometers wide. If we take it easy, we can map it safely. And who knows what we might find? This trip is an exploration mission, after all." Chris chuckled, "I like the way you think, babe." Jane tossed her luxuriant blond locks. "That's not all you like, hotshot." Chris replied, "You know it, sweetie. We better alert Copernicus about what we're going to do." Tripper touched a control on his panel.

"Shuttle One to Copernicus. Shuttle One to Copernicus. Over." Leonidas's tinny voice came over the intercom. "Copernicus here, Shuttle One. Over." Tripper leaned into the mic and spoke slowly and distinctly. "Request permission to enter Argo Chasma below the rim level to map more meticulously. Over." The reply came, "Standby, Shuttle One, over," Several minutes passed. Then, at last, the intercom crackled into life. "Shuttle One," came the voice of the first officer, "you may proceed with your mission. Proceed with all caution. Over." Jane laughed and leaned over and kissed Chris's cheek. "You had Spock when you said meticulously," she said. Tripper smirked. "I know."

Shuttle One sailed across the desolate surface of Charon like a vast white gull. Another orbit of the greyish orb left the craft again, approaching Argo Chasma's mouth. Chris Tripper oriented his vessel's approach to bisect the gaping canyon. Silently, the ship boat engulfed by the walls on each side. Slowly the light grew dim as the Chasma's cliffs blocked out the weak light of the distant sun. Jane Franke hit a switch, and powerful lights illuminated the fractured and twisted rock they could now see. Chris fixed the shuttle at one kilometer above the floor of the canyon. Data streams came over Franke and Tripper's screens from the craft's probing scientific beams.

Occasionally, one of Pluto's smaller moons would pass overhead, directing increased light into the darkness. Fantastic phantasmagorical shapes flashed from the Chasma's walls and floor. Half an hour later, the shuttle descended as it entered the deepest part of the rift. The canyon's walls also closed in. Suddenly, a light appeared on Tripper's board with a slight beeping noise.

"Hello?" said Chris. "What's this? I'm reading something metallic down there." Jane checked her screen. "I've got it too. Whatever it is, it's massive. It must be half a kilometer long. Do you get any reading on the metallic makeup of the thing?" Tripper studied the data stream and shook his head. "No, I don't," he admitted. "Whatever it is, the computer can't analyze its molecular structure." The navigator slowed down the shuttle until it hovered a kilometer above the mysterious structure. The craft's lights played over the surface of the roughly rectangular construction. A dull white under an icy covering of methane. "Do you think there is a way into that thing?" Asked Jane. Tripper shook his head. "We'd have to land and check the sides. Can't tell from up here." The two checked the information flowing through their screens and darted glances at the alien surface far beneath them for a time. "Well," said Chris. "We better contact Leonidas." Franke nodded her head in agreement. "Let me." Jane triggered a control on her board. "Shuttle One to Copernicus. Shuttle One to Copernicus. We have sighted an assembly of unknown origin over. " Immediately, the First Officer's voice came over the intercom. "Affirmative. We are getting your information now and will advise. Stand bye. Over."

The Communication Officer turned to Tripper. "Do you think they will let us land, Chris?" The navigator shook his head, "I have a feeling Captain Darkstrider won't. Too many unknowns." Excitement coursed through the two spacefarers. Finally, Leonidas's voice came back, breaking the silence. "Captain says, return to the ship at once. Do not land. Repeat, do not land. Over." Chris groaned, "Knew it."

Meanwhile, Shuttle Two continued its exploration of the minor moon Nix. "We've about finished mapping everything on Nix, Jason," said Francis Book. "What do you suggest we do next?" Riley glanced over at his companion. "I want to get another look at the Gates of Hell," he replied. "Suits me," said Book. Engineer Book's hands flew over the shuttle's controls and the craft curved in a graceful swoop. Twenty minutes later, the ship moved slowly over the vast open wound of Nix. Book and Riley gazed somberly at the tortured landscape a kilometer beneath them. "What do you think, Jason?" asked Francis. "Are Dante's nine levels of Hell down there?" Book rubbed his chin and quoted from Dante's Inferno.

"I thy guide

Will lead thee hence through an eternal space,

Where thou shalt hear despairing shrieks and see

Spirits of old tormented, who invoke

A second death."

Book looked at his companion in surprise. "I didn't know you studied the classics, Jason? And all this time, I thought you were eye candy who knew a bit about engineering." Riley grinned. "Thought wrong, didn't you?" Jason smiled back and asked, "Can you remember anything more?" Riley paused and reflected.

"Through me, you pass into the city of woe:

You pass into eternal pain through me.

Through me among the people lost for aye.

Justice, the founder of my fabric, moved:

To rear me was power divine,

Supremest wisdom and primeval love.

Before me, things created were none, save things Eternal and eternal, I endure.

All hope abandon ye who enter here."

Francis laughed, "Well, we're not about to enter, so we don't have to abandon hope." The shuttle continued its unhurried flight over the tumultuous terrain. "Franke and

Tripper get the plum assignments," remarked Riley. "They have Charon, and we get these tiny, sterile moons." Book glanced at his companion in amusement. "Don't forget Jason, whatever they discover, we all get credit for it. Remember what Spock said. There is no I on the team." Riley snorted. "Spock never said that!" Francis shrugged. "Well, if he didn't, he should have." For a few minutes, the two explorers sat in companionable silence. "You're right, Francis," said Jason. "This is the history we're making. No humans have ever gotten out this far, and no one has ever explored the moons of Pluto. This voyage is our legacy. People will read about us long after we're dead and gone." Book nodded, "Not to mention whatever we find on Charon and Pluto. The source of those transmissions came from Pluto itself. Who knows what we'll discover there? The captain will probably let us explore Pluto's surface as soon as we map the other two moons." Jason glanced down at the red disarray under them. "I'm getting a nasty premonition about this."

Suddenly, every light on their boards flashed, and alarms echoed in the cabin. Then, pressed back in their harnesses, their view of Nix blurred. "What's happening, Francis," shouted Riley. Engineer Book read the information from the data banks and struggled to interpret it.

"Nix has increased its rotation! It's flipped its entire rotational axis! And we're going along for the ride!"

On the control deck of the Copernicus, a beep sounded on Spiro Leonidas's board. "Captain," said the Science Officer. "We have an emergency call from Shuttle Two." Nancy Darkstrider glanced at Spiro: "Put it on speaker." Engineer Book's voice over the intercom: "Copernicus, we have a problem. Over." "Please state the nature of your problem, Shuttle Two. Over," replied Spiro.

"Lock forward viewscreen on Nix," ordered Captain Darkstrider. A greyish blob appeared on the screen, tumbling erratically against the velvet darkness of space. Engineer Riley's voice filled Copernicus's bridge: "Nix's rotational speed has increased fivefold. We are holding on with our tractor beam. We fear we might smash into Nix's surface if we release our hold. Please advise. Over." Nancy viewed the tumbling object, "Increase magnification on the Shuttle, Mr. Leonidas." The view increased till Nix filled the screen. A red patch appeared with Shuttle Two suspended above it like a fly caught in a spider web. "Why has Nix suddenly increased its tumbling, Mr. Leonidas?" asked Nancy. The First Officer studied his monitor. "Apparently, because of the chaotic rotation of Nix, at intervals, it can flip its entire rotational axis. This interval is one of those times, captain." Nancy pushed a button on her panel. "Stand by Shuttle Two, will advise. Over."

Ten minutes later, the First Office spoke: "I may have a solution. The computer has analyzed the rotation of Nix. I've downloaded all the specs that Shuttle Two has provided. If Book and Riley increase their engines to maximum power and then execute a 90-degree turn, they should break out of the moon's orbit. It's risky, but it's the only option they have." Nancy pondered for a few moments and slowly nodded her head. "Make it happen, First Officer."

Back on Shuttle Two, Engineer Book studied the data that First Officer Leonidas was transmitting. "OK, Jason, we have a plan. Rev up the engines to maximum, and I will turn when we're in the pipe." Riley turned an anxious look at his companion: "Francis, I've computed our odds, and we have a one in four chance of this working!" Engineer Book snorted, "Never tell me what the odds are!" Francis twisted the power toggle to maximum, and the cabin filled with the throbbing noise of an animal leashed. The tension crept up to unbearable levels.

Reaching a critical moment, Engineer Book gestured to Riley: "Now, Riley, cut it." With a last silent prayer, Jason twisted the directional control, and with a shudder, the shuttle lurched out of orbit. It threw two men back in their harnesses as the face of Nix rushed towards them. Seconds ticked by as the red open maw of Hell loomed. Then they passed, and the inky curtain of space filled the screen. Book and Riley let out a collective sigh of relief. "Piece of cake," remarked Riley. Book looked at his companion and laughed uncontrollably.

A Time to Map

Chapter Two

"Well, that was an eventful three days," remarked Captain Nancy Darkstrider. The crew of the deep space scout ship Copernicus in the main conference room had arranged themselves around a large table. "If you mean Francis and I almost dying," said Jason Riley. "I would incline to agree with you, Captain." Nancy looked at her two engineers sitting close together. "Yes, a close call. We almost lost you out there. Mr. Leonidas commuted the odds of a successful escape at only one in four." "Never tell him what the odds are!" stated Jason. Francis Book glanced at him and chuckled. First Officer Spiro looked at them strangely.

"Haven said that," declared Nancy. "You two showed commendable courage under extreme stress. I will write it on the ship's log." The engineers looked at each other: "Hear that, Jason," said Book. "We might be in for a medal." Leonidas directed a curious look at the two men. "You spent excessive time over the red anomaly on Nix's surface. What attracted you to it, and did you learn anything?" Then, after a brief pause, Jason Riley spoke, "We called the 'anomaly' you are referring to as The Gates of Hell." Leonidas nodded his head. "Named after Dante's Inferno?" Francis Book startled slightly and replied, "Yes, that's right, Mr. Leonidas. Something drew us there. But the moon went wild before we could discover what it was." "Perhaps before finishing our mission here, you might discover what that something is," said Nancy Darkstrider. "You both are lucky to be alive."

The First Officer stood up. "The Captain is correct. You were fortunate. Are you still willing to explore the outer two moons?" Book and Riley looked shocked. "Of course we are!" the two said together. Spiro Leonidas nodded his head. "Excellent." Captain

Darkstrider turned to the other two members of her crew. "Mr. Tripper and Ms. Franke, you also had an eventful three days. Tell us what you found on Charon." Jane muttered to Chris, "Glad someone is talking to us." Ignoring her Navigator, Tripper replied, "We had mapped almost the entire Southern Hemisphere of Charon and then descended into Argo Chasma." Leonidas pushed a button, and the view from Shuttle One filled the viewscreen. They could see the vast canyon of Argo filled with an odd purple mist. The landscape unfolded as the shuttle flew up the massive rent in the moon's crust. Pillars of tortured rock and ribbons of lava intertwined on the floor of the rift. The massive looming walls on either side were visible. "About halfway down the chasma, we encountered this," said Communications Officer Franke. A substantial white object covered with green and blue ice shimmered on the screen. "Magnify," ordered Captain Darkstrider. The alien artifact filled their field of vision. They could see no features through its icy shroud, roughly a half kilometer long. "Well, I'm stumped," said Engineer Francis. "What the hell is it?"

"That, Mr. Book, is the question," replied First Office Leonidas. Everyone on the bridge looked in puzzlement at Spiro. "Did Spock just make a joke?" whispered Jason to Riley. "Levity aside," remarked Nancy. "What we're dealing with is outside human comprehension. An alien artifact, made by an unknown civilization, at an unguessable date." The six crew members somberly viewed the object that crowded the screen. Finally, Captain Darkstrider asked, "What does the computer make of the data provided by Tripper and Franke, Mr. Leonidas?" Spiro touched a button on his workstation, and a scroll of numbers appeared on one side of the main viewscreen. Leonidas replied, "The structure appears to be made of an element on the order of 145 on the Periodic Table." Everyone turned in shock at the First Officer. "But that's impossible," protested Jason Riley. "The Periodic Table only goes up to 130!" "Yes, Mr. Riley," answered Spiro. "This is an unknown element of a density that was thought impossible by our scientists."

Looks of disbelief passed among the crew. "I know that elements of this nature are possible," said Francis Book. "But to encounter one out here. With our own eyes. Someone's going to win a Nobel Prize!" Jane Franke and Chris Tripper exchanged glances and smiled. "Maybe Engineer Book," replied the First Officer. "The real question is, where do we proceed from here?" Chris laughed. "We investigate the artifact." All eyes went to Captain Darkstrider at the head of the table. Nancy reflected and viewed the main screen with the alien structure and the column of figures beside it. "Not quite, Mr. Tripper," said the captain.

Shocks of disbelief and dismay appeared on Jane's and Chris's faces. "That thing is not going anywhere," continued Darkstrider. "We must finish our mapping first. Next, engineers Book and Riley can map the outer two moons, Hydra and Kerberos. Then, Navigator Tripper and Communication officer Franke can finish mapping Charon's northern hemisphere. That should keep us busy for several days. Then, finally, First Officer Leonidas and I will conduct a preliminary survey of Pluto's upper half. After that, we can investigate Jane and Chris's discovery." At this, the crew relaxed, and grins appeared on all their faces. Even Spiro allowed himself a small smile. "All agreed?" asked Nancy. "Then I would call this meeting over."

Later, in Copernicus's gym, the four younger members of the ship's crew were working out. Communication Officer Jane Franke was spotting First Navigator Chris Tripper as he did bench presses. "At first, I was angry at Captain Darkstrider for not letting us investigate the alien object we found, Chris," remarked Jane. "But she has a point. First, we should map the rest of Charon before attempting. Then, after that, who knows what we'll find?" Tripper grunted as he did 100-kilo reps. "I don't care, Jane. I say we should check it out now. It is the first solid evidence of extraterrestrial life we have ever found. So we are just going to leave it?" The First officer finished his set and switched places with Franke, who began a collection of 100-kilo reps herself. She smoothly pushed the weighted bar quickly. "As she said, darling, it's not going anywhere."

Engineer's Book and Riley were jogging on the treadmills across the gym. Francis glanced at the two crew members on the bench press. "I bet Chris is angry that they can't get at that thing they found on Charon Jason." Book looked at the two lovers and grunted, "I might feel the same way. The artifact is enormous. But we should finish our mapping before we tackle it." Jason looked eagerly at his companion. "Do you think the captain will let us help explore the object? Franke and Tripper think it belongs to them." Francis pushed a button on his machine, increasing the speed to 15 kilometers an hour. "I think she might. The enigma will not give up its secrets easily."

Jane and Tripper finished their reps and sat down on the bench to cool off. Franke wiped the sweat off her beautiful face and peered at the two engineers talking animatedly together. "I bet I know what they're talking about, Chris. They want in on our discovery." Tripper inspected the two men running full out on their treadmills. "Yeah, you're probably right. Well, it doesn't matter in the long run. We are the ones who discovered it. So the credit will go to us. Who knows? Maybe they will be useful. They are engineers, Jane."

Engineer Francis peeked over at the Navigator and Communications officers, who were now doing arm curls. "Why do they keep looking over here, Jason? Do they know what we're talking about them? I wish they would stop. They're making me nervous." Their machines pinged and entered the cool-down phase of the workout. Riley shrugged his shoulders. "Yeah, they can probably guess we want in on their discovery. But what do they know about structural weak points and spectrographic readings? And this is a metal we've never encountered before. Unless we can find a door, I doubt it will be easy to break in." Engineer Book gave his friend a puzzled look. "If it is a structure, why wouldn't it have a door, Jason?" The two treadmills halted, and the two men stepped off. "I don't know, Francis," said Riley. "I feel it will not be easy getting inside that ancient pile." The four crew members paused and smiled at each other from across the room.

Captain Darkstrider and First Officer Leonidas reviewed the ship's computer analysis in the Science Lab. Raw data from mapping the shuttles and the ship's sensors were being processed and printed. Suddenly, Spiro straightened up from his viewer. "Hello? What do we have here?" Nancy glanced over at her companion. "Did you find something, Spiro?" The first officer nodded, "Yes, Captain, that red area on Nix that Book and Riley spent so much time on. They may have found something." Darkstrider walked over to the First Officer's station and peered over his shoulder. "You see their data?" said Leonidas. "Methane, Argon, Krypton, Nitrogen, Hydrogen, nothing unusual." Nancy Darkstrider nodded. "But when the sensors probed deeper, this symbol came up," continued the First Officer. The captain frowned, and then recognition lit up her face, "That's the same symbol of the unknown metal that makes up the alien artifact Franke and Tripper found on Charon!" Spiro nodded, "Yes, a considerable amount of that metal buried deep in The Gates of Hell." Nancy turned that over in her mind for a minute and then said, "What is your best analysis, First Officer?" Leonidas hesitated for a moment and then replied, "I would hate to guess without more data, but I would venture that The Gates of Hell was not produced by a meteorite but by an alien object crashing into the surface of Nix's surface." Captain Darkstrider chuckled, "That should please the boys!"

As the night ended for Copernicus's crew, the enormous vessel continued its orbit around the dwarf planet, Pluto. The Plutonian moons carried on with their mad dance around their mother orb. Grim Charon moved majestically in its endless path. Morder, at the moon's peak, seemed to wait patiently, like a spider waiting for a fly.

It pleased engineers Riley and Book when they heard the news of the alien object's presence in "The Gates of Hell." The two kept nudging each other, glancing at Navigation Officer Tripper and Communication Officer Franke, who looked decidedly bored. "This is only pure speculation," cautioned First Officer Leonidas. "But I can't think what else might be down there. Something hit Nix's surface hard enough to splash Methane over a large area. And the ships' computers have ruled out a meteorite." The engineer's grins dampened somewhat, then Captain Darkstrider remarked, "But like the alien artifact that Jane and Chris discovered on Charon, it will have to wait until we have finished our preliminary mapping." Nods were all around the table as Nancy continued, "Ok, you are all aware of your assignments? Francis and Jason can map the outer two moons, Hydra and Kerberos. Chris and Jane can finish the mapping of Charon's northern hemisphere. And Mr. Leonidas and I will do a preliminary survey of Pluto's upper half. Questions?" There were none, and Captain Darkstrider said, "All right, let's get to work, people!"

Once again, the Copernicus crew assembled on the shuttle bay's deck. Franke, Tripper, Book, and Riley stood in their flight suits, holding their helmets and looking at each other warily. Some of the excitement of the previous mission was gone. As if they had realized the dangers they were facing once they left the ship. Captain Darkstrider and First Officer Leonidas faced them and watched the conflicting emotions as they appeared on the shuttle mission's explorers.

"Here we are again," said Nancy. "This time, you all know what to expect, which is to expect the unexpected. Don't relax your vigilance and don't take any unnecessary chances. It's a hard universe, and it doesn't reward mistakes. To reiterate, Book and Riley will map the outer two moons, Hydra and Kerobos. Next, Tripper and Franke finish up on Charon. Finally, First officer Leonidas and I will continue our survey of

Pluto. Questions?" There were no inquiries. Nancy and Spiro watched the four don their helmets and entered the two shuttles. A few seconds later, the shuttle doors closed.

Ten minutes later, Darkstrider and Leonidas watched the two craft as they left the shuttle bay and glided into space. A few seconds passed as the ships gathered speed and disappeared from view. Then, unconsciously, Nancy let a sigh escape her. Spiro heard the noise and glanced at her. "You sense something, Captain?" he asked. Captain Darkstrider considered her reply for a short time. "Yes, I feel trouble is coming." The First Officer nodded. "I feel it too."

Several hours later and 57,783 km from Pluto, Shuttle Two approached the Plutonian moon of Keberos. Engineers Book and Riley watched as the icy, double-lobed shape of Pluto's second-smallest moon appeared on their viewscreen. "Looks like a giant dumbbell, doesn't it?" Jason said. "Yeah, it kinda does," agreed Francis. Book's hands moved over the ship's controls, and the boat slowed on its approach. "We will not make the same mistakes we made on Nix," said Book. "These small moons are prone to tumble. Let's lock into a high orbit for our mapping." As if Keberos could hear Francis's words, it increased its tumbling. Flashes of light flashed from the rapidly moving object. "A Juggernaut!" exclaimed Engineer Riley. "I'd hate to get in the path of that monster!" Francis made final adjustments to his board.

"High orbit locked in now." Gracefully Shuttle Two soared in large circles around the oscillating moon. "What do we know about Keberos, Jason?" asked Francis. The Chief Engineer Book studied his readout. "Kerberos has a double-lobed shape and is approximately 19 km across its longest dimension and 9 km across its shortest dimension. Its shape is probably the result of two objects merging. Possibly Keberos, like the other moons of Pluto, formed from debris around Pluto." The two engineers studied their boards and carefully adjusted the controls as Kerberos slowed its oscillations. Finally, Francis Book looked up. "This is pretty routine. We will not learn much from this ice cube, Jason." Riley nodded. "Yes, Francis, but we must map every square meter of Kerberos. You better believe the astronomers back on earth will pour over our data."

Idly Engineer Book looked out the viewscreen at the constellations whirling like pinwheels. Against the soft velvet of space, the pastures of heaven were caroling stars. Francis sighed, "I can't get over how beautiful the scenery is out here." Jason looked up at his control board. "Yeah, the stars seem brighter somehow. Maybe it's because we're so far from the sun that there is less light pollution. Or something like that." The two engineers busied themselves with their controls and readouts for a time. "We're so lucky to be here, Jason," said Engineer Book. "Every engineer in the fleet applied for this mission. And we get it." Riley looked up. "Well, we have put our time in the fleet. Twenty-five years apiece doing routine grunt work. It's about time we got a plum assignment. We've earned it."

Francis smiled as he reminisced, "I remember it like yesterday. A year ago, I was at my job in the Martian colony. Then I got an official notice from Space Fleet that they had approved my application for the Pluto expedition. Well, I was on the journey's shortlist. Then came weeks of interviews and tests and finally two months of training before I knew I had made it. I still can't believe it. The happiest day of my life, Jason." Engineer Riley pored over the readings on his navigational computer. "Pretty much what happened to me, except I was on Titan station around Jupiter. I had given up hope of ever going on an important assignment. I thought they had passed me over. So when I got the news of my selection, I almost cried. My second happiest day ever." Engineer Book, "Only the second best day ever? What was the first Jason?" Engineer Riley looked over and grinned. "The day I boarded The Copernicus and met you, Francis." The two men smiled and grasped hands.

"Charon orbit in seven seconds. On my mark, the orbit has begun," said First Navigator Chris Tripper. "Roger that," replied Communication Officer Jane Franke, "Charon orbit locked in." The two young people gazed down on the grey crust of Pluto's largest moon. "Oz Terra," said Chris, "The oldest part of Pluto. Four billion years old." The Northern hemisphere of Charon unfolded beneath them. "Two craters coming up," said Jane. "Leia Organa and Skywalker." Chris laughed, "Star Wars!" Franke echoed his laugh, "That's right, Chris! Funny, we know a one hundred- and fifty-year-old movie, isn't it?" Tripper scrutinized the two craters and adjusted several controls. "Still a great movie Jane; our spacecraft don't nearly have the capabilities theirs had." An hour went by as the shuttle passed over almost featureless terrain.

Finally, a large dark crater appeared on their viewscreen. "Wow!" exclaimed Tripper. "That's one immense crater!" Franke examined the large irregular area. "Yes, Ripley crater. Named after the character in the Alien movies. That large canyon bisecting it is Nostromo Chasma." Chris chuckled, "The name of the ship that Ripley flew in. A deep space mining ship, I think."

Shuttle One flew over the undulating highlands of Charon. The distant sun made the ship glow like a floating iceberg in space. "Charon has a kind of austere, almost ascetic beauty, doesn't it, Chris?" mused Communication Officer Franke. "Jane Franke," said Chris in surprise. "You are a philosopher!" Jane frowned. "I know I've talked about this before, but I still can't believe we're here. When I applied for this mission, I never thought I would get chosen. So many people were in the running. Officers with far more experience and training than me. How did you feel, Chris, when you found out that you were going to Pluto?" Tripper laughed and bent over his controls. "I knew, Jane. I'm the best navigator in the fleet! Who else has my skill? My determination? My courage, steadfastness, drive, and coolness."

"Modesty?" suggested Jane, with an arched eyebrow. "Yeah," replied Chris mulling, "That too."

"An enormous crater coming up," said Tripper. "According to the chart, it's called Vader," said Franke. "Afer Darth Vader in Star Wars." The two space explorers watched Vader's crater grow beneath them. "Kind of ominous-looking, isn't it, Chris?" asked Jane. Tripper laughed. "That's just your imagination, Jane. It doesn't look any different from many of the craters down there. Or do you feel a disturbance in The Force?" Jane Franke shrugged her slender shoulders but made no reply. Time passed in silence. The monotonous scenery continued, relieved by a few features. "Here we go, another crater," said Officer Franke. Chris studied his readout. "This one is called Dorothy Gale. After Dorothy in the Wizard of Oz. Two hundred thirty kilometers wide and 6 km deep." Jane thought that one over. "Well, Toto, I don't think we're in Kansas anymore." Chris laughed. "You can say that again!"

Several hours passed, and a significant depression in Charon's crust appeared on the horizon. "Caleuche Chasma," announced First Navigator Tripper. "The mythological ghost ship that sails the seas around the small island of Chiloe Islands, off the coast of Chile, collecting the dead, who then live on board in perpetuity." Jane remarked, "That's a cheerful thought, isn't it, Chris?"

Passing over the canyon, the rim of a vast crater loomed in the distance. "Pirx crater," said Jane. "Named after Pilot Pirx, the main character in a series of short stories by Stanislaw Lem." In the eerie silence of space, Shuttle One flew over the vast crater. "Can you imagine, Chris, the size of the meteorites that created such vast craters?" asked Franke. Tripper shook his head slowly. "No, I can't. The birth of Charon must have been one unholy delivery."

Officer Jane Franke sat silently for several minutes as the harsh landscape unfolded beneath them. Then, "Chris," she said, "I just had the marvelous idea." Tripper let out a groan.

Copernicus First Officer Leonidas was speaking to Captain Darkstider on the bridge. "Orbit over the Northern Hemisphere of Pluto in ten seconds, captain. On my mark. Locked in." Nancy replied. "All right, let's map Pluto, First Officer." Below the enormous bulk of the Copernicus appeared two irregular splotches. "First up," said Spiro. 'Yutu and Luna Linae. They are long, dark, or bright marks appearing on a moon's surface." Nancy studied the two dark areas. "Luna, I know, but what is Yutu?" The First Officer replied, "Yutu means 'Jade Rabbit' in Mandarin." For an hour, the ship passed over almost featureless terrain. A large plane appeared. "Lowell Regio or region," intoned Leonidas. "Named after James Arthur Lovell Jr., commander of the Apollo 8 and 13 missions." Nancy nodded. "I remember reading about Apollo 13 in school. It's a miracle they got back to earth after their oxygen tank exploded."

Spiro reflected, "The Apollo program might have ended right there. But it continued with four more missions. Then starting in the early 1970s, a series of Russian space stations, the United States Skylab station, and many space shuttle flights. Next was the International Space Station in the year 2000."

"Yes," agreed Darkstrider. "Many probes to all the planets, especially Voyager 1 and 2. Hubble Space Telescope in 1990. The James Web space telescope in 2022. The Xuntian Space Telescope in 2024. Plato in 2026, and then the Nancy Grace Roman

Space Telescope in 2027." Leonidas gave one of his rare smiles. "I thought you might be fond of that last one." The captain glanced at her first officer. "Nancy was my Great-Great Aunt. My name is hers. It's because of her I joined the Space Corp."

Captain Darkstrider and First Officer Leonidas were silent as they contemplated the rich and turbulent history of space exploration and travel. "Then exactly one hundred years after the first moon landing, the establishment of the Lunar colony in 2069," said Spiro. "Followed by Mars Base in 2085, and then Titan Space station in 2101."

Below them, two long dark streaks appeared on the viewscreen. "Djanggawil Fossae, Yolngu creation figures from the Island of the Dead," reported Leonidas. Nancy frowned, "What is the Yolngu?" The First Officer adjusted a control before answering, "Aboriginal Australian people that inhabit north-eastern Arnhem Land in the Northern Territory of Australia." Another large plain moved into view. "Venera Terra, "said Leonidas, "Named after the first landers on Venus." Silently the Copernicus glided over a new vista, an enormous crater hovering into view. "Burney crater," said Spiro, "Named after Venetia Burney, who first proposed the name of Pluto." Another large landmass was visible on the viewscreen, scored by two long canyons. "Viking Terra," said the Frist Officer. Captain Darkstrider laughed, "Yes, I know, named after the Viking program of orbiters and landers. It was one question in my finals at the Space Academy." Leonidas smiled, "Did you get the question right, Captain?" Nancy affected a look of nonchalance, "I don't recall." Spiro turned away, grinning.

The two space explorers watched the panorama as it unfolded below them. Then, finally, Captain Darkstrider broke the silence. "Amazing how varied the surface of Pluto is. When Clyde Tombaugh discovered Pluto in 1930, they knew almost nothing about its surface for decades. Even Hubble could only see some light and dark areas. I remember seeing a picture of a schoolboy's paintings of the planets from the 1960s. All were quite good, but Pluto was black. I guess the child's imagination did not extend into the unknown." Spiro looked up at her. "Yes, when the New Horizons probe approached Pluto in 2015, they felt Pluto would prove relatively featureless. What a surprise the world got when the first images of Pluto's surface beamed back. Pluto's heart was especially astonishing. Though, of course, its shape is just a matter of chance. Some news outlets at the time speculated an alien presence put it there. Romantic nonsense, of course." Nancy glanced sideways at her companion and smiled.

A large dark area infringed on the right of the viewscreen. "Voyager Terra," said Spiro. "Named after the Voyager program, the first probes to Uranus, Neptune, and then into interstellar space." Next, a long valley bisected by a crater swam into view. "Kupe Vallis," said Leonidas. "Named after Kupe, the legendary discoverer of New Zealand." Finally, they could see a gigantic mass of sparkling mountains at the bottom of the screen. "Al-Idrisi Montes," said Darkstrider. "Named after Muhammad al-Idrisi, a medieval Almoravid explorer." Spiro frowned and said, "I hate to admit my ignorance on any subject, but what was an Almoravid?"

Nancy laughed, "I'm amazed that I know something you don't, First Officer. The Almoravid dynasty was an imperial Berbere Muslim dynasty has its center in the territory of present-day Morocco in the 11th century." Leonidas whistled silently, "Go into space, and you learn something new daily!" Nancy adjusted a control, and the shimmery blue lobe of Pluto's heart sprang into view. "All down the left of the heart are a series of mountains. Below Al-Idrisi is Baret Montes. Named after Jeanne Baret, the first woman to have completed a circumnavigation voyage of earth's globe. Below us is the Zheng He Montes. In honor of Zheng He, a medieval Chinese explorer. Then those two long ranges are Hillary and Tenzing Montes. Named after Sir Edmund Hillary and Tenzing Norgay, the first to scale Mount Everest." Leonidas nodded, "Ice mountains that can exist because of Pluto's low gravity. The Tenzing Montes reach up to 6.2 km. They are the highest Plutonian mountain range and also the steepest."

The deep-space scout ship Copernicus moved smoothly across the face of Pluto. Then another sizeable plane moves into view. "Pioneer Terra," said the First Officer. "Named after the Voyager program. The first probes to visit Uranus, Neptune, and then on to interstellar space." "Pioneer 10," mused Nancy softly. "Launched 150 years ago. I wonder where it is now?" Spiro shrugged his slim shoulders. "No one knows. It left the Sol system and entered interstellar space long ago. It headed in the direction of the star Aldebaran. Pioneer 10 must be sixty billion kilometers out by now." They could see several craters puncturing the terrain below Pioneer Terra. "Farinella, Coradini, Safronov, and Giclas craters," reported Leonidas. "Named for Paolo Farinella, an Italian astronomer. Angioletta Coradini, an Italian planetary scientist. Viktor Safronov, a Russian astronomer, and Henry Giclas, an astronomer at Lowell Observatory." Captain Darkstrider noticed a ridge defining the blue lobe of Tombaugh Regio. "What's that dark line in the left lobe of the heart?" The First Officer adjusted his eyepiece. "Cousteau Rupes. An escarpment named after Jacques Cousteau, the undersea explorer and co-inventor of the aqualung."

Nancy noted two low hills below Cousteau Rupes. They stood out on the shimmering vista of Pluto's blue heart. "What are those hills, Leonidas?" Spiro was quick to reply, "Challenger Colles and Columbia Colles. They named them after two of the space shuttles. They lost both in terrible accidents. All crewmen lost as well." The captain nodded her head. "It is fitting here on the solar system's fringes; their memory lives on." After a time, another plane emerged. "Hayabusa Terra," said Spiro. "Named after the first spacecraft to return to earth with a sample of an asteroid. Those craters that you see are Drake, Hollis, and Kowal. They named Drake crater for Michael Julian Drake. He was an astronomer who chaired the committee that approved the New Horizons mission, the first satellite to reach Pluto, you remember?"

"I seem to recall," said the captain dryly. Then, ignoring Nancy's remark, the First Officer said, "Charles Kowal was an American astronomer who discovered the first centaur. Centaurs are populations of small bodies, similar to asteroids in size and to comets in composition, that revolve in the outer reaches of the solar system, primarily between the orbits of Jupiter and Neptune. Then, finally, we have Hollis crater, named for Andrew Hollis, a British astronomer." Darkstrider's eyes went to a dark, elongated region above Hayabusa Terra. "What is that streak above the plain, Mr. Leonidas? It looks similar to the Cousteau Rupes. Another escarpment?" The reply came, "Eriksson Rupes, named for Leif Erikson, the Icelandic explorer who first set foot on the shores of North America. In Labrador in present-day Canada."

Captain Darkstrider let out a sigh and leaned back in her chair. "Well, that completes our preliminary mapping of Pluto. Next, the computers will have to analyze all the data we have fed into it." First Officer Leonidas nodded, "Meanwhile, the Copernicus will continue in orbit doing a more detailed exploration. I'm glad, though, we completed the preliminary work." Nancy cupped her chin in her hand. "I wonder how our chicks are faring?"

"Ok, Francis," said Jason Riley, "next up. The wonderful moon of Hydra." Book glanced at his companion, "What's so wonderful about this moon in particular, Jason?" Riley grinned at his friend, "It's the last one!"

Slowly the Plutonian moon Hydra filled their viewscreen. The brilliant white of its surface reflected light from the distant sun. It rotated on its axis as Shuttle One approached it.

"What do we know about Hydra Francis?" asked Jason. Engineer Francis Book studied the readout on his computer station. "H'm, Hydra is irregular, measuring 51 kilometers along its longest axis and 30.9 km across on its shorter axis. The moon has systematic dimensions of 51 kilometers by 36 km by 31 km. Hydra is the second-largest moon of Pluto, after Charon, being slightly larger than Nix." Riley mused, "Hydra, named for the Hydra, the nine-headed underworld serpent in Greek mythology. I wonder if this isn't a subtle reminder that Pluto was once the ninth planet before the International Astronomical Union reclassified it as a dwarf or minor planet in 2006 C.E.?"

"Could be," replied Francis Book, "Ok, locking in orbit on my mark. Now!" Shuttle Two settled into a high orbit around the tumbling moon.

Gracefully, the ship swam through space on wide curves. The two men studied the celestial object through their monitors. "We're nearly 65,000 km out from Pluto, Francis," said Engineer Riley. "I feel kind of isolated. But then Hydra is the outermost moon of Pluto." The two men busied themselves with their instruments as the surface of Hydra unfolded beneath them. "The surface of Hydra is so bright it almost hurts my eyes," remarked Engineer Riley. "Hydra's surface is lustrous due to water ice on its surface, Jason," replied Francis Book. "The water ice on Hydra's surface is comparatively pure and shows no noteworthy darkening compared to, say, Charon."

Suddenly, Hydra tumbled violently. "I expected that after our experience with Nix. Luckily we're in high orbit," said Jason Riley. "I will compensate for the increased rotation." Gradually, the moon slowed down. "Lots of cratering down there, Jason," said Book. "Yeah," agreed Riley. "Evidence provided by the New Horizons probe estimates the surface of Hydra to be four billion years old." A large dark patch slowly appeared to the two space explorers. "That's interesting and huge!" exclaimed Engineer Riley. Francis Book peered through his viewer. "10 kilometers across. Could be a crater or something else entirely."

The two engineers were silent as they studied the black area on their viewscreens. "I'm going to take us in closer, Jason," said Francis Book. "Closer!" exclaimed Riley. The shuttle spiraled gracefully nearer to the Plutonian moon Hydra and settled into an orbit fifty kilometers above the icy object. "Don't worry, Jason," said Francis. "We're not close enough to be in danger when Hydra tumbles again." Riley shook his head and looked pensive. "I hope you're right, Book."

At this distance, the black pool filled the shuttle's forward viewscreen. Featureless, it gleamed a glossy black. "It's like a black hole Jason," said Engineer Book. Riley nodded his head. "I was thinking the same thing." The two scientists busied themselves with their instruments and analyzed readings. Patiently, the black enigma waited for the two Earthmen. Finally, after an hour, Jason Riley sighed and sat back in his chair. "I don't get it, Francis. My spectrograph can't make out the composition of the surface of that material. An unknown substance, like that structure on Charon that Franke and Tripper found." Engineer Book agreed, "Yes, the readings I'm getting show nothing I've ever seen. I don't know if we're looking at a rock, liquid, or something in between."

"A liquid?" exclaimed Jason. "At 23 Kelvin, even gases freeze. So nothing could exist as a liquid at that temperature! Except for helium, of course." Francis frowned. "You mean nothing we know about yet?" For a time, the engineers contemplated the Stygian paradox below them. "Are you thinking the same as I am, Francis?" asked Riley. "Yeah, I think so, Jason," replied Book. "Let's send a probe down into that thing." Engineer Riley inputted some instructions into his computer and triggered a switch. Immediately, an opening appeared below the shuttle, and a small device fell to the surface of Hydra. After several minutes, the space explorers held their breath as the probe checked its speed as it approached the surface of the unknown entity. To their shock, the satellite immediately passed out of sight as it slipped below the surface.

Jason Riley studied his scope. "I'm still in contact with the probe. It's passing through some medium. I can't tell what. The temperature is still 23 Kelvin. Visibility is zero." Francis Book busily scrutinized his readouts. "Could it be some super condensed gas? A holographic projection of some type? We're feeling our way in the dark here, Jason."

Engineer Riley read a figure on his screen. "Not for long. The probe is almost 31 kilometers inside. Whatever it is, it must go through the whole moon. We should see the satellite in a few seconds, Francis." After a minute, Riley frowned. "That's odd. The probe says it's 40 kilometers deep but hasn't appeared on the moon's far side." Book asked, "How is that even possible, Jason? Could the probe be producing a false reading?" Jason shrugged his shoulders. "Anything is possible, Francis." Half an hour passed. "The satellite is showing it's at a depth of 1000 kilometers; the temperature is still 23 Kelvin," said Jason Riley. Engineer Book glanced briefly over at his companion but had no comment. Another half hour passed.

"Ok," said Riley, "passing 2,000 kilometers now. Our signal is getting weak, weaker, increasing speed now, weaker. I've lost contact with the probe Francis. The final depth reading was 2,232.6 kilometers." The two friends studied the black, fathomless darkness with frustrated, puzzled looks. Finally, engineer Book sighed, "Ok, let's get out of here, Jason." Riley smiled, "I'm with you, Francis."

Gracefully, the Copernican shuttle veered out of the orbit of Hydra and headed back to Pluto. "I wonder how the two lovers are doing on Charon?" mused Francis. Behind them, the black pool's surface oscillated with red rings.

"You want to run that great idea by me again, Jane?" asked Chris Tripper. Communication Officer Franke shook her head irritably, sending her blonde hair flying. "It's simple, Chris. We've finished our preliminary survey of Charon. So before we return to the Copernicus, let's fly again through Argo Chasma and look at that artifact we found." Navigation Officer Tripper smiled grimly, "There's one place we haven't been to yet, Morder." Jane glanced at her companion and then looked away. "And we won't ever go there. I have a nasty inkling about that place." With a sigh, as if consigning himself to the inevitable, Chris said, "All right, I guess it can't do any harm. So I'm setting our route to Argos Chasma. And may god have mercy on our souls." Franke laughed and tweaked Tripper's cheek, "That's my lover boy!"

An hour later found Shuttle One flying over Vulcan Planum. The smooth plain undulated under their gaze. "I wonder why this plain is so smooth compared to the rest of the moon, Chris?" asked Jane. Tripper mused, "I'm trying to remember something I read once about an ice flow. Oh well, it will come to me." An enormous mountain loomed on their viewscreen. It gleamed like an iceberg in the distant sun's weak rays. "Kubrick Mons." said Tripper, "the highest mountain on Charon. They named Kubrick after Stanley Kubrick, a film director from the 20th century. It is 4 kilometers tall and forty kilometers wide." Shuttle One soared gracefully, like a seagull, over the massive mountain. Jane exclaimed, "A moat surrounds it! How odd!" A look of intense concentration came over Chris' face. "Yeah, it's coming back to me now. The subsistence of a chamber of water and ammonia caused the moat." Franke looked puzzled. "But that type of chamber you're describing would be full of lava. Kubrick doesn't emit lava, does it?" Tripper shook his head. "No water. I remember now that Kubrick is a cryovolcano."

As if hearing his words, a mighty blast of water erupted from the maw of the rancorous mountain. First, it engulfed the two space explorers' craft in a liquid spray. Then, instantly freezing, it wrapped them in a steely web. Finally, the shuttle's controls exploded in a spate of alarms. A warning klaxon filled the cabin. Immediately, the shuttle glided toward the moon's surface. Navigational Officer Tripper cursed. "Chris!" exclaimed Jane. "What happened? What's going on?" Tripper's hands flew over the controls. "My fault Jane. I should have remembered that Kubrick was a cryovolcano. Now covered in ice, I've lost control. We're on a slow glide down to the surface of Charon." Communication Officer Franke wrung her hands. "Where are we headed, Chris? Where are we going to land?" Tripper looked in fear at his lover, "To Morder!!"

First Officer Spiro Leonidas pondered the data stream coming from the monitor of his computer. Captain Darkstrider gazed upon the spectacle of the complex view of Pluto's surface as it rippled below her on the main viewscreen. A look of almost dreamy contemplation was apparent in her startling green eyes. Then a light flashed on Leonidas's board. Frowning, Spiro said, "That's odd." Nancy stopped her reverie and looked over at her First Officer. "What's odd, Mr. Leonidas? Is Shuttle Two in trouble again?" Spiro shook his head. "Book and Riley are fine. They've made an interesting discovery and are heading back. No, it's Shuttle One with Franke and Tripper. We've lost communication with them."

Darkstrider swiveled her chair to face the First Officer. "Explain, please. What is their current location?" Spiro tapped his board. "That's just it. No communication, and the homing beacon signal on the ship is gone. So they have vanished from our view."

Nancy Darkstrider turned to her computer screen and rapidly scanned the data. "Yes, I see Shuttle Two, but Shuttle One is no longer there. What can you tell me about the last known whereabouts of the shuttle?" For several minutes, Leonidas reviewed the data the ship's computers had received from Shuttle One. Finally, the First Officer straightened from his monitor and faced his captain. "Franke and Tripper finished their mapping of the Northern hemisphere of Charon. Then they deviated from their prescribed flight path and swept into the Southern hemisphere. They flew from the Pirx impact crater, and their last transmission was over Kubric Mons. Then they vanished." Darkstrider traced a line of Shuttle One's flight path on her monitor. A grim look appeared on her face. "They headed back to Argo Chasma. They wanted another look at the alien artifact they found. I bet this was Franke's idea, and Tripper went along." Spiro arched his eyebrows. "Brilliant deductions, captain. I believe that happened. But it does not explain what happened to the shuttle, how it could suddenly vanish. Even if it crashed, the homing beacon would still emit a signal. It is virtually indestructible."

Captain Darkstrider rubbed her face in thought. "What can you tell me about Kubrick Mons, Mr. Leonidas?" The First Officer mentally reviewed the information he had stored in his memory. "Kubrick Mons is the biggest and tallest of Charon's mountains. Four kilometers tall and forty kilometers wide. A one-kilometer-deep moat surrounds it. There is speculation that Kubrick may be something else." As a horrible realization came over him, Spiro's words trailed off into silence. Nancy glanced at her First Officer, "A what, Mr. Leonidas?" Spiro looked at Nancy determinedly, "A cryovolcano Captain Darkstrider." Nancy turned her chair back to the main viewscreen. "Contact Shuttle Two immediately, Mr. Leonidas. Inform them that Shuttle One has crashed into Charon's surface. Possibly encased in ice." The First Officer opened up a frequency, "As per your orders, Captain." A look of sadness flitted across Nancy's face. "May Lam Lha, the Tibetan goddess of travelers, protect my poor chicks."

"Any luck getting through to the Copernicus Jane?" asked Navigator Tripper. "No," replied Communications Officer Franke. "The ice must shield us from receiving transmissions. I can't break through!" Chris looked through the viewscreen in front of the shuttle. The landscape appeared strangely distorted by the thick ice and ammonia coating it. "It wouldn't surprise me if the ship also lost our homing beacon signal. I doubt they know where we are. I don't know how we will get out of this one."

Like a silver bullet, Shuttle One curved a shallow path down to Charon's surface, light sparking off its icy blanket. Tripper analyzed the data on his monitor. "At least the mapping instruments are still functioning. We will cross the border of Mordor in ten minutes, Jane." Franke looked out the viewscreen as a line of red appeared on the horizon. A look of determination has replaced her earlier fear. "Can we survive the crash, Chris?" Tripper also surveyed the growing field of reddish brown as it filled their view. "Unknown, tholins cover Morder, but to what depth no one knows? Strap yourself in, Jane. The landing is going to be bumpy!"

Shuttle One crossed the perimeter of the landscape of Mordor. Lower and lower, it sank, looking like the legendary Flying Dutchman about to meet its fate. The shuttle plowed into the tholin topography, traveling two hundred kilometers an hour. The spacecraft, enveloped in red earth, rebounded off the surface and then hit again. In the shuttle, the two crewmen strained against their harnesses. It smashed another cloud of tholins off the moon's face as the red-brown shuttle hit for the third time. Tripper's teeth clashed in his mouth, and Franke's hair formed a nimbus around her head. This time, the spacecraft skidded forward as it plowed a hummock of tholins ahead of it. Finally, Shuttle One stopped, almost completely covered in a reddish-brown sheath. In the now-blackened interior of the spacecraft, the two space travelers looked at each other in relief. Jane smiled weakly, "If I'd not met you, Chris, imagine what I'd have missed."

Morder

Chapter 3

Aboard Shuttle Two Engineer Francis Book spoke, "Getting a voice communication from the Copernicus. I'll put it on speaker, Jason." Francis pushed a toggle, and the voice of First Officer Spiro Leonidas filled the cabin. "Attention, Shuttle Two. We have lost contact with Shuttle One. Their last known whereabouts were over Kubrick Mons in the Southern Hemisphere of Charon. Strongly suspect that Kubrick is a cryovolcano that has enveloped the shuttle in ice and crashed somewhere on Charon's surface. Proceed directly to Charon and Kubrick Mons and start a search

pattern. Speculation is that they headed back to Argo Chasma. Questions? Over."
Engineer Jason Riley keyed his mike, "No questions, Mr. Leonidas, over." A burst of
static came over the 65,000 kilometers separating the two craft. "Good hunting,
Shuttle Two," said Leonidas, "over."

Francis Book entered data into the Navigational Computer, "Course set for Charon,
estimated duration of the trip, 6.2 hours." Jason Riley gazed out of the shuttle's main
viewscreen at the distant grey orb that was Charon. "I only hope we will be in time,
Francis."

On Copernicus, Spiro Leonidas flipped off the switch to Shuttle Two. He turned to
Captain Darkstrider and formally announced, "Shuttle Two is on its way to search
for Shuttle One on Charon Captain. Do you think we should leave orbit and join in
the hunt?" Nancy pondered the question for a time and then shook her head
negatively. "No, taking the Copernicus out of orbit would use much of the fuel
reserve we need for our return journey. So until we get more concrete information,
we will stay here." Leonidas nodded and turned back to his monitor. Captain
Darkstrider looked sadly out the viewscreen at the grey specter of Charon. "I pray
I'm doing the right thing."

"Damage report, Officer Franke," demanded Navigator Tripper aboard Shuttle One.
"We did not come out too badly, Officer Tripper," reported Jane formally. "Life
support systems are functional, and hull integrity appears intact. Our fuel reserves
are at 50% full. We have air and water for a week. Of course, Kubick encased us in
ice, and Morder covered us in tholins." Chris grinned ruefully, "Yes, if we had landed
anywhere else, we would have ruptured the hull, and we would be dead now.
Luckily the tholins are meters thick and provided a soft landing for us." Franke tried
to peer out the main viewscreen but could see nothing out of the red earth covering
it. "What is Captain Darkstrider doing to find us, Chris?" Tripper did not look up
from his monitor but answered, "Well, the emergency protocol would be to alert
Shuttle Two. They would then start a search pattern. They probably know from our
data stream we were over Kubrick Mons. But we're a long way from Kubrick Mons
and, for all intents, invisible." Jane Franke looked restlessly around the darkened
cabin. "So, as far as they know, we could be anywhere. The surface area of Charon is
4.6 million square kilometers, almost half the size of the old United States. That's a
lot of ground to cover, Chris."

Tripper reached over and patted the back of his companion. "We sit tight, and they
will find us, Jane. Never tell them I said this, but Book and Riley are the best two
engineers in the fleet. If anyone can find a needle in a haystack, those two boys can."
A red light flashing on her board attracted Franke's attention. She frowned as she
read the new information appearing on her monitor. "We don't have a week, Chris.
The hull sustained a minor breach, and we're losing oxygen. We only have enough
air for 24 hours!" Tripper rubbed the back of his neck and winced. "Jason and
Francis better hurry, Jane!"

6.2 hours later, Shuttle Two entered orbit around Charon. "Charon orbit on my mark," said Engineer Riley, "Now. Locked in." Smoothly, the spacecraft began sailing over Charon's unremitting red, grey, and brown topography. "That's Butler Mons below us, another cryovolcano," said Engineer Book. "Look at the size of it! And that enormous crater beside it is Aldrin. Named for Buzz Aldrin, the second man to have walked on the moon. Pluto and Charon have some outstanding features for a minor planet and a small moon." Vulcan Planum unfurled below them, with Kubrick Mons bulking hugely on the horizon. "Ok," said Francis, "here we go. I will increase our altitude to 100,000 meters to get a good look at Kubrick. Plus, we will not make the same mistake Shuttle One made. If Kubrick blows, we'll be out of range." Like a white dove, the space shuttle spread its wings and gained height until it was over the center of the massive cryovolcano.

"I thought Butler Mons was huge," remarked Jason. "But Kubrick has it beat. How will we find Shuttle One down there in all that ice?" Filling their viewscreen, Kubric Mons displayed a long, sharp central bulge with sharp ridges running down its flanks. A caldera beckoned its maw for the unwary in the middle of the crest. Surrounding the monstrous pile was a deep moat lost in shadows. Engineer Book's hands danced over the controls, "Difficult or not, that's our mission, Francis." For several minutes, the two men pored over their instruments. Then, finally, Jason straightened up. "Right, there is evidence of a recent ice flow within 24 hours. The captain was correct about Shuttle One. It's blasted. But where did they go?"

Francis moved several switches. "I'm going to lower our altitude to 50,000 meters and put us in a circular search pattern. If they're down there, we should be able to pick them up." Like a descending falcon, the spacecraft curved over the massive mountain in lazy circles.

In meticulously planned rings, the spacecraft maneuvered over Kubrick Mons. Gradually, Book and Riley worked their way out from the central crater. Two hours later, Francis exhaled audibly. "Nothing Jason. Nothing but ice and ammonia with a few organic trace elements. I don't think they are down there." Jason looked at his friend. "You may be right, Francis. If they headed towards Argo Chasma, we should break off our search after our last sweep and fly in that direction." Engineer Riley nodded his head. "Yeah, I agree. We will find nothing here. Hello? What is this?" Book sharply twisted his head, "What's up, Jason? Did you find something?"

Riley scrutinized his readings. "Affirmative, I'm reading an ion trace. Similar to the ion vapor left by a shuttle's engines." Francis shook his head. "Such a trail would have disappeared hours ago. So why is it still here?" His companion quickly answered, "The cryovolcano eruption left crystals in the thin atmosphere of Charon. That, and Charon's almost negligible gravity, has left a signpost for us. Let's see if we can find the ion trace on our next sweep." Ten minutes later, Riley exclaimed, "There it is again! An ion signature! Now, if we can find it once more in our next circle, I think we'll know something."

A short time passed, and Engineer Riley crowed triumphantly, "Knew it! There it is again! Another ion trace." Engineer Book studied the data, "I've extrapolated the path the ion traces are following, and they did not head to Argo Chasma Jason." Riley frowned, "They're not? So then, in what direction are they going, Francis?" Engineer Book turned fully in his chair and regarded his partner. "To Morder!!"

On Copernicus, First Officer Leonidas watched as the newest data appeared on his monitor, "Transmission from Shuttle Two Captain. They have searched Kubrick Mons and found an ion path leading North to Morder. They will continue in that direction, looking for signs of Franke and Tripper." A look of anxiety clouded Nancy's face. "To Morder? What madness drove them to go there?"

In the dim interior of Shuttle One, Jane and Chris were endlessly attempting to find a solution to their crisis. "It's been twelve hours, Chris," said Franke. "Do you think the crew has any idea where we are?" Tripper's eyes were busy reviewing data on his screen. "I don't know, Jane. Of course, Book and Riley know we didn't crash on Kubrick Mons by this time. But do they know we're in Morder? That's the big question, and time is running out."

Communication Officer Franke moved wearily back into her chair. "We must face the possibility they may never find us, Chris. We may die here." Tripper reached over and touched his lover's shoulder. "That's true, Jane, but look at the positive. We were the first to land on Charon. The rest of the crew can't say that. Besides, when you signed up for the Space Corp, you knew the dangers. Lots of people die out here." Jane smiled at Chris' words. "Yes, we were the first to land on Charon. However, the crash might be a better description. Why did you join the Space Corp, Chris?" Tripper reflected inwardly, "This is going to sound silly, but that old television program inspired me, 'Star Trek.' It seemed like a great way to explore the universe. Remember, I got you to watch a few episodes with me?" Franke nodded in remembrance, "Not quite my cup of tea, Chris; I prefer holo features to antiquated television."

Tripper looked at the walls of the shuttle in frustration. "If only there were some way to break out of here! We have to break the ice that is cocooning us. But how?" Jane said thoughtfully, "Star Trek, Star Trek, I remember one episode you made me watch was of an Enterprize shuttle that had crashed on a hostile planet." Chris nodded, "The Galileo Seven. Is this a good time to talk about old T.V. shows, Jane?" Franke did not reply at first but tapped the walls of the shuttle. "I remember they used phasers to convert energy into fuel to escape." Tripper grimaced in frustration. "Yes, but we have enough fuel. That's not our problem, a lack of fuel." The Communication Officer turned to her companion. "I was building up to that. In the end, the creatures held down the shuttle, attempting to take off. So they electrified the shuttle to make the creatures let go." A look of amazement crossed Chris' face. "Go on, Jane!"

Jane smiled pleasurably. "If we electrified the hull, it would heat, weakening the ice. If we applied full power, the ice might shatter, and we could escape." Tripper rubbed his face in astonishment. "Brilliant. Flawlessly logical and inventive. It just might work. It will take hours to rig the engines to electrify the hull." Jane laughed. "What are we waiting for?"

One hundred kilometers North of Kubrick Mons, Shuttle Two sailed easily over Charon's surface. "We have just lost all trace of the ion path," reported Engineer Riley. "Never mind, Francis," said Engineer Book. "It has held steady up to now. We will continue in this direction until we find something." Then, serenely, the spacecraft swept over the tortured surface of Pluto's largest moon.

Four hours later, Jason exclaimed, "God, this crater is gigantic!" Francis nodded. "Yeah, Dorothy crater, the largest crater on Charon. Two hundred sixty-one kilometers wide and 6 kilometers deep. We should see the edge of Morder any moment now." As he spoke, a faint red line appeared on the periphery of their screen. Soon the edge of Morder was below Shuttle Two. "Lots of craters down there, Francis," said Jason, "How are we going to find Shuttle One?" Book eyes scanned his scope, "We have found nothing metallic on our way here, Jason. If our reasoning was correct, then they must be somewhere below. Look for anything out of the ordinary." For fifty kilometers, the two space explorers scanned the crater-scared landscape. "I see nothing resembling the shuttle Francis," complained Engineer Riley. "Could we be wrong? Could Franke and Tripper headed for Argo Chasma?" Book shrugged his shoulders, "It's possible, but let's not give up yet. We'll give it another twenty-five kilometers, and then we'll open up our search pattern. I have a hunch they are down there somewhere."

An hour later and twenty-five kilometers more, plunging into the jaws of Morder, found the two spacemen increasingly frustrated. "I think you're right, Jason," said Francis. "We're on a wild goose chase. I will start another search pattern 10 degrees to the west." Riley's fingers moved over his controls. "It's the best thing we can do. There's nothing down there—Wait a minute. Hold on!" Book glanced at his companion, "What have you found, Jason?" Assistant engineer Riley tweaked a button, and a section of Morder flew into high relief. "Look at this," said Riley. "That's no meteorite crater. It's too regular." On the screen, a roughly rectangular depression punched into the red soil of Morder. "And look at this." The view moved forward, and another identical depression appeared 100 meters further. "And finally, cast your eyes on this, Francis," said Engineer Riley. The view expanded again, and north of the two depressions, a long skid mark carved a mark in the red hide of the Morder beast. A small hillock ended the scrape.

"By Jove, you've done it again, Holmes!" joked Francis. "How do you know these things?" Jason winked. "Good looks, talent, extreme intelligence, and modesty." Book laughed, "Yeah, I buy the modesty." Francis touched a switch. "Shuttle Two to Copernicus. We have found something of interest. Sending a screenshot to you on my signal. Over."

Copernicus First Officer Leonidas said on the deep space scout ship, "I have received a message from Shuttle Two Captain. They think they may have found Shuttle One.

They have sent a screenshot." Nancy Darkstrider faced forward in her chair, "Put it on the main viewscreen, Mr. Leonidas." A segment of Morder replaced the view of Pluto's surface. Two depressions, a long groove, and a barrow stood out in stark contrast. "That's it. The shuttle is there," said Captain Darkstrider. "Prepare to leave orbit First Officer." Spiro grinned from ear to ear, "By your command, Captain!" Then, majestically, Copernicus left Pluto's orbit and sped toward the dwarf planet's grim companion.

"Hand me the spanner, Jane," said Navigator Tripper from the depths of the engine compartment. With the access panel removed, only Chris's legs were visible, sticking out. Communication Officer Franke grabbed a spanner and passed it through the panel opening. She heard a muffled appreciation. Two long cables snaked out of the access hole, and Jane busied herself using a screw gun to attach them to both sides of the cabin against bare metal. Affixing the last screw, she tugged at a cable to ensure it was secure. Satisfied, Franke turned her attention to Chris, who heard mumbling and occasionally cursing. "Do you have much more to do, Chris?" asked Jane. "We only have an hour of oxygen left." Tripper's reply came ghostly through the wall, "I know, I know! It's a much harder job than I thought.

Give me a few more minutes, will you?" Franke sank wearily into her chair and stared into space, "A few minutes is all we have, darling." Chris slid from the engine compartment five minutes later and climbed to his feet. Grease and sweat covered his face. Sitting down in his seat, he turned to his beautiful workmate. "Give us a kiss, Luv," Tripper said, grinning. Franke recoiled in mock horror. "Not on your life, buddy!"

Tripper put on his helmet, "Put on your helmet Jane; it's going to get boiling in here soon. Our suits will protect us from the temperature." With his helmet on, Chris tapped the side earpiece, signaling Jane to turn on her communicator. "Ok, Jane," said Tripper, "here we go. I'm going to turn on the engines. They attach directly to the jumper cables to the walls. It will directly convert energy from the engine to heat. I hope we have enough fuel to get free." The Navigator turned on the engines and heard a rumbling from the opened hatch. After a few minutes, the two space explorers could see the shuttle sides turning color to bright yellow. Even though their flight suits, they could feel the increased heat. "Shuttle skin is 1173 degrees, Kelvin," said Tripper. "I'm going to engage the controls to see if we have lift-off." The Navigation Officer pushed a button, and the shuttle rocked but did not move. "1350 Kelvin now," said Chris. "Engaging lift-off now." Again, the spacecraft swung but failed to advance.

The surface of the shuttle was now glowing a brilliant orange. With sweat pouring down their bodies, the space explorers steeled themselves. "1500 Kelvin," shouted Tripper over the roar of the engines. "We can't stand much more of this! One more try!" Now the color of the shuttle's skin was an angry cherry. Desperately, Chris stabbed down on the controls. Then, with a shudder, Shuttle One ripped itself from its ice envelope. Red dust and ice blocks showered in all directions as the craft erupted upward from its nest. Franke and Tripper grinned widely at each other in triumph. "We're free!"

Five kilometers away, Book and Riley were startled to see an object enveloped in red dust and shedding ice chunks explode from the surface of Morder. "What the hell is that!?" exclaimed Francis. Jason laughed, "It's them, the toothsome twosome! Contact Copernicus that we have a visual on Shuttle One!"

Aboard Shuttle One, the grins on Franke's and Tripper's faces faded as quickly as the heat in the cabin. Shuttle One looked like a flaming meteorite; the spacecraft traveled upwards at 300 kilometers an hour. Chris read the fuel gauge and cursed. Jane looked up in alarm. "What's wrong, Chris? We're free, aren't we?" Tripper glanced at his co-worker miserably. "Oh, we're free, all right. But taking off took all our fuel. So we can't achieve orbit." The Communications Officer paled, "You mean we're going to crash, Chris?" Tripper nodded, "That's the usual result of an uncontrolled trajectory Jane." The two held hands as the spacecraft reached the apex of its flight and then fell faster and faster. Calmly, the two lovers watched the surface of Morder growing in the forward viewscreen. "It was a smart gamble, Jane," said Tripper. "It's too bad there was no one to see Shuttle One's last flight." Franke looked at Tripper devotedly. "I love you, Chris." A crooked smile filled the young man's face. "I know."

"Shuttle One! Shuttle One! Shuttle Two is calling! We have you in sight. Can you read us? Over." Communication Officer Franke eagerly answered, "Roger Shuttle Two, we can read you! But, unfortunately, we are out of fuel. Can you assist us? Over." Instantly the answer came back, "Understand your problem, stand by, over." Chris looked out the viewscreen at Shuttle Two approaching them like a merciful angel. "What can they do? Shuttles don't carry tractor beams strong enough to catch us. Have they contacted Copernicus? Does the captain know what's going on?" Now the hellish landscape of Morder was rushing towards them. "Stand by, stand by, over," came Engineer Book's voice over the shuttle intercom. "For what?" growled Navigational Officer Tripper. "We'll never survive the impact." A last loving look passed between the two compatriots. "This is it," said Chris. "Seven seconds to contact." Suddenly the two space voyagers jolted violently forward in their harnesses, and the shuttle came to a dead stop fifty meters above the surface of Morder.

"Got you!" shouted First Officer Spiro Leonidas over the shuttle's com. "Shuttle One, we have you in our tractor beam. What is your condition? Over." The vast bulk of Copernicus hovered in sight, blocking off the light from the stars and distant sun. "We're fine, Copernicus," answered Jane exaltedly. "But we have oxygen for only thirty minutes. Over." Leonidas's voice came quickly back in a burst of static, "Roger. We will return you directly to Copernicus' landing bay. Welcome back, Shuttle One. Over." Chris and Jane hugged each other. "Glad to be back, over!"

Four days later, the crew of the Copernicus met in the ship's main conference room. The six sat in their chairs encircling the round table. Captain Darkstrider looked briskly at each member of her team. "Well," said Nancy, "we've had an eventful week. First, Engineers Book and Riley have made an interesting discovery on Hydra. Mr. Leonidas, if you please?" Spiro touched his controls, and a hologram of the Plutonian moon Hydra sprang into existence over the center of the table. The image sharpened to the dark pool that stained the side of the satellite. "You may remember we noted this black patch when we first entered the system," said Leonidas. The captain nodded her head. "Yes, will the engineers tell us what they found?" Francis and Jason glanced at each other before Francis Book spoke. "The pool is ten kilometers in diameter, captain. Its surface temperature is 23 Kelvin. Our spectrometer readings told us nothing, so we sent a probe down."

Jason continued the dialogue. "The probe vanished beneath the object's surface and gave depth reports for the next sixty minutes. When contact stopped, it was at a distance of over 2232.6 kilometers." Exclamations of disbelief exploded around the conference table. "That's impossible!" interjected Navigational Officer Tripper. "Hydra, at most, is fifty-one kilometers wide. Are you sure your instruments were working properly? Were they able to analyze the medium your probe was passing through?" Engineer Book gave Chris a noncommital look. "As far as we could tell, the probe's instruments were working perfectly. It's just what it was passing through is unknown to our science. Like the artifact you found in Argo Chasma?"

At the mention of Argo, Tripper and Franke winced slightly. "Any speculation on what it is, men?" asked Darkstrider. "And why was your probe registering a depth it could not have reached?" Engineers Book and Riley glanced around the table before they answered. "We've come up with several possibilities, Captain Darkstrider," said Jason. "A hologram, a black hole, an illusion, or black matter." Again, startling cries filled the sterile atmosphere of the room. "Black matter?" said Communications Officer Franke. "They theorized black matter one hundred and fifty years ago! Could you have found the first evidence of its reality?" But, first, Officer Leonidas touched a control, and the image of Hydra disappeared. "An excellent question, Yeoman Franke. A find of this caliber would be monumental. As you know, twenty-seven percent of the universe is black matter."

Nancy focused her laser-green eyes on Jane and Chris. "Now we come to the exploits of the Shuttle One crew. What did you think about abandoning your fight plan and taking a pleasure cruise toward Argo Chasma? And flying over a cryovolcano in the process?" Tripper and Franke straightened up in their chairs. "No excuse, Captain Darkstrider," said the Navigation officer. "We'd finished mapping the Northern Hemisphere and quickly looked at the artifact we had found. I had no notion that Kubrick Mons was an active volcano." Captain Darkstrider tapped the table with her forefinger. "I know this mission is fraught with risks, but some risks are not worth taking. You were lucky to escape with your lives. It took the engineers three days to repair the damage you had done to your shuttle. Not to mention you owe them your continued existence for finding you."

Chris and Jane reddened visibly. "We only meant it to be a side trip, Captain," said Yeoman Franke. "We were then going to complete our mission by mapping Morder."

Then, first Officer Leonidas spoke, "The Captain has relieved you of that responsibility. Since your shuttle was out of commission, Engineers, Book, and Riley mapped Morder." Chris straightened in his chair. "But Charon is ours to map!" yelled out Tripper indignantly. Nancy cut the Navigational Officer's tirade short with a curt gesture. "Wrong, Mr. Tripper. I will decide who gets what mission. Is that understood?" Cowed, both young people nodded their heads.

Captain Darkstrider turned her attention to her two engineers. "Let's see what you discovered in Morder. Mr. Leonidas, if you please. The First Officer touched his controls, and a holographic map of Morder sprang over the conference table. Yet, even in its disembodied state, an air of menace extruded. "What can you tell us about Morder Mr. Book?" said Nancy. "Morder is a reddish-brown macula that is 475 miles in diameter," said Francis. "A central plateau dominates it. One gigantic crater is to the South-West of the plateau." Jason took up the narrative. "66 craters pierce Morder, with two of them being especially bright. On the extreme West and East are two prominent conical hillocks."

"Excellent summary, gentlemen," said Captain Darkstrider. "As you know, it is customary first for the first cartographers of previous unmapped territory to propose names for certain features. Do you have any names in mind?" Book and Riley looked at each other and smiled. "Yes, Captain," said Francis. "We propose the large central plateau, Nancy Darkstrider, and the enormous crater to its SouthWest, Spiro Leonidas. The two bright craters we christened Book and Riley." Jason continued, "We dub the two large conical hills Tripper and Franke."

"Interesting choices for nomenclature," said the captain. "I will put forward your suggestions to the IAU. The International Astronomical Union. I think the names are acceptable. And thank you for my inclusion and the rest of the crew." Nancy unbent slightly and addressed the visibly deflated navigation and communication officers. "Don't worry; you'll get your chance. There is a macula at Charon's South pole. You can map that." Smiles appeared on the faces of Chris and Jane. "Now, let's talk about the next order of business," said Captain Darkstrider.

The holo map of Morder winked out, and a holographic image of the artifact in Argos appeared. "Since the Copernicus is in orbit around Charon earlier than planned, we can proceed with the next order of business," said Nancy. The magnification of the alien artifact increased until it filled their view. "The Copernicus will take a position 10 kilometers above Argos Chasma, direct its lasers down onto the structure, and disintegrate the ice cover. Then Shuttles One and Two will land on each extremity of the construction, and their crews will examine it on foot." Captain Nancy Darkstrider scrutinized each of her crew with eyes like emeralds. "We must find a way into that thing."

Ten minutes later, Engineers Book and Riley left the conference room to find Navigator Tripper and Yeoman Franke waiting for them. An uncomfortable moment passed. Finally, Jane said, "We never thanked you for saving our lives." The two engineers looked pleased. "Thank the Captain and the First Officer. They're the ones who grabbed you with the ship's tractor beam," said Jason. "We already have thanked them," rejoined Tripper. "And now we're thanking you. If you hadn't tracked us down, they would never have been in the right spot to rescue us." In unison, the four space explorers saluted each other and held the pose for a long moment. Chris grinned, "Named us after conical hillocks? Why didn't you call them after Jane's breasts? Or didn't you two think about that?" Book and Riley smirked. "Oh, we did, but we didn't think the I.A.U. would accept it." Yeoman Franke stepped forward, hugged each engineer, and kissed them. "Thanks again, Jason. Thanks, Francis." Jane and Chris turned and walked out of sight around the corner. Engineer Book whistled. "Jane is lovely, isn't she, Jason?" His boon companion looked mildly at him. "For a woman, I mean."

The sun rose above Charon's surface, looking like a giant star; its weak light sparkled off the hull of the Copernicus. The ship's 1500meter length continued its stately procession around the curve of the satellite. Beyond Charon, its four brothers and sister moons continued their mad capering around mother Pluto. Against the inky backdrop of space, the stars glowed like a treasure chest of jewels strewn carelessly on a velvet curtain. Constellations pirouetted and danced as if in a god's vast studio. Comets streaked like fireflies on their nuptial flight.

Yeoman Franke and ship Navigator Tripper lay in each other's arms in their cabin. Exhausted after their lovemaking, they gazed contently at the ceiling, lost in thought. "I'm glad the Captain didn't come down on us too hard for disobeying orders and almost losing the shuttle," said Jane. "Yeah," said Chris. "But how is she going to punish us? Send us to Pluto? We're already here!" Franke chuckled and nestled sleepily on Tripper's chest. "I'm still mad about the two boy toys stealing Morder from us and taking all the best spots for themselves, the captain, and Spock. And what do we get? Two lumps! I think they are calling us pillocks, Chris!" Tripper stroked Jane's lustrous blonde hair. "Well, we cracked Shuttle One, and they repaired it. Besides, we get the South Pole Macula to map. And then we get to pick the names!" Beside him, the Communication Officer snored gently.

Down the hallway, the Copernican engineers Riley and Book were lying on bunks in their cabin. Jason was flat on his back with his eyes closed as he listened to the music. Francis regarded his friend with mild irritation. "How can you listen to that retro crap? That is so 2090s!" Without opening his eyes, Riley responded, "Hey! I'm two years younger than you, grandpa. Would you rather listen to that garbage that the gruesome twosome enjoys? Martian skittles? I'm telling you, Francis, the younger generation doesn't know what delightful music is!" Engineer Book turned on his holovision projector and watched a program from the Titan Space station. "Spock said the captain has put us in for medals for our part in the Shuttle One rescue." His intimate waved his finger in the air as he followed the song's rhythm. "As well she should," said Jason, "We were heroes! Though I must admit that jury rig they dreamed up to free themselves from the ice was a bloody good bit of engineering!" Francis dipped his head in agreement. "And they were good enough to thank us for saving their lives. Though I don't think Franke needed to hug and kiss us." Riley snapped his fingers as his music launched into another song. "I see your point. If we had been wearing our medals, her big boobs would have crushed them!" Both men laughed uproariously.

Nancy Darkstrider lay curled up on her bed in the captain's cabin. She had lain there for hours, but sleep would not come. Restively, she swung her legs over the side and sat with her chin cupped in her hands. Nancy looked much younger than her fifty-eight years in her nightclothes and blonde hair unbound. Darkstrider stood irresolutely for a moment, then moved over to her nightstand and lowered herself into a chair. She stared at her reflection and into her remarkable green eyes for a time. "Old girl," said Nancy, "those eyes have seen a thing or two in their time, haven't they? Last cast of the dice. The final chance to make a significant discovery and create a name for me. But am I good enough? Am I strong enough? My shuttle crews have almost killed themselves, and we've barely started our mission. Thank god Leonidas has been a rock in all this. Is he in love with me? Sometimes I think so. I've known him off and on for thirty-five years since we were at the Space Academy together. But I can't allow myself to be distracted by romance. It's enough that I have two loving couples on board already. What will tomorrow hold, I wonder? Can we find an entrance into that strange thing that Franke and Tripper found? And what about Book and Riley's discoveries? What is that red-purple splotch on Nix? And can that black pool on Hydra be the black matter? So many questions and so little time to solve them."

The captain moved to the cabin's port and looked out into space. The minor moon, Pluto, slowly revolved into her view. At this distance, the heart of Pluto looked like the iris of a giant blue eye. Yet, unwinkingly, the heart stared at her. "The secret is there," said Darkstrider. "I feel that all our answers lay in the heart. But what price must we pay to get them?" Like the Eye of Sauron, the Heart of Pluto said the price would be very high.

Alone in his cabin, First Officer Leonidas lay in untroubled slumber. It erased the burdens of the day from his countenance.

And the deep space scout ship Copernicus carried them all, with their hopes, dreams, and desires safely stored within.

According to Copernicus's clock, dawn found the crew again assembled on the Shuttle deck. Barely contained excitement was apparent in the shuttle teams as they waited impatiently for the order to board. Finally, the shuttle door opened, and Captain Darkstrider entered, followed by First Officer Spiro Leonidas. She came to a halt in front of the two shuttle teams. "Well, eager beavers, I see. Impressive," said Nancy. "You know the drill. Put your ships on hover 10 kilometers from the artifact in Argo Chasma. We will inform you when we fire the laser cannons to clear the ice covering the alien structure. After we have finished, we will give you the all-clear, and you may proceed with your missions. Questions?" Navigation Officer Tripper grinned, "Piece of cake!" Captain Darkstrider smiled, "I hope you're right, Mr. Tripper. Now take off and be safe out there." The four space explorers entered their shuttles and closed the hatches. The Captain and her First Officer left the shuttle bay.

Fifteen minutes later, they watched as both shuttles cleared the shuttle bay and flew into space. "God forbid we have any accidents today," said Nancy. "Amen to that, Captain," rejoined Spiro.

An hour later, Copernicus positioned itself precisely over the artifact in Argos Chasma. "Both shuttles report they have taken their positions, Captain," reported Leonidas. Nancy regarded the main bridge screen as the alien building came into focus. First Officer Leonidas checked his monitor. "I estimate the ice is ten meters thick. I recommend a controlled laser discharge along the horizontal axis. Then we can make an assessment." Captain Darkstrider leaned slightly forward in her chair. "Make it so." Leonidas keyed a mike to the shuttles. "Attention, Fire in the Hole!" Forcefully, Spiro stabbed down on the laser firing button, and a vivid red beam of light leaped from the bottom of the ship and struck the monument. Large shards of ice erupted in all directions, and a haze of ice crystals formed a cloud. Slowly, the beam traced its way along the length of the massive pile. Reaching its end, the red stream of light abruptly stopped. Several minutes passed as the icy cloud dissipated in Charon's low gravity. The First Officer studied the readouts on his monitor. "About half the ice is gone, captain. Permission to repeat laser mission."

Darkstrider nodded her head. Again came the warning, "Attention, Fire in the Hole!" An angry streak of crimson smashed into the frosty shield for a second time. Bits of rime rained down like a shower of diamonds. Deliberately, the raw power of the laser stripped every vestige of crystal from the alien relic. Nancy could now see the vast superstructure free of its ice shroud for the first time in unguessable ages. "Fire mission complete, captain," announced the First Officer formally. "Noted, Mr. Leonidas," said Darkstrider.

The entity stood proudly on the canyon floor, an extraterrestrial antiquity blazing in white so bright it appeared to be tinged with blue. Spiro keyed his mike, "Attention, shuttle teams. You may land when ready, over." Agreements came quickly back. The two spacecraft resembled pale moths as they drifted down to a gentle landing by each end of the cyclopean complex. On Shuttle One, Yeoman Franke and Navigational Officer Tripper adjusted their helmets and prepared for their first foray onto the surface of Charon. The tinny voice of the Engineer Book came over their intercoms. "Shuttle One, the honor goes to you for the first step. Over." Chris acknowledged the honor being given to them, "Received Shuttle Two, and thanks, over."

Tripper touched his helmet to Frankes so she could hear him. "Well, Jane, we wouldn't be here if you hadn't devised your escape plan. So I think you should take the first step." Chris saw a tear running down Jane's face through her sun visor.

The two space explorers stepped into the small airlock and purged the oxygen. A light over the outside door turned from red to green. Franke pushed a button by the hatch, and the exit slid open, revealing Charon's sterile soil. Gingerly, she stepped from the shuttle and stood fully on the exotic moon's surface. The distant sun's rays caused a halo to form around Jane's helmet. "That's one small step for a woman. One giant leap for all humankind."

On Shuttle Two, Riley turned to Book. "Did you hear what she said? How are we going to top that?" Francis chucked, "We're not; let's get out there and go to work." From 10 kilometers in space, First Office Leonidas watched the four space-suited figures leave their craft and fan out the sides of the Brobdingnagian building. "What do you think of Yeoman Franke's first words, Captain?" Nancy pondered the question, "A derivation of Neil Armstrong's first words on the moon. But not bad, not bad at all." Spiro looked at his captain and smiled. "Perhaps when we land on Pluto, you will come up with an appropriate phrase? The first step on a planet always goes to the captain. That's been the tradition in the Space Corp." Darkstrider twisted her head and looked at Pluto on a side screen. "I will have to think about it, Mr. Leonidas."

Franke and Tripper walked over to the artifact and examined its surface. Ten meters high, the structure stretched for half a kilometer to the west of them. Just on the edge of sight, they could discern the figures of Book and Riley as they stood by their shuttle. Their two compatriots waved a greeting at them, which they returned shortly. Rileys' voice crackled over the helmet intercoms. "Attention, Shuttle One. We will take the south side while you explore the north." Jane spoke into her mouthpiece, "Acknowledged Shuttle Two, over." Yeoman Franke reached out her gloved hand and tapped the surface of the ancient relic.

"Anyone home?" she asked. Tripper's rejoinder came swiftly back, "Surprised if somebody was?" two spacers examined every square millimeter of the marble-like side with portable recorders. "The spectrographic readings concur with Leonidas's Jane," said Christ. "This metal is element is145 on the Periodic Table. Physically, it should not be able to exist, but here it is." Franke studied her screen. "Yes, incredibly dense. I don't know how we will get a sample for analysis." Navigation Officer Tripper took his blaster from its holder. "Stand back, Jane." As his companion watched, Chris fired a blast of white energy into the metallic flank. A blossom of red appeared briefly and disappeared. Tripper adjusted the weapon to its highest setting and fired again. Once more, an incandescent bloom appeared and then faded. Chris retired the blaster to the holder. "You're right, Jane. But, unfortunately, it is going to be hard to get a sample."

On the southern periphery, Book and Riley trudged along collecting data. Halfway along, they stopped and regarded the enigma before them. "I don't see any sign of a door, Jason," said Book. Jason studied his recorder, "I don't either, Francis. Can you believe the composition of this metal? The hardest substance in the solar system. I don't know how we will get in if we can't find an entrance. I doubt the ship's lasers could dent its surface." Engineer Book shook his head. "Maybe it's better if we don't get in. I'm worried about this." His companion looked at Francis in surprise. "We're scientists, old friend. I can feel the danger too. A foreboding, as if something is watching us, waiting for us to make a mistake." Book shivered in his spacesuit and looked at the chasma walls in the distance. A purple haze settled down, casting an eerie glow on everything around them. "The sun is setting, Francis," said Jason. "Let's finish up here and get back to the ship." The two men continued their lonely walk. Far-off canyon ramparts regarded the unwelcome intruders.

Yeoman Franke and Navigational Officer Tripper reached the end of the structure, turned the corner, and appraised the eastern end. Nowhere along the length had they found an opening. "Well, we came up empty," said Chris. "I had a feeling this would not be easy." Jane looked uneasily at the velvet mist falling around them. "Where does this vapor come from, Chris?" she asked. "Charon isn't supposed to have an atmosphere." Tripper looked in surprise at the gathering gloom. "Yeah, spooky, isn't it? It's like something out of Macbeth. I almost expect three witches to come skulking out of the darkness. Finished! Back to the shuttle!" Eagerly the two lovers hurried towards their alien craft. Behind them, the growing fog seemed to writhe with disembodied shapes.

At that exact moment, Engineers Book and Riley were regarding the western end of the alien structure. "Nothing Jason," said Book. "Not a crack, not a flaw, not a window in the whole place. I wonder if Franke and Tripper are having better luck?" Riley studied a large fragment of ice nearby. "I think we would have heard if they did, Francis. Let's take a core sample from that large slab of ice. The bottom is blue, which was the lowest layer on the artifact. See how it shades from blue to green to white? We should get an age for the artifact by calculating this ice fragment." Book turned on his helmet's light and played it around, searching through the purpling shadows. "Ok, but make it fast. The sun is almost down, and soon we'll be in complete darkness."

Jason took and small pick from his belt and chipped an ice sample from the berg. As Riley bent to his work, he suddenly grinned and said, "Hey, you know what this reminds me? That old movie we saw in the Holo Theatre last year on Titan Station. 'The Mist'? You know, a freak storm unleashes a species of bloodthirsty creatures in a small town. The purple stuff looks just like it." Francis groaned, "You would have to remember that now. Stop talking about it!" Jason dropped a sample of ice in his pouch and straightened up, "Ok, ok! Have no fear; Riley is here! Back to the ship Macduff!" With swift footsteps, the scientists marched steadily into the gloaming.

Back aboard the Copernicus, First Officer Leonidas listened to his headset. "Shuttle crews report they finished their preliminary surveys and are returning to the ship. They say the alien artifact has no discernable openings. Therefore, they could not get a sample of the hull. Nonetheless, both teams say they have gathered considerable data." Captain Darkstrider stood up and stretched her lithe body. Out of the corner of his eye, Leonidas watched her. "Well, Mr. Leonidas, let's call it a day."

The Door

Chapter 4

Twelve hours later, the Copernican crew assembled again in the main conference room. Around the table, the three couples made small talk. Eventually, Captain Darkstrider called the meeting to order. "OK, we have a lot to discuss. Mr. Leonidas, If you please." The First Officer busied himself on his monitor, and a holographic image of the artifact in Argos Chasma appeared floating above their heads. Spiro rotated the structure to show all its aspects: length, width, and upper surfaces. Nancy continued, "Mr. Leonidas has evaluated all the data gathered by the shuttle crews. It appears not to have a means of entry. An unbroken structure of an unknown element may be impregnable to anything we can throw against it. However, we are certainly going to try. First, it is undoubtedly not a solid rectangle but a hollow one. The question is, why is there not a door? Does anyone have any ideas?"

Uneasily, the team members looked at each other with blank countenances. Darkstrider swept her green eyes around the group. "Come on. You are all veteran space explorers. Surely someone must have an idea. Don't be afraid to give an opinion, no matter how outlandish it might sound. Now, why can't we find a way in?" Jason Riley glanced at his companions and said, "I have something, captain. It is going to sound weird, but I think it's possible. It involves two old movies I saw on the retro holo channels. 'Lord of the Rings and 'The Day the Earth stood still.'" Nancy rested her chin on her cupped hand. "Go on, Mr. Riley." Encouraged, the engineer said, "The spaceship on 'The Day the Earth stood Still' had a door that vanished after the alien Klaatu, or Gort the robot, exited or entered. And in 'The Lord of the Rings,' the Fellowship could not enter the Mines of Moria through an invisible entrance until they spoke a magic word."

For thirty seconds, the group stared at the nonplussed engineer until First Officer Leonidas commented, "You are speaking about a molecular door, aren't you, engineer?" Jason relaxed slightly. "Yes, Mr. Leonidas, a molecular door. That's how the aliens got in and out, and that's why we can't see it." Nancy considered, "An eloquent solution, Mr. Riley. Let's assume there are one or more molecular doors in the structure. How do we find them, and how do we open them? I don't think magic words or spells will work, even if there was an atmosphere to carry them." Engineer Book said, "We'll have to throw everything we have at it, captain. Radiation, heat, sonic beams, pressure cannons, even the ship's lasers. We must hit on the right method to force the door to that thing." Nancy Darkstrider nodded and said, "Yes, I agree. We'll have to use all our ingenuity to find a door."

Francis said, "It will take a day for Engineer Riley and myself to get the equipment ready, Captain Darkstrider." The captain frowned. "Very well. The shuttle teams will fly down to the moon's surface the day after tomorrow to set up the equipment." Nancy looked curiously at her two crew members, that had been uncharacteristically silent. "Navigator Tripper and Yeoman Franke, you two have said nothing. Don't you have anything to offer? The first two spacers who stepped onto Charon should be more vocal. 'That's one small step for a woman. One giant leap for all humankind,' I believe I heard one person say."

Two lovers spared a look between them. "I agree with Jason's idea of a molecular door, captain," commented Chris. "Jane and I examined every square millimeter of the monument's sides. She even tapped on its side." Yeoman Franke said, "I had the impression it was hollow, Captain." Nancy Darkstrider smiled, "I think you're right, Yeoman." The captain turned to the First Officer. "Mr. Leonidas, I believe you have some information you wish to share?" Spiro smiled slightly. "Yes, Captain, I have analyzed the core sample that Engineers Book and Riley collected. The deepest layer of the ice is of incredible age, on the order of a billion years."

Exclamations of surprise and shock exploded around the room. "A billion years! That's amazing!" said Navigator Tripper. "That would mean the artifact must be at least that age!" Spiro inclined his head to the younger man. "You are correct—at least one billion years. And the structure looks like they could have built it yesterday. No evidence of weathering at all."

For a minute, there was silence around the table as the crew mulled over this latest information. "Why would aliens leave outposts on Pluto and Charon a billion years ago," asked Jane. "What was earth like back then?" Leonidas was quick to answer. "Earth was in its Proterozonic Age, Yeoman Franke. The continents joined into one supercontinent, Rodinia. Life comprises single-celled organisms. The earth is spinning faster than it does now. A day was 18 hours." Jane thought that over. "Earth sounds like it was a boring place, Mr. Leonidas. No wonder the aliens never visited." The First Officer touched a button, and the holographic image of the alien artifact disappeared. "Yes," said Captain Darkstrider, "the earth wasn't as exciting as a Saturday night in Lunatic City on the Moon. Which you and Mr. Tripper can probably attest to." Jane reddened slightly in embarrassment. Chris looked ruefully at her.

"Captain Darkstrider," said Tripper. "Book and Riley won't need our help to prepare the equipment tomorrow. May Yeoman Franke and I have your permission to map the macula at Charon's southern pole? It's the only area left to map in Pluto's system." Nancy gave the ship's navigator and communications officers a penetrating look with viridian green eyes. "Very well. Prepare a flight path and submit it to me when you have completed it. And don't fly over any cryovolcanoes!" Chris laughed, "We won't, captain. Don't you worry about that!" Darkstrider smiled, "All right, I won't. Then, if there is nothing else, let's end this meeting and go to dinner."

The crew of the Copernicus left their chairs and headed down the corridor to the ship's galley. Below them, now free of its icy shroud, the alien artifact squatted like a predatory beast waiting for its prey.

Yeoman Franke picked listlessly at her food in the dining hall a half-hour later. "This grub has no taste, Chris. I wouldn't feed it to my cat!" Tripper busied himself with another forkful of vegetables. "It's been in stasis for a year, Jane. Some flavors have leached out, I guess. It tastes fine to me." Jane put her fork down in disgust. "Why can't we have replicators like they had in Star Trek? I bet their food tasted better than this garbage!" Chris took a drink of coffee before answering. "The same reasons we don't have transporters or holodecks on board. They don't exist." Jane glanced at the nearby tables where Engineers Book, Riley, First Officer Leonidas, and Captain Darkstrider were eating. "It was good that the captain will let us map the macula on the Charon's south pole tomorrow, Chris. And we get to come up with names of the things we find!" Navigational Officer Tripper busily stuffed more food into his mouth and didn't comment.

At their table, Engineers Book and Riley animatedly talked as they ate. "Busy day for us tomorrow Jason," said Francis. "We must rig the sonic and pressure cannon, a light pulse gun, and a heating device. Plus, anything else we can dream up." Jason glanced surreptitiously at Frankes and Tripper's table. "Look at those two. Jane is picking at her food, and Chris is stuffing his face as usual. Oh, right, the equipment? I think we can knock it together in a few hours, Francis. We'll finish before dinnertime tomorrow if we get an early start." Engineer Book speared a carrot on his fork and nibbled on it. "A molecular door. That was an inspiring idea, Jason. All those thousands of hours you spent watching those old movies were good for something." Book sipped apple juice. "It's inspiration if I'm correct. I don't think the captain will be too pleased if we spend a lot of time looking for a door that does not exist."

"A molecular door," said Captain Darkstrider. "Do you think we can find it? If it is there at all?" First Officer Leonidas swallowed a mouthful of souvlaki and replied, "I don't know what else it could be, captain. The artifact is a building of sorts. There must be a way in." Nancy looked around restlessly as she drank her tea. "We can only afford a few days finding our way inside. Our primary mission is to find the beacon on Pluto. And we do not know yet where that might be." Spiro sipped his ouzo. "I think what we potentially find in the artifact will help us a lot when we find the beacon." Darkstrider picked up a fork and turned her attention to her meal. "That's if we find a way into the alien structure. And if we find the beacon. And if we can find a way into it." Spiro smiled, "That's a lot of 'if's,' captain."

The following day, Captain Darkstrider and First Officer Leonidas were on the shuttle deck with Navigator Tripper and Yeoman Franke. The two young people held their helmets under their arms as they listened to the captain's last instructions. "Now remember, "said Nancy. "Map the southern macula, but don't attempt a landing. It would be best if you were back in time for dinner. And please don't fly over any cryovolcanoes. They may permit you to name the features you find there." Chris smiled, "Understood, captain, and thank you." Jane saluted, "Aye, aye, captain, and goodbye!" Darkstrider hid a grin as she returned the salute. With no more ceremony, the shuttle crew turned and entered the spacecraft; the captain and her first officer left the hangar deck.

Fifteen minutes later, on the bridge, Nancy and Spiro watched as the shuttle cleared the shuttle bay and flew into space. Then, turning gracefully on its side, the vessel sped south towards Charon's pole. "All I ask is a tall ship and a star to steer her by," murmured Captain Darkstrider. The first officer arched his eyebrow but had no comment.

In the Engineering Machine Shop, Book and Riley were hard at work. Francis had a glossy black gun-like machine panel open and was tinkering inside. Riley was under a squat device that resembled a large turning fork. Other machines lay scattered around the room. "What's the calibration on the sonic cannon, Francis?" called out Jason. "It's 20,000 PSI," answered Book. For a time, the two busied themselves industrially on their machines. Equipment and piles of spare parts covered the floors and walls of the room. Then, a banging noise came from under the sonic beamer where Jason was working. Francis carefully inserted an instrument into the open panel on his machine and made adjustments. Now satisfied, he closed the hatch and straightened up. "That's the pressure cannon ready now, Jason," he said. "I'm going to work on the heating device now." Again, from under the machine came a muffled "OK." Wearily the Chief Engineer Book walked over to a bench and sat down. He took a handkerchief out of his pocket and wiped some grime off his face. A few moments later, a cry of success came from the still-invisible Riley. He pushed himself from under his machine on a wheeled trolley. Jason saw his friend on the bench and joined him.

"Well, we have calibrated two machines and are ready to deploy," said Engineer Riley. "I'll tackle the heating device next while you're working on the light pulse gun." Book nodded and leaned back against the wall. Jason hunched forward with his head in his hands and contemplated their handiwork. "It's hard work getting those rust buckets to work," said Riley. "Like everything else in this ship, they are almost antiques." Book smiled, "Including us, Jason?"

Jason replied with a mock indignant look, "Speak for yourself, grandpa! But remember, I'm two years younger than you." Age was a standing joke between the two men. Francis opened his eyes and peered around the compartment. "I wonder if any of this equipment will work against the artifact. Its metal is extremely dense. Tripper said he tried to blast a hole in it with his sidearm. Didn't even scorch it." Jason flexed his fingers as if holding a weapon. "He always was a cowboy. So why was Chris carrying a blaster in the first place? What did he expect to find? A bug-eyed monster? I didn't carry mine." Engineer Book looked reflective. "Just the same; I think we should carry our sidearms tomorrow when we're down on the surface of Charon. I got a nasty inkling when that purple haze started descending." Riley shuddered slightly. "Yeah, Francis, I think you're right. Blasters are the order of the day. And I pity and green-skinned alien that crosses our path!" Book laughed, "I thought they were bug-eyed monsters?" Jason drew and aimed an imaginary weapon. "I'm no xenophobe, Francis. I'll shoot anything."

Five hundred kilometers away, Shuttle One was approaching the border of the south pole macula. A thin red line appeared on their viewscreen. "Approaching southern macula," announced Navigator Tripper. A look of discontent crossed Yeoman Franke's face. "That is such an awkward description, Chris. We can come up with a better name than that, surely?"

Tripper watched as the macular spread to fill the horizon. "What do you suggest, Jane? And don't call me Shirley." Franke laughed dutifully, "There is Morder at the

North Pole; why not have the Mines of Moria at the South Pole?" Chris whistled. "Not bad, babe, not bad at all. The Mines of Moria it is!"

Like a tremendous reddish-brown throw rug, the Mines of Moria macula spread beneath them. "Right, here we go," said Tripper. "Note those four large craters in a row." Jane grinned, "John, Paul, George, and Ringo craters." Chris smiled tightly, "Interesting choices, Yeoman; now we are approaching a large central plain." Franke gave a tinkling laugh. "Strawberry Fields." The Navigational Officer turned to his companion. "Let's hold off on naming for a while until we finish our survey, Jane." For an hour, the shuttle flew above the smooth landscape. "That's odd," said Chris, "in that entire tableland, only one small, lonely crater. Strange." With a mischievous look, Jane said, "Pete Best." Tripper let out a groan, "Oh my god."

Several hours later, Shuttle One had completed its mapping of the newly named Mines of Moria macula. "Mission accomplished," intoned Navigator Tripper. "We have a macula 325 kilometers in diameter. Four large craters and 45 smaller ones. A large central pain and two ridges." Jane smirked. "And two hard-boiled eggs." She poked her companion in the ribs. "And two hard-boiled eggs. Will you stop with the jokes, Jane? This is serious!" demanded Chris. Franke sniggered, "And one duck egg." Tripper wheeled the shuttle around and set it on a course out of the macula. "I think you've gone space happy, Jane." Jane simpered. "I'm always happy when I'm with you, darling." The Navigation Officer let out a small sob. "Oh, my god!" Like an old-time sailing ship, the white-hued spacecraft hoisted her sails and navigated into an ocean where oars never dip.

Captain Nancy Darkstrider relaxed at a table in the forward lounge and regarded the view of the large window covering one side of the room from top to bottom. The Milky Way spilled like a furl of bleached silk across the sky. In the subdued lighting, Nancy could see the beauty of the universe as it unfolded before her. Sipping a glass of red wine, Darkstrider heard the door slide almost noiselessly open and footsteps crossing towards her. "Good evening Mr. Leonidas," said Nancy without turning her head. "Get yourself a drink if you like and join me." The First Officer sat at Nancy's table with a glass of ouzo. He glanced out at the vista.

"I never tire of looking at that panorama. It's as if a god went mad with a brush full of white paint." Slowly the view rotated out of their sight, and several moons of Pluto came into their vision. "You know what this reminds me of?" asked Spiro. "When we were at the Space Academy, we took a trip to Vancouver, Canada. Remember that dinner we had at that revolving restaurant? The Harbourcenter Tower, I think it's called." The captain's eyes became misty for a moment. "Yes, a long time ago. Thirty-five years. Another time, a different place." Then, as if sensing this topic that Darkstrider did not want to pursue, Leonidas changed the subject. "I checked with the engineers. They report they are just finishing up their maintenance on the machinery. And Shuttle One has finished mapping what they call the Mines of Moria macula. They suggest several other names I'd rather not get into now." Nancy took another sip of her wine. "The Mines of Moria? I like that. An effective counterbalance to Morder on the opposite pole."

The two old friends sat in comfortable silence. On the edge of the screen, the minor planet Pluto steadily crept into sight. The white and blue lobes of the heart scintillated in the light of the far-off sun. Abruptly Captain Darkstrider spoke, "The beacon Spiro! Where is it? It's the whole point of the mission! Where can we find it?" The First Officer took a few seconds to collect his thoughts. "The heart, Nancy. It was always going to be the heart." A look of understanding passed between the two old intimates. Eventually, Captain Darkstrider said, "We are of one mind, Mr. Leonidas." Spiro looked curiously at Nancy. "And when you find what you seek, captain. Will that be enough to satisfy you?" For a long moment, Nancy considered the glowing heart and said sadly. "The roses of the past. I have the thorns of the present. I am the captain."

An hour later, Captain Darkstrider and First Officer Leonidas stood in the Engineering machine shop. Four giant automatons stood in gleaming black, red, yellow, and blue. Engineers Book and Riley stood proudly at attention as the two bridge officers inspected their devices. "Most impressive," said Nancy as she stood by the black apparatus. "What does this machine do again?" Francis stepped quickly to her side. "This is a light pulse gun, captain. It sends out bursts of photons." Spiro studied the glossy black hide of the mechanism. "Perhaps you can show us how this contraption works, Mr. Riley?" Jason grinned, "Gladly, First Officer!" The engineer climbed into the machine's control cabin, and shortly after, the black beast crawled forward on its caterpillar tracks. Francis passed goggles to Darkstrider and Leonidas, then donned a pair himself. Intense light pulses from the gun's barrel splashed into the room's wall. A strobing light display washed over the spectators.

At last, the gun ceased fire, and Riley climbed out of the cabin and rejoined the group. Captain Darkstrider took off her goggles and smiled. "Now, let's see what else your creations can do."

The yellow sonic cannon's turning fork fired sound vibrations through the air. Wearing ear protection, the three listeners could hear the sound waves echo from wall to wall. Finally, the wheeled brute moved backward and came to a stop by the group. Nancy gave a thumb up to Engineer Book, who returned the gesture from the cabin window. Next was the turn of the blue-tracked pressure cannon. It crept forward, its caterpillar tracks resting its muzzle against a large steel cylinder. A roar filled the air, and the barrel crumpled under the onslaught. Then, finally, the massive juggernaut returned to its place. The compartment window opened, and Engineer Riley's hands appeared clasped together in victory. First Officer Leonidas gave him a snappy salute.

The red heating device rolled forward on interleaved wheels until it faced the ship's secondary hull. A blinding rod of fire leaped from its snout to the cold steel. Slowly, the metal turned from cherry to white hot. Finally, the fiery discharge ended. The cerulean monster wheeled around, rolled forward, and stopped by the muffled observers. Francis lowered himself from the cab and joined his crew members. Captain Darkstrider removed her ear and eye protection and inspected the two builders with green beryl eyes. "Men, I think you've earned your pay this week."

After dinner, the crew of the Copernicus met in the conference room. Captain Darkstrider swept her team with her astonishingly green eyes. Tapping a pencil on the table, she faced Navigator Tripper and Yeoman Franke. "Right, so you managed a flight without crashing. That's good. Now tell us what you found in the Mines of Moria." First Officer Leonidas manipulated his computer controls, and a holographic image of the south pole macula appeared suspended over the round table. "OK," said Chris, "the macula is 325 square miles in diameter. That large central plain is called Strawberry Fields. The long ridge to its north is the Great Wall." Jane continued the narrative, "Those four large craters we named John, Paul, George, and Ringo." Nancy frowned, "Why those particular names?" Surprising everyone, First Officer Leonidas answered, "They're the first names of a musical group from the 1960s called The Beatles." Darkstrider looked at Spiro, "You continually surprise me with the things you know, Mr. Leonidas." A blank expression fooled no one materialized on the first officer's face. "That other escarpment in the west we call Neverland," said Tripper. "Add 45 other craters of various sizes, and there you have it." Captain Darkstrider smiled for the first time.

"A fine report. Concise and informative. I commend you two." Franke and Tripper glowed with pleasure. Nancy turned her attention to Jason and Francis. "Engineers Book and Riley have finished preparing the machines we will transport to Argo Chasma. The shuttle crews will use them to locate and open the proposed molecular door. The spacecraft only has room for a unit in its cargo compartment so the work will take two days. Any comments, men?" Jason assumed a confident air, "Smasher, Wilful Death, Viper, and Dreadnought, stand ready!" Grinning at the colorful names, Darkstrider said, "It's been a long day, and we have an even longer day tomorrow. I suggest you all get as much rest as possible." Pushing their chairs from the table, the crew of the Copernicus got up and filed from the room.

The following day on the Shuttle deck, Captain Darkstrider and First Officer Leonidas watched as they loaded Blue Wilful Death and Yellow Smasher into the back of the shuttles. Tripper and Book emerged from the cargo compartments and sealed the back doors. The two joined their partners, who were conversing with Nancy and Spiro. Captain Darkstrider eyed the two teams. "OK, you know the drill by now. Use your machines to find an entrance to the artifact. If you find one, do not enter; report your findings immediately. Well, that's it. Always be alert to danger and come back safely." Navigation Officer Tripper grinned, "Piece of cake!" Saluting, the shuttle crews turned and entered their shuttles. The hatches closed, and Darkstrider and Leonidas retraced their steps and left the hangar deck. Fifteen minutes later, the Captain and her First Officer watched from the bridge as the shuttle bay doors opened and the two shuttles launched, one after the other. Nancy sighed.

"I must go down to the seas again, to the lonely sea and the sky,

And all I ask is a tall ship and a star to steer her by,

And the wheel's kick and the wind's song and the white sail's shaking,

And a grey mist on the sea's face and a grey dawn breaking."

Spiro looked at his captain with approval. "Beautiful poetry, captain. Did you write that?" Darkstrider shook her head. "No, written a long time ago. It's called Sea-fever by John Mansfield."

An hour later, Engineer Riley watched from the side of Shuttle Two as his partner Book backed Yellow Smasher out of the back of the spacecraft. Then, a kilometer away, Navigator Tripper carefully maneuvered Red Wilful Death out of the cargo compartment under the supervision of Yeoman Franke.

The yellow sonic cannon rolled forward until its tuning fork was within meters of the side of the artifact. Jason paced beside the canary-colored beast. From the machine's cabin, Francis gave his friend a thumbs up. Riley returned the gesture and turned his attention to the side of the monument. Sound vibrations came throbbing from the fork carried by the thin methane atmosphere. Again and again, they rebounded from the structure's surface. Nothing happened. Jason caught the eye of his compatriot and shrugged. Slowly, Yellow Smasher traveled along the length of the massive pile, caressing its flank with sonic discharges.

On its interweaved wheels, the red heating device approached the side of the alien relic. Navigator Book took careful aim at a spot midway on the superstructure. Yeoman Franke observed the proceedings from a safe distance. Suddenly, a blazing beam of fire leaped from its nose to splash the icy surface. Waves of heat blossomed on the hull and died. Again and again, fire licked out, engulfing the cyclopean complex. Shading her eyes, Jane could not see any change in the unbroken veneer. From the cab, Chris looked out at his space-suited colleague. Franke pointed east and made a stabbing motion. Tripper nodded his understanding. The crimson-pigmented Wilful Death moved along the superstructure's extremity, bathing it in flames.

Far above, the ancient stars watched the young magpies as they played their meaningless games. They had been old when even the ancient relic in the Chasma had been young. From each side of the canyon, the walls were also vigilant. Finally, after unthinkable ages, a species interrupted their peace. Brooding, they seemed to wonder when the brash intruders would go away and leave them to their solitude.

Ten kilometers above, on the Copernicus bridge, Nancy Darkstrider listened to First Officer Leonidas' report. "The Shuttle crews report they have almost completed their examination of one side and end of the artifacts' walls and are starting on the other. No sign of any entry. They will continue their work until completion." The captain considered the main bridge screen at the yellow and blue dots moving around the alien relic on the Moon below. "Tell them to keep up the good work."

Arriving back at where he had started, Engineer Book shut down the engine of the Yellow Smasher. His companion, Jason, slowly trudged by the vehicle and keyed his helmet intercom. "Well, looks like we came up empty, Francis. We've been all over this enigma and have found nothing. Let's get back to the ship." High in the cabin,

Francis keyed his intercom. "I think you're right, Jason. There's always tomorrow, my friend." Book turned the engine on the amber mechanical beast and headed to the open cargo bay of Shuttle Two.

A kilometer away, at almost the same time, the vermillion Wilfull Death trundled over to a stop by the ramp to Shuttle One. Navigator watched as Yeoman Franke climbed the ladder to his cab and looked at him through the window. "Nothing Chris. We didn't find the golden goose this time." Tripper touched the window in front of Jane's face. "Right you are. Nothing ventured, nothing gained. I'm signaling the ship we are returning to the ship." Turning the engine back on, Chris navigated the scarlet monster up the ramp and into the shuttle's cargo compartment.

Around both shuttles and the solitary figures, the velvet curtains of mist curled down to announce the start of Charon's night. A low moan permeated the thin atmosphere. Then, hurriedly, the space-suited shapes entered the shuttle's side doors. Billows of purple fog rose to cover the spacecraft as they lifted off.

Two hours later, Captain Nancy Darkstrider studied her exhausted crew in the rec area on the Engineering Deck. Book and Tripper sat hunched over on a couch with cups of coffee in their hands. Tripper and Franke leaned against each other on a nearby settee with closed eyes. Perched on an overstuffed sofa, Nancy and her First Officer gave each other a rueful glance before Darkstrider spoke. "OK, I know you're tired, but you did fine work today. True, you found nothing, but you eliminated two methods of finding the entrance into the artifact."

Navigator Tripper responded, "Thank you, Captain." Nancy smiled briefly at Chris, "But we can't stop now. Tomorrow we will take the other two machines to the chasma and test the walls of the alien relic." Slumped on Tripper's shoulder, Jane murmured, "I like the 'we.'"

Pretending she didn't hear the Yeoman's words, Darkstrider went on. "At 0900 hours, the shuttle teams will take the... what were their names Book?" Francis shook his head to clear his thoughts, "Viper and Dreadnought, Captain." Nancy rolled her chartreuse-colored eyes, "Yes, black Viper and the blue Dreadnought. Colorful names. If that doesn't work, we will use the ship's lasers and see if we can blast a hole into that billion-year Gordian knot." The captain lapsed into silence. Then, finally, First Officer Leonidas spoke for the first time, "Don't worry, somehow we will find a way into that thing." Jason piped up, "You can count on that!" The informal meeting broke to general laughter, and the crew went to dinner.

Later, in their cabin, Chris and Jane lay on their bed in tired postures. "I hope we find the door, Chris," said Franke. "I think we've earned it." Tripper yawned, "Book and Riley worked as hard as us today, Jane. I'll be happy if one of us finds it." The Yeoman thought, "I guess you're right, Chris." Jane rolled over and circled Chris's ear with the tip of her finger. "Do you want to make love?" Tripper grinned. "Do you need to ask?"

"What do you think our chances are tomorrow, Francis?" said Riley from under his blankets on his bunk. "Is there a door?" Book put down the novel he was reading and looked at the lump that was his friend. "You came up with the idea of the molecular door, Jason. Yes, I know it's there, somewhere." Engineer Riley emerged from under his blankets. His head looked like the chewed-up end of a pencil eraser."Goodnight, Francis." Engineer Book clapped his hands to turn out the lights. "Goodnight, Jason."

In the captain's cabin, Nancy Darkstrider sat on a chair by the window port in her nightdress, peering at the image of Pluto. "Soon, my precious," breathed Nancy. "Soon, my precious, soon." The blue eye of the heart stared, unwinking back.

Alone in his cabin, First Officer Leonidas lay in untroubled slumber. Loud snores came from the Greek First Officer.

A shadow blackened the whiteness of the extraterrestrial antiquity as the massive bulk of the Copernicus passed overhead. It had held its secrets for a billion years; it could keep them longer.

At precisely 0900 hours in the morning (9 AM), a small group of Captain Darkstrider, First Officer Leonidas, Navigational Officer Tripper, and Engineer Book stood watching on the floor of the shuttle deck. The entrance to the Engineering Machine Shop yawned open, and the glossy black Viper and cobalt blue Dreadnought crept forward on their caterpillar tracks. Then, purposely, they slithered up the shuttle ramps. The shuttle compartment doors closed, and after a time, Engineer Riley and Yeoman Franke emerged from the side hatches. Carrying helmets under their arms, Jason and Jane joined the other members of the crew. Captain Darkstrider scrutinized the shuttle teams, as in the morning before, with her exotically colored green eyes.

"This is the last morning of our artifact inspection," said Nancy. "We must find the door into the alien relic. After that, there is no excuse for failure. Any comments?" Chris grinned, "Piece of cake!" Darkstrider smiled, "One day, I must try this cake of yours, Navigator. OK, you have your orders. Good luck, and be safe out there." The four shuttle members entered their spacecraft as the captain and First Officer left the Shuttle Deck.

Fifteen minutes later, Nancy and Spiro watched the main bridge screen as the Shuttle Bay portal opened and the two shuttles, one after the other, emerged and gathered speed. Swiftly, the two silver bullets sped from view against the backdrop of Charon. Captain Darkstrider spoke:

"I must go down to the seas again for the call of the running tide

It is a wild call and a clear call that may not be denied;

And all I ask is a windy day with the white clouds flying,

And the flung spray and the blown spume, and the seagulls crying."

A look of melancholy consumed Nancy's face. "Saint Drogo, patron saint of shepherds, please look after my lambs." Grimly the First Officer concurred, "Amen to that."

An hour later, two shuttles parked themselves at the east and west extremities of the alien artifact. Navigator Tripper oversaw his teammate Communications Officer Franke back, the glossy black light pulse gun down the shuttle ramp. Exiting entirely on the surface of Argos Chasma, Jane turned the black beast on its caterpillar tracks and crawled toward the west end of the monument. On her intercom, Franke heard Chris's voice, "Steady as it goes, Yeoman Franke. You may fire when ready." Intense pulses of light shot from the gun's barrel to the metal of the massive pile. Fantastic shadows flashed over the landscape. The menacing chasma walls appeared in sharp relief. Again and again, Jane punched the fire control, and light pulses splashed the superstructure. Finally, after a few minutes, Tripper's tiny voice came.

"Nothing on the east end, Jane. Let's continue down the north side." Then, like a giant black caterpillar, the black beast Viper crawled on its journey. Chris Tripper followed in its wake.

Engineer Book waited patiently as his friend and colleague Riley drove the blue-tracked pressure cannon on its caterpillar understructure. Spinning around, Jason placed the muzzle of the pressure cannon against the side of the cyclopean complex. The blue juggernaut increased the pressure until the cerulean machine's engine raised in protest. Riley increased the magnitude of the gun, and pressure waves became visible on the walls of the artifact. The pressure cannon slammed into the metal over and over. Riley glanced out the cabin window at Francis, making cutting motions across his throat. Reluctantly, the younger engineer cut the engine to hear his friend.

Book's voice sounded in his ear, "There's nothing here, Jason. Work your way to the south perimeter and proceed with testing." Like the Jawa crawler in Star Wars, the blue juggernaut lurched forward. Engineer Book kept pace in its wake. Behind them, the smooth white walls of the alien relic glinted in the sun's distant rays, totally unmarked.

Far above, on the deep space scout ship Copernicus, First Officer Spiro Leonidas listened to situation reports from the shuttle teams. "Shuttles One and Two are reporting they have completed half their tasks. They are now proceeding on schedule." As the black and blue specks moved around the extraterrestrial sphinx, Nancy glanced at the side viewscreen. "I hope they find something." She spared a look at Pluto hanging on the main bridge screen. "Time is running out."

Twelve hours later, Engineer Riley cut the engine on the blue-pressure cannon juggernaut. He wearily left the machine's cabin and climbed down the short ladder. With heavy steps, he plodded to where his significant other, Francis Book, was standing. Quick puffs of dust stirred at each stride. Behind them, Shuttle Two lay expectantly with its cargo compartment lowered. Jason and the equally tired Francis faced the east end of the white-faced monolith. "Three days of trying to get into this bastard," complained Riley. "Three days, and what have we found? Nothing! A complete waste of time!" Engineer Book gently patted the back of his space-suited friend. "We have accomplished something, Jason. We know what won't work. That may come in useful one day." Riley did not reply but eyed the black shadows creeping from the distant canyon walls. He nervously placed his hand on his sidearm as the first purple streamers of haze fell from the sky. "I think we've done all we can here, Francis," said Riley. "Why don't we inform Spock we've completed our mission and request permission to return to the ship?" Book nodded but replied, "We must wait for the last test. The ship's lasers, remember? But take the blue juggernaut aboard the shuttle." Turning on his heel, Jason retraced his steps to the hulking machine.

"Back to where we started, Chris," said Yeoman Franke. "There is no door, molecular or otherwise. "The two sweethearts were standing by their glossy black pulse gun. Behind them, the yawning maw of the shuttle's cargo bay awaited hungrily. Navigator Tripper searched the smooth facade of the west end that towered above them like the White Cliffs of Dover back on earth. "You're right, Jane. Why don't you take your cute behind and move the black beast back onto the shuttle?" Franke giggled as Chris familiarly patted her on her bum and went to reclaim the midnight-colored Viper.

Thirty minutes later, the two shuttles lay parked side by side, and the crews stood in front of them regarding the west extremity of the silent monolithic structure. Over their intercoms, they heard Leonidas's voice. "Prepare for laser discharge. Fire in the hole!" The four crewmen held gloved hands in front of their visored faces as a red beam of intense light shot down, hitting the ivory artifact. Again, the metal blushed with a rosy glow.

Similarly, the ruby-red cone of light smashed into the unyielding surface. Once again, the effort was to no avail. One last time, a crimson streak of destruction washed over the entire end of the milky white facade. An angry rash covered the snowy expanse. It, too, faded.

Yeoman Franke peered between her fingers after the third strike of the ship's laser. "That's pretty," she thought regarding the pinkish-hued metal. Then, to her surprise, an oval outline appeared on the wall. Before her eyes, the shape faded as the color left the rampart. First Officer Leonidas's voice boomed into their ears. Disappointment tinged his words. "Test firing complete. No result. Return to the ship, over." The two engineers turned and walked toward their shuttle. Navigator Tripper swiveled but stopped when he noticed Jane looking at the artifact's unmarked expanse. "What's up, Jane? Did you see something?" The Communication Officer walked the 100-meter distance to the artifact. "Follow me, Chris."

Beside Shuttle Two, Book and Riley noticed the two young people moving towards the side of the monument. "What's up, guys?" asked Jason Riley. "Not sure, Mr. Riley," replied Tripper. "Stand by." Approaching the dove-white wall, Franke stared intently at its surface. "It was here, Chris. When the metal was crimson, I saw it."

Tripper ran his eyes over the relic's exterior. "Saw what, Jane? What did you see?" Franke turned her head to Chris, "A door. I saw an oval door. Right here."

Chris turned this new information in his mind for a while. "Even if you saw a door, Jane, we've explored every square meter of this exterior. We've thrown everything we have at it. How do we get it open?" Franke thought, "Remember Lord of the Rings, what Frodo said when the Fellowship stood in front of the entrance to the Mines of Moria? Say 'friend' and enter." Tripper frowned, "Yes, I remember. You're not suggesting we try that here, are you?" Jane's brow knitted in thought, "What is the elvish word for friend?" Over their intercoms, they heard the tinny voice of Riley: "Melon." Yeoman Franke faced the wall and said, "Melon," knocked on its surface. To everyone's astonishment except Franke, an oval door materialized before them.

First Officer Spiro Leonidas's voice came again over their helmet com links, "Attention Shuttle One, Shuttle Two. What is the hold-up? Why have you not taken off and returned to base? Over."

Excitedly, Chris spoke into his transmitter, "Jane has done it! She found a door. We have a way in! Over." An intoxicated Babbel of voice flooded the airways. Finally, Captain Darkstrider's vocalization broke through. "Quiet, everyone! Shuttle One, ensure your entry method and both shuttles return to base. The sun is setting. Good work, everyone, and especially you, Yeoman Franke! Over." Jane and Chris realized that while they were communicating, the door had disappeared. Tripper said to his helpmate, "Let me try, Jane." The Navigational officer reached forward and knocked on the metal. Instantly, the oval door reappeared. Chris grinned at Franke and said, "See Jane, you don't have to say, Melon, you just have to knock." The Communication Officer shrugged her beautiful shoulders and replied, "Too bad. I liked it better the other way."

"You just had to knock on the door? And it opened?" exclaimed Nancy in a rueful tone of voice. "Three days of exploring and testing and using every method at our disposal, and that's what it took. A knock on the door?" First Officer Leonidas spoke up, "Apparently, that is correct, captain. Even the pressure cannon delivered the wrong type of force. The door opened to a knock." In the conference room, the Copernican crew members gathered for debriefing. Two hours had passed since Jane Franke's momentous discovery. "Jane was on the right track all along, Captain," said Tripper. "On the first day, she walked up to the artifact and knocked on it. Unfortunately, no door there."

Nancy Darkstrider faced Jane, "Brilliant work Yeoman Franke. I will put you in for a citation. You deserve it." A slight blush lit up Jane's face. "Thank you, Captain Darkstrider. But both shuttle crews deserve the praise too. We all worked together as a team." The captain nodded, "Noted and well said. Now our next order of business. Both shuttle crews will enter the alien artifact tomorrow and explore it. Make sure your helmet cameras are working. And make sure you carry your sidearms. It's been a billion years, but who knows what dangers you might encounter? Questions? No? Since there are none, I call this meeting to a close." Yawning, the four younger crew members got up from their chairs and filed from the room.

After they had left, Captain Darkstrider remarked, "I'm surprised at Yeoman Franke. I had her down as nothing more than a Communication Officer. She is quite brilliant." A look of mischief appeared on Spiro's face. "It's one of our society's last prejudices. Stunning women must be stupid. You must have encountered that yourself many times, captain." Nancy turned her lovely features with emerald green eyes to her First Officer and whispered, "Mr. Leonidas, shut up, please."

The four shuttle team members were relaxing in the sauna in the ship's gymnasium. Naked, they lay sweltering on the benches. Engineer Book had positioned his head on his friend's thigh. "That was great work today, Jane," said Jason. "I didn't think we would ever find the door. I had about given up." On the opposite bench, Franke lay with her head in her lover Chris's lap. Sweat beaded her magnificent body. "Thanks. I owe the idea to you. Your reference to the Mines of Moria inspired me." Tripper wiped the moisture off Jane's face with a cloth. "I don't think I was ever more shocked than when that door suddenly appeared before our eyes. First, it wasn't there. Then it appeared in the blink of an eye." Engineer Book ladled more water onto the hot stones, causing hot steam to fill the sauna. "Well, it was our first look at a molecular door. And tomorrow, we get to see what's inside that billion-year-old curiosity." Chris poured water over Jane's breasts, "Piece of cake!" Everybody joined in the laughter.

What Lies Within?

Chapter 5

"Here we are, once again," said Captain Darkstrider. "Thanks to Yeoman Franke, we can access the artifact." Gathered, the six members of the Copernicus met in the shuttle bay at 0900 hrs. "Thank you, captain," said Jane. "You're most welcome, Yeoman," replied Nancy. "Mr. Leonidas, give the shuttle crews their orders, please." The First Officer spoke, "The shuttle crews are to land 100 meters from the door to the artifact. You are to use a standard two-by-two cover formation. One team moves forward while the other gives cover. You will, of course, carry your blasters. Whatever the temperature or atmosphere of the interior, your helmets stay on. Switch on your cams and keep in constant communication with the ship. I think that is everything. Remember, this is the first time humans have ever explored an alien relic, so be prepared for anything."

Tripper looked puzzled. "How do we do that, Mr. Leonidas?" Spiro gave the ship's navigator a blank look. "I don't know." Then, amid general laughter, Darkstrider said, "Ok, that's it, and good luck. Watch out for face-huggers." The four shuttle team members stiffened slightly and then moved toward their vehicles. A minute later, they had entered and closed the hatches.

First Officer Leonidas frowned. "Should you have made that remark about face-huggers, captain? They are on edge now." Nancy smiled grimly. "Good, I want them to be. We don't know what they are going to find in there. They will be on their guard now." Spiro nodded at the logic and followed his captain out of the shuttle bay deck. They watched from the ship's bridge ten minutes later as the gateway to the shuttle deck yawned open. Out of its gaping maw flew the two shuttles. The two spacecraft did an intricate dance about each other, like a pair of mating dragonflies. Then, turning, they dived to the surface of the moon below. Captain. Darkstrider placed an elbow on the chair's armrest. She then rested her cheek on her palm. Nancy softly recited:

"I must go down to the seas again for the call of the running tide

It is a wild call and a clear call that may not be denied;

And all I ask is a windy day with the white clouds flying,

And the flung spray and the blown spume, and the seagulls crying."

A voice beside her intoned another stanza of John Masefield's sailor's poem, "Sea-Fever."

"I must go down to the seas again to the vagrant gypsy life.

To the gull's way and the whale's way where the wind's like a whetted knife;

And all I ask is a merry yarn from a laughing fellow rover,

And quiet sleep and a sweet dream when the long trick's over."

The two old shipmates looked at each other, speaking no words. However, what was in their eyes spoke volumes.

Spiro, "I know, captain. I'm worried for them, too."

An hour later, the four crewmen of the Copernicus stood in front of the pristine whiteness of the alien entity they were about to violate. Thin shadows swept across them as one of Pluto's moons tumbled overhead. Communication officer Franke's comlink crackled in her ear, and she heard the small voice of Tripper. "Ok, Yeoman. Show us the way in." Jane lifted her hand and said the word "Melon" as she knocked briskly on the side of the massive structure. Instantly, an oval door appeared to the gaze of the quartet.

"An oval door! Whoever heard of an oval door!" exclaimed Engineer Riley. "The Bella Coola region's bear clan of the Nuxalk used oval doors in their longhouses," said the Chief Engineer Book. "How do you know that, chief?" asked Navigator Tripper. The answer hissed into the younger man's ear. "Because I am Nuxalk, Mr. Tripper." Chris grinned at his crewmate. "That's right, so you are."

"If we can focus on the business at hand?" said Yeoman Franke. "Sorry, Jane," mumbled Chris. Franke examined the entrance into the alien edifice. "There is a blue shimmer effect in the door opening. It is a stasis field to keep the atmosphere from leaking out. I am putting my hand through. Yes, my hand passes through easily. I will now enter." Urgently Tripper spoke into Jane's comlink, "Take out your sidearm Jane!" Visibly irritated, Yeoman Franke replied, "Oh, all right!" The communication officer continued her narrative. "I step through the portal. Copernicus, are you seeing this? Over." First Officer Leonidas's articulation came instantly, "Yes, we have a good visual landing party. Over."

Yeoman Franke was in a room bathed in an eerie red light. Her helmet spotlight swept over the bare walls. Behind her, Chris Tripper had entered and was crouching with his blaster in his gloved hand. He seemed to be ready for any danger. Jane laughed, "You look ready for a shootout at the OK corral Chris." The navigator scurried about the room. Engineers Book and Riley had come in and gazed about with awed expressions. They had not bothered to take out their sidearms. "This place is dead, Tripper. Whatever was here was gone a long time ago," said Jane. The First Officer Leonidas' intonation caught their attention on the comlinks, "Atmospheric and temperature readings, shuttle crews."

Engineer Book studied the readout on his recorder. "Atmosphere 24% oxygen, 75% nitrogen, and trace elements. Temperature 288.15 K or 15 degrees Celsius, Mr. Leonidas." Spiro acknowledged, "Noted, oxygen-rich and on the cool side but within earth norms. But keep your helmets on. Over."

The four space adventures moved around the chamber. It was large, 100 meters long, and 25 meters wide. Lost in their sight was the ceiling. The red light cast strange shadows as they moved cautiously around. "What kind of light is this?" asked Tripper. "Some kind of infra-red, but not one I'm familiar with since we can see by it," said Francis Book. The only visible furnishings were chest-high benches or shelves fixed to both sides of the cubicle. Chris holstered his blaster and walked over to one stand. "What is this? A bench, maybe?" With an effort, he heaved himself onto the shelf, his feet dangling. Giggling, Jane joined him. Book and Riley also availed themselves of the luxurious accommodations. For a minute, they sat and swung their feet two feet above the ground, feeling oddly like children. "If these are benches," said Book. "The aliens must have been gigantic."

The four jumped down and looked around uneasily. As if expecting to see an alien leap out at the landing party. "Shall we move on?" asked Yeoman Franke. The four intrepid explorers walked to the far wall, which proved blank. "Can I try the secret knock?" said Engineer Riley. "Be my guest," said Navigator Tripper. Jason stepped up to the wall and said, "Melon," knocking firmly on the metal.

Instantaneously, the now familiar oval door materialized in front of the tetrad. "No stasis field this time," said Jane. "Makes sense since the temperature and atmosphere are probably the same within the building."

One after the other, the ground crew filled through the oval opening, which closed behind them. The dim red light increased, and the band could see this room was twice the size of the previous one. A large metallic, rectangular slab dominated the center of the space. The shuttle teams gathered around the vast object. "This reminds me of the monolith in 2001: A Space Oddysey," said Tripper. "Except this is white, and the monolith was black," pointed Jason. "I'm not suggesting they are the same engineer!" exclaimed Chris in mock anger. "Chest high again," said Francis. "You mean breast high," said Jane mischievously. "These creatures must have been over 2 meters tall," said Riley, awestricken. The four advanced scouts played their helmet flashes around, revealing more blank walls. "Nothing more to see here," said Navigational Officer Tripper. "Let's go on."

"Interesting data coming from the advance party," said Spiro Leonidas. "Temperature and atmosphere can support human life." Nancy thought that over. "It seems like an incredible coincidence that the aliens resemble us. At least regarding what environmental factors they need to exist." The first officer looked over at his captain. "Not that great a coincidence. You've heard of Carbon Chauvinism, no doubt? However, that carbon-based life exists throughout the entire universe." Captain Darkstrider frowned. "I thought that silicon-based life forms were possible as well." Spiro nodded. "Silicon can form four covalent bonds, similar to carbon. The possibility of silicon-based life forms has been the basis of many works of science fiction."

Darkstrider tapped her forehead. "I remember watching an old retro program when I was a child from the 1960s television show Star Trek. A silicon monster was attacking the Enterprize crew." The First Officer smiled. "A Horta, I also saw that program when an infant in the Martian colony. Amazing that the old TV show got so much right. And so much wrong as well. To answer your question, it would have to exist in a specialized atmosphere for silicon life to develop. That does not appear to be the case of the atmosphere in the artifact, so it's safe to conclude the aliens were carbon-based lifeforms."

Nancy got up and restlessly patrolled the bridge. She studied the extraterrestrial antiquity on the main screen. "Well, it's comforting to know they breathed the same air as us and liked cool temperatures. But that's all we know about their appearance so far." Leonidas had turned back to his computer console. "Engineer Book has reported that the structures they've found in the artifact could seat enormous creatures. On the scale of 2 meters tall or more." Captain Darkstrider returned to her chair and sat down. "Put their cams on the main bridge screen on multiple aspects. I want to see what they are seeing." Spiro made some adjustments, and the bridge screen split into four segments, each showing a camcorder recording from one of her crew.

"Is it ok if I say the spell now?" asked Chief Engineer Book. "I think we should all take turns. There is also some risk of being the first through the door." Chris looked at Francis in irritation. "You don't have to say the word. Knock." Francis smiled. "I know, but it's more fun that way." Then, turning to the door, the older man knocked and pronounced, "Melon."

Soundlessly, the oval aperture assumed its usual shape. Engineer Book entered the next room. His teammates followed closely behind them. "This is different," remarked Jane. The lights on their helmets revealed a medium size room with cabinets arranged around the sides. Yeoman Franke walked over to the nearest one and examined it. About 1.5 meters high, it has a small oval protrusion on its face. Grasping the projection, she gave it a hard pull. The container remained shut. "At least we are not dealing with a molecular door this time," said Chris. "There is a seam around the sides of the front." Each member of the shuttle crew stood in front of one case, of which they were twenty. "I think they are all locked," said Jason. "How do we get them open?"

Franke reached forward, knocked on her cabinet, and said, "Melon." Gripping the handle, she pulled hard again. "Still locked, I'm afraid." Tripper laughed. "Surprised if that trick had worked twice. Let's try a more direct approach." Taking his blaster from its holster, Chris took deliberate aim and fired at the oval knob. An angry red efflorescence spread over the face of the container. It faded rapidly, leaving the case unmarked. "Well, that didn't work," said the navigator. "They made everything here of the same impervious metal." Chris reached and gave the knot a slight pull. The door swung open. "It worked!" Tripper peered eagerly inside. On shelving, translucent cubes filled the case. Chris picked one up and examined it. The three other crew members stood at his shoulder and regarded the strange object. As he turned it over in his gloved fingers, Tripper could detect a kaleidoscope of colors that whirled and intertwined. One or two of the pigmentations were of a nature unknown to him. The Navigational Officer felt dizzy and stopped looking into the cube's depths. "Ok, I'm putting a few of these things into my specimen pouch. Everybody gets their firearms out and opens these cases!"

Each Copernican took out their blaster and moved from cabinet to cabinet, firing as they opened up the hatches. Tripper and Book found themselves side by side in front of the last two containers. Chris grinned. "Chief, let's test our fast draw again. Ready?" Francis retired his blaster to its holster and nodded. Watching them, Jane shouted, "Go!" Engineer Book drew his blaster, fired accurately with incredible speed, and returned the firearm to his holster before Chris cleared his gun. Tripper gaped at the First Nation's man with an open mouth.

"You lose Kemo Sabe."

The space explorers found five of the twenty receptacles with the lambent cubes. Collecting more specimens, the two engineers went the next door. Twisting his head, Francis called on the come link, "Quickdraw. It's your turn to try a door." Jane touched her helmet to Tripper's and muted her mike. "Chris, I don't think you should call Book chief. We consider it an insult to the First Nations people." Tripper protested, "But he is a Chief Engineer." Franke remonstrated, "I'd think it over if I were you." The navigator nodded, "Ok, I will. Oh, and by the way, Jane. Don't tell

Book and Riley I said they were the best engineers in the fleet." Jason and Francis turned to the two lovers grinning and exclaimed, "Why thank you, Mr. Tripper!" Yeoman Franke laughed, "Chris, you left your com link on!" The Navigational Officer groaned, "Oh my god!"

"What do you think those odd cubes are, Mr. Leonidas?" asked Captain Darkstrider. The First Officer shrugged his shoulders, "Could be anything, tools, batteries, toys. I'll know better when I get a specimen to analyze." Nancy watched the bridge screen as the landing party recorded images with a slightly jerky motion. "So far, so good."

It was the turn of Navigation Officer Tripper. He stretched out his hand and knocked on the blank wall. As before, the oval door was there instantly. Without a word to his companions, Chris entered the next room. The others were close behind him. Without a sound, the egress sealed itself. Chris looked around in surprise. Covering the walls were an intricate series of long colored markings. A dozen high metal square objects scattered around the room attracted their attention. "You know what? These streaks resemble the streaks we found on the moon Styx!" said Jason. "I knew we were right when we thought there was a pattern to the Styxian streaks," agreed Francis. "Which came first, men?" asked Tripper. "The streaks here or on Styx?" The two engineers looked at each other and shrugged helplessly. "We don't know, both, maybe."

Yeoman Franke had been studying the patterns. "Is this art to you suppose? Did the aliens come here and sit on those metal cubes and look at the colored streaks?" The Navigational Officer walked over to one of the metallic objects and hoisted himself aboard into a sitting position. "Only one way to find out. Each of you grabs a seat."

The foursome sat as comfortably as they could manage and surveyed the walls. For a time, nothing happened. Then the red light increased in intensity, and the colored streaks drifted in an intricate dance. Like a skein of variegated wool, the colors entwined and broke apart. Jane gasped. "Is this real? Are the streaks moving?" Chief Engineer Book studied the readouts on his recorder. "According to my data, they are not moving. It is some holographic projection or illusion that is beyond our technology." The Communications Officer gaped as she took in the magnificent display. "Whatever it is, it's beautiful!" All engineer Riley could say was, "The colors, the colors!" Finally, after 15 minutes of an incredible iridescent panorama of paints, the navigator jumped down, "Right, I've seen enough. Let's get on with the job." The other three reluctantly climbed down from their perches and followed Tripper to the far bulkhead.

"Looks like I'm up again," remarked Franke. Steadily she reached forward with her fist and firmly knocked while uttering "Melon." Almost routinely now, the accustomed egress took shape. As if sensing danger, Jane leaped through the door with her blaster and crouched like a coiled cat. Alarmed, her three teammates followed suit with their weapons drawn as well. "What's wrong Jane, what do you sense?" whispered her lover. Franke swept her eyes all over the red-lit domicile. "I don't know, Chris. But my feminine intuition is tingling. Follow my lead." The

Yeoman observed two long metal ellipsoidal objects that lay on the floor. At right angles, metal barriers joined the walls to the rectangular bodies. To reach the far bulwark, they would have to pass down the center between the twin monoliths that were one meter high. Slowly, Jane moved forward, weighing every possibility, every danger. Her crew was at her back, alert for anything.

Now the Communication Officer had reached the foot of the menhirs. A series of facing wall recesses drew Franke's eyes. Jane pointed. "There, high on the paneling. See them?" Deliberately Navigator Tripper reached into his pouch and brought out one cube he had collected. Flashes of red light instantly stabbed from each recess, vaporizing the collectible. Jane sighed. "A trap for the unwary." Jason Riley shook visibly. "How do we get across?" Franke laughed grimly, "Easy, we crawl."

"Did you see that?" exclaimed First Officer Leonidas. "The aliens laid a programmed trap. Why would they do that?" Captain Darkstrider considered, "So far, the rooms in the artifact have held nothing of real value. Perhaps the laser guns are guarding something of consequence." Spiro nodded, "That's possible. That also could mean that there are more pitfalls ahead. By the way, did you notice how Yeoman Franke has taken charge of the landing party?" Nancy smiled. "I noticed. Once a dormant bud, she's blossomed into a beautiful flower." Spiro examined his captain curiously. "Lovely poetic imagery. Who wrote that?" Darkstrider grinned, "I did."

"Keep low, everyone," said Communications Officer Franke, "If you lift your backside too high, you're going to lose it." The four space people grunted and wiggled along the alien room's floor. Instant death waited on either side. In the Indian file, Jane went first, followed closely by Navigator Tripper. Engineer Riley was next, and Chief Book brought up the rear. Panting and puffing, they covered the 100 meters to the end of the monoliths. Groaning, the shuttle crew got wearily to their feet. "Joint the Space Corp," said Engineer Riley sarcastically, "see the universe, my old dad used to tell me." Francis laughed. "You're 5.0 billion kilometers out. How far did your old man ever get?" Jason scratched his chin, "Usually just down the street to the pub." Amid chuckles, Jane motioned to Chris, "Chief Book, I believe this is your turn. Engineer Riley, join him. We will use the standard two-by-two cover formation again. Mr. Tripper and I will be at your back. Ok, people, let's move and go in with blaster's hot."

Book tentatively held his hand and knocked hesitantly, saying, "Melon." Francis stepped inside, followed closely by Jason and the bridge crew, his body silhouetted by the blue-lit oval door. The four spacers looked about them in mild amazement. Seeing no immediate danger, Yeoman Franke took a stride forward. Instantly, two sentry guns sprang up from the floor and sprayed laser bolts! Only the fact that the rusty guns were a billion years old saved the Copernicans. A fraction of a second before they opened fire, the landing party hit the deck on Franke's shout, "Down!" Sizzling harbingers of death passed just over their heads. Francis and Jason opened fire with their sidearms, putting the two ordinances out of commission. Two more sentry cannons revealed themselves from opened side panels. Executing combat rolls, Jane and Chris evaded their fire and silenced them with accurate return fire.

The dazed quartet lay sprawled on the floor. "Laser guns?" said Chris. "Like in the movie Aliens? Are we in some alternative universe?" Ignoring him, Yeoman Franke inquired, "Anyone hurt?" Engineer Riley grimaced. "Yeah, I took one in the leg." Jane opened her med kit and examined the wound. "Not too bad. It's just a scrape. I'll disinfect it and put a pressure bandage on it. I'll use medical tape to close the rip in your suit. It should hold when we go back to the ship." Her crew members looked on in admiration as Jane worked efficiently. Soon Chris and Francis were helping Jason to his feet. "Can you walk?" asked Chief Book. Riley tested his weight." Yes, I can march." The four explorers moved past the still-smoking sentry guns to the next hidden door.

Over every comlink, the captain's voice came urgently. "Attention, ground crew. You are to break off your mission and return to the ship. Your injured party needs more medical help than you can provide. You've accomplished enough for today. Good job, all. Over." The quartet looked at each other with irritation, relief, and resentment. "Well, you heard the lady," said Jane. "Back to the shuttles. Mr. Tripper, Mr. Book, give Jason a hand."

Several hours later, the crew of the Copernicus were in the conference room watching a holo recording of the landing parties' exploration of the alien artifact. The view centered on one cabinet filled full of hexahedrons. Captain Darkstrider held one of the enigmatic cubes in her hand and peered into its depths. "Fascinating. I wonder about its purpose. And I don't recognize some of these colors." First Officer Leonidas, "Those colors don't appear in our spectrum. Why we can even see them is unknown. The ship's lab is still working on its composition. So far, our tests have yielded no valuable information. What is their purpose? Also unknown." Nancy's forehead knitted in perplexity. "So many unknowns and so few answers." The holo recording showed Chris Tripper throwing a cube at its instant destruction by laser. "You were very alert, Yeoman Franke, to spot those recesses," said Darkstrider. "Thank you, captain," replied Jane smugly. Beside her, Chris gave her a nudge in the ribs. Franke returned the gesture with so much force Tripper gave out an audible, "Ooff!"

Every crew member straightened in their seats as the sentry guns began their barrage of laser blasts. The holographic projection became full of red streaks of fire from all angles. As the holo aspect filled full of smoke, Spiro turned it off. Nancy looked at her crew with beryl green eyes. "A lot of excitement, to be sure. Luckily for you, the sentry guns were slower than your reflexes. How's your leg, Mr. Riley? Are you able to go on with the mission tomorrow?" Jason grinned and tapped his calf. "Good as new Captain!" Darkstrider chuckled, "That's nice to know, engineer. Any speculation about why the laser array trap and sentry gun ambush were in place? It seems like someone had a lot of trouble protecting something."

Navigational Officer Tripper said, "I think the answers might lie in the edifice's next room, Captain." Leonidas snapped on the holo viewer, which showed a section of a blank wall. "I've marked the progress the landing team made through the alien artifact, and I calculate there is one room left to enter. As Mr. Tripper said, the answers may be there. The question is, what lies within?" Nancy stroked her chin in a habitual gesture. "Indeed. What lies within?" Chief Engineer Book said with a straight face, "Hopefully not a face-hugger, Captain." Wild laughter exploded around the room. Tension drained away as the Copernican crew filed from the chamber.

Below them, the sinister shape of the cyclopean complex waited patiently for the return of the interlopers. It had one more card to play in its deadly game of chance. And the moon, Charon's parent Pluto, awaited its turn. The secrets she held had been hers for a billion years. The minor planet would not give them up quickly.

After dinner, the landing party sat naked two hours later, relaxing in the ship's hot tub. Engineer Riley massaged the synth flesh on his calf. "Thanks again for patching me up, Jane. I thought I was a goner when that laser hit me." Yeoman Franke lay back with her eyes closed. "Not a problem, Jason. You were lucky, though. If that blast had hit you an inch lower, it would have taken your whole leg off." Navigator Tripper slowly stroked Franke's stomach with his hand and muttered. "Sentry gun. Who would have ever suspected sentry guns? If the cannons had been shooting bullets rather than laser bolts, it would have been a scene out of the movie Aliens. Excellent shooting, everyone. I think we earned our pay today." Chief Engineer Book chuckled, "Yes, it was like a wild west shootout. Except for this time, the Indians won." Everyone joined in the general merriment. Jane noted with anticipation that Chris was moving his hand lower.

Captain Darkstrider and First Officer Leonidas exercised on stationary bicycles in the shop's gymnasium. As they pedaled, Nancy remarked, "The landing party was fortunate today. They could have lost one or more killed between lasers and guns." Spiro increased the tension in his cycle. "Yes, and kudos to Yeoman Franke. She expected the dangers. Feminine intuition, she told me. Whatever it was, she saved lives today." Wiping the sweat off her face with a towel around her neck, Darkstrider said, "Jane deserves a promotion. After they finish their investigation of the alien relic, I will promote her to acting lieutenant."

Leonidas pedaled furiously. "I'm sure she will be pleased. She hasn't had an increased rank since she was a cadet." The captain increased her speed to match her First Officer. "I wonder what the landing party will find tomorrow? I think the whole key to the artifact lies beyond the door. Once we have discovered that, then we can move onto Pluto." The two exercise cycles entered the cooling-off phase. "Yes, Pluto, it's the main reason we're here; the key is the heart," said Spiro. Nancy stepped off her two-wheeler.

"The best and most beautiful things in the world cannot be seen or even touched - we must feel them with the heart."

The First Officer also stepped off his exercise device. "Is that yours, captain?" Nancy smiled, "Helen Keller."

Another day rose on Charon. The distant sun cast its feeble light on the icy plains, vast craters, and tall mountains of Pluto's largest moon. But deep in Argos Chasma, the shadows persisted. The bleached alien edifice slumbered in its billion-year nap. But the last chapter was about to be read.

The cold plates of Copernicus's hanger deck echoed the sounds of footsteps. The six crew members gathered in a small group before the ship's shuttles. They spoke in low conversational tones for a time, and then the two spacecraft crews separated and faced Captain Darkstrider and First Officer Leonidas. Tripper, Franke, Book, and Riley appeared excited but wary in flight suits with helmets under their arms. Darkstrider, "Ok, keep in mind the dangers you faced yesterday. Who knows what you might encounter today? Exercise extreme vigilance when you enter the last room of the artifact." Jane looked pensive. "What lies within?" she said. "Yes," echoed Nancy. "What lies within? So good luck and be safe out there." With no more ceremony, the landing party turned on their heels and entered the shuttles. The captain and first officer filed out of the cavernous hangar.

A short time later, Nancy and Spiro watched as they purged the hanger deck of atmosphere. The First Officer noted a reading turn from red to green. "Bridge to Shuttle One and Two. The hanger deck doors are now opening, and you are clear about launching. Over." Swiftly the acknowledgments came back, "We copy bridge, over." The bridge team observed as, one after the other, the Copernican spacecraft swept through the gaping aperture. Then, wheeling like luminescent dragonflies, the two crafts descended to the moon below. The captain sighed.

"As if the Sea should part

And show a further Sea—

And that—a further—and the Three

But a presumption be—

Of Periods of Seas—

Unvisited Shores—

Themselves the Verge of Seas to be—

Eternity—is Those—"

Leonidas cocked an eyebrow. Nancy smiled, "Emily Dickinson."

An hour later, the shuttles lay outside the massive pile. Inside the extraterrestrial antiquity, the landing party stood in front of a featureless bulkhead. Shrugging and smiling ruefully, Navigator Tripper knocked on the wall and uttered the word, "Melon." As the oval opening appeared, he said over the com links, "For luck." With blasters drawn, the four space explorers entered the last gallery. They could see the empty chamber as their eyes adjusted to the ambient red light. Suddenly, to their astonishment, a large sphere of pulsating blue light appeared in the middle of the room. Yeoman Franke shielded her vision from the flashing orb. "What do you think it is?" The Chief Engineer Book studied his recorder. "I don't know. It does not register as anything we have on record. An energy that is unknown to our science." Navigator Tripper stared at the mysterious object. "I have an uneasy inkling about this." Engineer Riley said, "I have the same feeling."

On the Copernican bridge, the crew viewed the spinning vortex with concern. "Shall I pull the crew out, Captain?" asked the First Officer. Nancy cupped her chin in her palm. The flickering radiance was no less intense than the twinkling in her brilliant green eyes. "No, let this play out. I don't think they're in any danger yet."

For several minutes, the landing party studied the indigo spheroid. "What do we do now?" asked Jason. "How do we figure out what that thing is?" Jane said, "There is only one way to find out." She took a step forward. Then, like a lightbulb going out in ample space, the red-lit surroundings disappeared, and the foursome stood in the middle of a vast plain. In the far distance, improbably tall purple mountains reared. Twin suns, one orange, one yellow, hung in the gathering dusk. A light chilly wind swirled the dust at the space explorer's feet and tugged at their clothing. "Toto," said Jane. "I don't think we're in Kansas anymore."

"Holographic illusion," said Book. Tripper scowled, "You mean this is not real?" Jane tittered nervously, "That's what the man said, hotshot." Engineer Riley rotated in a circle, "I've been in holo suites a lot, but this is far and away the most complex reality I have ever experienced. It's like we're here, where ever here is." For several minutes, the landing party senses drank in their habitat. "Look at the height of those mountains!" said Jane. "They must be 10 kilometers tall!" The Chief Engineer Book examined his recorder. "Fifteen kilometers if I can trust these readings. Plus, the atmosphere and temperature are the same as in the artifact. Makes sense since we are still there." Chris was studying the setting of the twin suns. "You know those twin suns remind me about something, but I can't quite put my finger on it." The four space travelers considered the dual sunset. Jason laughed, "I get it! It's the famous twin sun scene from the movie Star Wars!" A look of incomprehension crossed some of the landing party's faces. "Listen," said Engineer Riley, busying himself with his recorder, "look at the suns and hear the music for the scene. The old composer John Williams wrote it." The four tuned in to the sunset and listened to the music with rapt expressions. "Well," said Jane. "That was special."

"What are they doing?" asked Nancy Darkstrider. "They are just standing around. Not doing much. They even ignore that blue flashing sphere." The First officer said, "The crewmen are staring at something. But there's nothing there but a blank hull." The captain considered, "They don't seem to be in immediate peril. Leave them alone for now."

"Where do you think we are?" asked Engineer Riley. "I know we're still in the room, but what is this landscape supposed to represent? Why did the aliens make this?" Lost in thought for several minutes while the twin suns set. Then, just as the sunset ended, a new day began as a small red sun peeked above the horizon. "Got it," said Navigational Officer Tripper. "This isn't a binary star system; it's a trinary. Yellow, orange, and red stars? We're standing on Proxima Centauri b, the planet of the sun we see rising." Chris's companions made exclamations of astonishment. "Alpha Centauri is 4.37 light years away! Forty trillion kilometers!" yelled the Chief Engineer Book. "How do you know this is Proxima Centauri b, Mr. Tripper?" said Yeoman Franke. "Doesn't Proxima possess two other planets?" Tripper nodded, "Yes, but planet d is too close and hot to support life. Life as we know it, anyway. Planet c is too far away and thus too cold. So, no, this is Proxima b for sure."

"It all hangs together," said Jason. "But why did the aliens make this holographic reality? We're not here." Chris shrugged his robust frame. "Homesickness maybe," said Jane. I understand these aliens. Forty trillion kilometers from hearth and home. Away from their families for decades on end, maybe. This illusion was a way of getting back to their roots." Francis Book stooped and picked up a handful of dirt. "This is good soil. My people, the Nuxualt, could grow good crops here. Speculation is fine, but there is one thing we have not considered. How do we get back?" Everyone looked around. Riley pointed at a thin red oval that hung in the air some distance away. "There it is, hard to see, but that's the door we came through. It's the way back to reality."

"Ok," said Captain Darkstrider. "They are taking too long. Contact the landing party and tell them to return to the ship." The First Officer fiddled with his earpiece and replied, "Captain, we have lost communication with the shuttle crews." Nancy looked at the figures on the screen with concern. "This does not bode well."

"Right," said Tripper decisively, "Now we know what we're about; what do we do from here? I'd better contact the ship for instructions." Chris keyed his comlink. "Come in, Copernicus. Landing party reporting. Over. Come in, Copernicus, over." Tripper stared at his colleagues, shocked, "We've lost contact with the ship!" Nonplussed, the comrades regarded each other. "What do we do?" asked Jason. "Do we go back?" After a moment, Communication Officer Franke said, "No, this is too great an opportunity. The landing party has discovered what we believe is the origin of the aliens and what their planet resembles. We can find out more information. We're only a short time into the day's mission. I say go on. We are explorers, after all." Nods of agreement came from the quartet.

"First off," said Jane. "Let's open up the visors on our helmets. The atmosphere can support us here or back in the room." Tentatively, the foursome opened their visors. Each took deep, appreciative breaths. "The air smells delicious!" said the Chief Engineer Book. "After breathing in canned stuff for a year, this is wonderful!" Navigation Officer Tripper sniffed. "Cold and oxygen-rich, but yes, this is fine." The landing party luxuriated in filling their lungs with life-giving air. The red sun rose higher in the sky, casting a rosy glow on the landscape. "Now we know why the light was red in the artifact," said Francis. "Their home planet has a red sun." Tripper shaded his eyes as he looked at the carmine globe.

"Interesting, I've read about Proxima Centauri. It's only about 134,000 kilometers in diameter. Why does it appear to be as big as our sun?" Engineer Riley enlightened the young officer. "It's because Proxima Centauri b is only 7.5 million kilometers from its sun. It's all a matter of perspective." Chief Engineer Book, "Another fun fact. Because Proxima burns fuel so slow, it will remain on the Main Sequence for 4 trillion years, as against 10 billion for our sun."

"Four trillion years?" Jane Franke ejaculated. "The universe is only 13.7 billion years old. So Proxima Centauri sounds like it's immortal!" Jason smiled at the Yeoman. "Proxima is immortal."

The group surveyed the landscape. Ten kilometers away, there appeared a large rock formation. "Why don't we walk over there?" said Chris Tripper. "Not that far, and it's about the only notable thing on this empty plane." The others agreed with the Navigator Tripper's suggestion. Francis Book took a small device from his helmet. "I'm leaving my homing beacon here so we can find our way back to the door." Setting off in Indian file, the shuttle crew began their trek. The wind increased, blowing dust into their faces. From above, the four space-suited figures seemed lost in the immensity of the desolate plain. Like lost souls in purgatory, they advanced in the hope of salvation. The land was not as flat as it appeared at first. The landing party walked up and down a rolling terrain. In places, they crossed shallow gullies. After an hour, the pile of rocks seemed to stay far away.

The red sun had climbed higher in the sky, casting a rose-colored complexion to the white-clad space farers. They were traversing a particular deep gulley when Yeoman Franke made the discovery. "A plant! Look!" The Copernican crew gathered around a sickly-colored purple plant. Chief Engineer Book crouched low to examine the vegetation. "I can't see much difference between this and earthy flora." Jason Riley bent over. "If there is life, then there is water nearby." Yeoman Franke stroked the herbage with a gloved hand. "Proxima Centauri is in the Goldilocks zone. Water can exist in liquid at just the right distance from its sun."

The troop resumed their journey. Now, the rocky promontory seemed closer. The land dipped into a hollow before rising again. A small body of water materialized in response to Engineer Riley's words. The band of spacers stood next to the small pond and peered into its depths. Purple scum obscured their vision; small vermillion insect-like creatures skated on its surface. Yeoman Franke scooped up one creature and examined it. It looked back at her with long questing antennae. "It would be exactly like a Daddy Long-Legs if not for the color." Tripper ran his hand through the water, stirring it up. "Watch it, Chris, there could be a face-hugger lurking," joked the Chief Engineer Book. Carefully, Jane set the insect back on the water, and the landing party continued.

The quartet, at last, reached the rock outcropping. They carefully climbed to its top and peered out the other side. What greeted their eyes astonished them. The land fell away into an enormous plain that stretched to the horizon. Dotting the ground, thousands of animals grazed on sparse vegetation. The space adventurers examined the nearest ones. They were large, about the size of cattle, reddish-purple ungulates. They possessed formidable horns and differed from earth cows with spiked tails and six legs. One creature lifted its head and stared at the Earthers with bovine indifference. "My god," exclaimed Engineer Riley. "look at those things! Six legs!" The spacefarers drank in the vista with thirsty eyes. The beasts milled about, quietly cropping the purple grass. Disconcertingly, they would make an occasional honking noise like geese. "If you think that is interesting," said the Chief Engineer Book, "look at what's guarding them." Riding into view were three life forms on orange lizard-like animals. At that distance, it was hard to discern what features they possessed. They appeared to be very tall on their steeds. They held long poles or spears in their hands. Silvery tunics on slim forms. Long metallic objects strapped to their backs. Expertly, the beings guided their charges into compact groups using the goads. "Aliens!" breathed Jane. "Our first aliens!"

"It looks like a cattle drive," said Chris Tripper, "and they're cowboys." Jane pointed, "Those things they carry on their backs. I think they are weapons." The landing team studied the alien cowboys briefly as they worked their cattle. It appeared they were getting ready to move the livestock out. "You know," said the Chief Engineer Book, "I'm puzzled by the primitiveness of these creatures. I know this is a billion years ago, but this society possessed inter-stellar capabilities." Jane chuckled, "Even today, earth cowboys drive cattle with horses Engineer Book." Francis glanced at the Yeoman in surprise, "How do you know that, Jane?" Franke tossed her head back, forgetting she was wearing a helmet, "I grew up on a ranch Chief."

"I wish we could get a closer look at one of those cowboys," said Jason. "Oh, I don't think you have to wish long for that to happen," his friend Book said. "Why do you say that Francis?" asked Engineer Riley curiously. The Chief Engineer had turned and had his back to the group. "Because one of them is standing behind us."

The other three whirled so quickly that Jason fell flat on his face. Ten meters away, a Proxima Centauran sat on his lizard-like ride, spear in hand. The alien slowly got off his mount and walked a few steps toward the foursome. Three meters tall, his head was level with the landing party where they perched on the rocks. Calmly, he studied the newcomers. A weather-beaten reddened face with large oval, golden iris eyes, flat nose, and lipless mouth.

Colorful tribal scars or pigments adorned his countenance. From his scalp hung green mossy filaments that reached almost to his waist. The alien's body was virtually tubular with six-fingered hands. A silvery tunic covered in odd symbols clothed him from neck to knees. Thick purple, hide-covered gloves protected his six-toed feet. The creature addressed them in a strange, sibilant language that sounded like maggots dropping from a corpse hanging from a rafter and hitting the floor. Chief Engineer Book stepped forward with his right hand raised. "We are people from Earth. We come in peace." The tall alien reached forward and poked the shuttle crew with his long prod as if reassuring himself that they were real. Then he half-turned and pointed back to where the team had come. Without another glance, the Proxima Centaurian mounted his steed and rode away toward his fellows.

"Well," said Yeoman Franke, "That was special." Navigator Tripper addressed the Chief Engineer, "Why didn't you say, 'Take me to your leader'?" Book laughed scornfully, "That is so clichéd." Jason Riley tapped his face. "You know, he looked more like an Indian than a cowboy. With all that war paint, I mean." The four returned to their vigilance. They could see their alien talking to his mates and gesturing to where they stood on the rocks. "Why do you suppose the Centaurian was pointing the way we came?" asked Jane. "I think he was giving us a warning," said Chris. "We should move back to the door as fast as we can." Something in his tone alarmed the space explorers, and they quickly climbed down from their perch and hurried, following their outward footsteps. The small crimson sphere overhead had long passed its zenith and was now shining in their faces. Their bodies cast long shadows as they hurried across the endless expanse.

"This is so strange," said Captain Darkstrider. "They keep marching from one side of the chamber to the other with their helmet visors up. Then they spent ten minutes staring at something that wasn't there." First Officer Leonidas, "Not to mention Chief Engineer Book holding up his right hand and speaking to something he could see, but we could not." Nancy got out of her seat and paced in frustration. "Now they are marching faster than ever as if they feared something. Could the blue-spinning spheroid be affecting their minds?" Spiro studied the bridge view screen with its four split views. "It would be almost comical if it wasn't so deadly serious. The landing party is still not responding to my hails. Whatever is happening, I think we're approaching the climax." Darkstrider stopped her pacing and faced the screen. "I feel it too."

The black shadows of the four wanderers were longer now. The scarlet orb of the sun dropped quicker toward the horizon. "How much further do you think?" asked Jason Riley, panting. Chris Tripper consulted his recorder. "I see the Chief's homing signal. About 2 kilometers to go, men." Lithely Yeoman Franke bounded across the dusty ground, enjoying the wind on her face. Francis Book struggled to keep up with his younger crewmates. "Is all this haste necessary, Mr. Tripper? What are we running from?" A low rumbling echoed across the vast empty spaces. "There's your answer, Chief Engineer," said Chris grimly. "Look behind us." By common consent, the intrepid space explorers stopped and turned. A vortex of jagged horns, heads, and mailed tails suddenly destroyed the smooth line of the far horizon. A low honking came to their ears like a distant automobile jam from the 21st century. "Stampede!" yelled Engineer Riley.

Swiftly the landing party tore across the acrid soil of Proxima Centauri b. "Now we know what our alien was trying to tell us," said Yeoman Franke. "The herd was coming, and get out the way we came!" Jason, limping on his injured leg, replied, "That was good of him. He is a good Indian." Francis puffed, lagging. "That's almost racist, Jason. The only good Indian is a dead Indian, was the saying in the bad old days. Well, we might all be dead in a short while." Then, finally, navigator Tripper spoke, "I keep remembering that this is an illusion. We're not here. The artifact's chamber is where we are. So we aren't in danger." Francis replied, "I wouldn't bet on that, Chris."

Two hundred meters away, the red outline of the antechamber's door flickered in the waning light. "The door!" yelled Jason. "It's going out!" Navigator Tripper grimly concurred. "It must be on a timer. We have to get there before it closes!" By now, outriders of the quickest purple bovines were passing them on each side. Abruptly, geysers of dirt kicked up at the fugitive's heels. Jane risked a look over her shoulder. "Those cowboys. They're not trying to hit us. Just having a little fun." Navigator Tripper shouted commands. "Jane, you're swiftest. Go through the door first. I'll follow, holding Jason. He's exhausted. Chief, I'm afraid you must bring up the rear. Good luck, everyone!" With a leap, Franke was through the reddened aperture. Stumbling, Tripper and Riley followed through the closing entry. Chief Book paused and turned. A huge red-purple bull was charging him with horns lowered. Twenty-five meters away, the alien they had first encountered sat on his mount. With a stoic expression, Francis raised his palm to the Centaurian. The creature inclined his head. Then, with a desperate twist of his body, the Chief Engineer hurled himself through the shrinking portal.

Francis sprawled with his friends on the floor of the blackened sentry gun's room. Exhausted, they lay panting. "Well, we made it," said Jane. Chris turned on his back and groaned, "I thought you were going to say, 'That was special.'" Uncontrollable laughter echoed in the chamber for the first time in a billion years.

Pluto

Chapter 6

"Good to see the four of you back and in one piece," said Captain Nancy Darkstrider. The disheveled and weary landing party peered back at her. Copernicus's main conference room again was the setting for a critical tableau. "May I ask why you were out of communication for several hours?" continued Nancy. "And why you walked about at random in the chamber with the blue sphere?" The quartet looked at each other furtively. Navigational Officer Tripper opened his mouth to speak, then closed it again. Then, finally, Chief Engineer Francis Book said. "We were in a holographic projection captain. The pulsating azure ball created a virtual reality. We knew we were out of contact with the ship, but thought exploring while we had the opportunity was important." First Officer Leonidas tapped a pencil on the table. "If you knew experiencing something that was not real, why think it was so important to continue? What did you expect to learn? Where did you think you were?" Communication Officer Jane Franke answered, smiling, "We were on the alien's home planet, Mr. Leonidas, Proxima Centauri b."

Startled exclamations exploded from the higher-ranked bridge crew. "Proxima Centauri b?" said Spiro. "How did you know it was that alien planet and homeworld?" Engineer Riley took up the narrative. "The ambient reddish light matched that in the artifact. Plus, the planet had three suns, red, orange, and yellow, a trinary." The captain leaned forward in rapt concentration. "And you were seeing all of this? It's too bad that your camcorders documented what they were seeing and not what you were visualizing."

Navigator Tripper spoke for the first time. "It was beautiful, captain. But, unfortunately, when we appeared, the twin suns were setting." Nancy sighed, "It sounds beautiful, Mr. Tripper. I would have liked to have seen it for myself." Engineer Riley gave out a chuckle. "You can experience the next best thing, captain. I have a clip that closely matches the reality we had. I can download it to Mr. Leonidas's computer, and he can project it." Darkstrider leaned back in her chair and smiled slightly. "By all means, Engineer Riley, go ahead."

Jason got out his recorder and pushed a few keys. "Data coming in now," said First Officer Leonidas. "Visual and audio recording complete. I am hitting play." The hologram of a figure in desert clothing appeared. Twin suns hung in the sky. A look of anguish played on the face of the young man as the music washed over the scene. The two spheres bloated as they set, and clouds scudded across their faces. After a last view of the youth, the visual ended. Mr. Leonidas laughed shortly. "I recognized it as a scene from that old movie, Star Wars. It still appears occasionally on the retro channel. I saw it when I was six. Great movie, still holds up." Darkstrider slowly exhaled, "First time for me. I don't remember seeing that scene or watching that movie before. And you're saying that is what you saw on the planet?"

Yeoman Franke answered, "A little more reddish sky, and there you have it, Captain." The Chief Engineer Book broke in. "Plus, while the twin suns were setting, a red sun arose."

"It sounds a lot like Proxima Centauri b," admitted Leonidas. "Go on with your story. What else did you experience?" Francis said. "We saw a rock outcropping about ten clicks away, and Mr. Tripper suggested we walk to them. There were 15-kilometer tall purple mountains in the far distance, but they were out of reach." Chris continued, "Jane found a plant. The first sign of life we have discovered so far. And further on, we found a pond that has purple scum on it and red insects."

Riley took up the thread of the narrative. "Eventually, we reached the outcropping of rocks and clambered up them. It was then we made a momentous revelation." Jason paused and became reflective as if reliving the moment. "Yes," asked Nancy impatiently, "what did you find?" Yeoman Franke looked at the captain with her blue eyes, "Large animals like cattle, except they were purple-red and had six legs. But that wasn't the biggest shock." Now it was Jane's turn to discontinue. First Officer Leonidas said gently, "What was there, Yeoman, that stupefied you to such a degree?" Jane cast a look of triumph at the first officer. "Aliens! Aliens are acting like cowboys on orange lizards guarding the animals!"

They left Nancy and Spiro speechless at this announcement. "Aliens are acting like cowboys perched on orange lizards?" commented the captain. "It sounds like something you would read in a cheap science fiction novel." The First Officer touched a key on his board, and a hologram image of one of the landing party's cams sprang into existence. "This is the recording from Mr. Riley's camcorder. As you can see, the landing party marched up and down the blue sphere chamber for a considerable time." The four younger crew members colored slightly at their antics of endless walking. "Now we can see the shuttle crew looking intently for several minutes at something. Then Chief Engineer Book turns, holds up his hand, and speaks. Who were you talking to you?" Francis grinned. "I spoke to an alien who had come up on us unawares."

"You spoke to one of them, Chief?" said Captain Darkstrider in awe. "I wish we had a visual of that historic event." Francis turned and addressed his younger colleague, "We have something. Mr. Riley used a 3-D program to construct an image of the alien. He is downloading it now." Leonidas pressed control, and the likeness of the Proxima Centaurian on its mount winked into view and slowly rotated. "3 meters tall, reddish complexion with multi-colored stripes. Oval golden eyes, truncated nose, slash for a mouth, mossy, long, cornrowed hair, pipe-like body, six-fingered hands, and six-toed feet. Clad in a silvery tunic. Carrying a prod or spear with a rifle device strapped to his back. Mounted on an orange, komodo dragon-like lizard."

"Exotic creatures are riding dragons. We sure got our money's worth," said Nancy, shaking her head. "Please continue with your spiel. I'm fascinated." Navigational Officer Tripper took up the tale. "The alien pointed back to where we came and departed. We were feeling uneasy and hurried towards the door. Chief Book had left a beacon." Darkstrider nodded, "Most sensible." Chris said, "We had covered about eight clicks when we heard a rumbling."

"A stampede!" broke in Jason excitedly. "The aliens were driving their six-legged cattle onto us!" Jane admonished her older crewmate. "We don't know that for a fact, Jason. That may have been their regular drive, and we got in the way." Chris made a motion with his hands. "We barely got back. Chief Engineer Book covered the rear as we all passed through the portal as it was closing." First Officer Leonidas cast a look of appreciation at the First Nations man, "Very brave of you, Chief." Francis shrugged, "I was the slowest. A bull was almost on me. I could see the alien we had first encountered watching us on his dragon. He nodded as I leaped through the door just as it closed." Engineer Riley said indignantly, "They were shooting at us with lasers!" Jane laughed, "They were firing at our heels. They are just a bunch of cowboys having fun. If you had lived on a ranch, you would understand." The Chief patted his mate's shoulder. "Jason said they reminded him of Indians, not cowboys. I think he was right. I felt a connection with the alien." Riley whispered, "So it attracted you, the war-painted freak." Book spoke sotto voce, "Oh, don't be jealous. He's been dead a billion years."

Captain Darkstrider shook her head in disbelief. "An incredible adventure. It certainly reads like science fiction. You broke standing orders. When the landing party lost contact, they should have returned." The shuttle crew visibly diminished but perked up when Nancy said, "But you have accomplished wonders. We now know the alien home world's origin and appearance. You are all commended for showing initiative."

Captain Darkstrider swept her crew with the gaze of her hypnotic emerald-green eyes. "So, I know you are thinking, what next?" The Copernicans exchanged quick looks. "Where do we go? The goal of our mission. We are going to land on Pluto!" Nancy's teammates erupted in cheers. "Pluto!!!" Darkstrider waited patiently for her charges to settle down. "Ok, the First Officer and I have worked out a few likely landing zones. Remember, our task is to find the beacon. That, of course, is why we're here. We are using both shuttles again. Same crews as before."

Nancy paused for a moment in thought. "I think we could use some input on the landing sites. After all, you did incredibly well on Charon. Mr. Leonidas. Could you put up a holo map of Pluto, please?" First Officer Leonidas toggled a switch, and a map of Pluto materialized about the conference table. "You may each pick one site. But, remember, as captain, I have the final say. So what is it to be? Where do you think the beacon hides? If it is hiding?"

Each member of the crew pored over the map of Pluto. Its terrain was an incredible complex of low colles, vast craters, ditch-like fossae, dark maculae, steep montes, and extensive terra. "It's like finding a needle in a haystack!" exclaimed Engineer Riley. Yeoman Franke laughed, "Finding a needle in a haystack is easy. Just jump in one, and it will find the needle will find its way into your bottom." Amid chuckles, Captain Darkstrider said, "Ok, you have had some time to think about it. I don't think any additional time will help. What are your choices?"

"Burney crater," said Chief Engineer Book. "Why that option, Chief?" asked Spiro. Francis considered his answer. "It's wide. When a satellite passed over it, the beacon would have a wide range of motion to track it." Darkstrider said, "Excellent reasoning." The Chief continued, "Named after Venetia Burney, an 11-year-old girl who proposed the name, Pluto." Captain Darkstrider, "Yes, we know, Chief. We have spent the last few weeks mapping Pluto's surface. Yeoman Franke? You look like you're ready." Jane pointed to a place at the bottom of the map. "Pandemonium Dorsa, the capital of Hell in the poems of John Mills." Leonidas studied her preference. "Any reasons for that spot, Yeoman Franke?" Jane tossed her luxurious blonde mane back. "Just a hunch."

Next up was Navigator Tripper. "Pioneer Terra. It's near the top of Pluto and perfectly situated to intercept any spacecraft." Nancy nodded, "Good preference. Mr. Riley, are you ready for your guess?" Jason stabbed confidently upwards, "Tartarus Dorsa, from Greek mythology, the pit of Hell." Chris grinned broadly around the table, "Well, I would say we are all going to hell tomorrow." Groans abounded around the room at the young officer's quip. "For me, I want Balrog Macula," said First Officer Leonidas. "It's black, and they could hide anything there and pass unnoticed." Yeoman Franke shuddered, "A balrog? The demonic creature from Lord of the Rings?" Spiro spread his hands in a helpless gesture. "For me," said Captain Darkstrider, "Tombaugh Regio is where I want to land. Straight to the heart." The crew of the Copernicus exchanged glances. "I think that covers it," said Nancy. "Thank you, everyone, for today, and get some rest. We're leaving Charon early tomorrow to resume our orbit of Pluto." As the crew pushed their chairs back and arose, Darkstrider said, "Oh, Yeoman Franke, there will be a small ceremony tomorrow involving you." Taken by surprise, Jane could only gape, "Yes, Captain Darkstrider."

An hour later, Captain Darkstrider and First Officer Leonidas sat in the ship's holo theatre. The two had just finished watching the old movie Star Wars and now was halfway through the second feature, The Empire Strikes Back. "I find it hard to believe you have never seen these movies, Captain," said Spiro. "They are cult classics. I'm surprised they are not required viewing at the Space Academy." Nancy munched on some popcorn and sipped her beverage. She almost seemed to be a young girl again. "I have heard of them, of course. I was too busy to indulge in recreation somehow. The first movie, Star Wars, was enjoyable. Incredible special effects for the time. The planets look just as they do from space. I liked the woman, Princess Leia." Leonidas smiled. "Yes, I imagined you would identify with her. But let's stop talking. An important scene is coming up that will shock you."

On the screen, the duo heard, "No, Luke, I am your father." Captain Darkstrider cried in amazement, "Oh my god!"

In another part of the ship, the four younger crew members were relaxing at a table in the ship's lounge. "It's so much better to sit together and have drinks," said Yeoman Franke to the engineers. "After all we have been through today, I feel much closer to you guys." Chief Engineer Book drank some of his whiskey. "I know what you mean, Jane. You showed your mettle today. You saw the laser trap and reacted to the sentry guns first. I don't think we would have survived without you." Jason tipped his beer in a salute. "And you patched up my leg as good as new." Franke lowered her eyes in modesty, "Really, gentlemen, you are going to make me blush all over." Jane hid her embarrassment by taking a sip of her wine. Chris Tripper chose his moment and said, "If you are going to blush all over Jane. Let's head to the hot tub so we can all see!" Franke gasped and choked as her drink went down the wrong way. Finally, the Yeoman plotted her revenge. Jane waited to see the smile on her lover's face until he raised a glass of port to his lips. Then, adroitly, she reached over and tilted the bottom, making the liquor run down his front. Sputtering for a moment, Chris joined in the general laughter.

Captain Darkstrider lay on her back on her bed in her nightdress. With her arms folded behind her head, she contemplated the ceiling of her quarters. A ping sounded from her computer, alerting her that a message was coming in. Swinging slender legs over the bunk sides, Nancy switched on the play button on her PC. A small holo image of Darkstrider's son appeared. The facsimile spoke, "Hi, mom; Greg here again. Everybody at the Space Academy talks about the artifact you found on Pluto's moon, Charon. The mobile video stations are short on details, so I'm not sure what you have discovered. Mom, leave the exploring to other people. Your job is to command. We have a betting pool going to when you find the beacon. I'm not allowed to bet because they say I have an inside track. Well, that's all except to say I love and miss you. See you in about 15 months. Greg out."

Darkstrider restlessly sat on her chair by the cabin's portal. The multi-hued minor planet Pluto swam into view below her. The luminous body's heart throbbed before Nancy's gaze. Its blue, unflinching iris reached out. It seemed to say, "So you have come at last?" Nancy cupped her chin in her hand, "Tomorrow, my love. Tomorrow we will see if you can keep your chasteness from the strength of my ardor." Tossing and turning, First Officer Leonidas lay on his bed. Then, abruptly, he awoke and sat up. "I feel a disruption in the Force."

The four billion-year-old dance of mother Pluto and her children continued. Like fireflies, the smaller moons tumbled and careened while grey Charon moved sedately on its course. The distant sun's rays sparkled off the husband of Persephone's mountains and plains. The glossy white and blue halves of Pluto's heart lie beckoning for its lover.

On the Copernicus' hanger deck, the four younger members of its crew stood rigidly at attention. Captain Darkstrider and First Officer Leonidas stood before them. "Yeoman Franke, you showed exemplary leadership during yesterday's mission. Your outstanding courage and attention to detail keep your crew out of harm's way. Therefore, it is a great pleasure to promote you to the rank of lieutenant." The captain moved forward and attached the lieutenant's pips to the collar of Jane's flight jacket under her spacesuit. "Congratulations, Lieutenant Franke." Jane seemed about to burst with pride.

The other landing party members crowded around Franke. "Good work Jane," said Navigator Tripper. "It took me five years to make lieutenant, and you did it in two. But that's ok." Jane laughed and patted Chris's cheek as Jason and Francis slapped his back in mock sympathy.

Spiro stepped forward, carrying a clipboard. "Ok, break it up. I have your assignments. Burney crater for Book and Riley. Tombaugh Regio for Tripper and new lieutenant Franke. Questions?" Chris held up his hand, "Yes, one, Mr. Leonidas. Tombaugh was Captain Darkstrider's choice. Why are we going there?" Nancy smiled. "Because I'm going with you." Spiro grinned, "Does anyone have a problem with that?" Jane laughed, "Ok with me, captain!" Tripper stuttered a bit, "No, of course not. None." Leonidas made a sweeping motion with his arm, "Then off you go." As the five walked towards the shuttles, Chris mumbled to Jane, "I wondered why the Captain had her flight suit on and was carrying a helmet." Franke whispered back, "So now you know. Happy now?"

A short time later, First Officer Leonidas stood on the ship's bridge as he watched the shuttles leave the landing bay. Feeling oddly lonely, he observed the twin white doves circle, then descend gracefully to the planet below. Discontentedly, Spiro sat at his science station and continued his work. Finally, he muttered, "Come back home safely, Nancy."

"We're crossing the outer rim of Burney crater in 5 minutes, Jason," said the Chief Engineer Book. A low range of hills rose from the chaotic terrain of Viking Terra. Just visible on the left were the trench-like Inanna and Dumuzi Fossa. Francis noticed his friend's interest in the trench-like features. "Inanna and Dumuzi Fossa are Sumerian fertility gods that descended into the underworld." Jason laughed. "If I had names like them, that's where I would go." Book pulled a lever, and the spacecraft rose. "I'm going to increase our altitude to 25 clicks. Then we can see what we have to work with." The exploratory ship gained height at a steep angle and leveled off after several minutes. The tract of the crater spread itself beneath them.

"Burney is big, with lots of smaller cratering inside," said Engineer Riley. "One hundred and fifty-five kilometers from brim to lip," said the Chief. The two cohorts studied the alien topography. "Hey," said Jason, "look at that gigantic crater that looks like an eye up near the top. Then lower and to the right, two small holes that look like nostrils. Then below them that the ellipse-shaped basin resembles a mouth. Looks like a stylized portrait of a female face, doesn't it, Francis?" Book's eyes narrowed to slits as he attempted to conjure up the vision of his confidant. "Yeah, it does. Well, where shall we land, my partner in crime?" Riley pointed through the viewscreen, "To the mouth, my better half, to the mouth!"

In a long lazy spiral, the white-winged pegasus that was Shuttle One descended to the smooth expanse of Tombaugh Regio. Polygonal convection cells divide its surface. "The white, western side of Tombaugh, where we head, is Sputnik Planum, after the Soviet space program," said Navigator Tripper in the pilot's chair. "The heart's eastern, or blue, lobe is nameless." Lieutenant Franke beside him, "There is an austere beauty about this land. An almost timeless allure." Captain Darkstrider spoke from a seat behind them. "You have a very poetic nature, Lieutenant Franke. I never knew that about you." The Communication Officer glanced over the mirror over her head at her captain's reflection. "I read a lot of poetry, Captain Darkstrider. My favorites are Elizabeth Barrett Browning, Emily Dickinson, and Sofia Snowden of the Martian colonies." Nancy peered between their shoulders at the growing Plutonian plain. "I am a big fan of Sofia Snowden as well." Chris leveled out the shuttle's descent. "Captain, is there a particular destination you would like to name our first landing?"

Darkstrider considered the question, "Soyuz Colles, named after the three cosmonauts who died on the Soyuz 11. So centrally placed on the Sputnik Planum and a good place to start our search." Jane nodded to a series of distant hills on the horizon. "Soyuz Colles, it is. Entering course now in the Nav computer."

Shuttle One sunk slowly to its rendezvous with ice, floating like a white feather one hundred meters from the Soyuz hills. Navigator Tripper gave a running commentary to Copernicus. "70 degrees. 70 degrees. Eight hundred meters, 45 down. 30 degrees. Five hundred meters down at 19. Three hundred feet down at 6. Drifting slightly to the right, corrected. 210 meters. One hundred meters, readings are showing green. Seventy-five meters, things are looking good. The landing field is coming up, clear of obstructions and drifting right, corrected. Contact made. Ok, the engine is off. Shutting down controls and locked. Magnetic brakes are in place, over."

First Officer Leonidas voiced over the intercom, "We read you, Shuttle One, over."

"Copernicus, Shuttle One here. The Eagle has landed, over."

Captain Darkstrider gave a silvery laugh. "Eagle? Since when have you been calling the shuttle that?" Chris gave a rueful smile. "Since two seconds ago when I thought of it." Jane patted Tripper's shoulder. "Never mind, lover-boy, I'm sure Neil Armstrong would have been proud." The shuttle crew got out of their seats and stretched. A short distance away, the Soyuz Colles loomed like icebergs in a frozen sea. Lieutenant Franke stared in wonder at the icy ramparts of the hills, like the battlements of a medieval castle. "What caused these hills, I wonder," she said. Tripper chuckled, "If you are prepared to listen to a long technical exclamation, lieutenant. The nitrogen ice glaciers on Pluto carry isolated hills that are fragments of water ice from Pluto's surrounding uplands. The colles are miniature versions of the much larger jumbled mountains on Sputnik Planum's western border. Ice made of water is less dense than ice, primarily composed of nitrogen. So they float in a sea of frozen nitrogen like the ice shelves in Earth's Antarctica Ocean. Soyuz Colles follows the margins of the hexagonal cells' conventional movement." Jane stared at Chris in wonder. "Since when did you turn into a walking computer?"

Nancy had been staring out the viewscreen at the frozen tableau. "Let's secure our visors and prepare to leave the shuttle." Chris and Jane glanced at each other. "Captain Darkstrider, we think you should be the first Terran to step onto Pluto," said Franke. Tripper nodded. "It's the captain's privilege, after all." Nancy bowed her head. "I am honored." The three space adventurers stepped into the airlock and listened as the air purged into the main cabin.

Captain Darkstrider pushed a button by the airlock door when the warning light turned red to green. The egress slid aside, revealing the stark panorama of Sputnik Planum. The reflected light from the distant sun and stars flooded the darkened cubicle. Darkstrider took a deep breath and boldly stepped into contact with the thin skin of Pluto's body. Nancy directed her gaze at mother Earth, a blue dot in the sky. "Clyde Tombaugh, we are here."

"Did you hear that, Jason?" asked the Chief Engineer Book. "What the Captain just said?" Engineer Riley snickered. "I'm sitting right here, so, of course, I heard it." Francis mused, "'Clyde Tombaugh, we are here.' Powerful stuff; give her that. She knows how to turn a phrase." Jason busied himself with his control panel. "On that note, we are drawing near Mouth Crater, initializing landing protocol." Then, with elegant ease, the pure-white egret gently flew to a soft landing. The rim of Mouth Crater took shape a kilometer away. Riley looked curiously at his companion. "Did you plan a pronouncement when you stepped onto Pluto, Francis?" Book laughed, "Yes, I was going to yell Geronimo! But now I've had second thoughts." A mischievous look entered Engineer Riley's eyes. "Let's both say it!" Chief Book, "Oh, why not? How can they punish us? Send us to Pluto?" Five minutes later, the two men stepped onto the soil of Pluto for the first time.

"Geronimo!"

A hundred kilometers away, the engineer's shouts did not escape notice. "Did you hear that, Chris?" asked Communication Officer Jane Franke over the helmet comm. "What Book and Riley just said?" Navigator Tripper chuckled, "Geronimo? Well, it is appropriate since Francis is a First Nations." Standing with her younger crew, Captain Darkstrider swept her gaze over the stark expanse of Sputnik Planum. An eerie glow suffused the endless bone-white prospect. A labyrinth of stars wheeled overhead. Directly above their heads, the Copernicus hung in the sky like a stranded Moby Dick. Lieutenant Franke interrupted Nancy's vigil. "Captain, Mr. Tripper and I have been thinking. The surface area of Pluto is over 7.6 million square kilometers. That's greater than old Russia on Earth. How can we cover all that on foot, even with the shuttles?" The captain's disembodied voice hissed over their comms, "Way ahead of you, lieutenant. Come with me, you two." Five minutes later, the three spacers had the cargo bay door of the shuttle open. They inspected the object that Chris had just rolled down the ramp. A compact, cabin-enclosed vehicle with large solid rubber wheels. "A moon chariot?" asked Jane. "I didn't know we carried any." Nancy gestured to the vehicle. "Well, now you know. The engineers loaded them on the shuttles this morning." Navigator Tripper ran his hand along the hood. "What are we supposed to accomplish with this baby, captain?"

Captain Darkstrider gestured to the underside of the machine. "There is a powerful metal detector installed. We will know if we come within 10,000 meters of any alloy. Pluto is just rock and frozen gas with no metal at all. That's how we will find the beacon." Jane Franke walked to the passenger side of the auto. "I guess Francis and Jason have one too?"

"Wheeeeeeeee!" yelled Engineer Riley. He and Chief Engineer Book traveled along the floor of Burney crater in the moon buggy at 100 kilometers an hour. A cloud of dust kicked up by the vehicle's tires hung in Pluto's low gravity. An ellipse-shaped crater opened up in front of them. "Hang on, Jason!" yelled Francis, and the moon chariot sailed over the lip of the depression and crashed down its side without losing speed. Down the 45-degree slope, the cart careened. The vehicle hit bottom with a thud and sped along its lower level. It was darker here, and some of the strange purple haze first seen on Charon swirled about them like fog.

After a journey of about 5 kilometers, the rising slope loomed. Up and up went the two intrepid space explorers. Leaving the crater flying, the vehicle reconnected with the ground with a thump. "So much for the Burney's mouth," exclaimed Jason. "Nothing there." Now the moon chariot was approaching two deep holes that formed the nostrils of Burney's face. "Don't enter one of those," warned Riley. "They're too steep." The Chief's voice cracked over the helmet intercom. "Wasn't planning to enter them. I'm steering a course between them."

On board, the Copernicus First Officer Leonidas watched the progress of the two moon chariots as they raced on Pluto's exterior. A look of concern consumed Spiro's face as he noted the extreme speed the two engineers were traveling. Finally, keying his mike, he spoke, "Come in Shuttle Two, come in shuttle Two. You are moving at over 100 clicks per hour. Is this advisable? Over." The response was immediate, "We are perfectly safe, Copernicus. There are a lot of areas to cover, over." Spiro acknowledged the transmission and turned his attention to the Shuttle One crew. "Now, what are they up to, I wonder?"

"Did you hear that, Captain?" complained Navigator Tripper. "Shuttle Two has their chariot pushing 100 kilometers per hour." From her seat behind her two crew, Jane keyed her mike, "Maintain your speed of 60 kilometers. Unlike them, we are traveling over ice."

Soyuz Colles reared its flanks out of its surroundings. "But Captain Darkstrider," said Jane Franke. "Ice at 40 Kelvin is like concrete. We will not slide." Darkstrider responded swiftly, "When we enter the hills, we will need a lower speed." The moon chariot hit the sloop of the first of the Soyuz Colles. Up it traveled along the incline. Cresting its summit, Chris steered a course between two steeper prominences. The vehicle's two right tires left the ground as the driver swept into a valley. Shadows engulfed them as they plunged through the darkness. Their headlights cut swathes of light through the blackness. The valley ended in a switchback, and Chris cut his speed to navigate the tortuous path. The small vehicle burst into the morning as they gained altitude.

An indifferent universe looked down on a small moon chariot as it hurried along Burney's crater. A dust plume lazily floated down behind it in Pluto's thin atmosphere. Aboard this mighty craft, two flowers of adulthood were conversing. "I should have gone to the fresher before we left," said Jason. Francis steered a path between the two gaping pits. "Yes, you should have. You'll have to hold it in." The twin nostrils of Burney's face behind them, the intrepid space explorers raced towards Burney's Eye, 75 kilometers away. "If you had told me two years ago that one day I'm riding in a moon chariot in a crater on Pluto, I would have said you were mad," said Engineer Riley. The Chief Engineer Book snickered, "Maybe you are crazy. But then, I'm not one to judge. Since I'm here with you in the driver's seat."

The younger man shifted his left buttock to relieve a cramp. "Yeah, about that. I want to have some fun too, Francis. Let me drive the buggy Tomorrow, ok?" Francis laughed. "Since you always drive me buggy, I can accommodate you." Jason shifted his right buttock. "Wow, that sounded like it could almost be humor. But knowing you, it wasn't. God, my butt hurt!" The Chief Engineer Book lifted his eyes in mock dismay. "Oh no. Stop the mission. Jason's bum hurts!" Engineer Riley let out a peel of laughter. "Now that was funny!"

For a time, the two bosom friends rode in comfortable silence. "Do you think we can find the beacon, Francis?" asked Jason. "Even with the chariots, we can only cover a small portion of Pluto's terrain." Francis Book thought it over for a span. "Well, we can eliminate places where it isn't: the macula and the ice mountains. I think Captain Darkstrider is right. I think the beacon is in the heart." Riley appeared puzzled. "Then why are we here and not in the heart?" The Chief gave his head a slight shake. "Because it might be here. I had a hunch. Buckle up, buttercup. I see Burney's eye approaching."

"Oh, my god!" exclaimed Lieutenant Franke. The moon rover had unexpectedly rocketed off the last high pass of Soyuz Colles and soared through space before it slammed on the downward slope. Now traveling more than a hundred kilometers an hour, it rushed towards Sputnik Planum. Through gritted teeth, Captain Darkstrider spat out, "For heaven's sake, Mr. Tripper, slow down!" Immediately Chris arrested the velocity of his car at a more sedate pace. "Sorry, Captain, I got lost in the moment and got carried away." Nancy nodded her head. "Lost in the moment and got carried away. We'll all get carried away if you keep this up. On stretchers!" The moon buggy, reaching the bottom of the slope, continued its way onto the vast ice plain. "Where now, Captain?" asked Jane. "Coleta de Dados Colles, named after the first Brazilian satellite," replied Nancy Darkstrider. "It's about a hundred and fifty kilometers ahead of us. The Way Navigator Tripper drives; we should be there in five minutes." Chris grinned, "Coleta de Dados Colles, it is captain!" The tiny vehicle dashed along its path on the unforgiving ice plains of Pluto until it disappeared.

"Approaching outer rim of Eye Crater now," said Chief Engineer Francis Book. Engineer Riley pointed to a space between two rim spurs. "That gap looks good, Francis. Let's enter there." The Chief carefully positioned the moon chariot in alignment with the rim aperture. At sixty kilometers an hour, the vehicle burst through the cranny and winged its way through space. After several seconds, the rover banged onto the descending slope and hurled down into the bowl. "I'm glad they made these babies durable," said Francis. "We're sure banging it up a lot." Busily wedging himself into his seat, Jason replied, "I like how you say we. I'm not driving this thing." Book laughed, "Oh, I suppose you could do better?" Engineer Riley darted an indignant look at his friend. "You bet I could. I'm not such a poor driver myself." The Chief patted Jason's knee. "Well, don't fret. You'll get your chance tomorrow."

The chariot left the slope with a hard bounce and entered the horizontal portion of the eye's iris. "In twenty minutes, we will meet the eye pupil," said Chief Book. Jason stared out his window at the passing scenery. "It's interesting how differentiated the soil is here. Greys, blues, greens, and reds. All frozen gases mixed with tholins, I guess." Francis carefully steered around a large boulder. "I'm sure Spock has an analysis of all the terra firma we are seeing. The Copernicus did map this region last week." The two space voyagers traveled in silence for twenty minutes.

"Would you look at that!" said Jason in a shocked tone. On the skyline, an ominous black hump was growing. "The pupil of the Eye in Burney's basin," replied Francis. "Could that be the beacon, you think?" queried the younger man. The Chief Engineer studied his readouts. "Negative, it's just a big rock. No metal at all." The small vehicle climbed the steep slope of the black monolithic rock at 70 kilometers an hour. "God, this pile is steep!" exclaimed Riley. "Since we're looking at the stars, Jason," replied Book. "You will get no arguments from me." The chariot's small engine protested as the incline increased.

The vehicle was creeping now, trying to get traction on the bare black rock surface. "Almost there," said the Chief Engineer Book with a set expression. "Almost there."

With the last lurch, the dynamic duo crested the pinnacle victoriously. "Made it!" shouted Riley. "Let's get out and look around." Francis cut the engine. "Ok with me." The two friends left their vehicle and surveyed the surrounding scenery. A broad plain splashed in a palette of colors greeted their eyes. Ahead of them was the emerging escarpment of the eye's crater, lost in shadows. Then, just on the edge of their vision, they could discern the faint blue line of the edge of Burney's caldera. Arms around each other's waists, the two confreres drank in the heady concoction.

A tiny white speck streaked across the whitish-blue surface of Sputnik Planitia. A casual observer would have noted its incredible speed, 150 kilometers per hour. Occasionally, as the mite hit the margin of the region's polygonal convection cells, it jolted into the sky. "Wow!" said Lieutenant Franke. "That last bump must have sent us 20 meters into the air!" Navigational Officer Tripper corrected the course that was deviated by the minor collision. "Sorry about that, everyone. You can't see those borders until you're right on top of them." Outside the cab of the moon chariot, the landscape rushed by with incredible speed. "Well, Mr. Tripper, you have set the land-speed record on Pluto," said Captain Darkstrider. "No, captain," grinned Chris. "This baby is a lot faster." Scowling, Nancy said, "How much longer to our destination driver?" Tripper consulted his board. "We will see it any minute, Captain Darkstrider. I will slow down."

Nancy tapped a button on her seat computer console. "In case you're interested, this is the appearance of the Coleta de Dados Colles we headed for." On the screen of their monitors, Chris and Jane studied an image that had appeared. A roughly triangular shape tapered to a very narrow neck that ended in a saucer-contoured head. "Good heavens," exclaimed Jane. "That looks exactly like a Klingon Battle Cruiser!" The three were silent for a moment. "She's right; it does," commented Chris. "I will grant you that," said Nancy. "But I don't think it is a crashed ship, frozen into the ice, like the one we saw in the movie Alien." Tripper gestured out the window. "Whatever it is, we are coming to it now." A tumble of irregular shapes rapidly expanded in their vision. "Right, here we go," said Chris. "Slowing speed to 40 clicks an hour. Entering the Coleta de Dados Colles now." With a slight bounce, the speeding moon chariot ascended the first slope. Passing over the hill's zenith, it immediately followed the downward slope into a deep valley. Chris maneuvered his way through several hillocks with a series of left and right turns. Finally, passing under an overhanging ridge of water ice, the chariot scrambled up the most prominent elevation in the area. Lieutenant Tripper paused on the flat plateau on top. Ahead of them lay the long, narrow neck of the colles. Beyond it, they could barely discern the saucer contour.

The vehicle plunged to the neck of the colles and sprinted along its length. In minutes, it had reached the last stage of formation, the saucer head. Chris weaved in and out of the motley collection of hills, valleys, and ridges of the hill formation. At last, the craft broke free of the tortured landscape and swept smoothly down onto the virginal surface of Sputnik Planitia. Tripper brought the ship to a stop and killed the engine. For a moment, no one spoke. "What now, captain?" asked Jane. Nancy gave them a blinding smile. "We've done enough for today, children. Back to the shuttle and return to the ship!"

"Ok, we've rested long enough," said the Chief Engineer Book. "Let's finish our mission." The twin white-suited figures climbed into their moon chariot and careened down the opposite slope of the eye's pupil. A phantasmagoria of shapes and tinctures blurred out their windows. After an hour, the eye's massive ramparts rose in front of them. "Francis," said Jason, "that slope looks too steep. We'll never make it!" Chief Engineer Book crowed, "Hang on! We're going up!" Sparkles of light flew from the white-hued sides of the moon craft. Higher and higher it climbed. As the chariot slowed, Francis incorporated a series of switchbacks to gain height. Finally, at almost a standstill, the vehicle topped the final prominence and whizzed down the other side. The two engineers grinned at each other in triumph.

"Where now?" asked Jason. Francis shouted, "We return to our shuttle and thence to that sweet bird, the Copernicus!"

"Well, that was an eventful 24 hours," commented Captain Nancy Darkstrider later in the Copernican boardroom. "Our first landfall on Pluto, and we've completed some preliminary surveying." First Officer Leonidas chuckled. "They inspired your quotes when you first stepped onto Plutonian soil." Nancy blushed slightly. "I hope it sounded ok?" Chief Engineer Book and his junior Riley beamed. "It was great, captain. Even better than our Geronimo."

Chris Tripper grinned, "You two set a top bar with that one." Darkstrider lasered the crew with her viridian green eyes. "I've decided it is time-consuming to travel back and forth from the ship. Therefore, we will ferry down parts for a shelter and continue exploring. The First Officer Leonidas will be in charge of Pluto base, and I will spend most of my time here coordinating everything." Lieutenant Franke held up her hand. Nancy laughed, "You don't have to hold up your hand to speak, Lieutenant Franke." Jane tossed her blonde hair back, "Does that mean not returning to the ship during this period?" Nancy thought this over, "No, but you spend most of your time down there. We have so much ground to cover." The holo map of Pluto appeared over their heads. "Where do we build the shelter, Captain?" asked Spiro. "In the center of a triangle formed by Soyuz, Astrid, and Challenger Colles," said Nancy. "First, we erect the shelter, which should take a day. Then Lieutenants Tripper and Franke will go to Pioneer Terra, our engineers, and the First Officer to Balrog Macula." Leonidas fidgeted, "About that, Could I change the destination to the blue lobe of the heart? The unnamed eastern part of Tombaugh Regio?"

Darkstrider gave her first officer a long look with jade green eyes. "Certainly you can. But why the switch?" Spiro Leonidas looked distinctly uncomfortable, "I realized I was mistaken. There is nothing in maculas but quicksands of tholins." Nancy nodded her blonde head. "I thought the same thing but left it up to you. Excellent choice." Jane snorted. "Am I hearing this right? Did I hear Spock admit he was wrong about something?" Spiro looked at the new lieutenant and said in a deadpan voice, "Even Vulcans can be incorrect sometimes." Loud laughter broke out, and the meeting ended. Pushing their chairs back, the crew of the Copernicus left the conference room.

Late that night, Jane Franke lay naked on her stomach on a massage table in the therapy room. Chris Tripper stood over her, working on her back muscles with practiced ease. "Well, Jane, tomorrow we help the engineers build the shelter, but we're on our own the next day in Pioneer Terra." Jane's muffled reply came back, "I hope we find something. This planet has many mysteries and little time to solve them." At an identical table, a short distance from them, Jason Riley was working on his naked friend, Francis. "That's true, Jane. I think finding that beacon will come down to luck." Chris finished kneading his lover's spine, "Ok, Jane, flip over, and I'll do your front. It's a dirty job, but someone has to do it." Riley pulled the towel off Book's ass and slapped him with it. "You too, cowboy, over you go!"

Spiro and Nancy were relaxing in the ship's hot tub with glasses of champagne. The blonde captain looked very fetching in a black one-piece swimming costume. First officer Leonidas wore a knee-length pair of garish orange shorts decorated with the Greek gods. "The shuttle crews did well today. They traveled faster than I think was safe, but they covered a lot of ground that way," said the captain. Spiro took a sip of his champagne. "Tripper and Book are excellent drivers. In two days, we will see what Franke and Riley can do."

Darkstrider leaned back and shut her eyes. "Time is the key. We must find the beacon before we miss our return window." The First Officer had nothing to offer to that. He sipped his drink while peering surreptitiously out of his eye's corner at Nancy's trim form.

In the vast vault of the heavens, the heart of Pluto beat to a distant drum.

Clyde Tombaugh's base

Chapter 7

Two days later, five members of Copernicus stood by the prefabricated shelter on Tombaugh Regio. In all directions, the irregular polygonal cells were dividing the blinding whiteness of Sputnik Planitia. Soyuz, Astrid, and Challenger Colles stood at equally spaced intervals on the horizon, looking like stranded icebergs. "Well, it took a lot of work from all of us, but the job's finished," said First Officer Spiro Leonidas. "The shelter is up with all its amenities, bunks, kitchen, a computer station, fresher." Navigator Tripper laughed, "It's so great I may live here permanently." Leonidas gave a tight smile. "Captain Darkstrider has instructed me to inform you that our shelter has a new designation." The Copernicans grew solemn as Spiro announced, "I now proclaim this habitat as Clyde Tombaugh's base." Then, the space explorers heard Nancy's metallic voice over their coms, "Hear! Hear!"

"OK," said Leonidas, "We know our assignments. Mr. Tripper and Lieutenant Franke are off to explore Pioneer Terra." Jane gave a mock salute, "Hasta la vista, baby!" The two lovers climbed into their moon buggy and soon were tearing due north across the alabaster plains of Pluto. Engineers Book, Riley, and the First Officer moved towards their vehicle. As Spiro was about to climb aboard, something on the edge of his field of vision arrested his attention. The Challenger Colles reared over the distant horizon with spires like an ancient cathedral. The hills sparkled in the rays of the absent sun. Book and Riley noticed their passenger had stopped and turned to him. "Something wrong, Mr. Leonidas?" asked the Chief Engineer Book. "Did you see something?" queried assistant engineer Riley. "It was a long time ago," said Mr. Leonidas, "in a faraway place. I was in the Rub' al Khali, or the Empty Quarter. A desert that's in the south of Saudi Arabia; it is home to the largest dunes in the world. Up to 300 hundred meters tall. When the sun struck their surfaces, they sparked like polished diamonds. That's what I remember when I see those colles. My Bedouin guide called the hillocks, 'The Mountains of Arabia.'"

"The Mountains of Arabia," repeated Francis. "One of the hottest spots in the solar system is the same as one of the coldest." Then, nodding, the two engineers climbed into the machine. Spiro took one last look at the effervescence lighting on the far skyline. "I sense something else, an existence I have..." Shaking his head, the First Officer entered the craft, and it quickly sped away.

With approval, Captain Nancy Darkstrider contemplated Clyde Tombaugh's base on the bridge screen. "The boys and Franke wasted no time getting the shelter up." She watched the twin insects that were her landing crews as they rocketed across Pluto's sterile surface. "I told you I'd seduce you," said Nancy to the minor planet. "Your maidenly reserve is no match for my passion." Nancy got up from her chair and patrolled restlessly around the bridge. "I have an instinct. We are close to solving the riddle. But time is running out. The window is closing." The captain stopped and stared at Pluto's heart. Its blue and white halves spoke to her in an unknown language. "What are you trying to tell me? Where are you hiding? Where is the beacon?" Catching sight of her reflection in a mirror above the science station, Nancy grinned. "First sign of insanity, talking to oneself." Darkstrider pondered her image in the looking glass. "Oh, what the hell." Reaching behind her hair, she loosened the bun. A cascade of molten gold flowed over her shoulders. She tossed her head, turning her blonde tresses into a loose mane. "Eat your heart out, Lieutenant Franke," said the captain, smiling.

Traveling 175 kilometers per hour flashed a speck on the frigid aspect of Sputnik Planitia. "A new Pluto land speed record," grinned Lieutenant Tripper. "I feel like Luke Skywalker in his X-34." Jane Franke held herself secure in her seat, "All you have to do now is blow up the Death Star, and you're all set." Ahead of the couple, a series of dunes became visible. "Looks like the ice is ending," said Jane.

"What's the deal with those dunes?" Chris slowed down the moon buggy. "Pluto's thermal winds blew solid grains of methane across Sputnik. They then accumulate at the base of the mountains. We have to cross them to get to Pioneer Terra." At 90 kilometers, the space vehicle entered the drift area. Wheels churning in the soft ground, Chris steered a course up the first hummock.

Cresting, the navigator plunged into the small valley beyond the hill. "Our moon chariot has turned into a dune buggy," laughed Tripper. "Have you ever driven a dune buggy, Chris?" asked Jane. "Yeah, in California and on Mars," answered Tripper. Now the compact craft traversed the next eminence. Streams of frozen nitrogen formed clouds in their wake. The two space explorers measured their progress by the deep ruts produced by their tires. "You know," said Chris. "Our tracks might last a million years. That's harming the environment." Lieutenant Franke angled the mirror above her head to view their wake. "Yeah, the atmosphere on Pluto is fragile. It could take that long for our wheel marks to disappear." Swiftly the minute car flew off a hummock's peak. "Excellent!" shouted the navigational officer. Chris had to fight for control with its two front wheels on the far slope. Finally regaining command, Tripper swept the machine along a narrow defile. "Hey!" shouted Jane. "I just remembered. I was supposed to drive today!" Tripper flashed a smile at his lover. "I'll let you drive on the way back." Threading their way, the two were castaways in a sea where no sail sets.

"I bet Tripper tries to break our land speed record," groused assistant engineer Riley. "Wasn't Franke supposed to drive today?" asked Chief Engineer Leonidas. "Yeah, she was," answered Francis. "But I saw Chris get into the driver's seat." First Officer Leonidas spoke from the back seat. "There will be no set of records as long as I am here. I value my life too much for that."

Chief Engineer Book sniggered, "Roger, dodger." Across the sterile-white plain of the white lobe of Tombaugh Regio, the Lilliputian craft scampered. Its solid rubber wheels found adequate traction on the concrete-like surface of Pluto's heart. Periodically, driver Riley dodged a solid nitrogen boulder at the polygonal cell borders. "Glad to have you with us, Mr. Leonidas," said the Chief Engineer. "Really?" answered Spiro. "I think you would have preferred upper management not to be breathing down your necks when exploring." Book glanced in his review reflector at the Greek first officer. "Not at all. We rarely talk to you on the ship. Perhaps we can talk more freely here." Jason added, "Yes, Mr. Leonidas. We would enjoy basking in your wisdom." The First Officer tittered, "Right. What would you gentlemen like to know?" Jason and Francis flashed a look at each other. "What are the chances of finding the beacon, Mr. Leonidas? Pluto is a minor planet, but as Lieutenant Franke pointed out, its area is bigger than old Russia. We're searching in random areas. Is that the proper system?" said the Chief Engineer Book. "Believe me, there is a method to our madness," said Spiro. "First, we have eliminated that are unlikely sites for the beacon. The ice mountains and the maculas, for instance. Also, we can forget about the valleys and the smaller craters." The moon chariot hit a rut and was momentarily airborne. There was silence until assistant engineer Riley brought it back in control. "Why can we give those areas a miss First Officer?" asked Jason.

"The beacon would need a range of movement to track an overflying satellite. Small craters and fossae would restrict that too much," said First Officer Leonidas. "The four terras are too wide. Copernicus would have seen the beacon if it had been in the open." Book grimaced, "But Franke and Tripper head to Viking Terra right now!" Leonidas peered out his window at the flashing scenery. "I know. We can indulge our wishes to a limited extent. Besides, we know nothing for sure. The beacon might be there." Assistant engineer Riley said, "Where do you think the beacon is, First Officer? You were in a brown study back at the base." Francis gave out a laugh. "You're the one who would be in a brown study, Jason. Since you are brown yourself." Riley gave his friend a dig in the ribs. "So are you, my First Nations friend!"

Leonidas smiled. "Since we are on a mission together, you can call me by my first name. For this trip." The broken hills, defiles, and valleys of the blue, unnamed lobe of Tombaugh Regio took shape ahead of the speeding vehicle. "As you wish... Spiro," said Francis.

The chariot containing Franke and Tripper left the dune sea and entered an uneven, differentiated area. In their path lay a slight depression. "Farinella crater," said Chris Tripper. "Named after Paolo Farinella, an Italian astronomer." Jane sat upright in her chair. "You don't mean Paolo Farinella, the Italian astronomer!?" The Navigational Officer looked at her in surprise. "Yes, I do. You have heard of him?" Franke slumped back in her seat, "No." Chris laughed, "I don't understand your sense of humor, Jane." The new lieutenant patted her darling on his shoulder. "And you never will, lover."

"Right," said Lieutenant Tripper. "Here we go." At 80 kilometers an hour, the little craft flew over the lip of the crater and landed on the downward slope a hundred meters further down. The vehicle bounced on its oversized wheels and up into the air again before settling on its course. "Bumpy ride, "commented Jane Franke. "How big is Pablo's crater anyway, Chris?" The chariot jolted as it reached the bottom of the slope and continued along the crater's floor.

"This is Paolo's crater, Jane," said Chris. "And about ten clicks." Then, smoothly, the cramped conveyance rolled swiftly towards the far walls of the bowl. The ground was a mixture of dull greys, calm blues, and fiery reds. Shattered rock and fractured ice lay scattered about the field. Soon they were making the last assault on the crater's apogee. Then, like a mirror reflection of its entry into the cavity, the moon chariot left contact with the earth and hurled furiously through space. Finally, the car's wheels safely landed with terra firma. The sleek-looking vehicle rebounded like a rubber ball and soon settled down to a smooth ride. "This is the only way to travel!" giggled Jane.

"Entering the blue lobe of Tombaugh now," said the Chief Engineer Book. The three men's moon chariot entered a world of shades of blue. Their vehicle climbed a kilometer higher from the western lobe of the heart. They entered a world of craters, canyons, rills, and glaciers. "It's beautiful here, isn't it?" asked assistant engineer Riley. "Yes, it is," answered the Chief Engineer Book. "Like a winter wonderland, all decked out in festive colors." The first officer tapped the back of the spacesuit helmets of his confreres. "Let's not let this beauty distract you from our job. Finding the beacon." Jason expertly piloted his auto up on the tongue of a small glacier. On either side, aquamarine ramparts rose to frame them in a narrow defile.

Frozen waterfalls of methane flowed down the walls at intervals. Then, reaching the glacier head, Jason steered his vehicle onto a plateau with cracks and piles of nitrogen blocks of ice.

Carefully, he threaded his way through the potential minefield. "You've known Captain Darkstrider for a long time, haven't you, Spiro?" asked Francis. "Yes, as I told you back on the ship. Since our academy days. We have often served together on the same ships," answered Leonidas. "You two have great chemistry together," said Book. "We get along well, that's true," responded the First Officer. "That comes from a long working history, I suppose." The chariot left the plateau and entered a long defile. "Captain Darkstrider has certainly kept up her appearance. She could pass for mid-forties," observed assistant engineer Riley. "She has always been beautiful," said Leonidas. "When she was younger, it got her a lot of unwanted attention. Nancy is outstanding in her field now." Through their helmets, the two engineers shared a grin. "You like the captain, don't you, Spiro?" Catching the bantering nature of their questions, Leonidas responded with a long, drawn-out, "Could be." From far above, the universe observed a pure-white Arc of the Covenant carrying three pilgrims on their quest.

"There it is," said Chris Tripper. "Pioneer Terra." A thin grey line appeared from their perspective. "Looks kind of boring," commented Jane. "Boring or not, we must explore it thoroughly," said the Navigational Officer. "Pioneer Terra is near the north pole of Pluto. so it's situated perfected to house the beacon." The moon chariot carrying the two lovers crossed the outskirts of the vast basin and descended to the vistas below. They entered a landscape of irregular plains, craters, narrow valleys, and low plateaus. The two Copernicans weaved their way through a monotonous landscape unbroken by any other color. "Did you find having the captain in our chariot difficult?" asked Tripper. "First time we have ever been alone with her."

Jane thought for a bit. "Not really. After all, she gave me a promotion to lieutenant. And she's a fellow woman. Girl power and all that." Chris chuckled, "Girl power, eh? But, I have to admit, she's not one to flinch. I went through those colles as quickly as I could." Franke laid her hand on Tripper's thigh. "Just the same; I'm glad we're alone again." The car swerved slightly as Navigator Tripper said, "If you move your hand any higher, we're going to crash." The dove-white chariot left the plateau and entered a deep ravine. Billows of purple fog flowed around their vehicle. The end of the gorge twisted sharply to the left and followed a steep incline. Soon, the travelers were moving through an area of broken rock and pillars of ice. "This is fun," said Franke. "I keep reminding myself that we are the first humans here."

Chris maneuvered around a bolder shot-through with seams of burnt sienna and raw umber. "First humans, but the aliens beat us by a billion years. We're like Christopher Columbus following in the steps of Homo habilis." Jane laughed and moved her hand higher up Chris's leg. "My caveman!" Again the moon chariot swerved in its tracks as Tripper exclaimed, "Oh my god!"

Three days later, the five members of the crew, minus the captain, were relaxing at Clyde Tombaugh's base. "So," said navigator Tripper. "We've achieved nothing so far." Chris was sitting on a prefabricated couch with Jane's head in his lap. First Officer Leonidas faced the couple in an easy chair. The two engineers, Book and Riley, sat at the table playing chess. "I disagree, Mr. Tripper," answered Spiro. "I think we've achieved a great deal. We've mapped enormous areas of the Sputnik Planitia, Burney crater, Pioneer Terra, and the blue lobe of Tombaugh Regio. I think we've accomplished a great deal." Assistant engineer Riley moved a chess piece. "Yes, but we've covered only a small part of Pluto's surface, and we have little time left. We will have to choose our last sites for exploration carefully." Chief Engineer Book moved one of his chess pieces, taking one of Jason's. "We have Tartarus and Pandemonium Dorsas left from our original choices. Will you accompany one of the chariot crews again, Mr. Leonidas?"

Spiro covered a yawn with his hand and looked sleepily at Francis. "I think not. I will stay in the shelter and process the information we have gained." Lieutenant Franke rubbed her eyes with the knuckles of her fist. "I'm looking forward to exploring Pandemonium. It was my choice, after all." Jason moved his knight, threatening Book's king. "Check Francis. While Francis and I are exploring Tartarus Dorsa, we can check out the Sleipnir and Sun Wukong Fossas within the plateau borders." Leonidas brightened perceptibly. "You will find Sleipnir Fossa most interesting. It is part of the so-called spider of Puto, Mwindo Fossae. The name Mwindo comes from the Nyanga people of the Congo. It follows Mwindo on his journey to the underworld to end the cruel chieftainship of his father. Six extensional fractures converge to a point near the center. Sleipnir is the longest at 579 kilometers. Three legs of the Mwindo spider radiate into Hayabusa Terra, the other three into the bladed area of Tartarus." Franke grimaced. "I hate spiders."

Chris played with Jane's blonde locks. "Those are colorful names, Jason. Where are they from?" Riley considered his next move. "Sleipnir is the horse the Norse god Odin rides to the underworld. Sun Wukong was the Chinese Monkey King who found himself in hell." Franke shuddered. "Those sound like creepy places, Mr. Riley. I don't envy you. Aren't fossa long twisting deep ditches?" The younger engineers captured an enemy castle with his knight, putting Book's king in check again. "Check Francis. Yes, Jane, but I don't think we will find any trolls there." Leonidas laughed, "I certainly hope you don't find any trolls or other nasties."

Sweating slightly, Francis moved his bishop to block Jason's knight. "After we explore those areas when then, Mr. Leonidas?" The First Officer crossed one leg over another. "We chose new areas of course. And continue our exploration until we find the beacon. We cannot afford to fail. We must find the beacon troops!!" The Navigational Officer ran his fingers over Jane's face and throat, "We've already found the alien artifact on Charon. Locating the beacon with be the icing on the cake. I think we're getting close." Assistant engineer Riley crowed. "Checkmate!" Francis's face twisted in disgust. "Oh, not again. Congratulations, Jason!" Riley set up the chess pieces on the board. "Another game, old friend. Or have you had enough abject failure for one day?" Chief Engineer snorted, "Oh certainly, I love humiliation!"

Jane and Chris got off the couch, stretching. "We're going to have a shower before we go to bed. Does anyone need to use the fresher first?" asked Franke. The other three shook their heads. Then, hand in hand, the two lovers disappeared into the fresher cubicle. "I hope they're not as noisy as yesterday," said Jason, smirking. "Oh, I don't know," replied First Officer Leonidas. "I seem to remember hearing a great deal of commotion when you and the Chief were last in the sonic shower." The younger engineer's brown face visibly darkened in embarrassment. "He has you there, Jason," laughed Book. "I'm glad we partitioned the sleeping quarters off. The First Officer doesn't need to see that." Suppressing laughter, Spiro went to the small kitchen nook. "Anyone wants a drink while I'm up?" Jason looked up, "Yeah, Mr. Leonidas, a beer, if you don't mind."

Spiro got a beer and a glass of ouzo for himself. He returned and sat down at the table with the two engineers. "When are you going to stop drinking that weak stuff, First Officer?" asked Chief Engineer Book. "This is ouzo, chief," replied Spiro. "Back in the Nuxualt nation, that's lemonade," said Francis. He lifted his glass. "Now, this is a drink for fearless space explorers like myself." Leonidas examined the chief's drink. "Canadian Club whiskey?" The chief nodded. "Little old ladies in Pireus drink that, the sweet old dears," said the First Officer, smiling. From the fresher came the sounds of vigorous lovemaking. "Knew it!" said the Chief Engineer Book in exasperation.

Two thousand four hundred kilometers above the surface of Pluto, the deep space scout ship Copernicus continued its measured orbit. A lonely, sad figure wandered its empty passageways. "With the crew all gone, the ship seems so empty," thought Captain Nancy Darkstrider. Wearing her shipside uniform, with her hair still unbound around her shoulders, the captain wandered. Restlessly, she looked into the ship's gymnasium, dining hall, and conference room.

Eventually, Nancy found herself in the engine room at the very back of the vessel. She listened to the throb of the massive Hydrogen-Ram engines as they converted mass into energy. Darkstrider seated herself at a small table and put her elbows on its surface. Cupping her chin in her hands, she allowed her mind to drift. Her eyes were aware of a minor, sealed door on one side of the compartment. "That's the door that Jason insists he hears noises emanating from," Nancy mused. A rhythmic thumping sound came to her ears from beyond the bulkheads as if hearing her thoughts. "Now I'm hearing it," said Darkstrider aloud. Moving towards the door, the captain was aware her heartbeat had increased, and she was slightly sweating. "Am I afraid?" asked Darkstrider of herself. "What do I expect is behind that hatch?" Arriving at the egress, Nancy put her palm on its surface. Immediately, the thumping noise began. She could feel the vibrations through her hand as if someone or something were knocking on the other side. Chilled to the bone, Darkstrider thought, "If that is a Xenomorph from the movie Aliens standing there, I am going to be very upset." Belatedly, Nancy realized she was alone on the ship.

The pounding resumed. "OK," said Nancy, "Another minute of this. I am out of here and locked in my cabin." A look of comprehension slowly filled the captain's lovely face. "Is that morse code?" She listened intently. "DANGER." Darkstrider rapped out in morse with a trembling hand, "Who are you?" Instantly, the rapping came back. "Danger. Danger."

Swallowing hard, the captain rapped, "Are you going to hurt me?" Once again came the response, "Danger. Danger. Radiation. Do not enter." Nancy collapsed against the hatchway in relief. "A computer warning program!" she said. "Somehow, it must have short-circuited! Riley and Book don't know morse code!" Then, laughing half hysterically and weak at the knees, the fearless space explorer tottered off.

The crew discussed the plans for that day at breakfast at Clyde Tombaugh's base. "Can Mr. and Tripper and I take our shuttle to Pandemonium Dorsa?" asked Lieutenant Franke as she drank her coffee. "It would save a lot of time. Traveling by moon chariot would take too long." The First Officer spooned some dehydrated eggs into his mouth and chewed thoughtfully, "That's true, lieutenant, but you can do a lot of exploring of the bottom of Sputnik Planitia on the way to the Dorsa. It's one of the last major areas of the heart left to survey." Navigator Tripper got up and got a milk container from the deep freeze. "Mr. Leonidas is right; we can't miss opportunities like this. It will be the only chance we get. Perhaps the only chance humanity will ever get. People may never get out this way again." Engineers Book and Riley were busy demolishing a stack of flapjacks, eggs, bacon, and toast with marmalade. Jane looked at them in wonder. "How can you eat all that rubbish? It's all carbs, sugar, and cholesterol." Jason spoke around a mouthful of food, "It hasn't killed us yet, lieutenant." Spiro sipped his tea and went on, "As for the engineers. They can skirt the north of the unnamed lobe blue area and explore the Pulfrich crater. From there, they will be at the entrance of Sleipner Fossa." Chief Engineer Book swallowed a considerable forkful of bacon and toast, "Works for us."

Conversation ceased as the landing party finished their repast and drank their last dregs of coffee, tea, and milk. Putting their dishes in the sonic dishwasher, they took turns going in the fresher. At last, they were ready. Climbing into their flight suits, the four explorers, without Spiro, entered the shelter airlock. They waited until the pressure button turned green, purging the atmosphere into the shelter. After exiting the habitat, the quartet moved to their chariots and climbed aboard. The metallic voice of Leonidas came over their helmet cons. "You know your missions. Take care and good luck." Two land speeders left quickly, speeding south and west, respectively. The First Officer watched them from the base window.

"O, Captain! My Captain! Our fearful trip is made,

The ship has weathered every rack, the prize we sought I won,

The port is near, the bells I hear, the people all exulting,

While following eyes the steady keel, the vessel was grim and daring;

But O heart! Heart! Heart!

O the bleeding drops of red,

Where on the deck my captain lies, fallen, cold, and dead."

Spiro scratched his chin. "That came out of deep memory. I had almost forgotten I knew it. Who wrote it again? Oh yes, Walt Whitman."

Across the vast plains of Sputnik Planitia hurled an ivory-tinctured meteorite. "198 ... 199 ... 200 kilometers an hour!" crowed Navigator Tripper. "Congratulations, Chris," said Jane dryly. "You are the uncrowned land speed holder of Pluto. Too bad it doesn't come with a trophy."

The navigational officer gave his lover a lascivious wink. "I'd settled for a pair of your pink, lacey panties." Franke laughed, "Pervert." For a time, the duo was silently marveling at the starkness of their pristine white environment. The chariot cleaved an invisible bow wave as it sailed through a sulfurous ocean. "I miss not having the captain with us, Chris," said the Communication Officer. "Now I know you're space happy," grunted Tripper. "No, I mean it," protested Jane. "Sometimes it's fun to share things with another woman." Chris rolled his eyes, "If you say so." Franke turned toward her consort, "You weren't kidding when you complained about me making lieutenant the other day. That what took you five years I did in two?" To their right, Hillary Montes bulked below the horizon. Reaching 3.5 kilometers above the Sputnik plain, the ice mountains scintillated in a dazzling display of beauty. "Well, I mean, promotion is always welcome. But I worked hard for that promotion. Not that I don't think you deserved it," answered Tripper. "After this mission, I think we will all get promoted," said Jane. Chris brightened, "I think you might be right, Jane." Franke reached over and patted her soul mate on the shoulder.

An hour later, another range of icy peaks loomed to the west. "What's that group of mountains called again, Chris?" asked Lieutenant Franke. "That's Tenzing Montes," said Chris, "6.2 kilometers above the surface of Pluto. They are Pluto's highest mountain range and the steepest, with a gradient of 20 degrees." Jane gazed wistfully at the splendid display. "They are so beautiful, Chris. It's like being in a fairytale, and I'm the beautiful princess." Tripper smirked, "And I'm the handsome prince?" Franke giggled, "I wouldn't go that far." Finally, a line of brown appeared from a distant perspective. "Pandemonium Dorsa coming up, said Chris."

A few hours before, the two-person crew of Book and Riley were moving parallel with the Challenger Colles at a distance of 20 kilometers. Book glanced out his side window at the formidable collection of hills. "Tough terrain. I'm glad it isn't our assignment, Jason." Riley peered over his friend's shoulder at the hillocks to the north. "I remember reading that the Challenger Colles is an extensive grouping of these hills. They measure 60 kilometers by 35 kilometers. The hills are near the blue uplands that we explored the other day. They breach the nitrogen ice at the end of the cellular cell region and may have stranded themselves where the ice is shallow." Francis stared at his boon companion in amazement. "When did you get so smart?" Jason snickered, "I'm not just a pretty face, you know." Chief Book muttered under his breath, "That's for sure." Then came the indignant reply. "I heard that!"

After traveling through the now recognizable features of the blue lobe, the two men approached Pulfrich Crater. The hilly terrain had melted away, and the elevated rim of the basin came into view. "Right there on the right, Francis," said Jason. "Do you see it? A notch in the crater wall." Chief Book corrected the land speeder's course. "I'm on it." Expertly, he guided his craft through the gap with a meter to spare on each side. And then plunged down an almost vertical slope! "Hold on!" shouted the Chief Engineer. With consummate skill, Francis tapped his brakes almost imperceptibly, slowing them. As they reached the bottom of the incline, the gradient lessened considerably.

With a groan of metal, the moon chariot navigated the transition and shot across the crater floor. The two friends let out pent-up sighs of relief. "That was too close, Francis!" exclaimed Jason. "I've never seen better driving." Book sighed, "It wasn't necessary. I should have stopped at the top of the rim and reconnoitered. I almost got us killed!" Jason patted his friend's knee. "This voyage was always going to be dangerous. We knew we might not be coming back when we signed on." The white chariot roared at 70 kilometers an hour across the level landscape.

"How wide is this crater, Francis?" asked the assistant engineer Riley. "About 30 kilometers," said Book. In front of them, the central uplift took shape. Soon it filled their viewscreen. Without warning, the Chief Engineer mushroomed the speed of their vehicle. "What's going on, Francis?" queried Jason. "I'm looking at this overlay map from Darkstrider's survey. There's a ravine splitting that mound!" came the terse reply. "Oh my god, will this never end!" yelled Riley. Finally, at 110 kilometers per hour, the small craft left the lip of the crevasse.

Soaring 100 meters through the thin air of Pluto, it barely cleared the bottomless expanse and landed safely on the other side. With a glazed expression, Jason turned to his friend, "And to think of all the fun I would have missed if we had not got together." Two men laughed. The far side of the hollow was visibly approaching. "The walls there look terraced. It should be simple to climb them and leave the crater," remarked Chief Book. "Well, thank heavens for small favors," said his friend. Soon an inconsequential vehicle zig-zagged up the terraces and out.

"Pandemonium Dorsa is coming up," repeated Chris. The honey-combed texture of Sputnik Planitia had ended, and the land rose. Navigator Tripper followed a long slope that grew increasingly brownish-red in complexion. Finally, their land speeder crested a low plateau, and Chris stopped. The two had a bird's-eye few of a vast tableau of a roughly rectangular ridge. An intricate collection of small craters, narrow ravines, valleys, and broken hills greeted their eyes. "Well, it's a nice place to visit," said Chris. "But I wouldn't want to live here." Jane snorted. "I will never understand your sense of humor." Tripper patted Franke's shapely thigh with a smile. "And you never will."The small craft wheeled along the ridge and down the reverse slope into a shallow valley. Ancient clouds of brown dust rose around their chariot.

"Interesting isn't it, Jane?" asked Navigational Officer Tripper. "On Pioneer Terra, we were near Pluto's North Pole. Now that we're exploring Pandemonium Dorsa, we are close to the planet's South Pole." Franke placed her hand on Chris's, which lay on her thigh. "I'm glad you find it interesting. I don't." The duo crossed an eroded crater's rim and descended into its bowl. "All never surveyed or charted land is interesting, Jane. Even if it seems boring," said Tripper. "I guess you're right, Chris. The main thing is to find the elusive beacon," replied Lieutenant Franke. A moving shadow momentarily darkened the cabin of their chariot. The two glanced upwards as one of Pluto's moons eclipsed the distant sun. "One thing that never gets boring," said Communication Officer Franke, "is the number of occultations here. Five moons! Who would have thought of it!" Tripper squeezed his lover's leg, "On Jupiter. It has 80 moons." Franke restrained the navigator's questing hand. "And Saturn had 83 moons. So I get your point, and watch what you do with your paw." Chris grinned, "Just returning the favor, ma'am!"

Book and Riley raced their chariot across a small, desolate plain in a similar landscape. Their vehicle's tires churned up brown dirt. They had the left blue lobe of Pluto's heart and were entering the bladed area of Tartarus Dorsa. Francis reached the edge of an escarpment and killed the car's engine. Pluto's spider sprawled below them. The feature waited to capture the space explorers in its web, resembling a crouching arachnoid. The ravines exposed a dark-red material. "A giant red spider!" exclaimed Jason. "And we're going to enter its domain!" The Chief Engineer considered the labyrinth of ditches. "I've seen this before. The spider resembles Venus's radially fractured centers called novae. Mercury's Pantheon Fossae formation also comes to mind." Riley shook his head. "The two inner planets, and we find the same out here. Someone in the universe has a sense of humor."

Francis pointed out the central hub from which the six legs of the spider radiated. "The left-hand lower leg is Sleipnir Fossa. That's where we are heading." Assistant engineer Riley shuddered theatrically, "Well, if we must put ourselves into the spider's maw, then that's what we'll have to do!" Book sent the land speeder in motion, and it purred down the steep slope like a giant cat and headed towards the small complex of canyons. Jason muttered on the seat beside him, "I still have a nasty inkling about this."

At Clyde Tombaugh's base, the First Officer sat at the computer station and pored over reams of data. Sipping a glass of the ever-present glass of ouzo, Spiro was feeling increasingly frustrated. "I'm missing something," he thought. "I've seen a clue to the beacon's position, and I can't think what it is." Leonidas ran his hand over his face and knitted his brow in thought. "It's something I've observed. I know that much. Not something I've read in all these print-outs, something I saw with my own eyes. But where? When was I mapping Pluto with the captain? When was I with Book and Riley in the moon buggy? Where?"

Like a will-o'-the-wisp, the tantalizing memory played at the edge of his consciousness and fled utterly. Spiro shrugged philosophically. "Oh well, if I leave it alone, it will come back to me." The thought of the captain gave Leonidas pause. "I should give Nancy a call. She's feeling all alone on the ship." Spiro touched the ship to shore com button, "Tombaugh's base to the Copernicus. Tombaugh's base to the Copernicus. Come in. Over." Darkstrider's melodious voice immediately returned, "Copernicus here, First Officer. Do you have anything to report? Over."

Unconsciously, Spiro lifted his eyes to the shelter's roof, where the vast bulk of the ship hung in orbit like a white albatross. "Just hunches, captain, nothing concrete yet. I was just wondering how you are doing aboard. It must be uneventful to have your squabbling children gone. Over." Nancy gave her silvery laugh. "It is quiet here. I will let you take command of Copernicus in a few days. Then I will take residence at Tombaugh's base for a time. Over."

The First Officer took another sip of his drink. "Anytime you want, captain, I will trade places with you. I miss the sauna. I feel the need to cleanse myself. Over." The tinny voice of Nancy came to Spiro's ears. "That's understood. If there is nothing else, I will wait till your next report. Over." Leonidas prepared to close the switch. "That's all for now, captain, over."

Darkstrider added a query, "Oh, incidentally, does either Book or Riley understand Morse code? Over." A look of bemusement crossed the First Officer's visage, "Not that I know. May I ask why the question? Over." The captain's last statement was swift. "No reason, Darkstrider out, over." Spiro sat back in mild astonishment. "Now, what was that all about?"

Deep inside Pandemonium Dorsa, the moon chariot carrying Lieutenant Franke and Navigational Officer Tripper moved methodically. Across the bladed topography, the large solid rubber wheels took them forward. Across vast craters, down steep valleys, along narrow ridges, and into fractured rock fields, their trusty steed bore them in safety, if not comfort. "My bum hurts," complained Jane Franke, twisting in her seat and rubbing the hurt body part. Chris laughed, "I guess I shouldn't have spanked you so hard last night, Jane." Franke smirked, "Well, I was a naughty girl. It's not that. It's just we spend all our time in these hard seats. I'm getting worn out." Tripper moved the speeder carefully through a rock-strewn debris enclosure. "I know it's tough, but we must stick it out. We're mapping and exploring these areas. The beacon might be well-hidden." Jane stared out the window. "It's so lonely here—a world where humans don't belong. I almost feel hatred towards us. As if we were strangers in a strange land." The chariot topped a ridge line and entered a narrow valley.

Red patches and sickly green streaks relieved the brown tincture at intervals. "We are strangers here, Jane," said Tripper. "But we're also explorers. We must go where no human has gone before." Franke eased her bottom. "Yes, but why does exploring have to be so uncomfortable? Why can't we prospect in a howdah on top of an elephant? Lying on cushions and sipping mint tea?" Chris chuckled, "Aside from the fact we are 5 billion kilometers from the nearest elephant, the temperature is 44 Kelvin, and nitrogen, methane, and carbon monoxide compose the thin atmosphere. Aside from all that, I think your plan is efficient. Ow! No slugging the driver!"

In lonely solitude, the ivory-colored chariot rolled through the savage garden of the cosmos, far above pirouetted necklaces of diamonds, strings of Halloween-hued suns, and the solitary red of a ruby star. The Navigational Officer moved the vehicle from ridge to defile to plateau with consummate ease. Then, finally, the two space adventurers entered a part of the twisted aspect that sunk into a vast hollow.

Tendrils of the cloying purple mist swirled around them as they ventured deeper into the haze. "Do you bring all your dates here?" asked Lieutenant Franke. "No, you're the first one. I only got my driver's license today," said Tripper. The land speeder maneuvered along a dimly seen path, threading around one rock column to another. Finally, after an hour, a fallen archway provided a way out of the Minoan maze. The small craft followed a ridge that traced an intricate helix. "Now I know why they called it Pandemonium!" laughed Jane.

On the Copernicus bridge, Captain Darkstrider watched the progress of the two landing parties on the main viewscreen. Tiny microscale dots crept along the bladed terrain of the Dorsas. "Leonidas seemed concerned when I spoke to him earlier," reflected Nancy. "He must think I'm going space crazy in my solitude. Luckily he doesn't know what I heard in the engine room or how I reacted." Darkstrider regarded the solid, silver circle on the Tombaugh's Base screen. "Spiro mentioned a hunch he had. He's had them before, and they turned out to be right. I hope he's not mistaken this time." The captain got out of her chair and paced back and forth on the deck plates. "I think we're getting close. This mission could be the discovery of the ages. We already have evidence of an alien civilization in the artifact. But I need to find that beacon. That will be the icing on the cake. Captain Nancy Darkstrider, discoverer of the Proxima Centauri civilization!" Restlessly, Darkstrider threw herself back in the captain's chair. Her eyes focused on the white dot in Tartarus Dorsa. "So, you're going to the spider? I pray you don't get bitten."

"Well, here we are," said the Chief Engineer Book. "Spider of Pluto, Mwindo Fossae." The moon chariot stood on the edge of a circular basin—the head and body of Pluto's spider. In front of the two, a fractured decline beckoned. On either side, two pinching headlands resembled the jaws of a beast. "Right, here we go, into the spider's mouth," said Francis. "All hope abandons ye who enter here. The six hundred rode into the valley of death," quoted assistant engineer Riley. The chief gave his friend a sidelong look. "That's what I admire about you, Jason. You're always so cheerful." Down into the abyss sailed the ghostly ship.

An hour later, two men in their cream-colored conveyance entered the thorax of Pluto's spider. They could see six entrances radiating from the central cavity through the windows. The battlements surrounded them like a vast arena. And as if they were the sacrificial Christians. Francis pointed to one particularly forbidding portal. It loomed among dark shadows like the doorway into a haunted house.

"That's the way, Jason. That's the gateway to Sleipnir Fossa." The moon chariot rambled over the uneven surface of the crater. Passing through the entrance of the towering gatehouse, the two adventurers lost themselves in the gloom. The chariot's headlights ignited, cutting swathes through the velvety curtains. "What does Sleipnir mean anyway, Francis?" asked Jason. "Sleipnir was the steed Odin rides to the underworld," answered Chief Book. "I had to ask!" groaned the assistant engineer.

The duo found themselves in a narrow ravine, perhaps 100 meters in diameter. Above them, the kilometer-high trench walls lost to sight, shutting off their view of the stars. The forlorn vehicle moved down the ditch, tossing red soil as it motored. A thin reddish mist settled around them and tore into phantasmagoric shapes. "At least the fog is reddish instead of purple," commented Riley. "Yeah, blood-colored murk is not freaky at all," said Book dryly.

Chief Engineer Book sped up to get a feel for the space he was traveling. Flanges of rock and ice seemed to reach out to clutch them. The rough ground given below chattered the men's teeth despite the solid rubber wheels of their speeder. Like a Formula One driver of the 21st century, Francis executed a series of rapid rights and lefts to conform to the twists and turns of the moat. Gradually, the path declined until they were two kilometers under the planet's skin. Now all the light from the stars and sun was gone, and they traveled through impenetrable darkness. The fug seemed to thicken and press upon their windows like the famous smog of 19th-century London. "We're making good time, Jason," commented Chief Book. "Good to know," replied assistant engineer Riley. "How long to the end of the spider's leg?" Francis turned the wheel violently to the right, and the chariot swung around and plunged down a steep incline. "About seven more hours," he replied. "Piece of cake!" said Jason brightly.

A small white vehicle perched on the edge of a vast brown plateau. Navigator Tripper and Communication Officer Franke stood by their moon buggy and contemplated the featureless plain far below them. A hundred kilometers to the west of them, they could barely discern the evil darkness of Cthulhu Macula. "OK," said Chris, pointing to the north, "this is the plan. We skirt those two dark spots and pass between Norgay and Hillary Montes. Then it's on to Sputnik Planum and home." Jane studied the two dark patches sprawling in front of them. "What are those black areas called Chris?" she asked. "They named the nearest one Quidlivun Cavus, the land on the moon where the souls of the dead find rest. That comes from Inuit mythology," explained Tripper. "The second is Morgoth Macula, a figure of evil from the book The Silmarillion by J. R. R. Tolkien." Franke shuddered, "Morgath, as in Morder from Lord of the Rings?" Tripper chuckled, "If that works for you, yes." The Navigation Officer then turned to his feminine companion and, holding his arms wide, made ghostly sounds, "Whooo-whooo!" This noise continued until Jane punched him in the stomach. "The pain! The pain!"

At that exact moment, the other landing party was transiting through the last stretch of the gorge. On each side, tall ice pillars stood in rows to the narrow exit, which they could see one kilometer away. The posts were beautiful in bright shades of green and blue. They had stood for perhaps a billion years on guard. "This gorge is gorgeous," quipped Jason. "Oh, for god's sake," groaned Francis. "You and your jokes!" Feigning anger, the assistant engineer elbowed his chief in the ribs. This action was unfortunate timing as Francis completed the last turn around the nearest row of columns. The car swerved, momentarily losing control, and the trunk smashed into the fragile ice. With a tremendous crack, the collonade toppled over on its neighbor, also bringing it down. Like dominoes, the entire rank of obelisks marched toward the chasm's egress. "Step on it!" yelled Jason. "The whole place is collapsing, and it will trap us!" Keeping pace with the falling pillars, Chief Engineer Book floored his machine. Neck and neck with the plummeting ice cylinders, the land speeder slowly drew ahead. With a last burst of velocity, the land speeder cleared the exit. Behind them, massive chunks of ice piled up, filling the opening. The small craft slowed down and came to a complete stop in the bladed terrain of Tartarus Dorsa. Shakily, Jason turned to his friend, "Oops!"

The Hidden Ocean

Chapter 8

Several days later, the five landing crew members sat at the base's dining table. A monitor displays Captain Darkstrider, who is still on Copernicus. "Ok," said First Officer Leonidas," we've been exploring Pluto for five weeks. What have we learned?" The other members of the landing party looked at one another. "Nothing," came Nancy's voice from the monitor. "We have not found the beacon. The mission has failed so far." The Chief Engineer Book took a sip of his whiskey. "I would not go that far, captain. We have examined a large portion of Pluto's surface. We know where the beacon is not. And we can eliminate other areas because of their inaccessibility."

"That may be true, Chief Engineer, but the fact remains that we are fast running out of time," replied Darkstrider. "We have perhaps two weeks before we complete our mission and return home. If we miss our window, we risk getting stranded here forever." Lieutenant Franke tossed her blonde mane restlessly. "I don't want to get stuck on this ice cube. This world is a terrible place, so cold and barren. It does not mean us to be here." Navigation Officer Tripper patted Jane's hand. "Don't worry, Lieutenant. We won't get stuck here." Assistant engineer officer Riley poured himself a cup of coffee from a carafe. "Where do we go from here? What are our next missions? Chief Book and I are ready to do what it takes to complete our goals. If the beacon is out there somewhere, we will find it!" Darkstrider chuckled.

"Yes, the next two explorations, driven by Mr. Riley's enthusiasm, will have to be chosen carefully. First Officer Leonidas and I have examined the potential sites, and we have come up with two." Spiro pushed a button on the table keyboard, and two holographic displays flashed over their heads.

One image resembled a giant mouth surrounded by jagged teeth. "Piri Planitia, the 10,000 square kilometer bite mark of Pluto," said the First Officer. "A wall of cliffs borders the almost crater-free plains of Piri Planitia or scarp, one kilometer high, known as Piri Rupes. The cliffs break up into lonely mesas in several places." Franke stared in fascination at the gigantic mouth, "Where did the name Piro come from, Mr. Leonidas?" Spiro directed his attention to the young officer, "They name the area after Ahmed Muhiddin Piri, alternatively known as Piri Reis, a 16th-century Ottoman. He drew some of the first maps of North America. So which of the teams would like Piro?" Tripper grinned. "I'll bite. We'll take Piro, Spiro."

The two engineers examined the second holographic image, "What is that thing, First Officer?" said Francis. "It looks like an enormous eye, like the crater we explored in the Burney basin. But much, much bigger." The First Officer touched a control, and the crater increased in size until it looked like the eye of Sauron from Lord of the Rings. "Simonelli crater, at 300 kilometers across the largest crater on Pluto. They named it after Damon Simonelli, a Pluto geologist, and an American astronomer. The base of the crater is highly reflective and covered with frozen water. The large central peak is reddish. That's your quest, gentlemen." Jason exclaimed, "The quest for the Holy Grail!" Beside him, the Chief Engineer Book let out a groan. "No, he's right," came the sweet voice of Captain Darkstrider. "It is a quest for the Holy Grail. The beacon!"

Outside the shelter, on the pitiless plains of Sputnik Planitia, the two land speeders and two shuttles stood. A light wind rippled around them. A massive shadow darkened the solar panels of Clyde Tombaugh's base as Copernicus blotted out the far-off sun. On the horizon, the three ice islands stood sentinel on the lonely habitat. In the ink-black sky, the four small moons of Pluto whirled, danced, and tumbled in their endless frolics. Moving in majestic splendor, big brother Charon scorned his infant brothers and sisters' escapades. In his red cap of Morder, he slumbered. But the heart of Pluto was not asleep. The blue lobe, like an unblinking eye, waited.

The following day, the four landing party members climbed into their flight suits and put on their helmets. They all turned to First Officer Leonidas as he said, "Right. Your two objectives are too far to reach by land vehicle. So load them on the shuttles and fly to your destinations. Questions?" Assistant engineer Riley quipped, "Yes, what's the capital of North Dakota?" Spiro smiled, "Bismark. More questions? Factual questions?" There were none. The quartet sealed their visors and single-filed into the airlock. A minute later, Leonidas observed them through the shelter window, moving across the frozen soil to their chariots. Spiro approvingly saw the land speeders enter the cargo bays of the shuttles and the doors closing. Shortly afterward, dim figures moved about in the shuttle cabs. Then, like beautiful, pure-white gulls, the spacecraft leaped from the ground and soared out of sight.

A voice spoke behind the First Officer's back. "You didn't wish them good luck." Shocked, Spiro whirled to see Captain Darkstrider regarding him on the table monitor. "Captain Darkstrider! How long have you been there?" The image of Nancy peered into her First Officer with malachite-colored eyes. "Long enough. Well, they have their assignments. Do they know this is the last mission we have time for?" Spiro shook his head. "I didn't have the heart to tell them." Darkstrider looked beyond Leonidas to the window to the now departed shuttles.

"I must go down to the seas again, to the lonely sea and the sky,

And all I ask is a tall ship and a star to steer her by."

"John Masefield?" asked Leonidas. Lost in thought for a moment, Nancy collected herself and nodded.

"Land by that long fault, Jane," ordered Navigation Officer Tripper. "Yes sir, three bags full, sir," replied Lieutenant Franke. On the eastern edge of Piri Planitia, the pure-white shuttlecraft descended to land gracefully by the dreadful gash in Pluto's flesh. The two space explorers passed through the connecting door to the cargo bay and entered the land speeder. After lowering the cargo bay ramp, Chris backed out carefully and onto the surface of Spiro Planitia. The couple exited their vehicle.

Jane walked over to the crevasse brink and looked down. The depths were vanishing in a myriad of shadows. She marveled at the multitude of blue, green, and purple streaks of color that snaked down the sides. Chris joined her. "Beautiful sight, isn't it, Jane?" Franke turned to him and smiled, "Yes, it is; sorry if I was a downer this morning. I'm committed to this mission. What's the name of this chasm?" Tripper considered, "Inanna Fossa, it's a long extensional fault that cuts 600 kilometers from here diagonally to Sputnik Planum." The lovers walked to the front of their chariot and stared over the vast plateau that was Piro Planitia. A smooth, mottled surface spread before them. Far off in the distance rose towering purple cliffs that ringed the plain. "Why are some areas light and some dark, Chris?" asked Jane. "It's the nature of what's happening here. The cliffs we see, Piro Rupes, are on the edge of Vega Terra, which is rich in methane ice. Sublimation is the transition of a substance from a solid to a gas. Vega is sublimating into the atmosphere, revealing the ice of Piro Planitia. The dark areas we see are methane that has not dissolved yet." Jane laughed, "So we are really at the bite of Pluto! Hilarious!"

The duo got back into their speeder and proceeded across the landscape. The terrain was rolling here; light and dark areas passed beneath their wheels. Occasionally they would traverse the eroded remnant of a crater or parallel a deep volcanic rill. "The Holy Grail," mused Franke. "Captain Darkstrider called our mission a quest for the Holy Grail." Tripper steered the chariot around the pile of ice blocks. "Maybe for her, it is Jane. This assignment is a make-or-break for her. She has to find the beacon. We're at the beginning of our careers. She and Spock are at their end." Soon the blue line of Piro Rupes drew closer. The land rose and grew rougher. The buggy jolted as they passed over its uneven surface. Jane pointed over to their right. "Let's go in that direction, Chris. To that high mesa region." Two hours later, the land speeder had reached the cliffs that had broken into isolated mesas. The purple cliffs were much higher, rising a kilometer over their heads. Tripper entered a valley between two buttes. As they speed along the path, it engulfed their craft in a welter of shadows. Deeper and deeper, they delved into the broken terrain.

Three thousand kilometers away, the shuttle containing engineers Book and Riley flew over the rim of Simonelli Crater. Gently, the ghostlike machine settled down on the blinding white of the crater's floor. Then, with a pop, the shuttle's ramp opened up, and a moment later, the craft's land speeder backed out of its mother's womb. Assistant engineer Riley and the Chief Engineer Book climbed out of their chariot and looked about themselves. Behind them were the silvery cliffs of the basin's periphery. Their notched ramparts poked holes in the blackened sky. Fifty kilometers to their front menaced the red fortress of the central peak of Simonelli.

Rising five kilometers from the plain, it looked like India's famous Red Fort. Complete with crenelations. "Would you look at the size of the central peak Francis?" said Jason in a voice filled with awe. "It is impressive, isn't it?" replied the Chief Book. "It must have a diameter of 20 kilometers and an area of over 300 square kilometers." The assistant engineer grinned. "Let's circle that peak like we were Sioux Indians attacking a wagon train!" The Chief laughed, "Yes, Kemo Sabe!" The two warriors climbed back into their steed and rushed toward the helpless monolith. After an hour and 5 kilometers away, Francis turned the moon chariot to travel parallel with the peak's formidable slope. Quicker and quicker, the small vehicle moved in its gyrations. Soon it approached the speeder's maximum velocity.

"I feel the need for speed!" shouted Francis in exhalation. "Ah, Francis, don't you think we better slow down? We're almost going 200 kilometers an hour. This is dangerous!" said Jason. "I want to set the land speed record once and for all," replied the Chief Engineer. He looked at the craft's speedometer. "190 ... 195 ... 200 ... 205 ... 210 clicks an hour! A record! In your face, Tripper!" roared Book. "Slow down!" screamed Riley. The icy plain blurred outside the buggy's windows. It was still going at a tremendous speed when it hit a puddle of helium. Instantly, the car spun out of control. Leaving its wheels, it tumbled end over end. In their harnesses, it subjected the two friends to incredible g forces. Finally, the moon chariot came to a rest on its side. One tire still spun lazily.

"What a muddle," said Lieutenant Franke. "How are we going to find our way out of here?" The two lovers had been threading their way for several hours along a meandering path through the mesas. "We have a GPA, Jane. I know where we are. Relax and enjoy the scenery," said Chris. "You are on a scenic drive, free of the maddening crowd, and you are riding with the handsomeness man on Pluto. Can life be any sweeter?" Jane snorted but did not reply.

The chariot moved over broken humps of ice, along ledges, and up and down inclines and declines. On every side, tall mesas blocked out almost all light. The moon buggies headlights poked two holes in the curtain of Stygian gloom. "It's so spooky down here," complained Franke. "Can't we get on top of a mesa and get some light?" Tripper studied a map on the shuttle's monitor. A green dot fixed their position. "Yeah, all right. A ledge or path leads to the top of a mesa a kilometer further. I'll try to climb it." The navigator motored the moon chariot over a switchback and onto a series of broken ledges that pointed upwards. After a few minutes, the couple's vehicle emerged into the ambient light of the stars and the reflected luminosity from Sputnik Planitia. They found themselves on a broad terrace with an abrupt slope on three sides. Tripper drove his vehicle in the middle of the vast expanse.

Dismounting, they gazed about themselves. They stood amid a sea of mesas that stretched in all directions. A deep gorge separated from its neighbor on each tabletop. Five kilometers away, the escarpment reared its purple ramparts far over their heads. For a long time, the two lieutenants feasted on the view. "Well," said Jane, "this is special."

Captain Darkstrider contemplated her two landing parties on the bridge of the Copernicus. She noted that the silver speck in Piro Planitia has resumed moving after a brief halt. With concern, Nancy saw that the other particle had not. Darkstrider tripped the ship to shore intercom. "Captain to base. What is the condition of the landing party at Simonelli crater? Over?" Leonidas's reply came back. "Stand by Copernicus; I will check. Over." A minute passed slowly, and Spiro's voice rang from the mike. "Tombaugh's base to Copernicus. I have lost contact with Shuttle Two! Repeat, I have lost contact with Shuttle Two! Over!" The captain sat back into her chair and fixed her landing party with sad, leaf-green eyes, "Look, I am sending you out like sheep among wolves."

The light wind of Pluto tugged at two desolate figures that stood by an upturned land speeder.

One flight-suited shape turned to the other. "Are you ok, Jason?" The addressed spacer slowly rubbed his shoulder. "I'm ok, shook up a bit. How are you, Francis?" Chief Book ran his eyes over the underside of the vehicle. "I'm fine, but I can't say the same for the chariot. The axle broke." Riley walked over and stood by his friend. "Yeah, you're right. We have tools in the cab. Can we repair the damage?" Francis touched the broken piece. "I think so. Luckily, the chariot is on its side. So we can repair it and push it on its wheels. Well, let's get to work."

Two hours later, the two men looked at the axle in satisfaction. "Well, that's that," said Francis, "I think it will hold. Now let's push this crate onto its wheels." Grunting with an effort, the space adventurers pushed the edge of the chariot until it slowly toppled onto its solid rubber wheels.

The landing crew climbed in, and Book tried the engine. With a purring roar, it came to life. "The engine's fine. But the communications don't work," said Jason. "Let me look at them," said the Chief Engineer Book. Finally, after 10 minutes, the communications came on with a cackle of static. "Chariot Two, come in, over! Repeat, come in, over!" hissed the urgent metallic voice of First Officer Leonidas. "Chariot Two to base. Uh, everything's under control. Situation normal, over," said Jason. "What happened to you? Why were you out of communication for several hours? Over." demanded Spiro. "Uh, we had a vehicle accident, but everything's all right now. We're fine. We're all right here now, thank you. How are you? Everything copacetic? Over." answered the assistant engineer. "We're sending Shuttle One to your location. Over," said Leonidas. "Uh, uh... negative, negative," said Jason. "We had a systems malfunction. Give us some time to lock it down. An immense problem, no danger, over." The engineers heard a snort of laughter from the comm. "Ok, Han Solo. I don't know what you're hiding but return to base as soon as possible. Over." Riley keyed the mike, "Acknowledged, over." The two men looked at each other in silence. "Boring conversation anyway," said the assistant engineering officer.

"Quickest way to the shuttle is right across the central hub of the crater," said Chief Engineer Book. "Our transporter lies 40 kilometers away as the crow flies." In their viewscreen, the massive reddish peak complex dubbed Red Fort filled their field of vision. "We were going to map it anyway," answered assistant engineer Riley. "If we drive precisely down the middle, our metal detector will check the entire complex." The chariot reached the nearest slope, "Right," said Francis, "here we go. Entering the Red Fort now." Up the steep ascent went the duo. Reaching the top, they entered a world of fantastic ice shapes and odd formations. The chariot moved by truncated walls, collapsed towers, and broken masonry. All covered in a thin sheet of red tholins. "This is like Dante's Inferno," said the Chief Engineer Book. "I bet Shuttle One wished they made that remark when they crashed into Morder," replied assistant engineer Riley. "Well, it's too late now; I've said it," chuckled Francis. Entering the center of the peak contour, the engineers descended into a bowl-like depression. "If anywhere, the beacon would be here, but nothing," said Book. "Yes, we have no bananas," quipped Riley. At last, the two friends broke through the vermillion topography and descended to the reverse slope of the Red Fort multiplex. 5 kilometers away on the icy floor of the crater perched the welcome shape of Shuttle Two. "There she blows!" shouted Jason. "The white whale! Moby Dick!" Francis laughed, "Jason, you need locking up. You do, mate."

"I am shocked at you, Chief Engineer Book," said First Officer Leonidas later. "I am shocked that you would be so reckless as to travel at such speeds on uncharted ground." Francis looked suitably embarrassed. The five landing party members gathered around the dining table at Tombaugh's base. "I can imagine the younger members of the team doing that, continued Leonidas. "Franke, Tripper, and even Riley. But not you. I thought you were the sober one?" Francis took a large sip of whiskey from his glass. "I am the sober one, First Officer." Spiro's gaze hardened. "Did you figure out how you lost control? How do you spin out on a surface that's temperature is close to zero? The ice should have had the texture of concrete." Riley broke in, "Helium, Mr. Leonidas. We hit a pool of helium. Even at absolute zero, helium does not freeze." Surprised, the First Officer turned to the younger engineer. "Helium? I wasn't aware of that element on the planet. How do you account for its presence?" Book and Riley looked at each other and shrugged. "We can't. Perhaps it was part of the meteorite that created Simonelli crater," said Jason. "The helium may have been lying on the ground for a billion years," said Francis."That may be the case, Mr. Riley," said Spiro. "The important thing is that you two are uninjured, and the moon buggy suffered no permanent harm."

"Can you tell us our next assignments, Mr. Leonidas?" asked Jane. "Lieutenant Tripper and I are eager for our next mission." Spiro glanced at her. "None at the moment. Captain Darkstrider wants us to return to Copernicus for more discussions.

That means temporarily abandoning Tombaugh's base. We will relax and enjoy the ship's amenities."

The younger members of the crew looked at each other in delight. "When are we going, Mr. Leonidas?" asked Tripper. "Just as soon as you can pack your bags," said Spiro. As the meeting broke up, Tripper turned to Book and asked, "How fast were you going?" Francis grinned, "210 clicks per hour." Chris muttered under his breath to Jane, "Bastard."

That night, the entire crew of the Copernicus gathered in the ship's conference room. Captain Darkstrider examined each of them with sea-green eyes; she discomforted several of them with her stare. "Right, this has been a very eventful several weeks," said Nancy. "Not the least being Chief Engineer Book and assistant engineer Riley crashing their vehicle at over 200 kilometers per hour." Francis held up a finger. "210 kilometers, to be exact, captain." Under his breath, Navigator Tripper muttered, "Show-off."

Amidst the barely contained delight of several of the Copernicans, Darkstrider continued, "I stand corrected 210 kilometers per hour. Thank you, Chief. This rectification could mean a promotion for you. Or death." Nancy paused for a moment. "Now, all silliness aside, let's continue, ok? Mr. Leonidas, could you put up the holo map of Pluto, please?" Anticipating this request, Spiro pressed a button, and Pluto sprang into existence over their heads. "We have made a great deal of progress and have mapped more extensively a great deal of Pluto's surface," said the captain. On the map, the explored areas became shaded in red. "As you can see, we've covered almost all of both lobes of the heart and Pandemonium and Tartarus Dorsas. Plus Burney and Simonelli craters, Pioneer Terra, and the so-called bite of Pluto." Again Nancy paused and looked about the room, "But so far, no beacon. My question is, why? We are missing something obvious—a glaring something under our noses. Mr. Leonidas, you mentioned you have a memory you can't recall. About the location of the beacon. Have you had any luck bringing back that remembrance?"

"Sorry, captain, I can't remember. But it is the heart," said Spiro. "Well, that's been my impression, too," answered Darkstrider. "The answer was always going to be in the heart. Closer to the heart. Now let's concentrate. What's so special about the heart? What other qualities or properties does the heart of Pluto own?"

The company pondered heavily. "It exists in our reality. And it occupies a measurable space," said Spiro. "The heart possesses one blue and one white lobe," continued Lieutenant Franke. "It resembles a stylized heart," pointed out the Chief Engineer Book. "A broken heart," added assistant engineer Riley. "The heart's surface is smooth and devoid of craters," said Navigational Officer Tripper. The team became aware Nancy had picked up her glass of water and was staring at it with a strange intensity. She watched as ice cubes swirled around, clicking against the glass's sides. Captain Darkstrider's eyes blazed like green lasers, and the tension about the table became unbearable.

"Ishmael," said Captain Darkstrider. "Ishmael!"

Gasps of surprise erupted. "Ishmael? Like in the bible?" asked Jane. "Ishmael was in Moby-Dick," answered Tripper. "Call me Ishmael. Some years ago, having little or no money, I thought I would sail about and see the world's oceans," quoted First Officer Leonidas. "The sea, where each man, as in a mirror, finds himself," said the Chief Engineer Book, continuing the quote. "It's the sea!" cried assistant engineer Riley. "The sea! Under the ice plains of the heart of Pluto, there is a sea! That's where the beacon is!"

"I'm glad you've all come to the same conclusion. You are a brilliant crew," smiled Nancy. "Yes, the sea. We commented on it when we first came in-system a month ago. And then apparently forgot its existence." First Officer Leonidas deliberated, "It makes sense. The beacon could lie on the bottom of Pluto's ocean. A billion years ago, there was much more meteor activity than now. It's safe under the ice shield of the heart. Plus, the beacon would be difficult to detect for whatever reason." Jane took a sip of her white wine. "So the beacon transmits through Sputnik's ice layer? How thick is the layer, anyway?" Spiro checked his computer monitor. "The ice crust is 180 kilometers thick. The ocean is 120 kilometers in depth."

Exclamations erupted around the table. "And the beacon can get its transmissions through all that?" asked Jason. Leonidas spread his hands in an eloquent gesture, "Evidently." Then, with increased regard, the team examined the holo map of Pluto. "Right," said Navigator Tripper. "If correct, how do we find the beacon through all that ice?" Assistant engineer Riley taped the table with his finger, "Yeah, the ship's lasers can't cut through a fraction of that icy crust."

Lieutenant Franke pointed at Pluto's heart. "And there is no way of finding under what part of the heart the beacon is lurking." Chief Engineer Book tossed back the rest of his whiskey. "There is. With ground penetrating radar. We have two units on board." Heads around the table snapped to focus on the Chief Book. "Would your radar penetrate through 300 kilometers of ice and water?" asked Captain Darkstrider. "Yes, I believe so, captain. Riley and I can calibrate it to increase its range fivefold," replied Francis.

"How much area of the ocean's bottom would the radar impulse cover?" asked First Officer Leonidas. "The impulse spreads as the distance increases," said Francis. "By the time it strikes the ocean bottom, I would estimate the pulse would encompass 1000 square kilometers." Nancy put her elbow on the table and rested her chin on her palm. "And how big is Sputnik Panitia again?" It was Jason who answered, "840,000 square kilometers, captain. The same size as the country of Namibia on Earth."

A stunning realization came over the Copernicans. "840,000 square kilometers divided into one thousand square kilometers is 840 setups," said Chris. "It would take weeks to do that many, and we don't have the time." Francis gave an indulgent snort. "It would be Mr. Tripper if we had to set up on the ice each time for the shot. Then break down the radar unit and move it to a new location. But, no, we can wheel the ground penetrators into the moon chariots. There is a hatch at the bottom of the cars. We open the hatches and shoot through the holes. Then we drive the chariots 10 kilometers away and shoot again. I estimate, using both speeders, we could search 100,000 square kilometers in a day." A look of disbelief crossed Jane's lovely face. "Wheeling the ground penetrating radar units into the speeders? A hatch that just conveniently exists on the car's bottom. Shooting through the hole? What are the odds that all those factors just come together?" Chief Engineer laughed, "Pretty good, lieutenant, since we designed the moon chariots that way." A momentary silence followed.

"Well, isn't that special?" commented Jane.

Later that night, Tripper and Franke lay naked in each other's arms in their cabin. "Tomorrow, it's back to Tombaugh's base, and then we hunt for the beacon," said Jane. "Yes, I hope the captain's hunch is right. Because it is just a hunch," said Chris. "It makes sense, though," replied the Communication Officer. "If the beacon had been on the surface, I think the Copernicus or the speeders would have found it. But it's hiding in the heart's tears." Tripper chucked, "Tears of the Heart? Pluto's ocean? Very poetic, Jane." Franke ran her finger over the Navigation Officer's bare chest. "Chris, I was wondering. Do you think...?"

Tripper grabbed Jane's hand, "Yes."

First Officer Leonidas and the two engineers, Book and Riley, were soaking in the ship's hot tub. Sipping glasses of champagne, they relaxed after a hectic few days on Pluto. "You caught everyone by surprise, except me, when you mentioned the ground penetrating radar Francis," said Jason. "Well, I had to get some brownie points back after that dressing down I got from the captain for crashing the chariot," answered Francis. "It was pure inspiration, men," commented Spiro. "We should find the beacon in a few days. If it exists, and if there is an ocean. We don't know that for sure yet." Jason sipped his champagne. "Did you see the look of concentration on the captain's face? I thought green laser bolts would come out of her eyes." Spiro leaned back. "She has always been like that, very intense." Book arched an eyebrow. "Indeed. Why did you ship with her?" The First Officer smiled. "It seemed the logical course of action." The hot tub room resounded with hoots of laughter.

Captain Nancy Darkstrider sat in her cabin at the portal and gazed at Pluto's heart shimmering in the space below her. Dressed in her nightgown and with her golden hair unbound, she looked like a young girl. The blue lobe's iris crept into her soul. "I'll get you my pretty," said Nancy, chuckling. "And your little dog, too." An obstruction seemed to pass over the eye momentarily. "Wait, did you just wink at me?"

The following day, the Copernicus crew gathered on the shuttle bay deck. Captain Darkstrider, in her ship-board clothing, regarded five white-suited figures with their helmets under their arms. Nancy slowly passed her chartreuse-tinted eyes along her team. She weighed their strengths, weaknesses, traits, and tendencies. Finally nodding, she said, "Right, you know your mission. We loaded the penetrating radar units on the shuttles and were ready to go. Return to Clyde Tombaugh's base and start your search for the beacon. Then expand your parameters outwards. Mr. Leonidas has devised a computerized plan for every shot. As Chief Engineer Book predicted, we can cover 100,000 square kilometers daily. Maybe a little more. Questions?" There were none. "So good luck and be safe down there. And find me my beacon!!"

Darkstrider turned on her heels as the crew fixed their helmets and entered the shuttles. Fifteen minutes later, she watched from her seat on the bridge as the first one, then the other, shuttle shot from the gun muzzle of the landing bay aperture. Then, with dreamy eyes, the captain quoted Samuel Taylor Coleridge's "The Rime of the Ancient Mariner."

"It is an ancient Mariner,

And he stoppeth one of three.

'By thy long grey beard and glittering eye,

Now wherefore stopp'st thou me?"

From the bridge viewscreen, Nancy watched as the two silvery crafts spiraled gracefully to the planet below. Soon lost in the glare of Pluto's heart.

"Ismael," breathed Nancy.

Dawn at Clyde Tombaugh's base. The rising sun, 5 billion kilometers away, cast its weak rays onto a tableau of men and machines. Outside the shelter, a flight-suited First Officer Leonidas gave last instructions to his charges over the comm links. "Right, Franke and Tripper, drive 15 kilometers and begin your radar shots. Book and Riley will begin their first shoot here. After that, I will return to the hut and process your data with Copernicus' database. Then both of you move outwards in the pattern on your onboard computers. Good luck, everybody." Spiro returned to the shelter, and the four other members entered their land speeders. Immediately, Chris and Jane's vehicle sped away.

Freed of his space attire, Leonidas took his place at the computer station. He flipped on the connection to the chariot's radar output screens. Patiently, he waited for the data from the first shots to come through. In Chariot Two, parked outside the shelter, Chief Engineer Book and assistant engineer Riley were preparing for their first shot. "Ok, Jason, open the hatch door, extend the pulse gun, and power up the unit. We are in the green. Firing pulse! Passing through the ice. More ice. 75 kilometers now. This ice is very thick. There is more ice. We're passing 180 kilometers. 185 kilometers. We're through! We've found water!" Back in the shelter, Spiro lifted his eyes to the ceiling in exaltation. "Great work, Chariot Two. You've provided the first evidence for the existence of the underground ocean beneath Sputnik Planitia." Jason and Francis gave each other a thumbs up. Chief Book studied the readout. "Still passing through water. 200 kilometers. 250 kilometers. This ocean is deep; all right, 300 kilometers. 310 kilometers. Contact with the bottom! Pulse returning. Now we'll find out what's hidden at the bottom of the sea."

In Chariot One, Navigational Officer Tripper groused to Franke, "Great. So Book and Riley found the ocean. If we had the first shot, we would have been the ones to find it." Jane patted his shoulder in mock sympathy. "Never mind, lover-boy. I'm sure we will find something just as well."

On board the Copernicus, Nancy lifted her arms in triumph. "Knew it! I knew there was an ocean there! And Captain Nancy Darkstrider found it! Well, I had help, but it will be my name that history will remember." Darkstrider patrolled the bridge with her hands clasped behind her back. "Now we find the beacon. The chariot crews can cover a lot of ground. But the question is, is there enough time?" Finally, Darkstrider stopped pacing and turned to stare at the heart of Pluto that filled the screen. "You can hide, my friend. But we'll track you down. You can bet on that. And then you will be mine!" Nancy collected herself and laughed self-consciously. "Or maybe I am going space crazy?"

"Return pulse coming in," said assistant engineer Riley. "And here it is." On the dashboard screen, a green image emerged. "Well, well, interesting. It looks like the bottom of the Pacific Ocean. Abyssal plain, the edge of a seamount. Now something that looks like a guyot, a flat-topped undersea mountain. No beacon." Chief Engineer Book busied himself with the controls, sharpening the image. "Never mind, Jason. We're not finding it in the first shot. What would have been the odds of that?" Riley considered, "840 to 1?" Francis threw up his hands in mock surrender, "Ok Einstein, yes you're right, 840 to 1, preciously. That was a rhetorical question." The tinny voice of First Officer Leonidas came over their comms. "Good work, men. Our first images of the undersea bottom of Pluto's ocean. Not to mention the first physical proof of its existence. Not bad for ten minutes of work." Riley turned to the Chief Book. "Well, Spock's pleased at any rate. I expect the captain is happy too. You know how ambitious she is." Francis laughed, "Yes, I bet she is dancing around the bridge in her underwear." Jason stared at his friend in displeasure. "Funny kind of thing to imagine."

Fifteen kilometers away, a ping alerted Tripper and Franke to the location of their initial ground penetrating radar shoot. Chris stopped their vehicle, and he and Jane prepared for the shot. "Ok, Lieutenant Franke, slide the chariot's belly hatch open." The Communication Officer pushed a button, and an opening appeared at the bottom of the craft. "Do you think that hole's for the radar unit, Chris, as Book claimed? I always thought it was an emergency exit." Tripper busied himself with the controls. "Maybe it serves several purposes. It doesn't matter. Right, I deployed the pulse gun. We are powering up, powering up. I have green. Fire in the hole! Fire! Pulse is away! Now we wait for a minute until the pulse reflects on us." The seconds ticked away slowly. Finally, Jane complained. "Oh, what's taking so long?" Tripper smiled. "It's only been 50 seconds, sweetheart. Good things happen to those who wait. Remember last night in bed?" Franke giggled, "I don't think an orgasm and this are quite the same." Chris patted Jane's thigh. "Maybe not, maybe not. Stand bye. Pulse is returning. Let's see what we have."

On the speeder's dashboard, a circular disk glowed green. Faint images emerged. "Ok," said Chris, "there's the bottom. Much the same picture as Books and Riley's. Abyssal plain. The rest of that seamount, they mentioned. Oh, something new. The beginnings of an undersea trench. This crevasse may be the equivalent of Marianas's Trench in the Pacific. In irritation, Jane pointed at something on the screen. "Oh, what are those squiggles? Is there something wrong with the image?" Tripper frowned. "I see what you mean. I'll recalibrate to get those extraneous blips off. They could be echoes from the bottom. Odd, they are floating above the sea floor. Right, I've got the image recalibrated. Oh, my god!!!"

At Tombaugh's base, Navigational Officer Tripper's urgent transmission shook First Officer Leonidas out of his reveille. "Chariot One to Base! Chariot One to base! Come in, over!" Spiro keyed his mike, "Tombaugh's base to Chariot One. What is the nature of your transmission? Have you found the beacon? Over." Quickly the answer came back, "No, no beacon. Something even better! Over!" The First Officer examined the green disk from Chariot One on his monitor. "I am looking at your radar image. It's not clear. What are those worm-like things? Over." Jane's excited laugh came strongly over the intercom, "It's life, Mr. Leonidas! We've found life!"

"Life!?" repeated the First Officer. "You found life?" exclaimed Captain Darkstrider on the Copernicus. "Ah crap, they discovered life," said the Chief Engineer Book to his companion Riley.

"Yes," said Tripper. "Massive life forms. Maybe thousands. Our radar image has an assortment of specs, large and small. I can narrow our impulse and get a better image of some of them. Over." Nancy's quick order came from Copernicus's bridge: "Go ahead, Mr. Tripper. Fire another pulse, narrow beam. Over." From the captain's mike came the reply, "Aye-aye, captain! Over." Fifteen kilometers away, Francis complained bitterly to Jason. "Look! We have the same specs on our screen! Why didn't you figure out it was life?" Riley replied indignantly, "You made the same mistake! I thought it was extraneous data! We would have to have recalibrated like Tripper did to see them!" Book sighed. "You're right. I'm sorry, Jason." The assistant engineer patted his friend's knee. "It's ok. We discovered the ocean, after all. They can't take that away from us." The Chief brightened, "No, they can't, can they?"

"Ok, the second pulse is coming in," said Navigational Officer Tripper. On the screen, a new radar map appeared with distinct imagery. "Good god! Look at those things! They look like sharks, squids, and even plesiosaurs! Some appear like a nightmare!" exclaimed Communication Officer Franke. "Are those aliens or something else?" Chris twiddled with his controls, trying to sharpen the images. "Native Plutonians, I suspect. Remember, this ocean is many times deeper than the deepest part of the Pacific Ocean. This enormous volume could lead to creatures of tremendous size. I'm trying to get an estimate of their scale." Chris used the onboard computer to make calculations. "Wow, these things are big, all right, on the order of the earth's whales. Look at that thing! It must be a kilometer long! Its shape hurts me to look at it!" At his side, Jane shuddered violently. "Oh, Chris, I'm so scared. I don't want to go anywhere near those monsters!" Tripper looked at his lover curiously. "What makes you think we ever will be in their vicinity?" Franke stared back at him. "I'm not sure. We will before this is over, I suspect."

The five shore party members gathered that night at the shelter's dining table. They had placed a monitor on the tabletop so Captain Darkstrider could attend. "Right," said Nancy. "A lot has happened today. We have confirmed the existence of Pluto's internal ocean. Thanks to Engineers Book and Riley." Francis and Jason bowed their heads. "And we have discovered Plutonian aquatic life in the said ocean by the team of Chris and Jane." The two young officers wore broad smiles on their faces. "Now the first day's ground penetrating radar shots have completed. We've mapped and cataloged over 100,000 square miles of the ocean bottom. No beacon, but it's early days. Any comments so far?" First Officer Leonidas pushed a button, and a sizeable holographic circle appeared overhead. "This is the ocean bed we've mapped. As you can see, it's mostly flat, an abyssal plain. There are several seamounts and guyots. Cryovolcanoes, no doubt. A deep trench. Various scratches and indentations. What looks like an ancient meteorite crater? Very eroded and silted over."

Spiro looked up. "And then there are the creatures we found." A chill coursed through the assembled Copernicans. The First Officer touched another button, the map disappeared, and holographic creatures appeared. "As you can see, some of them resemble earth animals. Megalodon sharks, Colossal squids, and plesiosaurs from the time of the dinosaurs. Plus, a lot of things we can't identify." Darkstrider frowned. "Why are they so large? Is it because Pluto's ocean is so big?" Chief Engineer Book held up his hand. "I can answer that. The radar pulse spreads so wide it will only pick up enormous things. The ocean is full of medium-sized and smaller creatures. But we are too far away to capture their images." Lieutenant Franke interjected irritably, "You're discussing our creatures, Chief Engineer Book." Riley shot back instantly, "They're swimming in our ocean Communication Officer Franke!"

"Children, children," admonished Nancy. "Stop squabbling. We all share in the discoveries. Now back to the Plutonians. I find it interesting that some resemble our earth sea denizens closely. Is this an example of parallel evolution or something else?" Spiro lifted his eyes to the holographic display and squinted. "Unknown captain. The aliens might have visited earth a billion years ago, brought samples of marine life, and seeded Pluto's ocean with them. What existed in earth's oceans at the time was blue-green algae. From which all plant life on earth developed. And strings of molecules, the precursors to animals."

Jane gave a start. "Those monsters aren't from algae, Mr. Leonidas!" Laughter moved around the table. The image of Nancy on the table monitor looked at the younger woman curiously. "I'm intrigued, Lieutenant Franke. Why do you label them monsters? They are just newly discovered life forms, after all." Spiro touched a button, and the display changed. "Perhaps this will answer your question, captain." It altered the holographic display to reveal a creature of eldritch horror. All the Copernicans except for Spiro and Darkstrider looked away quickly. Then, with blanched cheeks, the First Officer said, "This is the kilometer-long creature Franke and Tripper discovered." Nancy gave Leonidas an amused smile. "I take your point."

Two days later, they found the beacon. The team of Chief Engineer Book and assistant engineer Riley made the discovery. "Stop your sinning and hide your women. Found it!" Exclaimed Francis. A metallic squawk came over the comm link. "You found it? The beacon? What is your location, Shuttle Two?" said First Officer Leonidas. "We are 200 clicks due north of Tombaugh's base. We are sending the first image of the beacon now," replied Jason. On Spiro's monitor, an image appeared on the ocean floor. "Immense, 5 kilometers wide," said Francis. "It appears to have stages. Difficult to discern from a bird's-eye view, but very tall."

"Excellent work, gentlemen," said Spiro. "Take several shots and then home for tea. You've earned it." Four hundred kilometers away in their moon chariot, Navigational Officer Tripper turned to his beautiful companion. "They found it." Jane stroked his cheek gently. "I know." Later, in the conference room, there was a celebration in progress. Several bottles of champagne, whiskey, and wine were drunk.

"We found it! We found it!" chanted Lieutenant Franke as she danced around. From the table monitor, Captain Darkstrider looked on indulgently on the monitor. On the couches around the room, the Chief Book, Riley, and Leonidas sat chatting with drinks in hand. Chris sipped his beer as he watched Jane's sensuous movements. "If I can have your attention for a moment," said Nancy. Everyone stopped and turned to the captain's image. "Tomorrow, I want the shuttle teams to take their chariots to the beacon's location. You are to take side-view pulse images of the beacon. Stand out 100 kilometers on each side and take multiple shots. We should get a good view of the beacon from that angle." The landing team all gave nods of assent. "Good. Now to quote an old phrase, party on, dudes!" Captain Darkstrider's image faded as the crew resumed their celebration. First Officer Leonidas and the two engineers looked on in alarm as Jane began a striptease.

The next evening, the shuttle teams were back from their mission. Seated again around the conference table, they watched in interest as the First Officer downloaded their radar images. Out of her monitor, Nancy peered intently. "Ok, here is the beacon as it appears from the side," said Spiro. A holographic image sprang from an immense black tower rising from the ocean floor. It loomed stage by stage upon the rampart of an obdurate alien metal—five kilometers high, a later day tower of Babel. Spellbound, the Copernicans stopped breathing. "Mission accomplished," said Tripper. Jane pointed to the bottom of the structure. "What's going on there?" Everyone looked to see what she was looking at on the screen. On either side of the frame, the heads of two enormous creatures were entering. "It's Megalodon and The Thing!" said Franke excitedly. "Mr. Leonidas, upload our later images. Let's see what they were doing!"

Dutifully, Spiro uploaded several more images. Against the backdrop of the tower, the two creatures appeared to rush together. The giant shark bit at The Thing with massive jaws. The creature wound tentacles tipped with claws around its opponent's head. In the last image, The Thing tore its rival in half. A silence descended on the group. "Well," said Jane. "That was special." From the monitor came Captain Darkstrider's voice. "Mr. Leonidas, tomorrow return to the Copernicus. I will visit Clyde Tombaugh's base for the wrap-up."

The morning saw Captain Nancy Darkstrider seated at the dining table in the shelter. The crew grouped around her in various stages of hangovers. Even First Officer Leonidas on the monitor looked decidedly ill. "Well," said Nancy. "You all look like you had a good time last night." Lieutenant Franke lifted red-rimmed eyes, "Please, Captain, don't speak so loud."

Darkstrider machine-gunned her team with leaf-green eyes. "I know Mr. Tripper said, "Mission accomplished" yesterday, but I'm not sure." Chief Engineer Book protested, "What more can we accomplish, captain? We've found an artifact, entered it, and identified the alien's homeworld. In addition, we have extensively mapped Pluto and all its moons."

"We found the beacon and have radar imagery of it." continued Francis. "Pluto's ocean is now verified. We have identified native Plutonians as inhabiting the said ocean. What else can we hope to find?" Darkstrider smiled. "Quite a list of accomplishments, I admit. I was hoping to enter the beacon and find out why it stopped working. And to learn anything else about the aliens from it."

Assistant engineer Riley held up his hand. "There is no way for us to travel through 300 kilometers of ice and water, captain. It just isn't possible." Nancy knitted her brows in frustration. "The aliens must have serviced the beacon. How did they access it from the surface?" The crew of the Copernicus looked blankly at each other. "A submarine," suggested Navigational Officer Tripper. "Teleportation," said Lieutenant Franke. "An elevator," said First Officer Leonidas decisively. Darkstrider looked at the image of her friend in mild surprise. "A 300-kilometer elevator Mr. Leonidas? Is it possible?" Spiro assumed a confident air. "Very possible, captain. Even probable." Chief Book tapped the table with his finger. "We've gone over the surface with our metal detectors for weeks. Neither from the ship nor our chariots have we detected a gram of metal. If the elevator exists, we would have found it by now." A minute passed, and Nancy sighed heavily.

"You're right, of course, Chief. All right, start packing up and breaking down the base. We have several runs with the shuttle ahead of us." Jane protested, "Can't we just leave the shelter here, captain?" Darkstrider shook her head. "No, I love this insignificant planet. When we leave, she will be clean!"

The landing party packed their belongings. Tripper noticed Nancy putting on her flight suit. "Going someplace, Captain?" Darkstrider put on her helmet and locked it tight. "Yes, while you people begin the disassembly, I will take one last ride in the chariot. But first, I want to say goodbye." The crew all nodded their understanding.

An hour later found Nancy in Chariot One on the ice precisely above the beacon far below. "I know where you are now, but I can't get to you. You've won," she said sadly. Then, blindly, the captain drove in a west direction. On the horizon, the ice islands of Challenger and Columbia Colles bulked. Stopping her vehicle, Darkstrider exited and stood on the naked ice. All around her, the unforgiving plains of Sputnik Planitia stretched beyond her vision. Nancy fixed her gaze on a tiny blue dot. "Well, blue marble, we're coming home." Darkstrider lifted her eyes and stared unseeingly into the velvet blackness of space. "I know we've accomplished much, but I wanted so much more. Well, Nancy, old girl, it's time to admit it. You've blown your last chance at greatness. You've failed." A tear trickled down her cheek.

For a minute, Captain Darkstrider had been aware in her subconscious that ticking noises were coming over her comm unit. "Oh, what now?" she thought. "Is the chariot's motor going to quit on me? That's all I need." Nancy walked over to the land speeder and stood by the hood. "That's odd. The noise isn't coming from the motor." With growing realization, the captain hurried into the vehicle. A green disk on the dash showed a red dot on its edge. "Metal!" exclaimed Darkstrider. "Ten clicks from here to the west." Nancy looked in that direction.

The majestic spires of Challenger Colles beckoned to her. Eagerly, she opened up the comm link to Tombaugh's base. "Stop packing! I've found the elevator!"

Missile launch

Chapter 9

A small convoy of two land speeders entered the Challenge Coles. Navigational Officer Tripper sat beside Communication Officer Franke in the first chariot. Sitting behind the two, Captain Nancy Darkstrider occupied the rumble seat. Following closely, Chariot One purred after Chariot Two, occupied by the Chief Engineer Book and assistant engineer Riley.

Nancy spoke to the built-in screen in the back of Chris's chair. On it appeared First Officer Leonidas, back on the Copernicus. "In retrospect, it's amazing no one thought of exploring the Challenger hills," said Spiro. "Yes," answered Nancy, "Pluto was too large to cover adequately in our time. We were making guesses, and our guesses were wrong. Did you ever figure out your hunch about the beacon's location?"

Leonidas looked embarrassed. "Affirmative. I was looking at Challenger Colles, and I noticed the spires in the middle were a different color than those around it." Darkstrider prompted her first officer, "And what caused the difference?" The First Officer continued, "Water ice is blue while nitrogen is white. The beacon transmissions forced nitrogen in the middle of the colles where it froze." Nancy frowned. "Radio transmissions do not cause physical disruptions of that nature." Leonidas nodded. "That we know about, yes. But the aliens are using strange technology. And the last two satellites crashed. Probably by something the beacon launched." The captain laughed, "You are overthinking, Mr. Leonidas. The beacon was transmitting to the first several satellites. Then sent a laser or missile at the last two. That's what fractured the ice." Spiro grinned. "That would be the logical answer, yes."

"Your premonition was correct, Jane," said Navigation Officer Tripper. "We are going to the ocean, after all." Franke shuddered. "As long as we don't run into megalodon or The Thing. Or something equally horrible." Chris patted his lover's knee. "We aren't going swimming with them, Jane. I'm sure the aliens could access the beacon in safety. Aren't you curious about what's down there?" The Lieutenant considered for a while, "Yes, of course. I am a space voyager. But I sense great danger. There is death waiting for us down there with open jaws. And the beast is hungry tonight."

The moon chariots climbed a steeper slope. Jumbles of ice boulders surrounded them. Fractured prisms of shining mirrors rose on every side. The space adventurers went deeper into the chaotic mixture of defiles, ridges, dells, and hollows. The engineers on Chariot Two were conversing. "It was clever of the captain to find the elevator if it was an elevator. How do we know what it is? It could be an alien dumpster," said Jason. "It makes sense; it's something to do with the beacon, though," said Francis. "In a horizontal direction, it's only 20 kilometers away." Riley stamped on the floorboard, "But 300 kilometers in the vertical. That's a long way." The Chief chuckled, "Whatever is in these hills, we would have to investigate it. It's the only metal we have found on Pluto and its moons. Not including the beacon, of course."

The land speeders crested a ridge and descended into a valley. Steep walls of glistening blue towered above them—kilometer after kilometer. The two vehicles forged their way into an endless winter wilderness. The metal director on Chariot One increased in volume. "We are getting closer," said Navigational Officer Tripper. "We're only two kilometers away in a straight line." Communications Officer Franke stared out the window at the fractured landscape around them. "Since when have we been following a straight line?" Chris peered out the front screen at an emerging mass of white spires. "This trip is going to get more interesting."

Captain Darkstrider spoke to her first officer at her back, "Are you still tracking us from the Copernicus? What's the terrain like ahead? Lieutenant Tripper says that the source of the signal is two kilometers away." Leonidas scrutinized the bridge's main viewscreen. "Yes, I can observe you. You are coming to the nitrogen intrusion of the colles. The topography is getting rougher. You may have to abandon the chariots and proceed on foot soon." Nancy smiled. "We know that. Tripper and Riley have mountaineering experience. They brought their equipment with them. We have it in the cargo compartment." Spiro's face assumed a look of approval. "Foresight indeed."

The two space vehicles stood at the base of a wall of white ice. It adorned its face with broken ledges and fractures. The five Copernicans roped themselves together and attached crampons to their boots. Each held an ice pick in their hands. The leader of the rope team, Mr. Tripper, addressed the rest. "Right, I will climb this chimney to the ledge we can see halfway up. Pluto's gravity is much less than Earth's, making it easier. But make no mistake, a fall here will kill just as effectively as a fall in our world. I will go first since I have experience in ice field climbing. Lieutenant Franke will be next, then the captain, Chief Engineer Book, and Engineer Riley will bring up the rear. He will be our anchor in an emergency since he also has past mountaineering. Questions?" Captain Darkstrider saluted Chris with her ice pick. "Carry on, Mr. Tripper, you are doing fine."

Without a word, Tripper inserted himself into a chimney and climbed upwards. Aided by the lesser gravity of Pluto, he soon reached a ledge halfway up. Stepping onto the shelf, he tapped an expansion bolt into a crack with his rock hammer and attached the rope. Then he leaned out and called, "Ok, now each of you comes up." The five explorers navigated the chimney until all stood on the ledge. Then, like flies on a wall, the lonely figures continued their ascent.

Up and up went the climbers. They approached the top of the wall using a series of ledges and chimneys. Now only a hundred-meter stretch separated them from the summit. "Ok," said Chris. "No more chimneys or ledges. I'm going to have to free climb. I see some handholds and cracks. It shouldn't be too difficult. I climbed El Capitan on Earth." Tripper started up. He hadn't gotten far when he lost his grip and came crashing back down on the ledge. Jane and Nancy grabbed him before he fell off. "Did you fall off El Capitan as well, Chris?" asked Jane dryly. Tripper grinned weakly, "Ok, I got a little careless. I've got this." The others watched, admiring the navigational officer moving quickly up the vertical face. Soon he had reached the crest and disappeared over. The young officer's voice came tinnily over their coms. "Right. I've anchored the rope around a boulder. I will pull you up one by one. Grab for hand and footholds on the way up." In twenty minutes, all five were standing on a white plateau covered with tall steeples and broken ice bastions. In his backpack, the Chief Engineer Book carried a small metal detector. "There," Francis, "that large hummock a kilometer away. The signal is coming in that direction."

Eagerly now, the landing party trooped towards their goal. Jumping over cracks and threading their way through an icy maze, they made their way. Overhead, the ghostly shape of the Copernicus watched their progress. Captain Darkstrider heard her first officer's metallic speech on her helmet com. "I place you at midway in the colles captain. You should be almost there. Over." Nancy acknowledged the communication. "Yes, this is not the end. It is not even the beginning of the end. But it is, perhaps, the end of the beginning. Over." Spiro chuckled, "Winston Churchill?" Darkstrider humorously spoke, "Do you know everything, Mr. Leonidas? Over."

Up the last slope, the group tramped. "I'm surprised we haven't run into a Yeti in all this ice," quipped assistant engineer Riley. "Or a Wampa," replied Communication Officer Franke. "Be careful about what you wish," cautioned Captain Darkstrider. "It might come true." After the last few steps, the fearless adventurers reached the previous summit. Pausing, they looked about themselves at the world. They stood on a large, circular white plateau adorned with spires and battlements.

Further out, the range of bluish ice hills spread out. They blazed like crystal chandeliers in the reflected light from Sputnik's plains. A nick on the plain's horizon was Clyde Tombaugh's base. "I feel like we've conquered Mt. Everest on earth," commented the Chief Engineer Book. "Or Mons Olympus on Mars. I've climbed that," replied Navigational Officer Tripper. "Well, we're here," said Nancy. "There's nothing to see. Except for the magnificent view, of course." The Chief Engineer Book turned up the volume on his com unit. The constant roar of his backpack's metal detector filled their ears, hurting them. He chuckled, "Look down, captain." All five looked at their booted feet. Like looking through a glass, they could see a black oval object ten meters below them. Nancy sucked in her breath. "So there you are."

Half an hour later, the Copernicans crouched in a trench-like depression. The hummock reared a hundred meters away. Captain Darkstrider spoke on her com, "Ok, Mr. Leonidas, you may fire when ready. Over." The First Officer's announcement was swift in its return. "Acknowledged. Fire in the hole! Fire in the hole!" A blinding red laser bolt smashed into the ice hummock. The five brave spacemen lay flat on their stomachs in their trench as ice shards rained down on them. Again came the call, "Fire in the hole! Fire in the hole!" For a second time, a crimson stream of destruction came hurtling down. A mist roiled over the fearless explorers. "Fire mission complete. Copernicus is standing down. Over," announced the laconic voice of the First Officer. Getting to their feet, the team saw the top of the hummock blast away. It exposed three meters of a black structure to their view. Their boots crunched on ice crystal debris. The five lined up in front of one side of the dark eminence.

Devoid of any damage from the lasers, it exuded an air of unguessable antiquity. "This looks more like the monolith from 2001: A Space Oddysey than the artifact on Charon, doesn't it?" commented Jason. "Yeah," said Tripper. "It does." Captain Darkstrider turned to her fair companion. "Lieutenant Franke, will you do the honors?" Jane stepped forward and knocked on the glossy black surface. "Melon."

Instantly, in front of their eyes, an oval door appeared. The now recognizable blue atmospheric force field filled the entrance. Captain Darkstrider spoke into her com. "Mr. Leonidas, we are entering the structure. We may be out of communication for a while. Over." Spiro's modulation echoed in their earpieces, "Understood, captain. Good luck, and I wish I had been there with you. Over." In a single file, the landing party passed through the blue shimmer and entered the maw of the black beast. Instantaneously, the door sealed itself behind them.

The group found themselves in an oval chamber, 5 meters in diameter—shelving they had first encountered in the Charon artifact projected from the walls. The same red ambient light lit up the interior. "Well," said Chris Tripper, "this is cozy." At his side, Franke said, "Odd, I was going to say this was special." Chris smiled, "I know." The Communication Officer stamped on the foot of her companion. "Bastard," said

Jane in a sotto voce. Chief Book studied his portable reader. "We might as well open our visors. Temperature and atmosphere are the same as in the artifact on Charon." With opened visors, the landing crew examined the walls. "If this is an elevator, how do we get it to work?" asked assistant engineer Riley. "Good question, Mr. Riley," said Captain Darkstrider. "We need to find the answer." For ten minutes, the Copernicans searched every square centimeter of the featureless surface.

Finally, Captain Darkstrider said, "Here's something." The others hurried over to see what Nancy was pointing. High on the wall were the faint traces of two sizeable six-fingered hands. One above the other. "Sharp eyes, captain." said the Chief Engineer Book. "I can barely see that."

Navigational Officer Tripper removed his glove and stretched to the limit of his reach, placing his left hand in the lower outline. Nothing happened. "You need six fingers for that to work," joked assistant engineer Riley. "I'm guessing the aliens were predominantly lefthanded," observed the Chief Engineer Book. "Interesting observation, Chief Book," said Nancy, "But it doesn't help us much." For a time, the quintet considered their dilemma. "I think I have a solution," said Communication Officer Franke. "Mr. Tripper and Chief Book are our two tallest. What if Francis places his left hand over Chris's in the pattern so they overlap and press hard? Would that give the impression of a six-fingered hand?" Everyone was dumbfounded. "That's so crazy it might work," said Captain Darkstrider. Once again, Tripper stretched and put his hand on the trace. Taking off his glove, Francis pushed himself into Tripper's back and stretched up to put his hand over the young officer's. "This doesn't mean we're engaged," he whispered loudly. Everyone except Jason snorted with laughter. The two men squeezed their hands together. The crew fell to the floor as the elevator rapidly dropped away. "I think it worked!" said Chris. "Ya think so?" asked Jane sarcastically.

On Copernicus, First Officer Leonidas used the bridge screen's extreme magnification. Then, with keen interest, he observed the five landing party members enter the black monolith. Instantly, the background noise of the open circuit to the landing party ceased. "Copernicus to Captain Darkstrider, come in, please. Over. First Officer to Captain Darkstrider, come in, please. Over." Spiro leaned back in his chair. "Well, they're on their way. To where, who can say?"

Abruptly, the g forces forcing the landing flat stopped. Shakily, they got to their feet. "I think this elevator adjusts itself for whatever organism rides inside it," said Navigator Tripper. "It had to compensate for non-aliens." Captain Darkstrider smoothed her blonde hair. "I think you're right, Mr. Tripper. Chief Book, how fast are we moving?" Francis was busy reading his recorder. "300 kilometers per hour, captain. We should reach the bottom in an hour." Nancy considered, "Ok, let's relax on these shelves or seats and get some rest. We should discuss what we're going to do next." The landing party jumped up and sat on the shelves. Riley and Franke lay down and closed their eyes. The other three, Darkstrider, Book, and Tripper, sat with their legs swinging. "I feel like a little kid on this shelf," said Darkstrider. "That's how we felt back in the Charon artifact," Chris replied.

The three sitting members looked at each other curiously. "I was thinking," said Tripper. "We could have landed the shuttle on the hummock and saved ourselves a lot of trouble." Nancy laughed, "True, but where would the shuttle have gone when the Copernicus blasted the top of the hummock? And once the ice was gone, the monolith took up most of it." The younger officer slapped the side of his helmet contrite. "Yeah, didn't think about that."

The captain smiled, "Forget it, Mr. Tripper. You did excellent work getting us up that wall to the plateau." Chris grinned, "Thank you, captain, but it was much easier than it looked. Pluto's gravity is only one-twelfth that of Earth." Francis studied his recorder. "Brilliant deduction on Mr. Leonidas's part. He thought there was an elevator, and so there was." Nancy swung her legs like a little girl. "Yes, there are no dummies on my crew. That's for sure." Silence descended on the trio. Jane and Jason looked like they were asleep. "I wonder what we'll find when the elevator stops? A submarine?" said the Navigational Officer. "Maybe an underground tunnel to the beacon," replied the Chief Engineer Book. "If it's a tunnel, we face a long walk. It's 20 kilometers from here to there," said Captain Darkstrider. "It will be mind-blowing if we can reach the beacon," said Tripper. "The aliens did not leave any technology of note in the artifact on Charon. That massive structure we're heading to must be full of scientific knowledge." Book considered, "Of course, we can't take much with us. We're limited in what we can carry. But we can photograph and record everything we see."

"Whatever is out there," said Nancy. "I'm sure it will be worth any risk to discover it. Am I wrong, or is the elevator slowing down?" The captain was not mistaken, and the elevator came to a halt. The communication officer and the assistant engineer woke and sat up.

Nancy, Chris, and Francis jumped down from the shelf, quickly joined by the other two. "It appears we've arrived at our destination," said Nancy. "Lieutenant Franke, if you will do the honors?" Jane walked over to the blank space on the bulkhead where they had entered. She knocked firmly, saying, "Melon." Immediately, the oval egress sprang into existence. The cast of the Copernicus filed through. But what was the name of the play they were performing? The troupe found themselves in a large square room lacking any furnishing. Opposite them, a sizeable ovoid opening confronted them. The atmospheric blue shimmer in the door prevented them from seeing what lay beyond. The landing party looked about them in the low reddish luminosity.

"This is the first room we've seen that was anything other than ovoid," said Tripper. "Yeah, sure makes for a pleasant change," replied Franke. "Here's another first," said Riley, pointing. "The first door that doesn't disappear." Captain Darkstrider took her blaster from her holster and checked it. "All right, now listen. Whatever is through that door, prepare yourself." Her crew drew their weapons with grim looks on their faces. "Let me go first," demanded Navigational Officer Tripper. Nancy smiled. "Captain's privilege. You all have taken enough risks on this trip. It's time I did my part." Then, seeing further protests on several faces, she added, "The only uncomfortable thing about being an officer is that occasionally you have to act like one. This one is mine." Then, with a firm stride, Nancy was through the nuanced blue portal.

Instantly she assumed a combat stance and searched her new surrounding. To her astonishment, Captain Darkstrider found herself in a red-lit tunnel stretched westwards into infinity. She was standing on a platform that overlooked a sunken railway. Lining up were six flatbeds on the trackway. Nancy peered up at a glass ceiling 5 meters above her head. Beyond that was a blackness her eyes could not piece. The other Copernicans had gathered behind her and were looking wildly around. "I was right," said the Chief Engineer Book. "It is a tunnel. And it's pointing at the beacon." Assistant engineer Riley stepped to the edge of the platform. "And those flatbeds take you there. You stand on one, and it goes. The other side of the trackway must be for returning stages." Lieutenant Franke pointed up at the ceiling. "The blackness beyond the glass. Is that ice or rock or something?" Navigation Officer Tripper followed her gaze. "You know what? I think it's the sea. We're under Pluto's ocean!"

Each landing party member gazed at the black depths as if searching their souls. "I think you must be right, Mr. Tripper, "said Darkstrider. "We're beneath the ocean. All 120 kilometers of it. The pressure on that material must be enormous." Nancy holstered her blaster and stepped onto the furthest flatbed. "Well, we better get going, people." The ambient red light went out at that moment, immersing the crew in total darkness. "What's going on?" queried Jason. "Who turned off the lights?" Suddenly, the dark world beyond the glass was swimming with many iridescent shapes, large and small.

"Fish!" laughed Jane. "They're fish!" Unexpectedly, the thin voice of First Officer Leonidas intruded into the crew's coms. "Copernicus to a landing party. Come in, please. Come in, please. Over." Nancy keyed her mike. "Captain Darkstrider to Copernicus. We read you. Over." A note of relief was apparent in Spiro's tone. "Glad to hear from you, captain. What is your situation? Over." Darkstrider glanced around. "We're in a subway station of sorts under the ocean. It leads to the beacon, we believe. We plan to take a flatbed to get there. Can you see what is on our helmet cams? Over?" Spiro's response was quick, "Yes, I can see them. Native Plutonians, correct? Fascinating. Brilliant display. Over." Darkstrider turned on her lamp and motioned for the landing party to step onto the stage. "We're proceeding with the next phase of our journey. I will stay in touch. Over." Leonidas sighed with regret, "Understood, Copernicus out. Over. "

At 10 kilometers an hour, the small stage with the Copernicans on it moved down the tunnel. It fascinated the crew with the strange radiant life swimming about them. "Look," said Franke. "There's a small squid—Salmon, trout, mackerel, and bass. Well, I don't know what the heck that is. Or that. My god, that's one ugly fish!!" The Chief Engineer Book told the captain, "Since these creatures were born in complete darkness and live out their lives without hue, they have developed the ability to produce light." Nancy laughed, "You mean they glow?" Francis assumed an expression of mock offense. "I believe I just said that." Darkstrider shook her head. 'You've been spending too much time with Mr. Leonidas. You sound like him."

Smoothly, the landing party sped along the trackway. "See that? The tunnel one kilometer ahead and beyond lit up with reddish light. I wonder why it's dark where we are?" asked assistant engineer Riley. "Perhaps because the creatures attract to the light?" suggested Chris Tripper. "See? Already some of those fish are paying attention to our helmet luminance." Communication Officer Franke shook her head. "The aliens weren't worried about the fish. They were worried about the apex predators. Like the titans we saw on the radar scans. They looked big enough to damage the tunnel structure. No matter how strong the glass is." Chief Book chuckled indulgently, "Inspired speculation, Lieutenant, but still speculation. Perhaps—."

Precipitously, every gleaming fish in sight went out. "Now what?" asked Jason. "The fish have turned off their lights! Why would they do that?" Tripper pointed to the side. "There's your answer. Look!" Far off, a tiny thread of light appeared. Slowly, it grew in size, revealing it to be a long, undulating, paddling creature. Even at that distance, it was a beast of vast proportions. Jane gave out a shout, "The Thing!"

The monster swam up to the tunnel surface and kept pace with the explorers. A kilometer long, it had a head like a slug containing two multi-faceted eyes that were as large as beach balloons. Huge paddle-like fins were propellers, and a forest of clawed tentacles grew from its back. The Thing extended its eyes on stalks until they pressed against the glass. The crew was terror-stricken. Out of a nightmare, the eldritch horror opened a mouth filled with crooked teeth as long as an elephant's tusks. For a long minute, the stand-off continued. Then, unexpectedly, the leviathan's gleam extinguished, and it was gone.

Weakly, the Copernicans collapsed to the floor of their conveyance. "Well," said Jane. "That was special." Chris looked at Franke in surprise. "You don't look scared, Jane. I thought the Thing terrified you." The Lieutenant shook her head. "I looked it in its eyes, Chris. I don't think it meant any harm. It was curious." Slowly, the group sat up. "Do you think that was the same behemoth we saw before?" asked Captain Darkstrider. "Maybe," admitted the Chief Engineer Book. "But there would have to be many to support a population. This beacon might be its hunting territory." Idly, assistant engineer Riley looked up and frowned. "That's odd. The Thing is gone, but the fish have not returned. Why are they afraid? Is there something else out there frightening them?"

A vast, dark shape hurled itself at the tunnel partition with a tremendous smash. Shocked, the quintet looked up. A lit creature appeared.

Two hundred fifty meters long, it had massive jaws. Now it turned, and with extraordinary speed, came at them again. "Megalodon!!" shouted Tripper. Once more, the tunnel resounded with echoes from the impact. Tiny cracks appeared on the surface of the tunnel. "Turn off your torches!" shouted Nancy. Hurriedly, each of the crew switched off their helmet lights. They held their breaths as the beast hung in place, wondering where they had gone. "One more hit like that, and we've had it," said Chief Book. Then, as if hearing him, the juggernaut gathered itself for the last rush. The next moment, it disappeared, carried away by a vast unseen shadow. "There's always a bigger fish," said Darkstrider.

The landing crew of the Copernicus, at last, reached their destination. I was stepping off their flatbed and onto the platform. "Why do you think The Thing saved us?" said Tripper. "We didn't see it." Franke smiled, "I know it was. I felt a connection with it. And don't call it The Thing anymore. I gave it a name." Chris laughed indulgently, "Or really? And what is The Thing's new appellation?" The Communication Officer said, "Well, it's big and ugly but cute. I call it — Chris." Tripper visibly started, "You named that thing, Chris? Is that supposed to be some joke?" Jane patted his cheek, laughing, "I wish it were, darling. I wish it were."

Assistant engineer Riley was examining the platform area. "This station is the same as the one on the other end. The same number of flatbeds. The same square room ahead with an ovoid entry. Same everything." Chief Book snickered. "What did you expect? That the aliens would build them differently? Like Piccadilly and Waterloo station in London?" Captain Darkstider pointed up over their heads through the glass. "Well, one thing is distinct. Look there." As one man, the Copernicus crew gazed upwards. Through the glass, they saw the beacon. An immense black tower rises from the ocean floor. It loomed, stage by stage, upon the rampart of obdurate alien metal. Lost in the gloaming, it gave off an unearthly glow.

"Well," said Jane, "that's special." The Chief Engineer Book gestured to the blue-tinged open door. "Let's go in. I believe that is the way to the control room." Tripper hesitated, "How do you know that, chief?" Francis turned to him. "Well, it's not the way to a tobacconist, is it?" The five landing party members trooped through the door into a square room. It proved identical to the one they had left 10 kilometers back. They passed through a portal into a wide corridor that continued out of sight on each hand. Finally, one last indigo-hued gate confronted them. Nancy made a follow-me gesture and passed through the entryway. The quintet found themselves in an ample, silent space. Around the cubicle's perimeter were panels covered with buttons of an indescribable alien color.

"At last, alien technology that looks like something we can work with," said Francis with satisfaction. The two engineers spent the next three hours examining the alien equipment. Captain Darkstrider stood behind them, watching their work, to their intense irritation. The other duo, Tripper, and Franke sat on the floor, bored. Finally, the Chief Engineer Book ventured, "You know what? I think we're dealing with a simple short-circuit." Nancy reflected, "Can you fix it and power up this beacon?" Assistant engineer Riley snorted. "Captain, the Chief, and I have over 50 years of experience. We can find a simple short-circuit."

Restlessly, Jane got to her feet and wandered over to an overlooked side panel. She noticed idly one dark button among the lit ones. "Could this be it?" she asked, pushing the button. Instantly, the boards flashed and the immense engines started.

A powerful vibration hummed through the deck plates. "Seriously?" said Jason. "You pushed one button that fixed the short circuit and powered up this entire beacon?" The Communication Officer could only shrug her shapely shoulders.

Chief Book had already attached a cable of the resurgent panel to his recorder. He studied the readout. "Captain, give me two hours, and I'll have the technical specs of this entire baby downloaded." Nancy smiled. "Make it so." Almost exactly two hours later, Francis removed the cable from the panel. "That's it. I'm finished." Navigational Officer Tripper said eagerly, "Captain Darkstrider, can I repeat it?" Then, as if twenty years had dropped from her face, Nancy nodded. "Mission accomplished," said Chris with great satisfaction. "Congratulations, Captain," came First Officer Leonidas's vocalization over the helmet coms. "Mr. Leonidas!" said the captain. "I thought our transmissions couldn't pass through this alien metal?" Spiro's smug answer came back, "Thought wrong, didn't you? Your transmissions come through the open doors."

Smiling and shaking her head, Nancy viewed her crew with intense delight. Her eyes blazed like bottle-green supernovas. "I want to tell you that, without a doubt, you are the finest crew I have ever served. I honor you." With that, Captain Darkstrider gave the Copernicans a long salute. Then, straightening into a military line, the crew returned the tribute. After a moment, the landing party relaxed and smiled. "What now, Captain Darkstrider?" asked Jane.

"Do we go back to base and load up?" asked Chris. "We accomplished what we wanted. And time is growing short." Francis held up his recorder. "I want to download this data into the ship's computers as soon as possible." Jason put his hand on his stomach and rubbed. "And I'm hungry!" Captain Darkstrider held her hand in mock surrender. "So many questions! Yes, I believe we can go now. I would have liked to examine the beacon more, but we lack time. So, mount up, and let's be on our way." At that moment, unexpectedly, the ambient red light in the chamber dimmed, and the engines above gave a surge of power. "What the hell was that all about?" demanded the captain. Nancy did not have long to wait. Over their coms came Leonidas's strident message, "First Officer to the landing party. Copernicus is under attack! The beacon just hit us with a pulse torpedo!"

First Officer Leonidas sat at his station on the Copernicus. Idly he watched from 100 kilometers in orbit over Clyde Tombaugh's base. Spiro regarded the white nitrogen plateau in Challenger Colles, where he had last seen the landing party. Then, to Leonidas's shock and amazement, the spires and battlements shattered, and a ball of energy burst from their midst. Transfixed with horror, he stared at the blob of green, super-heated energy as it sped toward him. Then, with a blast that rocked the ship, it hit the shields.

"Damage report Copernicus! What is your situation?" said Darkstrider in urgent tones. "I got the shields up with no time to spare. But our forward shield is down 40%. Over." replied Spiro. Then, again, the light in the cubicle dimmed, and the engines gave another intense discharge. "We've been fired on again! Here it comes!

A hit! The forward shield is at 25%. I don't think we can take another strike there, captain! Over," shouted the First Officer. "Take the ship out of orbit immediately, First Officer! Do not return until you receive my command! Do you understand? Over," instructed Nancy pressingly. "Understood. Copernicus is leaving orbit. Good luck landing party. Over," said Spiro sadly. The crew stood silently for a minute, waiting. Then, Captain Darkstrider let out a pent-up breath, "No more firings; the Copernicus must be out of range of the beacon. That simplifies matters; we are staying."

"I thought we were leaving!" protested Lieutenant Franke. "We could go now and make it back to base. But we could never return to the ship. That beacon would blast it out of space," said Nancy. "What do you suggest we do, captain?" asked Navigational Officer Tripper. "Engineers Book and Riley stay here and see if they can shut down the beacon's engine. After that, we three will investigate the rest of the complex," explained Darkstrider. "We have two days, and then we must leave." Assistant engineer Riley said plaintively, "What about supplies?" The captain pointed to his backpack. "We have enough emergency rations and water for a week." The younger members of the crew looked at one another. "What happens when the supplies run out?" asked the Chief Engineer Book. "We better be back on Copernicus before that happens," said Nancy grimly. "Since we'll be here for a while, I think we can discard our flight suits and wear our shipboard clothing. We can leave them here and our helmets for when we leave." The Copernicans quickly discarded their environmental suits and helmets and stacked them neatly in a corner.

Captain Darkstrider made for the portal. "Le's get started. Franke and Tripper follow me. Book and Riley, we will check in every hour. Good luck, everyone." Nancy and her two companions exited the lapis lazuli-colored gate and were gone. The Chief Engineer Book turned to his assistant Riley. "Ok, Jason, let's get to work."

In the corridor outside, the trio of Darkstrider, Tripper, and Franke took their bearings. To both sides, the red-lit passage curved out of sight. Ten meters wide and tall, composed of a glossy black, faintly glowing metal. "We'll proceed to the left," said Captain Darkstrider. "I'll take the point. Lieutenant Franke comes next, and Mr. Tripper can take up the rear." At a brisk pace, the trio started their journey. Finally, after two kilometers of unrelenting sameness, Jane said. "How long is this corridor, Captain Darkstrider?" Nancy replied, "Chief Book mentioned the complex was 5 kilometers tall and the same at its base. If we apply two pi r to get the circumference, we arrive at 15.7 k. A pleasant walk for us." Chris laughed, "We won't need to hit the treadmill when we get back to the Copernicus. We're getting our workout now." Franke replied darkly, "If we get back." On the outside corridor wall, an oval window appeared. The threesome placed themselves in front of the thick glass and looked out. A myriad world of luminescent creatures, large and small, presented itself to their view. They watched the tapestry of life unfold. Fish attacking, eating, and consuming in return. Spellbound, the space explorers were spectators to a perpetually dark, silent universe. A world that has been hiding away for over 4 billion years. At last, Captain Darkstrider said, "Recess is over; let's go, children."

Several hours later, the landing party had reached the midpoint of the great circle they were traversing. A recessed door appeared on their right hand, leading deeper into the core of the building. "Let's take a break before we attempt that door," said Darkstrider. Gratefully, the captain's two companions let themselves to the floor. After a moment, Nancy joined them. Jane glanced at the portal. "A molecular door?" Chris grinned. "That would be my guess." For a few minutes, the trio sat in silence. "You look pensive, Lieutenant Franke. Is something bothering you?" said the captain. "I was just thinking," replied Jane. "We are 10 kilometers from the engineers. 300 k from the surface of Pluto. Five billion clicks from the Earth. I feel alone. Like a flower dying in a desert."

Navigator Tripper had opened his backpack and taken out some food concentrates and a canister of water. The other two followed suit. The three ate and drank. "I know what you mean, Jane," said Chris. "We're about as isolated as humans can get from the rest of humans. The age of this complex is getting to us, I think. I felt the same thing when we were in the artifact on Charon. A billion years. The aliens were here a billion years ago. Built these structures and then left. It was so long ago our minds can't process the awful passage of time." Franke sipped some water."What do you think, captain? Why did the aliens come here in the first place? And where did they go?"

Nancy chewed thoughtfully. "I believe they set up this beacon for us to find. That is apparent. But I think they meant us to find something more." Jane knit her brow. "Something more? What else are we supposed to find?" Darkstrider smiled, "It's as Ishmael said, 'The sea, where each man, as in a mirror, finds himself.'" The younger woman turned that over in her mind. "We are to find ourselves? That's why we're here?" A silence fell on the lonely group. "It's as good an explanation as any," said Tripper, "I wonder how Book and Riley are doing?"

"Did you hear that, Francis? The captain and the other two found a door. They are exactly on the opposite side of the beacon to us," said assistant engineer Riley. "Yes, I heard Jason," replied the Chief Engineer Book. "They say they are going inside after a meal break. I could use one myself. We've been at this for three straight hours." So the two engineers attached their portable recorders to the alien consoles. "The trouble is that they based their numerical system on a 12-digit rather than a 10-digit method," said Jason. "Probably because they have twelve fingers and toes, and we only have ten," pointed out Francis. "Well, let's take a break." So the two men sat down against a wall and opened their backpacks.

Taking out food concentrates and fluids, they set to their repast. The two men studied the array of control boards that were flashing and humming with power. "Amazing any of this still works after a billion years," said Book. "The aliens sure built things to last." Riley squeezed a food tab into his mouth, "Yeah, not like the stuff we buy today. I bought a holodeck projector last year, and it broke down in six months." The two friends busied themselves with their meal for several minutes. "This floor is hard to sit on," said Jason. "I haven't seen a decent chair in either of the extraterrestrial habitats we've explored so far." Francis snorted. "Well, what do you expect? The creatures were 3 meters tall and very slender. Can you imagine what their seats must resemble? Those boxes we sat on in the colors room back on Charon weren't too bad."

"You know Francis," said assistant engineer Riley, "the aliens had a billion-year head start. This technology is only about one hundred years ahead of us." The chief engineer Book took a long drink of water. "I think you're right. Our recorders are not having any trouble downloading their data. Interpreting it is another matter." The duo thought silently. "I can't believe Franke powered on this array by pushing one button. I mean, what odds of that happening?" said Jason. "About a thousand to one against," replied Francis. "She got lucky. Jane could just as easily have overloaded the power plant for this beacon. I'm pretty sure there are using atomic power." Jason laughed, "Yeah, remember in the old movie Aliens? The nuclear reactor they were using blew up. At all costs, we avoid that." Chief Book studied the control panels, blinking in colors that his brain refused to register. "One way is to not press buttons at random. That is the path to disaster." Assistant engineer Riley chuckled. "That's for sure. I wonder when the beacon got power. Why did it shoot a pulse missile at Copernicus instead of a transmission? Poor Leonidas was sure shocked!" Francis pondered, "I think after a billion years, a sub-routine got corrupted. So instead of a message, it went into a defensive mood. If we can figure out where the problem occurred, we can hopefully repair it." Jason nodded. "Speaking about Spock, I wonder how he is feeling?"

"I have never been so frightened in my life," thought First Officer Leonidas. "One more hit on the forward screen, and I would have atoms." Spiro watched as the minor planet Pluto receded from him. He could see new holes in the nitrogen intrusion in Challenger Colles on maximum magnification. Shards of ice were still floating down from the violent passage of the pulse missile. Leonidas stopped Copernicus when it was two standard planetary diameters from the frozen world. "I'm out of range here," said Leonidas. "And I can still watch things." The First Officer studied his monitor. "H'm, shields have still not firmed up. I better go to engineering and see if the engines sustained any damage."

The corridors of the Copernicus echoed the footsteps of her first officer. "Who would think there would be an active weapon system on the planet after a billion years," said Spiro. "I hope the captain and the rest of the landing party are ok. They only have food and water for a week." Leonidas entered the engineer control room and sat down at a computer console. The Hydrogen-Ram engines throbbed powerfully behind the bulkheads at his back. "H'm," he thought. "The engine shields are firming up. In a few more hours and they will be back to normal. Then I can—what in the hell is that noise?"

The First Officer's attention drew to a small, sealed door at one side of the engine room. Getting up from his chair, Spiro walked over to the portal and listened intently. "There it is again. A rapping or tapping. Could the engines have sustained damage after all? Tap, tap, tap, tap, tap. Mr. Riley's ghostly knocking! No wonder he sounded frightened; this is spooky—tap tap, tap, tap, tap, tap, tap. Wait a minute!

That tapping is a morse code! No wonder the captain asked me if the engineers knew morse code! Could someone or something be back there and attempting no communicate with me? It doesn't sound at all credible, but there it is. I will rap a message back in morse. What is your name? Ok, let's see the response. DANGER. Danger. Am I in danger? Let's try again. Who is in danger? Right here we go. Danger. Danger. Radiation Do not enter. Oh, for heaven's sake. A computer warning program! Never a dull moment on this old ship!" Chuckling, the First Officer returned to his chair and resumed his studies.

Against the backdrop of the heavens, the ghostly Copernicus continued unhurriedly. But soon, it would have to return to its parent world or remain orphaned around its icy stepfather.

"Right, break time is over. Time to get going," said Captain Darkstrider. Getting to their feet, the advance party members assumed a stand in front of the oval hatch. Reaching out, Lieutenant Franke rapped firmly on its surface. "Melon." Instantly, the portal disappeared. Gingerly, the trio of space adventurers entered the room beyond. They found themselves in a large room filled with high 4-meter-long slabs. Small cubicles lay in front of each slab. In the center of the room was an elevated oval platform surrounded by a lower wall about 1.5 meters high. Between the wall and the venue, there was a meter gap. The crew wandered about, examining the strange furnishings.

"You know what?" said Tripper. This room is a dormitory for the aliens who live here. Nancy looked around. "I think you are correct, Mr. Tripper." Jane had gone over to a cubicle and examined it. The booths strongly resembled the ones they had discovered in the artifact back on Charon. Taking out her sidearm, she aimed a blast at the oval knob on its front. A cherry blossom bloomed and faded. Franke took hold of the bump and pulled. "Empty," said the communications officer. Chris was standing by the platform in the middle of the room. "I think this was their communal dining table. And this low wall is where they sat." Nancy pointed at the slabs that lined the walls. "And those were their beds where they slept. Look like mortuary slabs, don't they?" Jane giggled nervously, "That's a cheerful thought,

Captain." Navigational Officer Tripper gazed around the room, looking for something. "It's interesting that we haven't found a 'fresher. How did the Centuarians relieve themselves, do you think?" Captain Darkstrider shrugged. "They must have had some method. Luckily, our flight suits have built systems to eliminate our bodily wastes. I'd hate to find a bathroom in this billion-year-old pile."

The three crew members addressed their attention to an oval recess on the far side of the room. "Let's go, people," ordered Captain Darkstrider. The triad paced boldly forward. Coming to a halt, Tripper rapped on its surface. Another gap beckoned the triumvirate. Stepping bodily onward through the portal, Darkstrider, Franke, and Tripper confronted a pulsing, blue energy globe that hung in the center of the next room. "A holographic projection!" exclaimed Jane. "Just like the one on Charon!" Chris glanced over at the Darkstrider. "Do we want to risk it, captain?" Nancy turned a dazzling smile on them and stunned them with blazing green eyes. "Let's." The troika stepped forward and vanished. The players set the stage. Let the play unfold.

Alpha Centauri b

Chapter 10

The three Terrans stood in the middle of a vast plain. In the near distance, the tall purple spires of a city scraped the sky. Twin suns, one orange, one yellow, were setting. The red sun was climbing over their heads. A light wind moaned around the adventurers and chilled their faces. "Toto," said Jane. "I don't think we're in Kansas anymore." Chris laughed, "Jane, do you ever tire of saying that?"

The advance party drank in the view and feasted with their eyes on the glorious sunsets. "Magnificent," said Captain Darkstrider. "Just like that holotype of the Star Wars movie you showed me back on Copernicus." Lieutenant Franke pointed, "That's new. Look at that strange city! Never have I seen anything so exotic!" Her two companions followed her direction. "Yes. That's extraterrestrial civilization at its finest," said Navigation Officer Tripper. "I strongly believe that you were right, people. This scenario is exactly the depiction of Alpha Centauri b," said Nancy. The Earthers instinctively drew closer to one another for mutual support. "What now, Captain Darkstrider?" asked the Communication Officer. "Right," said the captain, "Lieutenant Franke, take out your homing signal and place it here by the outline of the portal. After that, we walk to the city. It's about 10 kilometers away. A pleasant stroll."

One after the other, the Copernicans marched towards later-day Xanadu. The land here was not wholly barren but dotted with purple-red sagebrush vegetation. The plain undulated as they walked. Soft, purple moss carpeted the hills and cushioned their steps. No life stirred their senses. "There were insects and those purple cows in the other virtual reality on Charon. Here there is nothing," complained Franke. "Don't be so quick, Jane," replied Chris. "Look up into the sky." The three spacers peered upwards. Far above them, vast red creatures wheeled and danced. They sported massive wings and tails. Occasionally, one would lose a jet of flames. "I do not believe it," said Nancy flatly. "Dragons? Seriously?"

Shaking her head, the captain motioned the other two to continue their trek. Finally, after a few hours, the strange metropolis loomed before them. After mounting a low hill, the alien city spread itself beneath. The municipality looked like being made of spun glass. Tall, purple, spindly towers reached two kilometers into the sky. Narrow, high-flung bridges connected the skyscrapers. A constant stream of airborne craft streamed at different levels. Lower cylindrical, rectangular, and cubic structures filled the gaps between their tall neighbors.

Unlike the cities of the earth or the Martian colonies, they could hear very little noise. Beyond the town was a rampart of high, towering red cliffs appearing on the edge of their vision.

"It looks like something out of a dream," said Lieutenant Franke. "I never thought something like this could exist." Navigational Officer Tripper chuckled, "Yeah, it's something you might read in a science fiction novel. Or see it in a movie. Is this the alien home world a billion years ago?" Nancy replied, "The original supposition was that this virtual reality would provide the Centaurans with recreation. By providing them the chance to return home while they were on Pluto. The only evidence we have that this is accurate is that there are three suns. Yellow, red, and orange. This arrangement is what we know about the Alpha Centauri trinary system."

"What's our next course of action?" asked Tripper. "Do we attempt to enter the city?" Nancy pursed her sensual lips. "That might be difficult. I don't see any roads in and any doors at ground level. How would we enter the buildings? But, of course, that's assuming we want to do that." Looking down, the captain pointed to the bottom of the hill. "We might try those." Beneath their feet was a low field containing about twenty yellow cylindrical crafts. As they watched, one rose 100 meters into the air and flew toward the city. Soon the shuttle merged into the maze of traffic. "Aerial taxis!" laughed Chris. "It's the only way to travel when you are abroad." Nancy replied, "Yes, I would say being 40 trillion kilometers from home would qualify as being abroad." The two women prepared to leave when they noticed Tripper gazing at the city. "Proxima Centauri spaceport: You won't find a more wretched hive of scum and villainy. We must be cautious," said the Navigational Officer. Jane tittered, "I bet you have been waiting your whole life to say that, Tripper." The Copernicans walked down the hill and entered the field of aerial vehicles. No one was attending the craft.

Close up; the taxis were 2.5 meters tall and 6 meters long. Carefully, Tripper grasped the oval knob and opened the equally oval door to the vehicle. "There aren't any controls or steering wheels in here. I think they are automatic. Once you get in, the taxi will take you to a pre-set destination. Look at those signs by each craft." Chris gestured to a board covered in a complex of squiggles in front of each alien shuttle. Lieutenant Franke studied the one in front of their vehicle carefully. "Don't tell me you can read what it says, lieutenant?" asked Nancy in amusement. "No, I can't," laughed Jane. "Pity, I would have liked to go to a mall to shop for shoes." Tripper muttered, "It's always about the shoes." The two women turned towards Chris. "What did you say, Mr. Tripper?" asked the captain. "Nothing Captain Darkstrider," replied the Navigational Officer. "I just suggested we get in and continue our journey." The three explorers opened the doors and climbed in. The shorter Earth people had difficulty getting up on the 1.5meter tall seats. After a few moments, their taxi rose to a set height and flew towards the city.

"I think I'm making some progress, Francis," said Jason. "I'm adapting my reader to read a 12 numerical system rather than the standard 10." His companion was silent at first. Then, finally, the Chief Engineer Book spoke, where he had his head in an open panel. "You're doing better than me, my friend," Francis replied. "I can't make any sense of these electronics, if these are even electronics." Jason eased his buttocks on the rigid floor plates. "I wish there were chairs in this place. We'll have to sleep on this hard metal tonight, you know." The chief laughed, "Would you like me to call up room service Jason?" His friend responded eagerly, "Would you do that, please, Francis? I'd appreciate it. And ask for a bottle of champagne while you're at it." The two men laughed. Laughter echoed through the room into the hallway, down corridors that had not heard a sound in a billion years. An expectation seemed to stir. The beacon, which had stood guard for eternity, did not take kindly to intruders. Even things made of metal can possess teeth.

From one planetary diameter in space, First Officer Leonidas viewed Challenger Colles. "What trigger point causes the beacon to fire an energy torpedo?" he thought. Spiro adjusted the bridge screen for maximum magnification. The white plateau in the collection of blue hills sprang into eyeshot. "Already that hole I saw earlier has gone," Leonidas thought. "The stresses of the ice on either side filled it up. If I didn't know that the beacon had punched a crater there, I wouldn't be able to tell." Restlessly, he got out of his chair and paced the bridge, unconsciously mimicking Captain Darkstrider. With his hands clasped behind him, the First Officer thought furiously. "I must think of a way to rescue them. I feel so helpless. Suppose it wasn't a standing order for one officer to be on the ship at all times? I'm missing so much stuck up here. A billion old alien technology, and I'm not part of it? This situation is annoying!" Stopping, Spiro fixed his attention on the planet below. "For god's sake, what is happening to Nancy?"

"Captain, I've been thinking," said Navigational Officer Tripper. "That's good, Lieutenant," replied Darkstrider. "I always encourage my officers to think. I find it can come in useful." Chris laughed dutifully, "Right. I was wondering. If we left and returned to base, couldn't we fly the shuttles out of range of the beacon?" In their alien taxi, the advance party flew toward the fast-approaching city. "I considered that, Mr. Tripper. We don't know the extent of the firing mechanism of this structure. At the very least, it would knock the shuttles out of the sky." Lieutenant Franke took up the discourse. "Couldn't Mr. Leonidas take a position with Copernicus out of the beacons' reach? And then we fly very low in the shuttles until it's safe to leave the planet?" Nancy shook her head. "Too risky. We must do all we can here before considering other courses of action. Haven made that comment; we will have to do as you suggested soon."

The shuttle, carrying the three members of the advance party, entered the city limits of the metropolis. Gracefully, the vehicle rose and eased itself into a traffic stream. The Terrans could barely get their eyes over the windowsills. With trepidation, they noted Proxima Centaurans in a variety of nearby craft. "Aliens again!" exclaimed Jane. "Yes," agreed Chris. "And these don't look like cowboys." Finally, at a kilometer's height, the shuttle passed the slender purple cathedrals they had noted before. The metropolis confronted the trio with a bewildering cacophony of life. "I scarcely know where to look," said Franke. "There is so much to see!" Tripper nodded, "Yeah, we better be careful we don't experience culture shock." The

Copernican marveled at several garish signages on passing landing stages. Sweeping by their eyes was an assortment of shops, restaurants, offices, and other buildings of unguessable usage.

The three crew members' craft settled down on a high platform. Then, the doors of the shuttle popped open, inviting egress. Uncertainly, Darkstrider, Franke, and Tripper exited their vehicle and stood on the platform's surface. All around, aliens moved about their business. The creatures were tall, averaging 3 meters in height, though many were shorter than this. One stalwart individual topped off at almost 4 meters in height. Most had silvery tunics covered in enigmatic symbols, but some wore more colorful garb. They wore their green locks in a variety of styles. Many Centaurans were wearing their hair in dreadlocks but swirled, helix, and bald was present. To their ears, the Terrans heard the harsh, sibilant language of the aliens— the sound maggots make when they fall from the belly of a corpse hanging from a rafter onto the floor.

"The creatures are not taking notice of us," said Lieutenant Franke nervously. "It's like they can't even see us. On Charon, the aliens certainly could." Captain Darkstrider examined the tall beings passing on each side. "Perhaps this is a noninteractive program. They designed the virtual reality room scenario you were in previously for participation. But I'm only guessing, of course." More relaxed now, the advance party strolled along the promenade. Nancy and Jane stopped in front of a storefront and examined footwear. The designer shoes were half a meter long and six-toed. Some colors were outside the human spectrum, but the women could see them oddly enough. "It's always about the shoes," muttered Chris. "What do you keep mumbling about, Tripper?" asked Franke crossly. "Nothing, my love," answered Chris. "Why don't we go inside, and you can try on a pair?" Jane slapped Tripper lightly on the shoulder, "Oh shut up."

The Terrans continued on their way. They gazed at the tall purple spires reaching another kilometer overhead. The red Proxima sun had reached its zenith and bathed the surroundings in a scarlet cloak. The wind was stiffer here, filling the trio's lungs with cold, highly oxygenated air. Chris walked to the edge of the walkway and looked down. The Navigation Officer's vision could not pierce the bottom's shadows a kilometer below him. Carefully, he edged back from the railless parapet. For an hour, the three Copernicans meandered among the many sights and delights of the promenade. "Captain Darkstrider," said Communication Officer Franke. "Aren't you concerned about the time we're spending here? As you pointed out, we have a few days before the window closes. After that, the portal back into our reality might also close." Nancy paused from a storefront of magical objet d'art she was examining. She turned to face the younger woman. "No, I am not Lieutenant Franke. The clock may not move back on the beacon. Or if the chronology is passing, it is dying slowly." Chris protested, "But back in the reality projection room in the artifact on Charon, time was moving as we lived it. In real-time." The captain smiled. "That is true. The clock was moving linearly. But this is a noninteractive play we are experiencing. The rules don't apply here."

Jane nodded and peered at a flying bridge spanning the awful chasm between the tall towers. "Let's cross over here. There might be some interesting shops on the other side." Chris joked. "More shoes?" Then, in sudden anger, Franke turned to her lover, "If you make one more crack about shoes, I'll..." The captain spread her arms, separating the two crew members. "Children, children. This setting is not a place for a lover's spat. Behave like the officers you are." A tall alien collided with Nancy's arm, spilling her to the ground. He walked on unconcernedly. "Oh, for the love of god!" spat Darkstrider. Chris and Jane helped Nancy to her feet. "Are you ok, captain?" asked Tripper. "I'm fine. Let's cross the bridge," said Darkstrider. Tripper looked across at the meter-wide, railless span and shuddered. "It has no handrails!" Franke laughed, "Don't worry, handsome, I'll lead the way!" Then, the three Terrans advanced over the terrible depths in a single file.

"The captain hasn't signed in for a while," commented assistant engineer Riley. "It's only been just over an hour," replied the Chief Engineer Book. "I'm sure they are all right." Jason paused over the panel readout he was studying. "What if they aren't all right, Francis? What then?" Book looked at his companion. "Then we go searching for them." Around the room, the panel covers were open, exposing their circuitry. "You know Francis; I took a walk down the right-hand corridor a while ago. That's opposite to the one the captain, Franke, and Tripper took," said Riley. "Yes, I know Jason," replied his friend. "Did you find something interesting?" The younger man put down his reader and glanced at his companion. "Yes, I found an elevator about 100 meters down the corridor." The chief engineer looked up in interest. "Really? Well, it makes sense. The aliens must have some way of accessing the upper floors." Jason got to his feet and walked restlessly to the chamber door. "I'm tired of being cooped up here all the time and missing out on all the action. When the captain returns, I want to ask her for one of us to go along on the next mission." Book did not look up from his recorder. "It's not an unreasonable request, Jason. Both Franke and Tripper have computer training. I think the captain would go along with your wishes."

The younger man nodded. "Yeah, she's been very reasonable so far. But I wonder what she and the others are doing. The last thing we heard, they had found a door and were going in. It's this massive pile of alien metal that is causing the problems. It makes transmitting so uncertain." Francis stretched his cramped arms and yawned. "Jason, you have a good idea. After you go, I'll ask the captain for a turn at exploring." Book got to his feet and joined his boon companion at the portal. He put an arm over his friend's shoulders. "Do you feel it too? The danger? As if this complex was a beast and is waiting to devour us?" Riley put his arm around Francis' waist. "Yes, I do. I may not have Jane or the captain's feminine instincts, but I feel the anger. It's all around us. It's as if, after a billion years, the beacon has developed a personality. And humans aren't welcome." Book nodded, "But not on this level; the peril is higher up, on the upper floors of this pyramid." Surprised, the younger man looked at his partner. "Knowing that you still want to go with the advance party? Into that jeopardy?" Francis laughed and chucked his friend under the chin. "It was your idea first. So you want to go too?" Riley smiled. "Oh yeah, that's right. I want to go."

"I wonder if I used the ship's escape pod, whether I could reach the landing party," mused First Officer Leonidas. "I know where the elevator is and how to get inside. Down the 300 kilometers to the bottom of the ocean. Then it's smooth sailing to join the crew at the beacon." The smile on Spiro's face faded. "Damn! I forgot the beacon again. Before I got near the Challenger Colles, it would blast the pod out of the sky. Well, it's still not a bad idea if they can just shut down that bloody machine. Or reprogram it; Book and Riley are fine engineers. Those two can do the job if anyone in the fleet can." The First Officer increased the magnification of the main bridge screen until the small hummock filled it. Then, gradually, Leonidas pulled the view back. "An open spot is half a kilometer from the hummock. I could land the pod there with no trouble. At least, I think I can. Never tried it before. Then it's a short hike to the elevator. All right, it's risky, I know."

The First Officer sprang out of his chair and rapidly left the bridge. Then, with quick steps, he hurried down the corridor. Reaching the end, he entered an elevator that took him to the ship's lowest level. Leonidas found himself in front of a small hatch at the end of a dimly lit curving passage. Above the sill was a sign reading, 'Escape pod: For emergency use only.' Spiro hit the button by the hatch, and it hissed open. A waft of stale air blew into his face. Entering the confined space, the First Officer sat in the only chair and strapped himself into it. Then, with acute attention, he studied the controls and switches. He moved the wheel around and experimentally pumped the floor pads with his feet. Then, satisfied, he smiled, "Piece of cake, as Mr. Tripper is wont to say." Unstrapping, Leonidas left the pod and pushed the button, sealing the entry. As he walked away, a thought occurred to the First Officer. He turned and regarded the pod's entrance and grinned. "I can fly that thing better than R-2 D-2 did."

"I wouldn't say I like this," said Navigation Officer Tripper through gritted teeth. The three Copernicans were midway along one of the alien cities' high-flung bridges. Aliens passed them continuously, ignoring them. Leading the way was Captain Nancy Darkstrider. Behind her was Tripper, with Communication Officer Franke bringing up the rear. "Just don't look down, my big, healthy boy," laughed Jane. "You've always known about my fear of heights," protested Chris. "Is that why you joined the Space Corp, Mr. Tripper?" asked Nancy mischievously. "Because you were afraid of heights?"

At last, the stalwart three reached the far end of the bridge, to Chris's profound relief. They continued along this new promenade. It consisted mainly of eating and drinking establishments. Smells came out of the restaurants that made them shudder and gag. At the nearest eatery, an alien server placed what looked like plates of live maggots in front of two patrons. With disgust, Nancy moved away and hurried to join her companions. For a time, the spacers walked along the high street, enjoying the sights and sounds of the alien city.

Eventually, Chris stopped in front of a run-down cantina. Discordant music floated out from the depths of the pub. "Let's go in there." Captain Darkstrider frowned. "Why do you want us to enter this place, Mr. Tripper?" The ship's navigator regarded his captain with a neutral expression, "I could use a drink." Nancy glanced at her Communication Officer, who shrugged. Then, with a resigned air, Darkstrider said, "Very well. Let's go in."

The trio went down a short ramp and found themselves in a bright antechamber with a darkened main room. Tripper, Franke, and Darkstrider stood at the bottom of the ramp and allowed their eyes to adjust to the low light. The adventurers were astonished to see the diversity of creatures inhabiting the establishment. Expecting to see just Centaurans, they noticed monsters with fur, fangs, and claws. Some looked like insects, and others looked like they belonged in the ocean. All sat at tables conversing in apparent harmony. Chris, Nancy, and Jane took an empty table and peered around. A group of simian beings played some genuinely awful music at a raised dais. "There is a multitude of intelligent species on this planet," remarked Captain Darkstrider. "My god," said Franke in a low voice. "Would you look at that thing?" Her two companions looked in the direction Jane was pointing and glanced away. "I'd just as well not," replied Tripper pointedly.

A tall insect carrying a tray stopped at their table and deposited three drinks with its pincers before hurrying off. "I wouldn't drink that if I were you, Mr. Tripper," said Nancy. Chris picked up his drink and gulped it down. "Too late." When the navigation officer failed to die, the women guardedly sipped at their drinks. Then, relaxing, Tripper looked around the darkened cantina with a puzzled look on his face. Monsters held drinking receptacles in claws, hands, pincers, and tentacles. None of the bipeds, quadrupeds, or multi-legged beings looked human. However, the simian band came closest. Chris's face cleared. "I get it! This bar reminds me of the cantina scene in Star Wars." Jane laughed. "If you see Han Solo and Chewbacca around, ask them if we can book their freighter." Tripper smirked, "The Millennium Falcon made the Kessel run in less than 12 parsecs." Nancy looked puzzled. "A parsec is a unit of distance, not time." Tripper and Franke both laughed. "Always wondered about that, captain," said Jane.

The Navigation Officer appropriated another drink from the tray of a passing server. "This is a fascinating city. I wished we had time to explore it more fully," said Tripper. "It seems so real," commented Communication Officer Franke. "I keep forgetting we're still in the virtual reality room back in the beacon." Captain Darkstrider sipped her drink. "If we are, that is. The Centauran technology is so advanced that I'm preparing to believe anything. But I'm being silly. We haven't traveled a billion years back and forty trillion kilometers from where we last were."

The simian band played again after a break. The group resembled a gang of Homo Habilis hominids but were much hairier. "Does that band only know one song?" asked Chris in irritation. "They've played it repeatedly five times!" A creature about the size of a man stopped by their table. It directed its attention to Jane. A biped, but with a nightmarish head. It had massive, golden multifaceted eyes on a vivid red face. An insect's antennae grew from its forehead. A large muzzle contained the nostrils and a fang-filled mouth. The creature spoke to Franke in a wheedling tone. When she did not respond, it put a plastic chit on the table in front of her. Then, after more of its incomprehensible language, it added a further chit. The communication officer shrugged, and the monster reluctantly moved away. Jane looked at her two companions, who were studying her in surprise. "I think the thing was trying to pick me up." The tall insect server swept by their table and scooped up the chits. "I guess I was wrong about one thing," said Nancy. "This program has some interaction in it." Tripper laughed, "Yeah, you're probably correct, captain. That critter wanted some personal interaction with Jane." Franke playfully slapped her lover. "Oh, hush."

Several more of the horrors had attempted to pick up Lieutenant Franke an hour later, and a couple had had a go at the captain. A pile of monetary plastic chits had grown in front of the two women. "I kind of fancied that last scaley one," said Jane. "Captain Darkstrider, I've been thinking," said Tripper. "What if we return to the base and set one shuttle on an automatic course to set down on Sputnik Planitia one hundred kilometers away? If the beacon does not shoot that craft out of the sky, we five pile into the second shuttle. Then we land, pick up the first shuttle, and return to Copernicus. Piece of cake!" Nancy mulled the suggestion. "I think your suggestion is brilliant, Lieutenant. Let's stay in the beacon until the last possible moment attempting repairs. Then, if we can't fix it, we will proceed with your plan. We don't have many options, do we?" The two younger people shook their heads. "Right," said Nancy. "I believe it's my round."

The cycle of life went on in the midnight ocean surrounding the beacon. Ten thousand types of fishy residents were born, mated, and died. All in perpetual darkness, other than the bioluminescence they provided themselves. On Pluto's oceanic bottom, unseen creatures crawled and burrowed into the organic-rich tholin seabed. Larger ones preyed on small fish in a complex food chain. Teeth bit, jaws gaped open and snapped. Tentacles gripped and strangled. It was a nature red in tooth and claw in this life and death arena. At the top of the food chain were the super predators. The colossal squid, two hundred meters long with a forest of tentacles armed with toothed suckers and a wicked beak. The megalodon shark, at two hundred and fifty meters and with rows of razor-sharp teeth and an insatiable appetite. And occupying the very apex of the food web was the nether horror known as The Thing. A full kilometer long and scarred in a hundred battles. Fearing little, it swam through its kingdom, knowing nothing about the world beyond the ocean's icy ceiling.

For a billion years, the five-kilometer-tall tower known simply as the beacon had kept its vigil on the bottom of Pluto's ocean. On its five-kilometer-wide base, it stood. Rising buttress upon buttress: bulwark upon bulwark: bastion upon bastion, the dark tower of obdurate metal from Proxima Centauri. At its muzzle was the transmitter twinned with a gun aperture of deadly force. Within this vast pile, it held secrets for the unwary. Not easily would it give them up, and the price would be very high.

The deep space scout ship Copernicus continued its unhurried swim around Pluto's silent, frozen world; the inaccessible sun cast sparkles along the glossy bulk of its snow-white sides. Whirling constellations poked holes in the smooth velour of the heavens; the universe cast its uncaring eye on the melodrama in six humans' lives.

"I'm repeating it, Francis; it's been too long now," said assistant engineer Riley. "Ok, we have not heard from the captain or the others in three hours," replied the Chief Engineer Book. "What do you suggest we do?" Jason looked up from his recorder. "What do we do? We go after them, of course!!" Francis glanced at his companion, "The captain said to remain here until the advance party returned. If we ignore that, we would abandon our posts." The two men worked in silence for a while. Eventually, Chief Book threw down his spanner. "Oh, all right! We'll go look for them!" Jason threw up his arms. "My hero!"

Ten minutes later, the two men were ready after gathering their supplies in backpacks and holstering their sidearms. They entered the hallway and proceeded to their right. The dimly lit corridor curved endlessly in front of them. Finally, one hundred meters on, they came to a recessed door. "This is the door I spoke about yesterday to you, Francis," said Riley. "I think it leads to an elevator." Chief Book examined the portal. "And you didn't check it? Let's do that now." Francis stepped in front of the entryway and rapped on its surface, saying, "Melon." Instantly, an oval door appeared. The two friends stepped inside and looked around.

"Yes, there is the six-fingered hand on the wall and another below it," said the Chief Engineer Book. "One for going up, the other for coming down. I've seen enough. Let's get out and be on our way." Returning to the passageway, the men continued their journey. A foreboding descended on the two engineers. Shadows seemed to gather in corners where there were no corners; the ambient red light was strange to their eyes. "Do you think we should turn on our torches, Francis?" asked Jason. "No, I don't want to make ourselves conspicuous," replied Book. Then, an oval window appeared on the outcurve wall to their right. Francis and Jason eagerly stopped and peered out. Two enormous eyes were peering back at them.

"Ok," said Captain Nancy Darkstrider, "it's time we left this fine establishment. Gather the chits; we may need them, but leave a tip for the server." Communication Officer Franke and Navigator Officer Tripper scooped the plastic chits into their pockets. There was an audible groan from the patrons as the three Terrans left the cantina. The Copernicans came out onto the promenade into the reddish light of the sun with blinking eyes. "Where to now, captain?" asked Jane. Nancy examined the storefronts ahead of them and pointed at one. "Let's try that one. It looks like an art gallery." Dodging the tall Centaurans, who continued to take no notice of them, the three entered the oval door of the gallery. The alien art consisted mainly of holographic images that hovered in mid-air. "I presume you buy these projectors and take them home," Chris said. "Then you turn them on, and presto, you have art." Nancy examined sculptures of unknown animals from strange translucent materials. She placed her hand on a giant flying creature that tried to bite her. Then, hurriedly, she took her appendage away.

Tripper and Franke were studying oval pictograms on the walls. Sometimes, the sentient beings in the holo pictures looked back at them and made crude gestures. "Just like the pictures in the Harry Potter movies," said Franke. "Hey! Stop that. Don't be rude!" Tripper grinned. "Well, I don't know art, but I know what I like. And I don't like this." Fascinated, the trio went from exhibit to exhibit, admiring even if they could not comprehend. Solitary Centaurans stalked around them, wearing what looked like beards and berets. "I just realized," laughed Jane, "we are in a virtual reality looking at holographic images. We're not there, and the things we look at aren't there either." Chris looked at her and smiled, "I think you just defined life, Jane." Franke swatted her companion lightly across the cheek, "Oh, don't go all philosophers on me, lover."

Out onto the esplanade again, the trio entered a restaurant. They seated themselves at a booth and looked curiously at a bank of buttons on the tabletop. Captain Darkstrider pushed one, and a holographic image of a purple-red steak appeared. Quickly Franke and Tripper bent to their controls, and soon a host of unidentifiable food items were hovering over them. Soon afterward, a couple of tall, insect-like servers, like the one in the cantina, came over with the food they had ordered. Nancy looked up and spoke to her two companions, "I wouldn't eat that stuff if I were you." Then, with their mouths full, the duo answered, "Too late!"

Shrugging her delicate shoulders, Darkstrider began her meal. First, however, she set aside the bowl of wriggling maggot-like creatures. Next, one insect returned with a giant pitcher of blue liquid and set it down with three glasses. "That stuff looks like the blue milk that Aunt Beru served at the Star Wars homestead," Chris said. Tripper poured himself a glass and drank. "Tastes like it too. No wonder Luke Skywalker was eager to leave the Tantooine."

"This is a unique opportunity here," said Captain Darkstrider. "We were living the life of a typical Proxima Centauran a billion years ago. When we return to Titan Station, we can provide a full report on an alien civilization. So not only are we the first to discover an extraterritorial culture, but we also have realms of information about it." Jane pursed her sensual lips. "Is that information valuable, captain? Wouldn't it be more useful to know about the present-day culture of Proxima Centauri b?" Chris drank off the rest of his blue milk. "I doubt the Centaurans are still there, Jane. Civilizations don't survive a billion years. But some other society may be there now."

Nancy looked about herself. "That's correct, Mr. Tripper. But unfortunately, according to current theory, intelligent species don't last more than a few thousand years. So sadly, all we are witnessing here has turned to dust long ago." The Copernicans contemplated this thought for a time. Then the navigational officer held up the blue milk pitcher. "Anyone for more blue milk? No? Last chance? Good, more for me then."

"This place reminds me of the Sunset Restaurant in Malibu, California," said Darkstrider. "Were you born in Los Angeles, captain?" asked Jane. "I moved around a lot when I was young, but I am a California woman," replied the captain. "I wish they could all be California girls," quoted Tripper. Nancy smiled, "The Beach Boys. They were trendy in my great-great-great grandmother's time." Franke studied the clientele of the eatery. "It's odd that all we see are the insect servers and the Centaurans. We saw at least a dozen different species in the cantina." The captain contemplated a wriggling thing impaled on her fork. "I've been thinking about that. I wonder if what we expect to see is influencing this holographic program. You and Mr. Tripper expected to see creatures out of Star Wars. So your mind supplied the reality of your thoughts." The navigational officer put down his glass of blue milk. "You mean those sentient beings we saw are not native to this planet? That our minds conjured them up?" Darkstrider nibbled at the squirming insectoid. "Who can say? I might be wrong about that. Everything is up for conjecture. If you like, try to use your thoughts to bring people you know into this tableau."

The three spacers fell to their meal. Nancy found even the larvae had a taste that reminded her of chicken. But then she recollected to herself everything tastes like chicken. "Except for chicken," she thought. "Isn't that odd?" Mentally shrugging the thought away, the captain harpooned a crab-like creature walking off her plate. "The trouble with this place," said Darkstrider. "is half your meal is trying to escape." Jane stared at the baby octopus entwining its tentacles around her wrist. "I know what you mean, Captain Darkstrider." Tripper pulled at a scorpion-like arachnid attached to his nose and refused to let go. "I agree. Ow! Leggo, my Eggo!"

In front of the window, the Chief Engineer Book and assistant engineer Riley stared helplessly into the enormous eyes of the sea monster. The size of a beach ball, a dead-white sclera surrounded black pupils. Unwinking, the demon held the two engineers in its hypnotizing gaze. "What the hell is it, Francis?" asked Jason. "I don't know, Jason. But I'm glad it is on the other side of this window," replied Francis. An enormous tentacular club appeared at the edge of the window. Deliberately, the creature placed its appendage on the surface of the viewing port. The duo could see two rows of suckers the size of dinner plates attached to the club's underside. Gnashing teeth filled the suckers.

"You know what? I think this is a colossal squid, like the ones back on earth," said the Chief Book. But much more significant, maybe ten times as large." Riley attempted to swallow a lump in his throat. "Maybe because Pluto's ocean is nine times deeper than the Pacific, the creatures in it grow much bigger." The Chief Engineer's face grew hard. "I'm tired of being scared on this trip. Hey, pal! Back off! We're not afraid of a piece of sushi like you!!" It seemed as if the behemoth heard the angry human. Slowly, one eye closed, and then suddenly, it was gone. "Did you see that?" said Francis in shock. "It winked at me!" Jason laughed, "Well, you are cute!"

The Copernicans resumed their journey. "I can't get used to how these creatures can turn their lights on and off at will," said the Chief Engineer Book. "You never know if the monsters are still there or not." Assistant engineer Riley carefully scanned the hallway ahead. "As long as there aren't any in this passage or rooms we go into." For several kilometers, the two trod down the floor of the endless corridor. Only the sound of their shipboard shoes broke the absolute silence of the ancient passageway. The awfulness of extreme antiquity hung heavily in the air and oppressed the men. Several more windows passed. After their previous experience, the engineers continued and did not peer out. But that did not stop invisible monstrosities from spying on the two humans. Unseen entities wondered at the Terran's presence and carefully noted their progress.

"There's another door," Jason pointed to a recessed oval on the curved wall. The duo had come six kilometers and were growing tired. "So it is," replied Francis. Shall we knock and see if anyone is home?" Jason grimaced. "I wish you would not joke about things like that, Francis. If there is anything alive in this vast mausoleum, we wouldn't want to meet it." Chief Book grinned, "I hear you. It's just my way of coping with the stress. I'm scared too."

The Chief Engineer knocked on the door, saying, "Melon." The two spacers stepped through the oval entrance. A large room unfolded itself before their eyes. Several translucent elliptical columns stretched from floor to ceiling. A kaleidoscope of colors, some beyond the human spectrum, whirled and danced inside the pillars. "These columns are like the cube we found in the artifact back on Charon," said Riley. "I wonder what they are?" Chief Engineer Book stood mesmerized by the brilliant display. Quickly lowering his eyes, Francis brought out his recorder. "I think they have something to do with power, a power source. It is strange we can see those colors. They register on my recorder as outside visible sight." Assistant engineer Riley studied his own device's readings. "Do you think this place is an auxiliary power station?" The chief wandered around the room, poking in the corners. "Here's a control panel, the only one in the place. Do you want to rip this thing apart?" Jason grinned, "Why not?"

First Officer Leonidas sat in Copernicus's darkened lounge, nursing a glass of ouzo. Waves of loneliness descended on the middle-aged officer. "This is good," Spiro thought. "Drinking alone. I should run on the treadmill rather than destroy my liver." Leonidas took another sip of his drink. "Make the most of this opportunity, Spiro. You're the First Officer on a good ship, and that's something that will not happen again after this trip. Subsequent retirement, the taste of dust, then nothingness." The First Officer gazed out the window at the panorama of the galaxy. Three of Pluto's moons tumbled by in his sight. Chaste Charon eased its grey bulk onto one edge of the screen. A spill of cream was the Milky Way. A tiny blue dot caught Spiro's eye. He raised his glass. "Here's to you, lads."

Captain Darkstrider sucked the last morsel of flesh from the carapace of a giant beetle. She placed the shell in a heap in her bowl. "These insects taste better than snails." Nancy set her soylent green eyes on her two crewmates. "If you finished your feast, let's be on our way. Leave a generous tip for the arachnid. The larvae were delicious. I hope they weren't some of his extra children."

Out again onto the boardwalk went the space adventurers. Captain Darkstrider noted the reddish sun had passed its zenith and was descending to the far horizon. Crowds of Centaurans were still passing the Copernicans. There was a distinct chill in the air. "Well," said Nancy. "Where should we go next? We have time for another couple of spots; then, we must leave." Franke pointed at a nearby store. "How about that clothing boutique?" Tripper groaned, "You want to buy a dress now, Jane? You realize none of this is real?" His lover confronted Chris with a defiant look on her face. "I still want to go in, and you can buy something for me." The navigational officer threw up his hands in mock surrender. "Sure, why not? The females average almost three meters in height. But I'm sure you can find something that will fit. Females always do."

The trio entered the store where Centauran females browsed, attended by their bored mates. Tall arachnoids hovered nearby. "I get it," said Tripper, "the workers in this world are all insects." Nancy nodded in agreement. "I think you're right. Either a domesticated species or another intelligent race." Lieutenant Franke was examining a silky gown that was much taller than her. The alien color of the garment was one humanity had never encountered before. Her eyes hurt to look at it. Jane turned to Chris. "I'm going to try it on." Tripper protested, "It's 2.5 meters long!" Nancy laughed, "Oh, let her try it on, Mr. Tripper. How often do you get to shop 40 trillion kilometers away from home?" A few minutes later, the communication officer exited a dressing room wearing the dress. She had great swathes of fabric gathered around her waist. Jane was radiant. Captain Darkstrider addressed a hovering 3-meter-tall arthropod. "Wrap it up, my good—insect. And the gentleman is paying."

Ten minutes later found the intrepid cosmos travelers tripping the boards. Navigation Officer Tripper was carrying an enormous shopping bag. Nancy considered her surroundings. "There," she said. "on that elevated platform. I believe it's a zoo." Lieutenant Franke laughed, "And we must cross a high bridge to get to it!" Chris groaned, "Oh my god!"

"In my wildest imagination or deliriums, I never would have guessed creatures like this existed," said Nancy Darkstrider a short time later. "It is something out of a nightmare," agreed Lieutenant Franke. "But I wouldn't have missed it for the world." Tripper rocked on his feet. "Is there someplace to sit down? My back is hurting." The Centauran zoo covered a square kilometer. Caged species from all over Orion's arm of the galaxy. Centaurans, with their families, strolled through the exhibits. It surprised the Terrans to see young aliens under 2 meters tall. One creature lay coiled in its cage with its head tucked under its wing.

Sensing their approach, the red beast opened its eyes and regarded them. "A baby dragon!" breathed Jane. The wee beastie let out a thin stream of fire that lapped around the bag Chris was carrying. "Hey, watch it! This cost money!" cried Tripper. Captain Darkstrider pointed to a sign in front of the exhibit. "That must be a warning to keep your distance in case of fire."

Next, the Copernicans came to a cage holding a massive purple-skinned gorilla-like creature 3 meters tall. It had an extra set of muscular arms. The look the thing gave the Terrans was so nasty it made them quail. "What did I ever do to you?" muttered Chris shakily. A cage over was a very tall red praying-mantis-looking insect. It fixed them with a rigid stare. Then, without warning, a stick-like appendage darted out between the bars and grasped Chris's bag. "Hey! Leggo, my Eggo!" shouted Tripper. With a cry, Jane leaped forward and karate chopped the offending limb. The arachnoid quickly withdrew its injured limb and danced around, making chittering noises. "Never get between a woman and her newly purchased apparel," said Darkstrider, amused.

The crew members moved to a darkened cage at the end of a row. They strained their eyes to see the thing that lurked in the shadows. Finally, it emerged. What they saw was so horrible that the advance party could not describe it afterward. "Ok," said Lieutenant Franke, blanching, "I'm ready to go back to the taxi and out of this city." Nancy was looking into the next cage. "I think you should see this."

The triad stood in front of a cage containing oddly familiar specimens. Seeing them, the animals within got to their feet and stood grasping the bars, looking out. "What are they?" asked Jane. "They're us," replied Captain Darkstrider. "Our remote ancestor, Homo Erectus, from a million years ago." The humans and hominids stared at each other in silence. "Well," said Jane. "This sucks." Nancy sighed with regret. "Right, time to go."

Several hours later, the advance party found themselves on the plain within a kilometer of the portal. Jane's homing signal, which she had left at the gate, was pinging louder. Without warning, a vast shadow passed over them. Chilled, they saw the red dragons wheeling and swooping toward them. "Run!" shouted Nancy. Racing over the soft carpeted mossy ground, the trio could see the oval of the portal. The entrance was blinking. "The door is closing!" yelled Jane. "Hurry!" A sheet of flame whooshed over their heads, knocking them down. Quickly, the three picked themselves up and hurled themselves forward. Captain Darkstrider took the lead, with Lieutenant Franke behind. Bringing up the rear and carrying Jane's clothing bag was a puffing Tripper. A massive red dragon plummeted down and pulled up just over their heads. The tip of one wing knocked Chris down head over heels. Another flying wyvern pounced on the hapless Terran with gaping jaws.

Jane stopped and pivoted, drawing her sidearm with one motion to shoot the tip of one of the creature's ears off. Screeching in pain, it flew off, wings flapping. "Pick up my bag, Tripper, and hurry!" Franke yelled. Cursing, the Navigational Officer picked up the parcel and ran toward them. Now three of the vast basilisks rocketed down, wingtip to wingtip. With a cry of triumph, the communication officer dove through the gateway, followed by Chris, still holding the bag. Captain Darkstrider paused on the threshold and looked at a boiling fire coming at her. Then, with a smile at the frustrated dragons, she leaped through the door just as it closed. Flames passed through the space.

Two hours passed, and the advance party was within kilometers of the room where they had left the engineers. "I am a fool," said Captain Darkstrider, "we haven't contacted our two crew members for hours. They must be sick with worry." Just then, a door in front of them opened, and Book and Riley exited, chattering and laughing. The two groups stopped dead in their tracks and stared. "Well, said Jane. "This is special."

Taking it to the next level

Chapter 11

"Want to run that by me again, men? Why did you abandon your post?" asked Captain Darkstrider. The Chief Engineer Book and assistant engineer Riley looked at each other guiltily. "We were worried about you, captain. You and the advance party were out of communications for several hours," replied Francis. "We came looking for you!" put in Jason.

"Really?" said Nancy. "Then why did we find you in a room kilometers from where you last heard from us?" Chief Book assumed a defiant expression. "We investigated a room on the way. It seemed pointless to ignore opportunities to explore." Darkstrider gave back Book's look with a sardonic expression. "We also found the elevator to the next level, Captain Darkstrider," Riley pointed out. "And here I thought you would be worried sick about us. How wrong I was about that!" laughed the captain. "What kind of room did you find?" asked the Navigational Officer Tripper. "An auxiliary control room," answered the Chief Engineer. "Similar to the main engine room, but much more compact."

"Well, you sure left this area in a mess," said Communication Officer Franke. The room was in great disarray, with opened panes, exposed circuitry, and tools lying on the ground. "Enough of our little adventure," said Jason hurriedly. "What did the advance party discover? Important things, I bet!" Nancy laughed at the assistant engineer's apparent deflection. "First thing we found was a room with a bunch of low rectangular slabs and one circular one," said Chris Tripper. "Beyond that was a space that contained one of those pulsating blue energy balls."

"Like the one on Charon!" said Jane Franke. "A virtual reality?" exclaimed Book. "Where did it take you?" Nancy smiled, "To a vast plain with a city ten clicks away. We walked toward it and caught an automatic taxi into the metropolis."

"We spent the next several hours eating in restaurants, drinking in bars, shopping for clothes, checking out an art gallery, and visiting a zoo!" said Tripper. "Weren't there any native Centaurans? Did they take notice of you?" asked Riley. "Yes, there was, and no, they didn't," answered Nancy. "We could have been invisible to all the attention they paid us. But the insect workers interacted with us. And the animals in the zoo knew we were there." Francis sighed. "Wow, you had an incredible adventure! And you suffered no mishaps? No moments of danger to make it interesting?" Franke tittered, "Unless you want to call running to the portal for our lives while being attacked by dragons! Does that count, chief?" The two engineers exploded with ejaculations of amazement. "Dragons? Fire-breathing ones? Was anyone hurt?" asked Jason. "Only Chris. And I could patch him up," said the communication officer with a smile. "He got scorched a little." The Chief Engineer frowned, "Singed? Where was Mr. Tripper singed?" Tripper colored with embarrassment. "On my bum!"

The other four Copernicans laughed, and Chris joined them after a brief pause. "And he lost my bag with my new dress!" lamented Franke. "I told you, Jane. The bag didn't come through the portal. So it wasn't real," pointed out the young navigational officer. "That's your story," said Jane darkly. "Getting back to you two engineers," said Captain Darkstrider, "did you find anything in the auxiliary engine room that would make up for the desertion of your post?" Book said, "Well, we showed you the place, Captain Darkstrider. Columns containing energy fluctuations and one control panel. But no, we learned nothing new."

Captain Darkstrider examined her engineers with a speculative look. "Has anyone ever told you, captain, that the lights in your eyes resemble moonlight on the Nile?" asked assistant engineer Riley. A startled look crossed Nancy's face, and her countenance softened into an amused one. "No, no one ever did, Mr. Riley. So, is that what you want to tell me?" There was complete silence for a moment. "No, he doesn't," interjected Chief Book with a quick jab in his younger friend's ribs. Nancy stared at the two men with eyes like jewels that sparkled.

"Jason's right. The lights in her eyes do resemble moonlight on the Nile." thought the Chief Engineer Book. "Where did he ever pick up a phrase like that? The kiss-ass never mentions my eyes unless they're bloodshot."

"All right, you scamps, I'll overlook it this time. But no more disobeying orders from now on. Is that clear?" asked Nancy. "Clear," answered Francis. "As clear as your alabaster skin," added Jason. "You can shut up now, assistant engineer Riley. Right, next course of action. We must form another advance party to explore the level above us," said Darkstrider. "Yes, about that, captain," interrupted Francis. Navigational Officer Tripper groaned, "Here it comes." Nancy fixed Francis with a piercing look. "Yes, now you have something to say about my cheekbones?"

Chief Book laughed shortly, "No. Well, you do have nice cheekbones, but no. Assistant Engineer Riley and I would like to know if one of us could be a member of the next advance party. We feel we are missing out on the big discoveries. Either Lieutenant Franke or Tripper could assist the engineer that stays. They both have extensive engineering training. And the next advance party after that could contain the other engineer, and the additional bridge crew could remain behind. That way, the advance parties wouldn't get stale, and the work parties in the engine room would gain a fresh perspective."

"Logical. Flawlessly logical," said Captain Darkstrider, shaking her head. "I was right. You are spending too much time with First Officer Leonidas. Very well. Assistant engineer Riley can be with tomorrow's advance party. Navigational Officer Tripper will stay here. After that, it will be the Chief Book and Lieutenant Franke's turns. Any comments?" Everyone turned to look at Jason, who reddened. "Good, well, get some sleep. If one can rest on these empty deck plates." The crew broke up and readied themselves for the night. "You never give me compliments about my eyes," complained Jane. "You have two of them; happy now?" replied Chris. "You saved our bacon just now," murmured Francis. "Where did you ever come up with that stuff?" Jason smirked. "Know how to talk to women, my son. A lady wants to be wooed, sweet nothings whispered in her pink, shell-like ears." Chief Book snorted, "And how would you know that?" Riley replied indignantly, "I read stories!"

Chris Tripper noticed Captain Darkstrider checking her weapon. "Are you going someplace, captain?" Nancy glanced at her young officer. "Yes, I'm going out into the tunnel under the ocean. Since the First Officer moved Copernicus, he can no longer receive our transmissions in this room. The angle isn't right." Chris frowned. "I better come with you." Darkstrider chuckled, "Negative; I'll only be gone for a few minutes. Get some sleep. You'll need it. You will work with the Chief Engineer tomorrow, and he's a hard taskmaster." Without another word, Nancy walked through the exit and into the corridor. Stopping midway, the blond-haired, green-eyed woman glanced in both directions. The corridor stretched endlessly in her view until it merged into shadows—no sounds came other than muffled noises from the engineering control room she had quitted. The ambient red light cast a sinister luminosity. Shivering slightly, the captain passed through the exit and into the antechamber.

Captain Darkstrider emerged onto the trackway platform. Everything seemed the same as they had left it the day before. Flatbeds still lined the venue, and the tunnel extended endlessly before her. Only the glow of the beacon illuminated Nancy's surroundings. Beyond the glass of the subway, an endless universe of life wheeled. An explosion of lambent sea creatures moved and danced in myriad directions—a cacophony of not sound but sight. Entranced, Darkstrider gazed in wonder at this silent world. Ending her wool-gathering, the captain spoke into her communicator. "Landing party to Copernicus. Come in, please, Over. Darkstrider to Leonidas. Come in. Over." Gratifying, the response came back quickly.

"Copernicus to the landing party. First Officer Leonidas here. Good to hear your voice, Captain Darkstrider. Over." Nancy smiled, "Good to hear your voice, Mr. Leonidas. How are you holding up? Are you still maintaining one standard planetary orbit over Tombaugh's base? Over." A burst of static filled the captain's ears. "Affirmative. I am monitoring the Challenger Colles. The hole created by the torpedo pulses has closed up. No permanent damage to the ship. What is your status? Over."

"The advance party explored the first level of the beacon. We discovered another virtual reality room identical to the one in Charon's artifact. Franke, Tripper, and I journeyed to a city on Proxima Centauri b. We investigated the metropolis and dragons chased us back to the portal. The engineers are making progress on fixing or shutting down the beacon so we can return to the ship. But could not affect repairs. Over," said Darkstrider. A note of concern was clear in the First Officer's voice. "Captain, you know we left only a few days in the window? Then you must return to the ship? Over." Irritably Nancy replied, "I am well aware of that First Officer. Mr. Tripper plans to fly a shuttle on auto to see if it draws the beacon's fire. We can return to the ship with all and sundry if it works. Over."

Now the alarm was strong in Spiro's tinny communication. "That sounds very dangerous. When you take off in the shuttles, I can take the Copernicus within range of the beacon's gun and distract it with lasers. Over." The captain noticed all the fish had turned off their lights. "Is there an apex predator near?" she thought. "Now it's you who are taking risks, First Officer. You are slurring your words slightly. Have you been drinking? Over." An injured tone entered Leonidas's voice. "Yes, I have. I am off duty, after all. Over." Nancy laughed, "Don't overdo it. Try not to be too melancholy. We will return to the ship in a few days. I will keep you monitored; Captain Darkstrider out. Over." Over her communicator came the first officer's metallic vocalization. "Understood. Be careful, Nancy. Leonidas out. Over."

Thoughtfully, Captain Darkstrider turned and walked back the way she came. "Spiro rarely calls me Nancy. He is distraught. I hope he is not drinking too much of his ouzo." Darkstrider passed out of sight into the next room. In the surrounding ocean at various distances, the colossal squid, megalodon shark, and The Thing winked into existence.

The following day the landing party picked themselves, groaning off the cold, rigid deck plates. "God, my bones ache. I am getting too old for this," complained the First Officer Book. "Have you considered taking a vacation to Pluto?" quipped assistant engineer Riley. "Humor!" Francis replied, "I recognized it." Lieutenant Franke stretched her lithe body. "I need a sonic shower," said the Communication Officer. "This girl smells. I haven't cleaned myself in two days." Navigational Officer Tripper rubbed his hand over his bristly face. "You and me both, babe. I am feeling like Robinson Crusoe." The words Robinson Crusoe triggered a dormant memory in the captain's mind. She crooned:

♫ Like Robinson Crusoe,

It's prehistoric, as can be.

For five stranded castaways,

Here on Tombaugh's Isle!♫

"I'm not sure you got the lyrics quite right, captain," said the Chief Engineer Book dryly. Nancy shrugged her slender shoulders, "Copyright laws, you know." Tripper laughed, "Who's going to care about them way out here?"

The three advance party members filled their backpacks with supplies and checked their side arms. Tripper and Book watched them in silence and trepidation. Then, at last, all was ready. Captain Darkstrider addressed her two remaining crew. "Right, men. We will be anywhere from eight to twelve hours. I will check in with you every two hours, if possible. Keep working on fixing this engine; it's vital. Goodbye, and see you tonight." Tripper, Franke, Book, and Riley embraced; shouldering their packs, Francis and Jane followed Nancy into the corridor. The Chief Engineer turned to the Navigational Officer. "Let's get to work."

The advance party turned right in the corridor and tramped over its icy surface. A hundred meters later, the recessed door to the elevator appeared. The captain stood before it and knocked, saying, "Melon." Miraculously, the oval door appeared as if in a prophecy. In the Indian file, the three walked in. Behind them, the entrance sealed itself. Nancy regarded the two six-fingered outlines high on the wall. "Ok," said Darkstrider. "you're taller than me, Lieutenant Franke. Reach up and put your hand in the upper outline. Then, engineer Riley, press yourself into her and place your hand over hers. Hopefully, this works." Dutifully, the two Copernicans positioned themselves. "You better not get an erection Riley," said Jane. Jason laughed, "I'll try not to, Lieutenant. But I am only a man."

The two squeezed their hands together, creating a six-fingered hand. As a result, Franke and Riley lost their balance and crashed to the floor when the elevator went forward. Jane and Jason gingerly picked themselves off the floor. "Why is the elevator moving forward rather than up?" asked the Communications Officer. The captain thought for a moment and then brightened. "I have it! This beacon tapers. The elevator is moving first in, then up." Jane laughed, "Yeah! They had elevators like that on the Enterprise in Star Trek."

True to the captain's words, the elevator abruptly stopped moving forward and ascended. Darkstrider said nothing, but looked at her two crew smugly. Finally, after several minutes, Franke remarked," This is a long elevator ride." Riley was studying his recorder. "Nothing to match the 300-kilometer ride we took in the Challenger Colles, but we have traveled horizontally 500 meters and almost one kilometer vertically." At that moment, the elevator came to a smooth stop, and the oval door appeared. Tentatively, the advance party exited and found themselves in a corridor identical to the one they had just left.

"Which way, captain?" asked Jason. "To our right," ordered Captain Darkstrider. "Any reason for going right Captain Darkstrider?" asked Jane. "Yes," said Nancy, "I am right-handed." So the trio advanced up the passageway, every sense alert. Presently, they came to an oval window on the outcurve wall. Gathering in front of the aperture, they looked out. A kilometer below, they could see the trackway stretching 10 kilometers into the far distance towards the base of the Challenger Colles. Its dimly red-lit interior dwindled to a thread in their perspective. The now familiar schools of brightly lit fish swirled in the ocean outside. "Beautiful view from up here," remarked Lieutenant Franke. "It will only improve," said assistant engineer Riley. "I believe there is a hallway for every kilometer of height." After a minute, the trio moved on. Behind them, an enormous eye on the end of a stalk slowly crept into visibility in the window.

"How far do we have to walk this time?" asked Communication Officer Franke. "My recorder measures the diameter of this level at 4 kilometers," Jason said. "So applying the formula two pi r, we get 12.56 km." Nancy laughed. "The distances are getting smaller all the time." So steadily, the advance party moved along the corridor. Kilometer after monotonous kilometer went by, broken only by the occasional window. Unbeknownst to the three, unseen entities were measuring their progress. The awful stillness of the circumambient air swallowed up their footfalls. The ever-present reddish light gave an unhealthy glow to any exposed flesh. Eventually, after a few hours, the Copernicans reached a point halfway from their starting point. 'Look, another door," pointed Jane to a recess on the curving wall.

Captain Darkstrider positioned herself in front of the portal and said, "Melon." The trio filed through the oval entrance. Darkstrider, Franke, and Riley looked around the large room composed of square cubes surrounded by about 20 oval metal daises.

"What do you imagine the aliens used this room for?" asked Jason. "It's the only one we've found on this level. It must have some importance." Nancy pointed to some cupboards that hung from the walls. "Check those out. The answers might be there." One by one, the Terrans opened the unlocked cabinets. They were all empty. Finally, Darkstrider came to the one that was locked. Taking out her blaster, the captain fired at the oval handle. A splash of red, like a blush, blossomed. Cautiously, Nancy opened the door to the shelving. Stacked inside were rows of disks. Curious, her crew gathered behind Darkstrider as she removed one disk from its holder. Nancy held the object to her eyes. It did not surprise her to see colors, some of which she could not recognize, mixing below the crystalline exterior.

"What do you think the saucer is for?" asked Jane. "Well, it wasn't for holding cups of tea," quipped assistant Riley.

Thoughtfully, the captain tapped the alien object in her palm. Then she glanced over at the oval dais. Striding to the nearest one, Darkstrider climbed on top of a tall metal cube and examined the surface of the oval tabletop. In the exact center of the veneer was an oval depression. Nancy leaned forward and placed the disk in the receptacle. The captain settled onto her seat; Franke and Riley followed her example and climbed on the metal cubes beside her. Then, not unexpectedly, a hologram appeared over their heads.

A Centauran wearing a clear visor around his eyes appeared. He appeared elderly and wore a purple tunic covered with a mathematical-like symbology. His red face had darkened with age, and he spoke with an air of authority. "I get it!" exclaimed Jason. "This is a library, and he's a teacher!" Nancy laughed, "Or a professor." Jane tittered, "Or maybe just a librarian. If you're right, and this is a library." The Centauran walked around his surroundings, which appeared to be their room. But much different in that there were holographic pictures on the walls, strange sculptures that moved, and were full of other Centaurans of various ages and sexes.

The advance party watched, enraptured, as the holographic image walked around his space, gesturing and lecturing in the sibilant alien language. "If we only knew what the alien was speaking," said Captain Darkstrider. "There may be a way, captain," replied Riley, fiddling with his recorder. "I am downloading the language the Centauran is speaking; when I get a large enough database, I think the universal translator will decipher it." Nancy frowned. "But scientists meant the universal translator for human languages. Do you think it would work on an alien one?" The assistant engineer grinned. "Only one way to find out. I suggest you ladies get all the rest of the discs and start playing with them. I need as large of a syllabic reservoir as possible." Like young girls, Jane and Nancy ran to the cabinet giggling and grabbed handfuls of discs. They moved from table to table, inserting the saucers. Holographic images sprang up all over the room. Soon, twenty scenarios involving animals, Centaurans, and planetary-wide vistas were bombarding the triad.

"Ok, Chris, prepare to receive this data I am transmitting," the Chief Engineer Book said. "Roger, Francis. I have the data and am cross-referencing," replied Navigation Officer Tripper. The two men were busy examining the exposed circuitry in the central control room of the beacon. "You have impressive engineering skills, Chris; I'm glad you haven't forgotten your training at the academy," said Chief Book. "Thanks, Francis; I always liked to work on my car engines when I was a teenager. Though this is the most sophisticated engine I've ever encountered," said Tripper. The Chief Engineer examined his recorder at some numbers. "This is the first time we have encountered alien technology. We lack a reference point, a way to think as they did. It's a tall order to understand a species that has been extinct for a billion years." Francis put down his recorder in frustration. "I know it's a corrupted sub-routine that caused the beacon to shoot at the Copernicus. But, unfortunately, I can't find it!"

Tripper grinned, "Jane will work in here tomorrow. Maybe she will find something. Remember, she found a way of turning on the engines." The older man frowned. "She just got lucky. Pushing a button at random was very irresponsible. It could have just as easily led to disaster." Chris pushed up the cover on another panel and peered inside. "True. But she has always been lucky that way. Jane seems to possess some intuition. Remember back at the artifact on Charon; she sensed the laser trap and sentry guns." The crew members were quiet for a time. "Ok, I'll grant you that, Mr. Tripper. Lieutenant Franke has proved herself invaluable on this trip. But tell me about your journey yesterday. What was the highlight of your trip?" Book asked Chris.

"There were so many I can't pick out one Chief Engineer. Drinking in the cantina with the Star Wars denizens and the alien zoo were sights I'll never forget," replied the young Navigational Officer. "Is it true you saw a family of Homo Habilis in a cage?" asked Francis. "Correct. The look they gave us is one I'll never forget. A look of betrayal," said Chris.

"And what was that thing you saw in that darkened cage? The captain and Franke refused to discuss it," enquired the Chief Engineer. Tripper shuddered and grew pale. "I can't describe what I saw. Can we drop it, please?" Francis smiled. "By all means." Tripper paused with his hydro spanner in hand. "One thing for sure. You can bet Spock on the Copernicus is working every moment to get us out of here!"

"Wait for it. I'm powering up. Target in sight. Fire! Damn it, missed!" In his cabin, the First Officer played an ancient video game on his computer. "I don't know why I bother with this game, Battlefield 2. It's over a hundred years old. I could go to a holo suite and play for real. But no, this game has a certain charm. I can't believe it! Another claymore? I'm always dying on those! Have no luck on the Karkand map." Spiro flipped to another screen. "Ok, I'm almost ready to crack the top ten in the world standings. Let's see who is ahead of me. Rohtez, Captain-Cuddles, Coolgirl, DefaultPlayer, Arclight, Billyhoo, Elite-Cyprio, JuliaJuul, Hallojohnson, and the number one, Sunnyghost. H'm Sunnyghost, Dutch, eh? Well, cheesehead, you're going down one day!"

Restlessly, Spiro got off his bunk and sat by the port window on a chair. Far below him, he could see the blinding whiteness of Sputnik Panitia. To his unseen eye, he imagined under that thick mantle of ice the forbidding hulk of the black beacon. How was the trapped landing doing? An intense look of concentration consumed the First Officer's countenance. "I'll get you out of there, people. Or die trying!"

Several hours later, the advance party was still in the alien library. Lieutenant Franke sat watching a Centauran western-type movie. Holo cowboys were riding dragons and herding purple-red, six-legged cattle. "Ride 'em, cowboys," she murmured. Engrossing Captain Darkstrider was a soap opera. In the holo images over the table, a tall Centauran female and an even taller male shouted at each other.

Then, suddenly, the female struck the male across the face. "Good for you, sister! You don't take crap from any man! You go, girl!" cried Nancy. The two women turned their attention to assistant engineer Riley when he shouted triumphantly. "Got it; I think I've cracked their language!" Darkstrider frowned, "How did you succeed, Mr. Riley when dozens of top linguists failed to decipher the signal the beacon sent to the satellites?" Jason looked up. "I believe it's because the beacon transmitted in binary based on 12-digit numerology. With no database, it was impossible to decode." Franke and Darkstrider jumped and walked over to Riley's dais. "Ok, Engineer. Let's see what you've come up with," said Nancy.

Assistant engineer Riley put a disk into the tabletop slot. "Here's a new one I found. It allows limited interaction." Jane laughed, "You mean we can ask it questions, and the image will answer?" Jason placed his recorder on the dais and adjusted a control. "Precisely." The image of the old Centauran they had seen before phased into view. He peered at the advance party through his clear, wraparound visor." I think those are glasses he is wearing," commented Franke. The holographic image turned to her. "They are."

The two women reacted in shock at the voice coming out of Jason's recorder. Riley looked happy. "It can talk!" said Jane. "Well, of course, I can talk; I'm a Centauran, aren't I?" responded the alien crossly. "Query: Holographic image. What happened to your civilization? Is it still functional?" asked Nancy. "Of course, it's still functional. The Proxima Centauri culture has lasted for five thousand years and will flourish for five thousand more. And don't talk to me as if I was a damn computer, young lady!" snapped the extraterrestrial teacher.

"Sorry," mumbled the captain, secretly pleased to be addressed as a young lady. "Master," said assistant engineer Riley. "Why did you build the beacon? And why did you place it where you did?" The red-faced alien looked flattered. "You have pleasant manners, at least. We build beacons in systems that harbor life. We place them in the ice body belt that surrounds every sun. Then we wait for a civilization to develop sufficiently to discover the transmitters. The beacon then sends a warp-bubble message back to our home planet. Now we know another race is ready to join the galactic federation of planets." Lieutenant Franke said eagerly, "So there was a United Federation of planets? Like on Star Trek?"

The tall creature looked at them strangely and adjusted his visor. "You ask odd questions that are common knowledge. You're not exactly Centaurans, are you? Who are you, and where are you from?" Captain Darkstrider said gravely, "We are humans from the third planet from this sun, which we call Sol. We have named our planet Earth." The aged alien looked confused. "But that's impossible. There are only bacteria and plankton on that rock. Wait a moment. How much time has passed?" The three Terrans exchanged glances, "One billion of our years as measured by our planet's rotation around the sun," said Nancy. The otherworldly being looked shocked. "One billion years? A billion years?" The creature looked at the crew sadly. "What took you so long?" The hologram dissolved into static and then disappeared.

"I think we're getting somewhere, Chris," said the Chief Engineer Book. "Look at these readouts. We can narrow down where the malfunction occurred in the circuitry." Navigational Officer Tripper studied his recorder. "Yeah, I see what you mean, Francis. If we run self-diagnostic programs here and here, I think we may have something." The two men busied themselves with tools and recorders. The banks of colored buttons and switches cast eerie lights over their faces. "Tell me again about that cantina Tripper. You said it reminded you of what again?" asked Francis. "The cantina scene in Star Wars. The captain thinks our thoughts influenced what we saw. We expected to see Tantooine creatures, so we saw them," said the Navigational Officer. "God, I wished I'd been there. I would have loved to have seen those beings. No Chewbacca or Han Solo, then?" asked Francis. Chris laughed, "No, sorry."

"Tomorrow, you get to be a member of the advance party yourself, Chief Book, as do I. So Franke and Riley can have a crack at figuring out this computer," said Tripper. "It will be nice to get out of this room. I haven't been on a scout mission since we were topside," replied Book. "Jason texted me and said the corridor levels in this complex are one kilometer apart vertically. So even if Franke, Riley, and the captain explore two stories today, that will still leave two levels for us tomorrow. That includes the very apex of this complex. I have a feeling that's where the action is." A small puff of smoke came from the open panel the Chief Engineer had been working. "Damn, not again!"

First Officer Leonidas sat in the ship's hot tub drinking ouzo. He contemplated the swirls of steam as they rose off the heated water. "I've got to watch my drinking," thought Spiro. "The captain even commented on it the other day. I must be tip-top to get down to the planet." Spiro took a sip of his drink and closed his eyes. "Nancy looked so beautiful in her black one-piece the last time we were together. When did we ever get into the friend zone? I'll never understand how or why that happened. She seemed keen enough on me before she made captain. Maybe that's it. The responsibility has changed her. Well, I guess age catches you in the end. The sea-witch's claws get us all, eventually."

Leonidas opened his eyes and stared unseeingly at the ceiling. "My gut is telling me something. I will have to fly the ship's escape pod to the surface. I'm as sure about that as I am about anything. The shuttles are much bigger than the pod. The beacon will blast them out of the sky. I have a chance, especially using Copernicus as a distraction." The First Officer scratched his hairy chest. "Am I doing this to show the captain how brave I am? That's part of it, of course. Afraid? I'm terrified. What is bravery? I was born in Sparta and proudly carried my ancestor's name, Leonidas. King Leonidas and his 300 held the pass of Thermopylae against a huge Persian army. Well, not quite. Another 7,000 Greeks were backing him up. Leonidas and the 300 died to a man. Was that courage or suicide? I don't know. Is what I'm contemplating suicide? Maybe I shouldn't think about these things." Leonidas picked up the bottle of ouzo to pour himself another drink. Nothing came out. He contemplated it sadly. "Another dead soldier."

"I think the thought of a billion years was too much for the teacher's logic program. So it shut itself down," said assistant engineer Riley. "Yeah, I think you're right, Mr. Riley," Captain Darkstrider said. "But we learned a great deal from him. We should move on, anyway. We have time to explore another level if we hurry." Lieutenant Franke looked up in distress. "But I haven't finished my cowboy program! I want to know if they get the herd to market!" Nancy patted the younger woman's arm. "It will have to wait. Duty calls, unfortunately."

After a knock on the door and a quick "Melon," the three found themselves back in the corridor. Turning to their left, they continued up the passageway. Several uneventful kilometers passed. Unrelieved except for the occasional window. If they thought their passage was unremarked, then they were sadly mistaken. Keen intelligence monitored every step of their progress.

After completing an almost full circle, the advance party arrived at the elevator to the next level. Now it was the turn of Jason to step forward and utter "Melon." Entering the hoist, Riley and Franke made the six-fingered hand. Instantly, the advance party felt their conveyance moving forward and then upwards.

"We made an amazing discovery back there," said Communication Officer Franke. "An ancient archive complete with talking librarians! And Jason decoded their language so we could understand what they were saying!" Assistant engineer Riley said, "Only my inherent modesty prevents me from agreeing with your accurate praise." Captain Darkstrider laughed. "Remarkably, you were deciphering a billion-year-old language. And we learned a lot from the old librarian. Can you reaccess his program, Mr. Riley?" Jason nodded his head; "Yeah, no problem. But, of course, we must be careful what questions to ask it." After a few minutes, the elevator stopped, and the oval portal appeared. The trio stepped into a passageway identical to the one they had just left.

"I wonder what lays ahead of us on this level?" asked Jane. "There is bound to be at least one important room. What is the circumference of this plane, Mr. Riley?" Jason checked his recorder. "It's 3 kilometers in diameter. We apply two pi r and get an answer of 9.42 clicks." Captain Darkstrider stretched her back. "Let's take a break and have something to eat and drink. After we finish this last tour, we will have walked 21 kilometers." With a sigh of relief, the advance party sank to the floor and opened up their backpacks. Removing canteens and tubes, the three ate food concentrate and drank. "So the Copernicans have placed these beacons on several solar systems. I'd love to know which ones and if they found life," said Riley. "So would I," replied Franke. "The librarian said Kuiper belts surround every star. I would guess they left transmitters around all the nearby suns to them." Nancy nibbled a food cube, "Inspired deductions. We could return later to the library and ask the master these questions."

The companions ate and drank in silence for a while. "I can't believe we saw humans in a cage back on the Proxima Centauri b," said Communication Officer Franke. "We didn't," answered the captain. "We saw what we expected to see. The same with the creatures in the cantina. Straight out of Star Wars." Assistant engineer Riley sighed. "I would have given almost anything to have been there."

"You were just as well not to have been there," laughed Nancy. "Dragons attacked us. We barely escaped with our lives. Luckily, Lieutenant Franke is a dead shot." Jane took a sip of water. "Do you think the dragons were real, Captain Darkstrider? That they existed on Proxima b a billion years ago?" Darkstrider shrugged her slim shoulders. "Who can say? It's hard to separate reality from fantasy. Especially if that fantasy is your heart's desire." Jason eased his bottom on the hard floor. "Fantasy or not, I wish I'd seen what you saw yesterday." Nancy smiled, "Stick around, engineer; you have seen nothing yet."

Chief Engineer Book and Navigational Officer Tripper were also on a break in the engine room. Sitting on the room's hard floor, the duo munched their rations and sipped their drinks. "So you think we will ever find out the problem, chief?" asked Tripper. "No discouragement, my friend. We've made a lot of progress. I feel we are getting close," answered Francis. "Well, we better find something soon. Either we shut down the engine or repair the corrupted sub-routine," Chris said. "If we leave here without doing either of those two things, we risk lifting off in the shuttles and getting blown out of the sky."

Tripper looked around himself and at the open panels, tools, and cables lying in disarray. He listened to the throbbing of the powerful engines above him. "I don't know why we don't just take our blasters to the control panels and blow them up. That would shut down the beacon's engine permanently." Book chuckled, "Yes, it would, but it would also end us for good." Chris examined the First Nation's man curiously. "What do you mean by that, Francis?"

"Listen, this entire complex is just one big nuclear reactor, correct?" explained the Chief Engineer Book. The younger man nodded. "Shut down its safeguards, and we are looking at an atomic explosion that will destroy everything out to 100 clicks." Tripper smiled weakly, "Hadn't considered that."

After the meal, the advance party stowed foodstuffs and beverages into backpacks. Then, slinging the burdens over their shoulders, they continued their journey. The space adventurers trudged down the empty corridor, bathed in eerie red light. So quiet that the trio could hear their breaths. And almost their hearts. Periodically, one would look behind them as if fearing some monstrosity was following. Finally, after a couple of hours of walking, the captain stopped at one of the oval portals and looked out; Nancy's two companions moved to her side. The trio looked at a galaxy of luminous stars representing Plutonian fish. The creatures formed an intricate skein of light, forming constellations that broke and wove into a brilliant tapestry. Far below them, the tunnel they had traversed was a ribbon of red. Sighing, the Copernicans resumed their trek. An hour later, something appeared on the inner-curved wall.

"There's a door," said Lieutenant Franke, pointing to a recess on the passageway's left-curving bulkhead. She stepped in front of the portal and knocked, saying, "Melon." The advance party hurried through the oval entrance, which disappeared behind them. The three found themselves in a large, oval room. Variously pieces of unknown machinery clustered on the floor, attached to the walls or hung from the ceiling. At intervals, metal cubes stood, on which stood a more delicate apparatus. The space explorers stared around in wonder. "A laboratory," said Captain Darkstrider softly. "Or a machine shop," replied Riley. Jane walked over to the nearest cube or table. She studied the intricate glassware on top. Seeing a button on the side of the stand, she hesitated, then pushed it. A green gas flowed into the tubing. "I can't believe this stuff still works after a billion years," exclaimed Franke. "Yeah, the aliens built things to last," said assistant engineer Riley. "Not like today. I bought a holoprojector, and six months later—." The women shouted, "It broke down!" Nancy chuckled, "We know, Mr. Riley. You've told that story a dozen times." Jason said discontentedly, "Well, it did."

The captain was checking out the contents of another tabletop composed of a squat-like machine with a small aperture. A colored light disk occupied a raised portion of the surface; Darkstrider pressed down on it. A purplish-red flame burst out of the hole. "Hello, bunsen burner," said Nancy. Assistant engineer Riley had found a gun-looking mechanism. He pressed a switch on its side. Instantly, the equipment emitted a throbbing noise, and orange-colored rings flew from it. The calls increased as they flew across the room and vanished in a collision with the wall.

Like kids in a new toy shop, the advance party moved from device to device. Soon the oval room filled with discordance of sounds, sights, and smells of an alien origin. Sheets of unearthly-colored flame enveloped the trio. The hooting of deranged beasts deafened them, and smells assaulted them so outside their experience to defy description. The trio agreed that they had had a great time. Eventually, at Captain Darkstrider's signal, they shut down all the devices. A deafening silence filled their workspace. Finally, the trio gathered at an empty cube for a conference.

"Well, Mr. Riley," said Nancy. "you're the engineer here. What do you think of all the things we have discovered?" The assistant Engineer smiled broadly, "There are more things in heaven and earth, Horatio, than are dreamt of in your philosophy." Lieutenant Franke laughed delightedly, "Shakespeare!" Jason smirked, "No, Hamlet." The Communication Officer swatted the older man across his cheek. "That's hilarious. Hamlet is Shakespeare." Riley assumed a knowing air, "What I mean is, we are dealing with things beyond your ken." Jane smirked, "Really? Well, your 'Ken' can kiss my Barbie."

The deep-space scout ship Copernicus sailed in its endless orbit with throbbing engines. Like a watchful parent, it supervised the antics of the smaller Plutonian moons. The grey nurse of Charon also stood guard on their foolery. The constantly changing sky constellations were a delight to behold. But on board the magnificent vessel, First Officer Leonidas was not happy.

Spiro sat hunched forward in the captain's chair on the bridge. Unshaven, he stared down at the heart of Pluto. "Another day will see them finish their exploration of the beacon. Then like salmon returning to spawn, they must return home," he thought. "I have to decide. Do I let them risk their lives in the shuttles, or do I take the escape pod down to the surface? But why? What can I do or bring to the landing party that they don't already have?"

Leonidas got up and restlessly patrolled the bridge. "I have to get it together. I'm drinking too much and not taking care of myself. If I'm going into action, I have to be ready. The landing party depends on me. I can't let Nancy down." The First Officer ran his hand over his bristly chin. "First things first. I need to shave and have a shower." Then, smiling for the first time in days, Leonidas left the bridge.

"Aside from your Shakespearean aspirations, did you learn anything from all this assistant engineer Riley?" asked Captain Darkstrider. "Yes, I did, captain. I have downloaded everything on my recorder. That should keep Earth scientists busy for months," replied Jason. "Am I thinking of the Nobel prize for Physics for Engineer Riley?" asked Lieutenant Franke mischievously. The older man looked at the young woman seriously. "You have never looked more attractive to me than now, Jane."

Nancy laughed and got to her feet. "Well, this is all very amusing. But if we're finishing here, I think we should head back. We've been gone for 10 hours, and it will take us two more hours to get back. I don't know about you two, but I'm getting tired."

"I just received a call from the captain, Chris," said the Chief Engineer Book. "They have finished exploring the next two levels and are returning. She estimates the landing party will be here in two hours, give or take a few minutes. Darkstrider says they have made some important discoveries. She will fill us in later." Navigational Officer Tripper was busy working on the small side control panel off to the side. Then, finally, his muffled voice came out from under the lid. "That's good. Then it will be our turn to explore the last two beacon levels. And Jane and Riley will stay here and work on this circuitry. Then we'll have some discoveries to talk about."

The tool Chris was working with dropped from his hand and hit the floor, rattling underneath. "Damn! Clumsy of me!" said Tripper. The young officer squatted and searched for his spanner—an "Oh my god," came from the shadows. Chief Book turned and asked curiously, "What's wrong Mr. Tripper? Did you find something?" Chris crawled out and stood up. He dramatically thrust out his hand, showing something. "Yes, this!"

The Green Hills

Chapter 12

"So, this was the source of all the problems?" asked Captain Darkstrider. Nancy stood in the middle of the engine room, holding a blackened and cracked cube. "Yes," replied the Chief Engineer Book. "Mr. Tripper found it under the side panel. It must have jarred loose at some point and fell out the bottom." Darkstrider walked over to the control panel and looked at the area Chris was showing. She carefully inserted the burnt cube into the vacant slot. It was a perfect fit. "I have to agree," said Darkstrider. "The cube came from here—some energy unit, I imagine. Well, the landing party on Charon found plenty of these. We have to put a fresh one in here. All four of the quartet took examples, as I remember."

Riley, Franke, Book, and Tripper looked at each other sheepishly. "What's the matter?" Why are you all looking at each other like that?" asked Nancy. Shamefully, no one of her crew could meet the captain's eyes. "Well, come out with it," said Darkstrider. "It can't be that bad. I won't bite." The Chief Engineer shifted his eyes to the captains, "All the cubes are back on the Copernicus!"

Captain Darkstrider threw up her arms. "Heaven protect children, sailors, and drunken men!! I beg your pardon; I always address the heavens in moments of celebration. And no one thought to bring one hexahedron with us?" The four all shook their heads. "Well, I didn't either, so I must take some blame. Pity; this complicates things a lot. But at least we know how to fix the computer that controls the beacon's engines. The trick is how to get another power unit." Franke lifted her hand, "Perhaps there are more in the levels we haven't explored yet, captain?"

"Perhaps there is, Lieutenant," said Nancy. "I wouldn't count on it. Now to business. I think it's pointless to leave personnel working here anymore. So all five of us will form the advance party and explore the last two levels." The couples brightened considerably. "We won't let you down, captain!" declared assistant engineer Riley. "I won't lower myself in your eyes."

Darkstrider smiled kindly. "Oh, that would be impossible, Mr. Riley." Chris, Francis, and Jane all laughed at Jason's bemusement. "Jane and I could return to the Copernicus and get some spare cubes Captain Darkstrider," said Navigational Officer Tripper. "We would be back within a day." Darkstrider shook her head. "And get shot out of the sky by the beacon? I don't think so. We will use your other plan in the last eventuality. But now we should all get some sleep. We have a big day and a long walk tomorrow."

The landing party prepared to bed down for the night. Chris noticed the captain checking her sidearm; seeing his scrutiny, Nancy lifted an eyebrow. Tripper smiled, shrugged, and turned away to Communication Officer Franke. "I'll be back," said Nancy. Captain Darkstrider strode through the portal into the corridor beyond. "There goes the Terminator," quipped Jason.

The captain once again found herself in the lonely passageway. On both sides, the corridor faded away into dark shadows. Nancy shivered. "I can feel the extreme age of this awful place when I'm alone," she thought. "The centuries, the millennia, the eons that have passed since the building of the beacon. And the weight of 300 kilometers of ice and ocean to the surface. Is there a more lonely place than this in the universe?" Collecting herself, the captain entered the square antechamber and onto the trackway platform. Darkstrider looked about herself and saw nothing different. She peered through the glass at the midnight ocean. A silver cavalcade of whirling dervishes spun before her eyes. Captain Darkstrider triggered her communicator. "Landing party to Copernicus, over. Captain Darkstrider to First Officer Leonidas, over." Instantly came Spiros' cheerful reply, "Leonidas here, captain. What is your situation, over?" Nancy smiled, "Good to hear you so chipper, Mr. Leonidas; we have completed exploring three levels of the beacon now. Tomorrow we intend to investigate the last two stories, over," Leonidas's tinny response squeaked in Darkstrider's ears, "Thats' gratifying to hear, captain. Have you repaired the beacon's computer, so it no longer fires on moving objects? Over."

"No, but we have figured out what is wrong. The computer station is missing one of the translucent cubes we found on the Charon artifact, over," said the captain. "That's wonderful, Captain Darkstrider! Have you completed repairs? Over," asked the First Officer. "No, we have not. Unfortunately, we left all the alien power units on the Copernicus, over," replied Nancy.

A silence descended, prompting the captain to say, "Mr. Leonidas, are you still there, over?" Spiro's metallic communication filled her ears. "I can use the Copernicus' escape pod to fly down within a click of the Challenger Colles elevator. I can make my way to you with spare cubes." Darkstrider instantly replied, "Negative, Mr. Leonidas! That is too dangerous; the beacon will blow you apart! You will not, repeat, will not attempt a rescue. That's an order! Do you understand? Over." Spiro's sullen reply came back reluctantly, "Understood, over." Nancy noticed all the fish lights in the surrounding ocean had gone out again. "Is there a predator nearby? This sudden absence of lights out happened last time, but I saw nothing." The captain turned the thought away. "Good, I didn't mean to be too hard on you, First Officer. I will check back tomorrow with the results of our last investigations. Then we can decide on a course of action. Darkstrider out, over." The First Officer replied, "Copernicus out, over."

Darkstrider turned to go when something drew her attention to the upper surface of the tunnel. A large Plutonian fish had illuminated itself and was swimming rapidly over her head. No sooner had it passed when the creature known as The Thing filled her vision, chasing. For a full thirty seconds, it continued to flow overhead. Nancy saw multiple flippers, bloated underbelly, ancient scars, and organs and orifices; thankfully, she remained ignorant of the latter's purposes. Finally, the two creatures dwindled to small illuminated dots in the distance, then disappeared. "Reminds me of the beginning of Star Wars," commented Darkstrider. Nancy turned her gaze upwards to the towering bulk of the black tower. Faintly glowing, it rose to Himalayan heights, stretching the limits of her vision. The captain studied the upper levels of the Brobdingnagian structure. "There is danger there. I sense it, and so do the others. Unless I use every skill I possess, there will be a bloodbath." With that pleasant thought, Nancy retraced her steps back to the landing party.

The following day, the landing party picked itself off the cold metalled floor of the control room. "Another beautiful morning in the Space Corps," groaned Navigational Officer Tripper. "Yeah, didn't the aliens have beds to sleep on?" asked Communication Officer Franke. "They must have taken their beds with them," said assistant engineer Riley. "I am getting too old for this," remarked the Chief Engineer Book. "Sleeping on a hard metal floor is not my idea of fun." Captain Nancy Darkstrider sat cross-legged and opened up her backpack. "Let's have some breakfast and discuss what we will do today, shall we?"

The quintet sat quietly, eating and drinking. Around the crew, the control panels blinked in various colors, some out of the human spectrum. Cables sprouted from the panel surface like spaghetti, and tools were strewn haphazardly around as if by a child. "How far do we have to walk today, captain?" asked the Chief Book. "Fortunately, the elevators are only one hundred meters apart on each level," answered Darkstrider. "So we don't have to walk around half of each circumference to access the next lift." Nancy consulted the calculator on her recorder. "If we did, adding the circumferences of the first three levels, 15.7 kilometers plus 12.56 km plus 9.45 k, we arrive at 37.72 kilometers. Dividing that in half is 18.86 clicks. But we've already explored the first three levels, so we don't have to walk all that distance again." Cheers resonated around the room. "Now, if the 4th level is accurate to form, to find the next room, and we have to traverse half of it, that's only another

3.14 kilometers," finished the captain. Nancy ignored the whistles that came to her ears.

"Walking that distance and investigating the 4th floor might take us most of the day," said Tripper. "I suggest we camp out in any rooms we find on that level and tackle the fifth one tomorrow." Darkstrider considered, "That's an excellent suggestion, Mr. Tripper. If what we find on the fourth floor takes a lot of our time. We finished our meal. Shall we start our road to redemption?"

"My duty is clear," said First Officer Leonidas," I will have to take the escape pod down to Challenger Colles. It was always going to be my course of action." Spiro looked at the half dozen translucent cubes in his hands and stuck them in a pouch in his spacesuit. "Now, to bring the Copernicus within range of the beacon, 100 kilometers should do it. I will program the ship's computer to take evasive action for 15 minutes, then fly out of range. That will give me enough time to reach Pluto's surface."

The First Officer marched down the corridor to an elevator and emerged on the ship's lowest level. With hurried steps down a dimly lit curving passageway, Spiro found himself once again in front of the escape pod hatch. Leonidas hit the button, and the hatch hissed open. Entering, he strapped himself into the chair and faced the control panel. Leonidas sat poised, as if waiting for something. Then, abruptly, he felt the ship lurch and shudder. Over his comlink to the bridge, the First Officer could hear the ship firing its lasers. He steeled himself, "Ok, here I go. It's show time!" Spiro stabbed down on a raised button. Explosive bolts ignited, and the escape pod fell away from the ship into space.

The five members of the landing party hurried along the curving hallway. Captain Darkstrider took the lead, followed by Franke, Tripper, Riley, and Book couples. They soon merged into the reddish light of the passageway. Within a hundred meters, the Copernicans had reached the first elevator. Knocking on the recessed panel and uttering "Melon," they entered the lift. Several minutes later, they emerged on the second level. Turning to their left, the landing party continued for another one hundred meters until they reached the elevator to the third level. Thus, the quintet proceeded until they arrived at the 4th level.

The landing party hesitantly stepped out into the unknown fourth corridor, as before, the passageway stretched out of sight on both sides. The ambient reddish light filled the space, and there was dead silence. "Ok, people," said Captain Darkstrider, "if I'm right, there is an elevator to the fifth level, one hundred meters to our left. The younger team members can check that out and return here." Tripper and Franke moved out and soon returned. "You were correct, captain," said Jane. "There is an elevator. Chris and I looked inside." Nancy nodded her head. "Good. Let's proceed to our right and see what there is to find on this level."

The team continued along the passage. Soon an oval window appeared on the outcurve wall. The five gathered in front and peered out into the black ocean. The usual clouds of fireflies that were the Plutonian denizens presented themselves to their eyes. Blue phosphorescence formed a halo around sea cucumbers and jellyfish. The shadow of a shark dispersed a cloud of herring. They could see the shoelace-sized red tunnel stretching out of sight. Forests of orange coral provided homes for many bright crabs and octopuses. Silvery rays flapped their wings, looking to harvest. After a few minutes, the landing party continued on their way. Then, outside the bottom of the glass window, a host of tentacles emerged.

The landing party continued its journey down the red-lit corridor. Just over an hour later, a recessed door appeared on their left. "Allow me," said Lieutenant Franke. She stepped forward and knocked, saying, "Melon." One by one, the quintet stepped through the oval opening which sealed behind them. The Copernicans stared about themselves at a circular, empty room. A dozen cubes occupied the middle of the space. "There doesn't appear to be anything here," said Navigational Officer Tripper. "Nothing except those cubes or seats," replied assistant engineer Riley. "You wouldn't think the Proxima Centaurans would create this room for nothing," observed the Chief Engineer Book. "Do we leave and keep exploring?" asked Communications Officer Franke. Captain Darkstrider laughed, "Children, children, you lack faith. Good things come to those that wait. Let's go sit on the cubes and see what happens." The five walked over to the dozen hexahedrons and climbed aboard. The Copernicans settled down when the lights went out, plunging the compartment into total darkness. "What the—?" exclaimed Jane. To their astonishment, the landing party was floating in the middle of a universe.

Like a stone thrown by a giant, the escape pod hurtled to the planet below. Green globs of plasma smashed through the pristine surface of Pluto's heart to strike at the darting Copernicus. Swearing, First Officer Leonidas attempted to stop the wild gyrations of his tiny craft. Finally, halfway to the surface, he succeeded. "God! It's hard to fly this thing! I almost lost my lunch!" Spiro looked out the window at the retreating mother ship. "Good, the Copernicus is out of range. The beacon has stopped shooting at her." Leonidas directed his sight toward Pluto's surface. "Not so good! Now, it's shooting at me!" With trepidation, the First Officer watched as a mass of green destruction reached out to him. "Wait for it. Almost there. Now!" shouted Spiro. Wrenching at his controls, the escape pod twisted sideways. The lethal dose of energy passed harmlessly overhead.

Leonidas studied the Challenger Colles that was rapidly growing closer below him. "I can see the clearing where I want to land," thought the First Officer. "It looks like such a tiny target. So striking that it is like Luke Skywalker hitting the thermal port on the Death Star with proton torpedoes. Or bulls eyeing womp rats in his T-16." Slowing his small craft, Spiro was within a kilometer of his landing area when another green ball of plasma broke through Sputnik's Planitia's icy exterior and swept toward him. Reacting too late, the First Officer increased the velocity of his conveyance downwards. Just missing, the escape pod triggered the murderous globe of annihilation's proximity detector. The resulting explosion tore into the small vessel. Like a wounded dove, it fluttered towards its rendezvous with the ground.

"Would you look at that?" asked Franke in awe. "We're floating in space, and the Milky Way surrounds us!" It was true; the five adventurers sat like a bubble in the foam of a milk spill. The stars spread out before them. As if a pirate ship's hold had broken open, spilling its load of barbarous jewels. The Copernicans marveled at the roaring furnace of red Belelguese and Polaris's icy splendor. A bed of smoldering rubies, emerald ovens, and the Coalsack's black emptiness. Orion was a spray of pearls; they swam with Aquarius, the water bearer.

"Look there! Look there!" exclaimed Jason. The three jewels in Aquarius's cup are Sadalsuud, Sadalmelik, and Skat. A blazing goblet poured a stream of stars across their consciousness. They burnt themselves on the fiery Southern Cross and rode the heavens with Auriga the Charioteer. At its center is Capella, the golden star. Lyra the lyre sang a song that pierced their souls. In its heart, scintillated Vega, the white diamond, with promised wealth. A stream of photons propelled them across the cosmos. The tangled web of Berenice's hair. A spider snare for the unwary. Pegasus, the winged horse. Markab, Scheat, Algenib, and Sirrah formed the square that gave that excellent beast flight.

The stars drew the space adventures closer. Beta Hydra, in the constellation of Draco the Dragon, is a water world. Here the ocean is so deep that most consider it bottomless. The twin red dwarf suns cast a bloody cast on its endless parade of waves. The core of a dead planet floated in splendor around Mizar in the handle of the Big Dipper. Beautiful but deadly, any spaceship would never leave its orbit; solid platinum formed its mass.

Supernovas flared and died; planets were born and crumbled to dust. The endless journey stretched the Copernican souls beyond sight and sound; they marched with the gods and despaired with the homeless. The quintet perished and was reborn countless times. The universe exploded in a tumultuous storm, shrank, and burst with force again.

At last, the five returned to the present. The lights went on in the room. "Well," said Jane. "That was special."

"Good," said First Officer Leonidas. "I made it down in one piece. That's all I can say about that." Spiro looked to where the pod lay half-buried in the ice. One side of the craft blackened and melted. "A few more centimeters and I would have had my atoms scattered to the universe," observed Leonidas. He looked at his vicinity. The landing pod's last resting place was in a blue forest of spires and battlements. Beyond the cerulean plateau were the rest of the Challenger Colles rolling hills. In the distance, the First Officer could observe vast sterile white plains stretching to the horizon. A series of black holes marked where the beacon had fired its plasma bolts. Spiro shuddered. A nick on the skyline must be Clyde Tombaugh's base.

Leonidas looked up into the velvet blackness of space. Copernicus keeps its lonely vigil two hundred kilometers above his head, looking like a seagull. "At least the ship is undamaged," he said, rubbing his shoulder. "That is, one of us is. I better make my way to the elevator. It's one kilometer in that direction on that low hummock."

Presently, Spiro cut across the trail of the landing party. He followed it over shallow ditches, towering precipices, and shallow ravines. Then, finally, the space explorer trudged up the final slope to where the black monolith thrust itself out of blue ice. The First Officer knocked firmly on the door and uttered, "Melon." An oval door materialized in front of his eyes. "Outstanding," said Spiro.

After stepping through, the portal sealed itself behind him. Leonidas observed the outlines of two six-fingered hand-prints high on the wall. "Just like the captain said," remarked the First Officer. "Luckily, I came prepared." Taking a rigid, five-fingered glove with extra appendages sewn out of his pouch, he pressed it to the lower handprint. Nothing happened. Spiro tried again with the same result.

Finally, the First Officer stood back with his hands on hips. "Well, if this isn't a kick in the head."

"Special is an understatement," said Captain Darkstrider. "I never dreamed I could experience something so real, so vivid. I feel I have just explored the universe." The rest of her crew chimed in. "I thought I had died, and this was heaven," exclaimed assistant engineer Riley. "The Proxima Centaurans must have explored a lot of stars to get such detail," observed the Navigational Officer Tripper. "Do you realize we were in that light show for ten hours?" said the Chief Engineer Book, checking his clock. The landing party exchanged looks of disbelief. "In that case," said Nancy. "Let's have a meal here and bed down for the night. We will tackle the fifth and final level tomorrow."

Sitting cross-legged on the metalled floor, the landing party broke open their backpacks and removed canteens and food tubes. "Not much water left, captain," said Chris. "We'll soon be down to our suit's recycled water." Jane made a face. "I hate that stuff. It tastes like piss!" The Chief Engineer looked at the young woman mildly, "That's because it is urine, Lieutenant." Francis's friend Jason looked at him crossly. "Do I have to you mention that while I'm eating? You will ruin my appetite." Chief Book snorted, "You? Lose your appetite? Not likely."

Companionly, the Copernicans set to their meal. Silence descended on the group for a time.

"I still don't know what we're going to do once we have explored the rest of the beacons," said Communication Officer Franke. "If we don't get that power cube, we can't deactivate or repair the beacon's computer." Navigational Officer Tripper sucked at a food tube, "Then it's Plan A; we will have to fly the shuttles very low and hope the beacon does not shoot at them." The Chief Engineer Book drank thoughtfully. "There is a Plan B. Spock could bring down some of the translucent cubes in an escape pod. He could pilot the pod to the white plateau and join us here. Fortunately, the craft is so small the beacon would probably ignore it." Nancy noted nods from some of her crew and shakes from others. "Negative; Mr. Leonidas has already volunteered for such a mission. I ordered him to stand down. It is too risky." More nods from around the circle. "Spock has guts; give him that," said Francis.

"I am a fool," said First Officer Leonidas. "The solution is obvious once you realize what it is." Spiro placed one hand on the lower handprint. Then pressed his other hand over it. Instantly, the elevator fell away. "Eureka!" shouted Leonidas. "I have found it! It was a Greek, Archimedes, who first coined that phrase. Ah, the Greeks, you can't beat us! Except in the World Cup of football, which we still haven't won in almost two hundred years!" Elated, the First Officer hopped onto the shelving and went to sleep.

The following day, the landing crew woke up after a restful, nourishing sleep. "My god, I tell you, I can't take much more of this," the Chief Engineer Book groaned. "I can't either, Francis. Our bunks back on Copernicus look like the Space Traveler's hostel back on Titan station," said assistant engineer Riley. "Uh! This liquid tastes horrible! Recycled suit water!" complained Communication Officer Franke. "Yeah, our rations are getting low," remarked Navigational Officer Tripper. "That's what makes my heart warm," laughed Captain Darkstrider. "A contented crew." Jason whispered to Francis, "Contented? Is that a joke?"

Finishing a hurried meal, the five space explorers prepared to move out. Nancy knocked on the door and spoke, "Melon." Then, trooping through the oval portal, the five turned left and walked down the red-lit passageway. After an hour and a half walk, the five arrived at the elevator Franke and Tripper had found the previous day. "Here it is, the lift to level five. A kilometer over our heads," said Captain Darkstrider. "Captain," said Franke. "Do you feel the oppression from above? Something up there is waiting for us. I feel it." Chris patted his lover's back reassuringly. "We all feel it, Jane. The captain knows."

Captain Darkstrider took out her sidearm and checked the setting. "I have about 50% charge remaining. How is everyone else doing?" The rest of the landing party was about the same. "That's unfortunate," continued Nancy. "Whatever awaits us. I hope we have enough firepower to deal with it. Don't waste shots, people. We will go in with the standard two-by-two formations. Tripper and Bank to the left. Franke and Riley to the right. I will provide a backup. Everyone understands the instructions?" Chris slapped his blaster. "Understood, Captain. Locked and loaded."

The captain knocked on the door, saying, "Melon." The five entered the elevator. Chris and Jane placed their hand over the upper handprint, and the lift moved sideways rapidly for 500 meters and then moved upwards. Nancy studied the faces of her crew. Their countenances were a mixture of resolution, fear, and determination. "I have the finest team in space," thought Darkstrider proudly. "If only Spiro were here."

"That was one long elevator ride," said the First Officer. "But considering I covered 300 clicks in one hour, I would say I made perfect time." Spiro jumped off the shelving, went to the portal, and knocked, saying, "Melon." He exited into the square antechamber. Peering about, Leonidas walked onto the trackway platform. He examined the railway stretching into the distance, the flatbeds, and the curved tunnel 5 meters above his head. "Look at all those fish! Oh, for a fishing rod right now!" Leonidas spotted the 250-meter megalodon shark in the distance. "Or maybe not."

The elevator came to a stop. Nancy knocked on its surface, saying, "Melon." Quickly, the five space travelers exited the hoist through the oval portal and into the corridor beyond. They found themselves in the usual wide, red-lit passageway, but with a difference. "Wow," said Jane. Would you look at this!" The entire facade of the outside curve of the hallway was glass, permitting an unobstructed view of the ocean beyond. Only the elevator they had just quitted, and the core of the building on the corridors inside curve was metal. "This level looks like an observation deck," observed Chris. Clouds of Plutonian fish cavorted in front of them and over their heads. Seeing no present danger, the quintet moved to the platform's edge. Looking down far below, they could see the red thread of the tunnel reaching towards the Challenger Colles. "I can just make out the trackway platform and antechamber," said Tripper. "God, we are so far up! Five kilometers off the ocean bed!" It was assistant engineer Riley who realized something else.

"Hey! The floor is moving!" he said. "So we are," remarked Captain Darkstrider. "How fast would you say we're traveling, Chief Book?' Francis consulted his recorder. The diameter of this level is one kilometer. So its circumference is 3.14 clicks. So we are traveling at 3.14 k per hour or one rotation in that time." Nancy sighed, "Just like the Harbor Center tower restaurant back in Vancouver." The Chief Engineer turned to her curiously, "What was that, captain?" Nancy laughed, "Oh, nothing. Just an ancient memory." Darkstrider peered down the hallway, stretching in each direction. "Nothing much to see here except the ocean. Let's proceed to our right and explore. Be alert, people!"

The landing party walked along the moving platform; the red ambient light colored their exposed skin a garish pink. Their ears could only hear their breaths and soft footfalls. At intervals, they passed sets of cubes that viewed the outside. Finally, Navigational Officer Tripper glanced through the glass over their heads. "Captain Darkstrider. There is one more level to this complex." The group stopped and looked in the direction the young officer was pointing. Above them, the beacon rose one hundred meters upward, ending in two peaks. The black metal glowed ominously. "I think one of those apexes is the transmitter, and the other is the plasma gun," said Chris. "If you're right, Mr. Tripper, we will find another elevator on this level going up," agreed Darkstrider. "And I believe you're also right about those pinnacles. We're almost at the end of our journey."

The First Officer Leonidas arrived at the beacon trackway terminus. Stepping off, he looked around. "A square room rather than an oval one! That's a first," said Spiro. "Well, let's see where it leads." Leonidas passed through the antechamber and into the corridor beyond. The space adventure stood in the middle of the red-lit, five meters wide and tall gallery. The First Officer looked left and right down the slightly curving passageway till it disappeared into the gloom. "This is a very spooky place," he said. "Ah! A door that does not close. Here goes nothing."

Leonidas passed through the oval portal and into the computer room. He gazed at the open panels, drooping cables, and tools strewn around by the landing party. "I can see the engineer boys have been busy here," Spiro said. "What a crazy setup! I can't even identify the colors on blinking switches and buttons. Why can I even see them? One of these boards must contain the slot for the cube. Well, I will not figure out which one it is right now. I'll leave that up to the Chief Book." The First Officer noticed flight suits, boots and helmets stacked more or less neatly at the side of the room. "The five of them discarded their outerwear here. I might as well do the same." Stripping down to his shipboard clothing, Spiro stacked his flight clothing by the others. "That's better. Now to find the elevator up to the next level." Leonidas stepped into the corridor and peered in both directions. "But which way do I go? Right or left?"

After walking half a kilometer, the landing party saw a recessed door against the bulkhead. "Let's check it out," said Jane. The quintet stepped off the moving walkway and onto the immobile perimeter. Jason said, "Look, there's a gallery up there." The other Copernicans raised their eyes to contemplate a curving window about 100 meters long. "Only one way to find out," said Captain Darkstrider. "Let's go in." Communication Officer Franke stepped to the door and said, "Melon." Stepping through the oval hatch, they walked up a short ramp. Arriving at the top, they beheld a large 100-meter square room full of clusters of cubes around oval tables with a long chest-high counter on one side. An opening in the counter gave access to what lay behind. Attached to the bulkhead at the back of the bar were empty shelves. "You know what?" said Chris. "This place looks like a lounge."

"I think you might be correct in your assumption, Mr. Tripper," said the Chief Engineer Book, sitting down at a cube near the window. Jane, Nancy, and Jason sat down with him. Chris went behind the counter. His voice came unseen from where he was out of sight. "Hey! There are fixtures and sinks back here. And a few metal oval cups and trays." The captain laughed. "The aliens didn't take everything with them." Then, again, Chris' disembodied vocalization came to their ears. "I don't believe it. There is some fluid flowing when I turn on these oval taps. I think it is a beverage for the Proxima Centaurans." Nancy frowned, "Well, don't drink it, Mr. Tripper. It might be poisonous, and it's a billion years old!"

A few minutes later, Tripper appeared behind the counter with a bottle on a tray with five oval cups. He sat the oval tray on the center of the table. "I didn't drink any captain," said Chris. "I'm not that crazy. I thought the Chief Book could analyze it." Francis got out his recorder and held it over the bottle. He frowned as he studied the readout. "It is a liquor of some sort. Not human, but it won't harm us. Extremely aged, of course. A billion years, give or take a million."

Captain Darkstrider studied the purple liquid. "I still wouldn't drink this stuff. Who knows what effect this alien secretion has—." Tripper downed his drink in one gulp. "Too late!" Francis sipped at his cup. "Tastes like Saurian brandy." Jason tasted his alcohol, "Romulan Ale." Jane took a swig and declared happily, "Aldebaran whiskey!"

Several hours later, the First Officer was still walking along the endless corridor. "I think I went the wrong way," he lamented. Finally, a recessed door appeared on his right. "Hello? This scenario looks promising." After knocking and speaking "Melon," Spiro passed through the portal. Leonidas saw a room with several slabs and cubes and an oval dais. "Looks like a dormitory." Spying another recessed outlet on the far wall, the First Officer crossed over to it. A quick knock and the word "Melon" got him into the next room. A pulsating blue sphere of energy confronted him. "The famous virtual reality room. Dare I? Well, they say, once in Rome—." Leonidas stepped forward, and instantly the room disappeared.

The First Officer stood in the middle of a vast plain. In the near distance, the tall purple spires of a city scraped the sky. Twin suns, one orange, one yellow, were setting. A red light was climbing over his head. "Superb!" exclaimed Spiro. "The acropolis in Athens was never like this!" Leonidas drank in the view for minutes as the light wind rustled his hair. Then a noise behind him caused Leonidas to turn around. Three Centaurans mounted on lizards had their spears pointed within a meter of his breast. "I have a nasty premonition about this."

For an hour, the Copernicans enjoyed their drinks and watched the panorama of life unfolding outside the double glass pane. "Of all the things we could have found on this level, star maps, power cubes, ancient records," said Nancy. "We find booze." Chris imbibed his potion. "Works for me!" The quintet sat in silence for a time. "This has been a pleasant break," said Captain Darkstrider. "As soon as we finish our drinks, we are on our way. There is still the elevator to the sixth level to find." Jane pointed, "Look! The fish have extinguished their lights. Something is coming."

A light thread appeared far off Pluto's ocean's inky depths. Slowly, it grew in size as a creature of vast proportions approached. Massive flippers propelled its undulating body, and a forest of clawed tentacles grew from its back. An enormous head full of misshapen teeth hovered into view until it filled the entire one-hundred-meter outer glass. Eyes on stalks as big as beach balls peered at them. "Chris!" declared Lieutenant Franke happily.

"I wish you wouldn't call that thing Chris," Tripper said irritably. "It is annoying, isn't it, darling," agreed Jane, patting the Navigational Officer on the cheek. "Interestingly, the creatures can always find us," remarked the Chief Engineer Book. "I think they are tracking us," said assistant engineer Riley. "You may not have noticed, but every time we look out one window, they appear after we leave." Nancy chuckled, "You have sharper eyes than the rest of the crew, Mr. Riley. So tracing our movements is what the creatures have been doing. They've been tracking us since we left the elevator at the bottom of Challenger Colles."

In the velvet blackness of the ocean, three vast megalodon sharks appeared in a blazing display of lights. Silently, they sped toward the unsuspecting one-kilometer animal suspended at the space explorer's window. Jane jumped up and rushed to the glass. Hammering it, she shouted and pointed, "Look out! Behind you!" Something of her urgency must have penetrated the creature's brain. It had half turned when the sharks tore into its bulk. As it reared in pain, the Thing grabbed one of its assailants in its mouth and bit down with jagged, sword-length teeth. The shark tore chunks out of the Thing's face. One of its other enemies ripped flippers from its bulk while the other carnivore rented a long gash.

Phosphorescent purple blood flooded the primitive scene as the four creatures sank out of view, locked in a mortal battle. "Oh, I hope Chris will be ok!" cried Franke. Her lover patted her shoulder, "Don't worry, the Thing is strong. It will survive."

The subdued Copernicans returned to the corridor. "Let's get back on the moving portion and keep walking," said Captain Darkstrider. "We should get to the next elevator in a short time." True to her words, an egressed portal appeared on the core of the beacon to their left. Stepping off the trackway, the five explorers stood in front of the lift. Jane stepped forward and uttered, "Melon." As in a dream, the oval portal appeared. The five stepped forward into the hoist. Chris and Jane stretched to put their hands in the six-fingered upper outline.

As the elevator carried them upwards, Nancy briefed her crew. "Same instructions as before, two-by-two formations. Get ready, people." After a hundred meters, the elevator stopped. Darkstrider knocked on the door, speaking, "Melon." Each couple leaped through the opening, going right and left. Nancy followed close behind with blaster drawn. The landing party stood in the middle of an empty, vermillion-colored passageway. Nothing moved. Through the glass sides and top, the summits of the transmitter and plasma gun appeared. "We're at the very top of the beacon," commented Jane.

"This passageway is just over 300 meters in circumference," said Nancy. "Let's move out to the right." So the five intrepid but frightened space adventures slowly moved forward. Then, after a hundred meters, Lieutenant Franke noticed a half dozen recessed openings on the sides of the corridor. "See them, Chris?" Tripper took an empty food tube from his pouch and threw it toward the recesses. Instantly, it vaporized in a welter of laser bolts emitted from the recessed openings. Sighting carefully, Tripper and Franke each blew up the laser stations. Each exploded in a mass of sparks and black smoke.

They were proceeding with even more caution as the Copernicans advanced. Another 100 meters passed. Without warning, from the passageway's floor sprang up two sentry guns! "Down!" shouted Nancy. On their bellies went the quintet as streams of destruction screamed over their heads. Book and Riley put half a dozen blaster rounds into each gun. Then, gratifyingly, each erupted into miniature smoking volcanoes.

Shaken, the space adventurers moved ahead with extreme vigilance. One more hundred meters went by. Then, in the lead, Jane triggered an invisible beam. Everyone tensed at the sound of a large click but relaxed when nothing happened. They had walked a dozen more steps when, with shocking suddenness, a dozen oval portals opened before and behind them in the corridor's walls. Out of the gaping holes stepped armored forms that instantly assumed a fighting posture. "The third trap! Attack robots!" yelled Captain Darkstrider. "Fire my children!"

Laser bolts of different hues ricocheted off the wall and floor. The Copernicans went down onto their stomachs or adopted a kneeling posture to return fire—the passageway filled with smoke and crisscrossing streams of deadly intensity. The smoke confused the robots and made it difficult for them to see their targets. Again and again, one would receive a blast to the chest and head and go down. Still, they came on like the mindless automatons they were. Then, moving along the wall, Nancy noticed a previously overlooked recess.

Reaching up, she knocked and was delighted to see a dark black oval appear. Over the roar of battle, the captain shouted, "Everyone! We're getting out of here! By twos, Riley and Franke, through the portal!" Now they took casualties. Turning, Jason took a glancing bolt to his shoulder. Jane grabbed him and supported him through the door.

Now it was Tripper and Books' turn. They each received superficial wounds to the leg and chest, moving backward, firing as they went. Stumbling, both of them left the corridor for the room beyond. Alone, Nancy stood erect with her back to the opened ingress. She laid down a series of bolts, creating more dense smoke. A ricochet toasted the end of her golden ponytail; rage filled Darkstrider's emerald-green eyes. "Not the hair!" she shouted. Two luckless machines went down with burst chests, exposing erupting circuitry. Then the captain leaped through the closing portal. Several blasts splashed harmlessly on its surface.

Inside the room, Nancy found Communication Officer Franke with her med kit, patching up her injured companions. The captain adjusted the intensity of her blaster and fired a long, continuous beam of energy around the outline of the door. The metal blossomed a cherry-red color and then faded. Noticing Jane's questioning look, Darkstrider explained. "I'm hoping the swelling metal will seal the door shut for a short time. That will give us time to prepare." True to her words, an ominous knocking resounded on the other side of the portal, which failed to open. As if in frustration, the pounding continued.

The captain took stock of her company. Tripper, Riley, and Book were now massaging their hurt areas. Jane had applied synth flesh to their wounds and bandaged them up. The three grinned at their captain. "Good as new, captain, thanks to Jane!" exclaimed Jason. Darkstrider scanned the empty room. There were no visible exits or even recessed doors.

"What is our weapon status, people? How many shots do you have in your sidearms?" asked Nancy. "I'm empty," said Lieutenant Tripper. "Same here, captain," said the Chief Engineer Book. "That makes three of us, Captain Darkstrider," added assistant engineer Riley. "I exhausted my blaster in the hall." Communication Officer Franke checked her weapon. "I have one shot left." The captain looked at her blaster's charge. "I used most of my weapons' charge, sealing the door. So I have just enough for one shot, too."

Nancy looked at the portal, where the pounding had increased in volume. "That is unfortunate. I counted the number of robots that we did not disable. By my count, there are four left." Tripper laughed grimly. "Four of the automatons and only two shots left." Riley examined his empty blaster. "Yeah, what are we supposed to use against them? Foul language?" Book stroked his chin in thought. "We can grab their rifles if the captain and Jane drop the first two robots." Franke trained her weapon on the portal. "That's a thousand to one shot. After that, the others will be right on their heels. And we don't know how their rifles work."

"Now listen, everyone, you all showed incredible bravery just now," said Nancy. "I didn't notice you being afraid, captain," replied Chris. "Standing up like that. You were the last one to retreat to safety." Darkstrider grinned. "Let me explain a few things to you. First, whatever comes through that door, remember, you are the crew of the Copernicus. And if this is the end, let us make such an end that space farers will remember for a thousand years." Jane looked confused, "But no one will ever know, captain." The captain smiled. "We will know, Jane." Then, outside the door, the pounding stopped.

"Right, children, this is it; Lieutenant Franke and I will form the first rank and fire at the foremost of the machine men. You others, well, wait for any opportunities that present themselves," said Nancy. "No one fires until I give the word." Tripper looked at Franke. "I love you, Jane." The Communications Officer smiled back saucily. "I know."

"Get ready," warned Darkstrider. "Here they come." Unexpectedly, the sounds of blaster fire came through the still-closed hatch. Then, the crew heard several heavy bodies falling. "What the hell is happening out there?" asked Chris. "Some sort of weapon malfunction?" suggested Jason. The sound of knocking came, and an oval black oval patch appeared on the wall. Smoke roiled into the room. "Wait for my signal," ordered Nancy. A figure appeared outlined in the smoke. "Hold your fire. Make sure of your target," said the captain. A shape stepped out of the vapor; the Copernican jaws dropped. Nancy and Jane lowered off their blasters in shock. "Hi," said First Officer Leonidas. "Is this a private party, or can anyone join in the fun?"

A look of extreme joy consumed the captain's face, and she held out her arms. "Leonidas! Spiro!!" Nancy's delighted smile faded when she noticed her crew's grins. Darkstrider frowned, "I am pleased to see you, Mr. Leonidas. I don't know how or why you got here alone." Spiro dug into his pouch and brought out a cube. "I brought this, captain. I figured you would need it." Franke, Tripper, and Riley gathered around their First Officer, clapping his back and hugging him. "Indeed, we do, Mr.Leonidas," replied the Chief Officer Book. "I cannot understand why there were so many safeguards for an empty room."

A voice behind them said, "I believe I can answer that." The space adventurers whirled to behold a 3-meter-tall hologram of Proxima Centauran. He dressed in a simple silvery robe that came to the floor. Captain Darkstrider stepped forward with her right hand raised. "Greetings. We are men and women from Earth. We come in peace. May I ask you how you speak our language?" The Centauran smiled. "I know what you imparted to the librarian. You come from the third planet, and a billion years have passed since we abandoned the beacon." Nancy frowned. "That still doesn't explain why you built this device."

The alien spread its hands. "My fellow beings, welcome. After your long journey, I'm sorry to give you only a holographic welcome, but we who built this beacon will have long turned to dust by the time you arrive. We will set the transmitter to send messages to any satellite that enters this system." Jane held her hand. "What do you mean by fellow beings? We are nothing like you." The tall Copernican looked at the young officer. "When we entered your system, we found simple plant life in the third planet's ocean. But no animal life and none that was likely to arise. So we did what we have done on multiple worlds in this sector. We seeded the primeval seas with our DNA." Darkstrider's hand flew to her mouth. "Your DNA? Do you mean that we—?" The alien nodded, "We have sowed the seed, and you are the crop. You are our children." In the shock that followed, the tall being smiled gently. "My brothers and sisters, Centaurans, I wish you well." With that, the image of the alien slowly faded away to nothing.

The crew of the Copernicus looked at each other suspiciously. "Isn't that a kick in the pants?" said Chris. "We came all this way to find the aliens, only to find out that they are us." Jane shook her head. "Ishmael, the captain said. Pluto's ocean is a mirror where we found ourselves." The First Officer Leonidas looked at Nancy. "You are strangely silent, Captain Darkstrider. Is there anything you want to say?" The captain thought for a moment and then brightened. "Let's get out of here."

An hour later found the sextet in the computer room. "Here goes nothing," said Chief Book as he placed the translucent cube in the empty spot on the side panel. Immediately, a new hum came from the machinery. Leonidas was listening to his comlink. "Captain, I'm in communication with Copernicus. She is receiving a transmission from the beacon." Cheers erupted from the crew. "We should have asked the Librarian or that other fellow, the Prophet, what the transmission was saying," said Tripper. "Yeah," said Franke, "Well, it's too late now." Captain Darkstrider looked around the room. "Now that the beacon works again, let's clean up this room and put it right. I want to leave the beacon the way we found it."

Now clad in their flight suits, the six space explorers rode the flatbed two hours later toward the Challenger Colles elevator. "Captain," said the Chief Engineer Book. "I've been reviewing the data I downloaded from the alien computer. I think I've deciphered what the transmission was saying." Nancy spoke from where she was sitting cross-legged on the moving platform. "By all means, chief. Enlighten us." Francis frowned. "It's a warning. Stay away from the beacon. Do not attempt access." Assistant engineer Riley groaned. "Now it tells us!" Darkstrider laughed. "I think we can expect smooth sailing from now on."

A tremendous crash just over their heads startled the Copernicans. Looking up, they were terrified to look into the malignant eyes of a megalodon shark. The enormous creature turned and smashed into the tunnel glass again. "I spoke too soon," said the captain dryly. "I don't think the tunnel structure can take much more of this captain," said Navigational Officer Tripper. "If the glass breaks, the ocean will flood, and we'll all drown." Outside, the 250-meter brightly lit length of the sea creature poised itself for another charge. It had no trouble seeing the crew in the nearly complete darkness. Just then, an enormous shadow enveloped the carnivore. "Chris!" shouted Franke happily. "Not this time," grinned Tripper. The attacking creature illuminated itself, revealing it as the 200-meter colossal squid. The ten-limbed animal had its arms wrapped tightly around the shark's body, and its beak was tearing chucks from it. Luminescent purple blood flooded out of gaping wounds in the megalodon's flesh.

"Aw! I was hoping it was Chris saving us!" exclaimed Franke. "I guess he is dead." The captain laughed, "No, he's not Lieutenant; he's over there." The landing party turned to behold the eldritch horror regarding them with another megalodon in its mouth. Wounds on its face still oozed blood. One eye closed and opened again, and then the beast swam away. "It winked at me!" squealed Jane. Francis laughed. "Welcome to the club."

Captain Darkstrider stood on the blue plateau, examining the blackened remnant of the escape pod. "This pod is a write-off," she said. "Do you know what escape pods cost, Mr. Leonidas?" Spiro knitted his brow. "No, captain. I don't." Nancy slowly nodded her head. "Well—it's probably a lot!"

"I'm afraid we didn't have enough time to dismantle Clyde Tombaugh's base," said the Chief Engineer Book. "The window for our return is too short. Once we arrive on the Copernicus, we must leave orbit in one hour. We've loaded what we could on the shuttles, and the moon chariots are aboard, too." Darkstrider examined the shelter and the white plains that stretched in all directions. "That's ok, chief; we should leave something of ourselves behind." Francis nodded and walked towards the shuttle, where his companion Jason was waiting. Franke and Tripper's spacecraft gracefully lifted off and flew into space. Nancy went to follow her crewmate when she stopped and stooped. She left a clear imprint of her gloved hand on the front of the icy surface. "Goodbye, Tombaugh," she whispered as a tear trickled down her face.

"I have laid in the course, Captain Darkstrider," said Navigational Officer Tripper. "On your order, we will leave orbit." Nancy sat on the Copernicus bridge and contemplated Pluto as it filled the screen. As always, the heart of the frozen world beckoned to her as if a lover. Darkstrider's sea-green eyes flashed. The brilliant blue lobe seemed to wink back. The bridge crew turned and regarded the captain. On her monitor, the engineers, Book and Riley, faced the captain's image on their screen. Communication Officer Franke smiled knowingly.

"Captain?" asked Chris again. "Your orders?" Nancy laughed. "Back, Mr. Tripper. Back to the green hills of home!"

The End.